EX-PATRIOTS

EX-PATRIOTS

A NOVEL

Peter Clines

Broadway Books
NEW YORK

BROADWAY

Copyright © 2011 by Peter Clines

Published in the United States by Broadway Paperbacks, an imprint of the Crown Publishing Group, a division of Random House, Inc., New York. www.crownpublishing.com

BROADWAY PAPERBACKS and its logo, a letter B bisected on the diagonal, are trademarks of Random House, Inc.

Originally published in paperback in the United States in slightly different form by Permuted Press, in 2011.

Cataloging-in-Publication Data is on file with the Library of Congress.

ISBN 978-0-8041-3659-4
eISBN 978-1-934861-88-2

PRINTED IN THE UNITED STATES OF AMERICA

Cover illustration: Jonathan Bartlett
Cover design: Christopher Brand

10 9 8 7 6 5 4 3 2 1

First Broadway Paperbacks Edition

EX-PATRIOTS

Prologue

NOW

THE NIGHT BREEZE swept the black cloak away from Stealth's body. As the folds of fabric opened up, they revealed the array of straps and sheaths crisscrossing her skintight uniform. Her boots shifted on the water tower's sloped peak until the warm wind died down and her cloak and hood settled around her again.

Her featureless mask looked down at the figures gathered around the base of the tower. They filled the streets of the modern-day fortress that had come to be known as the Mount. Some of them staggered and made awkward lunges at each other. Many of them were eating. Shouts and cries echoed up to her.

She shook her head and turned to the man hanging in the air near her. "This is a waste of time."

"No, it isn't."

St. George, once known to the world as the Mighty Dragon, floated next to the tower and ordered gravity to ignore him. A solid six feet tall, his body was well muscled but leaned toward wiry. His leather jacket, the same golden brown as his shoulder-length hair, was decorated with sutures and grafts. At this point it was two jackets stitched into one. A five-inch tooth was tied to the coat's ragged lapel with thin straps.

Stealth glanced over her shoulder at the building that served as her office and the de facto town hall. "We should be drawing up schedules for this week's construction. The north wall is close to done."

"It can wait," he said. "They all need this. They probably don't even know how bad they need it."

"So you keep insisting."

Below them, the celebrating people packed the streets and alleys. Families gathered on the rooftops. They cheered and laughed and called out to one another. Even the guards along the wall seemed more relaxed.

"You're grumpy," said Claudia. She picked her nose while she stared at Stealth.

Inside her hood, Stealth turned her head to the little girl perched on St. George's left shoulder. "I am practical."

"She is very grumpy," St. George told the child, "but we're working on it." He pulled his arm across her legs like a seat-belt and spun around in the air.

"Go higher!" yelled Timmy from the other shoulder.

"Actually," said the hero, "I think time's up for you guys. Down we go."

"No!" the boy shrieked.

"Good-bye, grumpy lady," said Claudia with a wave.

St. George drifted down to the crowd and handed the kids off to their parents. Dozens of little arms reached up but he waved them off. "No more rides for now," he told them. "Show's going to start soon."

A few yards away, the blue and silver form of Cerberus waded through the crowd. The battle armor towered over the tallest citizens of the Mount. Most of their heads didn't reach the American flags stenciled across its gleaming biceps. The metal limbs were extended out, and gleeful children swung from each massive forearm.

The titan's armored skull, with lenses the size of tennis balls, looked up at the sky, then back to St. George. The armored suit was androgynous, but after working with its creator for so long George tended to think of it as female. He gave her a thumbs-up and got back a nod from the helmet.

He looked up to the star-filled sky and keyed the microphone on his collar. "Hey, up there. You ready to do this?"

Far above the Mount, one of the stars swung back and forth through the sky, tracing zigzags and figure-eights across the night. Barry's voice echoed in St. George's earpiece. "Yep."

"No problems?"

"No, of course not. What could go wrong?"

"Didn't you say something yesterday about setting fire to the atmosphere?"

"Well . . . yeah," Barry said after a brief pause. "But the chances of that happening are really minuscule."

From inside the Cerberus armor, the voice of Danielle Morris echoed across the channel. "You could set part of the atmosphere on fire?"

"Not part of it," said Barry. "Look, the odds are slim to none, seriously. There's a better chance of one of us getting—wow."

"What?"

"I just got struck by lightning up here. What're the odds of that?"

"Quit it," growled Cerberus. She set down the children who were climbing on the armor.

"Trust me," said Barry, "everything's going to be fine. Make your little speech."

St. George gave the armor a smile as he drifted upward. Another round of cheers broke out as he spiraled into the air, and several upraised bottles saluted him. Matt Russell's home brew reserves would be gone after tonight. The hero gave the crowd a wave and soared back to the top of the water tower.

Stealth was watching the walls when he landed next to her on the sloped peak. "Are you certain all guards are on duty tonight?"

"Yes," he said. "And so are you, or you would've already dealt with it. Try to relax for one night, okay?"

She said nothing.

"Ladies and gentlemen," boomed Cerberus from below. With the suit's speakers at full volume she was louder than a bullhorn. The voices quieted.

"A year ago," she continued, "we'd barely been in the Mount for eight months. We were all still working around the clock just to make this place livable. There was no time for fun. No time for celebration. It was all about survival." She paused and let the echo of her voice fade. "And not all of us survived."

The crowd murmured its agreement, and a few more bottles were raised.

"So this year, we wanted to make sure everyone remembered the day and everyone had time to celebrate. We're alive. We're together. Happy Fourth of July!"

There was a rumble of thunder, and a bright red flower of light filled the sky. A moment later a white blossom appeared next to it, followed by a blue one. Cheers rose and spread out across the Mount. Hundreds of children screamed with joy. The lights faded and four more bursts went off in a row. The sharp thunderclap of a distant cannon echoed in the sky.

Barry's voice came over the radio again. "I thought you said you were going to do the president's speech from *Independence Day*?"

"No," said Cerberus, "you kept saying I should do it. I ignored you."

"That's such a great speech."

"Weren't you about to blow up again or something?"

Above the Mount, the night sky lit up with another burst of light. The applause echoed for blocks. St. George keyed his mic again. "How long do you think you can keep this up?"

"I can probably do another ten or twelve like this," said Barry, "maybe a dozen quick ones as a grand finale. You can't have fireworks without a finale."

"Not going to be too much for you?"

"I had a big dinner." Two more bursts lit up the sky, followed by another thunderclap. "Besides, this is totally worth it for the view. I can see most of North America. The top of South America, too, I think."

"Wow," said Cerberus. "How high up are you?"

"Pretty high. I just dodged a satellite."

"Wait," said St. George. He looked up at the sky and tried to spot Barry's gleaming form between the stars. "You're out in space?"

"Technically, yeah," Barry said over the speaker, "but I was joking about the satellite. I'm right about at the Kármán Line."

"Are you . . . okay with that?"

"Well, it's not like I need to breathe or anything. And this way we've got the ozone layer between me and Earth, just in case."

"Just in case what?"

"Hey, I'm letting off a lot of energy here. Some of it's

going to slip into the more dangerous wavelengths. Can't be helped."

"It is a wise precaution," said Stealth. She'd listened on her own earpiece without looking away from the Mount's defenses. "As you were, Zzzap."

"Yes, ma'am," said Barry. They could all hear his grin. A pair of gold flowers exploded across the sky and another cheer came from below.

St. George looked up at the display and pretended not to watch the woman next to him.

"If it matters so much to you that I take part," she said, not lifting her gaze, "please just say so."

He shrugged. "I just think it would be good for you, too. You need a morale boost as much as anyone else. Maybe more."

"I do not find it as easy as some to set aside my responsibilities for a few hours of frivolous entertainment," said Stealth. "Especially to celebrate the anniversary of a country that, in most senses, no longer exists. There are always more pressing concerns." She looked out across the dark metropolis.

He followed her gaze. Each burst of light illuminated the city. Beyond the high walls of the Mount, past the barricaded gates and the rows of abandoned cars in the streets, he could see the other inhabitants of Los Angeles.

The ex-humans.

The more distant ones staggered aimlessly. Closer to the Mount, where they could see the guards, they clawed at barriers and reached through gates. They made slow swipes with emaciated fingers. Not one of them reacted to the thunderclaps. Not one of them looked up at the brilliant display in the nighttime sky.

Not one of them was alive.

From the top of the water tower he could see tens of thousands of the walking dead—maybe hundreds of thousands—stumbling through the streets in every direction. During the flashes of light, he could pick out some with twisted limbs and many more stained with blood.

The sounds of celebration and the echo of Zzzap's fireworks almost hid the chattering. The constant noise that reached everywhere in Los Angeles; that echoed off every building and down every street. The mindless click-clack of dead teeth coming together again and again and again.

If Stealth's estimates were correct—and they almost always were—there were just over five million of them within the borders of the city.

St. George sighed. "You can really kill the mood sometimes, you know that?"

"My apologies."

The Doctor Is In

THEN

I WAS IN my private lab, gathering the notes for my one-thirty lecture. My teaching assistant, Mary, was dividing her time between searching for the flash drive that contained my PowerPoint slides and organizing a pile of correspondence and journals that had spilled onto the floor from my desk. To her credit, she'd let the papers fall and grabbed the photos of my wife and daughter.

My beard was scratching against my collar. I'd wanted to have it trimmed before the start of the semester and lost track of time. Now I was heading off to my fourth lecture and it still was a shaggy mess of too-much-silver hair. Eva hates it when my beard gets too long. It was short when we met in grad school. I needed to stop by the campus barber before I ended up looking any more like Walt Whitman.

I heard the door open behind me as I packed my briefcase, but thought nothing of it until I heard my name.

"Dr. Emil Sorensen?"

The speaker was a young man I didn't recognize. He wore a well-tailored suit he looked uncomfortable in. A double-Windsor-knotted tie. Tight, cropped hair above sharp eyes.

I'd seen this ploy many times. Every professor sees it at least once or twice a semester. There are a few different names for it, but here the faculty calls it the VIP Play. An undergrad tries to look or sound important to put themselves on equal footing with their instructor. Then they explain the extenuating circumstances behind a certain grade or exam result. They drop the names of people who would be disappointed because of it. Which all leads, of course, to the suggestion that they should be allowed to resubmit a paper, retake a test, or—in some bold cases—simply have their grade changed to something acceptable.

I was running late and it was too early in the semester for such schemes. "You have ninety seconds," I said. "Can I help you with something?"

Even as I spoke, two more men stepped in behind the first. They were larger and more solid than him. One carried an attaché case. All their suits matched.

Mary stopped looking for the flash drive. Her gaze shifted from me to the trio of men.

"John Smith," said the man. "I know it sounds like a joke, but that's really my name. I'd like to speak with you for a few moments, if I could." He had a broad smile I knew from fund-raisers and alumni dinners. A practiced smile, but not a well-practiced one.

"This really isn't the best time. I have a lecture in about ten minutes on the other side of campus, and—"

"I hope you'll forgive me," said Smith, "but I took the liberty of canceling your lecture."

It took a moment for the words to sink in. "Who the hell do you think you are?"

"John Smith," he repeated. The smile faltered as his hand fumbled with a leather wallet. He opened it to reveal a golden badge and a set of credentials with his photo. He was smiling in the photo. "Agent Smith, technically. I'm with the Department of Homeland Security, seconded to the Defense Advanced Research Projects Agency. Could we speak alone, sir?"

He said the last with a nod to Mary. She looked at me with wide eyes. We all spoke a bit too freely at times, and on a college campus paranoia and rumors about the Patriot Act ran like wildfire. "Doctor?"

I tried what I hoped was a reassuring smile. "Why don't you go see if there are any stragglers at Bartlett Hall," I told her. "Let them know this delay doesn't mean they're off the hook for next week's test."

She gathered her own papers and paused to make sure I saw the flash drive she'd uncovered. The smile graced Smith's face the entire time. He gave Mary a polite wave as she slipped out between the two larger men. They closed the door behind her.

"So what's this all about?"

Smith's face relaxed. As the smile faded, he gained several years. Not a young man, but cursed with the face of one. One of the other biochem professors had the same problem. A young face in a college town meant always being carded at the liquor store and never being taken as seriously as your colleagues.

"You're a very impressive man, Dr. Sorensen," he said. "You've got more doctorate degrees than I've got years of education. Physiology. Neurology. Biochemistry. A forerunner in molecular nanotechnology and—"

"I know my own credentials."

"From what I've read, you got cheated out of the Nobel Prize last year."

"It's not about winning prizes," I said. "Besides, the gene modification techniques Evans and the others developed are brilliant. They even helped my own work."

"Of course," Smith agreed with a polite nod. "You've received several grants from DARPA over the past twenty years. If I read the file right, your contract's been renewed a record-breaking seven times. In fact"—he gave a forced chuckle—"you started working for the government just before my eighth birthday."

"Can you please get to the point, Mr. Smith?"

The smile faltered again. "Well, doctor, the fact is they want to bring you on full-time and put you in charge of—"

"Not interested."

His face dropped. "You don't even know which project I was going to say."

"It doesn't matter," I said. "I'm comfortable with my arrangement the way it is."

"Are you sure?"

"Why wouldn't I be?"

Smith reached out to the side. The man with the attaché case opened it and placed a file folder in the waiting hand. "You've seen some of the headlines, I'm guessing?" He walked past me to the table and spread out some clippings and printed articles.

THE MIGHTY DRAGON PATROLS LOS ANGELES

"APE MAN" STOPS ROBBERY

SHADOWY FIGURE HUNTS RAMPART
DISTRICT CRIMINALS

I'd seen most of them before. A few of my grad students had been saving news stories and images for me since the Mighty Dragon had first appeared in June. I guessed we had twice as many articles as Smith did. Copies were on the flash drive, which reminded me to pick it up and drop it in my pocket. "Have you seen the ones about the electrical man up in Boston?" I asked him.

His eyes lit up like a child. "I have. What do you think of them?"

"I'm intrigued, of course, but until I see more concrete proof than a headline in the *Post* or some grainy photos on a blog, it's not going to occupy a lot of my time."

"But you've had your students saving news stories for you." His smile came back.

"What are you getting at, Mr. Smith?"

He avoided my eyes and looked around the lab. "I hate to sound suspicious, Professor Sorensen, but . . . well, some folks at DARPA have been wondering if you've had some success with your human enhancement research that you haven't told us about."

I felt a twinge of panic. Maybe Mary's paranoia wasn't that misplaced after all. "You think I had something to do with these people?"

Smith shrugged. "To be honest," he said, "I think they'd be thrilled if you had. It'd put the United States far ahead in the superpowers race."

"The what?"

"They're not just here, doctor," he said. "People with superhuman abilities are appearing all over the world. Did you see Vladimir Putin on the cover of *Time* last month?" Smith shook his head.

"I saw the picture," I said with a nod. They'd titled it "Superman of the Year." Putin had been bare-chested in front of the Kremlin, holding a car one-handed over his head. "I thought it was Photoshop propaganda."

"Most people did. Thank the CIA for that. But superhumans are popping up everywhere." Smith slid some more photos from the file folder. "England's got the Green Knight and the Scarecrow. Japan's got a whole team of super-samurais. There're two guys in Iran calling themselves Gilgamesh and Marduk. Hell, we got satellite footage of a dragon flying over Baghdad this morning. Wings, horns, tail, everything."

"A dragon?"

He shrugged. "Some of the agency folks think it might be some kind of metamorphosis or something." His tongue tripped over the word. "That something, maybe someone, changed into—"

"I know what metamorphosis means."

"Right, sorry. Anyway, don't you see, professor? That's why we need to get you back on Project Krypton. No more consults, no more outside evaluations. We want you working full-time with us on this. And you don't want to miss out on a chance like this, do you?"

"No," I found myself saying. I knew Smith was right. Eva and Madelyn were going to be angry with me. I'd promised them I wouldn't take on extra projects this year. "I thought Krypton was done for good?"

"The secretary of defense likes it. He brought it back two years ago, but it's been kept pretty quiet. The Future Force Warrior project gets most of the headlines on *Wired*, anyway."

"Then why bring back Krypton?"

"Well, Future Force is doing well," he said, "and they're also hoping to have that new exoskeleton project in the public eye in the next seven or eight months. But when it comes down to it, the vice president, the secretary, and the Joint Chiefs want to see the real deal in our corner and they think you're the man to do it."

I furrowed my brow. It's a bad habit. Eva says it's giving me wrinkles. "Our corner? I'm not sure I understand."

He gestured at the papers and images on the table. "All these other superhumans are answering to their country's government," he explained. "Almost every one of them. Some are even on payroll. I mean, think about it, doctor. There's no point in having superheroes in the United States if the government doesn't control them."

Two

NOW

THERE WERE AT LEAST three dozen more people in the shop than needed to be. A rumble of conversation echoed through the warehouse-sized room. The rolling tables and racks had been wheeled away. In their place, a single chair sat centered under the cleanest skylight.

St. George sat in the chair. His leather jacket had been tossed aside on one of the tables, revealing the cherry-red tank top that still made summer in Los Angeles feel too hot. He looked at the crowd, then at the handful of people who stood around his chair.

Jarvis tucked a sturdy hacksaw under his arm and clapped his hands. "All y'all, quiet down," he said. "No reason to turn this into more of a circus than it already is." He paused to scratch his chin beneath his salt-and-pepper beard. "We all know this ain't a one-person job. We drew lots last week and each of the winners is going to get a chance at him."

To St. George's left, Andy held a pair of well-worn bolt cutters, and by his shoulder a woman clutched a pair of bright blue tin snips. Billie Carter stood on the other side of the chair with a pair of wire cutters. Mike Turner had another set of bolt cutters. Right in front was a little Latina girl, Andrea, with a black set of wire cutters. She was bouncing up and down. St. George smiled at her and she blushed.

Jarvis turned to the hero in the chair. "Last chance to back out, chief."

The hero smiled. "I'm good," he said. "This is long overdue."

The older man shook his head and let his own hair settle past his shoulders. "Personally, I think it makes you look distinguished."

"Maybe," said St. George, "but it's too damned hot in the summer."

"You let it grow any longer we'd all start calling you St. Fabio," said Mike.

"St. Hippie is more like it," said Billie. She squeezed her wire cutters a few times for emphasis and a round of chuckles echoed in the room. She still wore her hair cropped military short.

Andy stepped forward and held up the bolt cutters. He moved behind St. George and began to gather the golden hair into a ponytail.

"*Et tu*, Andy?" St. George said with a grin.

"How could I pass up the chance to cut the hair off a legendary strongman?" Andy said with a smile. "If I ever get ordained, I could tell that story every Sunday to a rapt congregation." He settled the ponytail into the mouth of the bolt cutters, took a deep breath, and levered the handles together.

The hair resisted. Andy took another breath, threw his weight into it, and there was a crackle of sharp pops, like breaking spaghetti. It echoed through the shop and the ponytail dropped to the floor. The crowd hollered and applauded. Andy looked at the gouged blades of his bolt cutters and shook his head.

Mike wobbled forward. It had been eight months since an ex had tried to bite through his shoe and cracked half the bones in his foot. Dr. Connolly still wasn't sure if he'd ever walk without a limp. "Little off the top, boss?" he said with a wicked grin.

Over the course of the hour, they sawed and clipped and chopped at the hero's hair. In the end the tools were chipped and pitted, but the floor was covered with hair. There was a final burst of applause from the crowd as St. George looked at himself with a hand mirror.

"Reminds me of a haircut I got in college once." He set down the mirror. "Hope everyone had fun," he said, and gave Andrea a wink. "Time to get back to work. The day's wasting."

The crowd funneled away as he shrugged into the jacket. A few moments later he was alone with Billie and Jarvis. "We ready?" he asked.

She gave him a sharp nod. "Luke's got the extra fuel tanks loaded in *Road Warrior*. We've got overnight gear if we need it. Stealth's even letting us take three extra cases of ammunition. One nine millimeter, two of .30-08." She glanced at her watch. "Team assembles in thirty-nine minutes."

The hero glanced at Jarvis. "What's the armor situation? Did Rocky get those last three sets of sleeves done?"

"He did not," said the bearded man. "He says it's an art and it takes as long as it takes. I told him y'all wouldn't be pleased."

"Crap. What's that give us, thirteen full suits?"

"Yup."

"Not a great number," said Billie.

"No," agreed the hero.

"Half the folks just want to wear their leathers anyway," said Jarvis. "This whole armor idea still ain't going over that well."

"It's too damned hot for leather," said Billie. "Either people don't wear it or get heat exhaustion from it."

"Tell Rocky he gets chicken for dinner tonight if he can finish one more set before we leave," said St. George. "He's got my word on it."

"Hell," said Jarvis, "for a whole chicken I'll make the damned sleeves myself."

"What if he doesn't?" asked Billie.

"Then we'll have to make do with what we've got."

"Does that mean cutting three people or having three people go without armor?"

St. George wrinkled his brow. "Let me think on that one."

They stepped out into the morning light and took a moment to adjust their sunglasses. Off to their right was the Lemon Grove gate, and St. George reached up to rub the bladelike tooth on his jacket as he looked that way. "I'm going to check in with Zzzap and Stealth. I'll meet both of you at Melrose in thirty."

Jarvis nodded and loped away. St. George was about to leap into the air when Billie touched his arm. She gestured down the road.

A thin, shaved-bald man waited there with the little girl who'd cut St. George's bangs. When the man realized they'd seen him he switched the girl's fingers to his other hand and gave an awkward salute. He walked forward, still holding his hand up, pulling the little girl behind him. He wore a pair of fingerless gloves.

The hero waited for the salute to drop and then shook

the hand. "You were the one who actually won the drawing, right?"

"Yeah," said the man. He was young, twenty tops, and spoke with an anxious, eager voice. His bare arms were decorated with tattoos, and the hero could see the prominent number on the left shoulder. "Andrea's my niece. She's wanted to meet you since we moved up here."

"You were with the Seventeens?"

"Was in, yeah," the young man said, "but I'm out now. I'm Cesar. Cesar Mendoza."

Behind him, St. George heard Billie's boots shift. "Good to meet you, Cesar," he said, pumping the hand again. "You've got a beautiful niece."

"Hell-o," the little girl sang. She waved and ducked behind Cesar, blushing again.

"Yeah, I know," the young man said. "Look, I was wondering . . . could I talk to you for a couple of minutes about something?"

"Is it urgent?"

Cesar shrugged. "I mean, it's not life or death," he said. "Just wanted to talk about some stuff."

"What kind of stuff?"

"Just . . . you know." He shot a glance at Billie. "Stuff. Just something I need to get off my chest, you know?"

"D'you get bitten?"

"What? No!"

"Kill somebody?" asked Billie.

"No!"

"Steal something?"

"No! Well . . . no, not for like two years. Honest, man, nothin' like that."

"Can't be too pressing, then," St. George said with a smile.

He clapped a hand on Cesar's shoulder. "I've got a few things I need to take care of before we head out, but maybe later. I'll be around all day tomorrow if nothing comes up."

The young man nodded. "Yeah," he agreed. "Yeah, later'd be cool. Thanks, man." He hefted the little girl into his arms. "Say bye," he told her.

"Good-bye," she sang, waving at them.

"Still don't trust any of those people," murmured Billie as they walked away.

"Those people?" echoed the hero.

"Don't play the PC card," she said. "Less than a year ago the Seventeens were trying to kill us. Now we're sharing supplies with them."

"They're sharing with us, too, don't forget. Chickens, eggs, a hell of a lot more fruits and veggies."

She shrugged. "Okay," she said, "if you think they're so trustworthy why aren't any of them scavengers or walking the wall yet?"

St. George watched the young man and the little girl as they turned the corner. "You know, you're right," he said. "We ought to do something about that."

"I didn't say I have a problem with it," she said. "I wouldn't trust any of them with a weapon. Most people wouldn't."

"Well, you're going to have to," he said. "None of us are going to survive if we keep up this us-and-them mentality. Rotate someone out and put one of the Seventeens on the team for today."

"What?"

"There're a couple decent candidates. Nestor. Hector. Fernando. Who's the woman with the faux-hawk? Desirea?"

"Just to be clear, I started this by saying leaving them out was a good thing."

He smiled. "That's why you're picking who comes with us. Didn't they teach you about team-building in the Marines?"

"Yeah. They said if someone wasn't part of the team you should shoot them."

"Choose wisely," he said. He focused on a spot between his shoulders, and his feet drifted off the ground. "At Melrose in twenty-five. I expect to see at least one person with a tattoo."

"I've got three," she called up to him.

"You don't count."

"I'll let you see the third one," she offered.

He pushed down against the world and soared up into the air. The wind felt strange against his scalp, and it took him a moment to remember the new haircut.

Flying the three blocks south to the old Stage Four was excessive, but St. George still hadn't gotten past the thrill of flight. He'd been able to glide for years, but it wasn't until the war with the Seventeens and their undead army that he'd been able to make the leap, so to speak, to actual flight. The threat of losing everything they'd worked for, losing friends, and letting down the people who believed in him had made something click. Now he could fly, and he was stronger than ever.

And the thought of losing Stealth, he admitted, had probably had something to do with it, too.

He shot into the sky, high enough that he could see the beach a dozen miles away and the Pacific Ocean and Catalina Island far off to the south. Stealth had sent Zzzap out there six months ago. The island's little town, Avalon, was gone. About a thousand exes wandered the narrow streets and out into the hills. He stared out at the dead island and then dove back to the ground.

He landed outside Four. The air stank of ozone. Kids

came here at night to watch their hands glow with static electricity. Four had been a stage once, back when the Mount was a film studio. They'd stripped out the sets and linked it to one of the nearby power houses with heavy cables once used by lighting crews.

The other end of those cables ran to the object at the center of Four. It was a set of three interlocking rings, each wrapped with copper wire. They formed a rough sphere that looked like a seven-foot gyroscope. Someone had dubbed it the electric chair while it was being built. The nickname had stuck.

Hovering inside the rings was the form of a man. It was a reversed silhouette, like looking at the sun through a man-shaped cutout. Arcs of energy shot from the brilliant figure to snap and pop against the copper-wrapped sphere. St. George could tell his friend was staring off into one of the stage's empty corners.

Well, I'm still getting used to it, said Zzzap. His voice was somewhere between a kazoo and pure static, and it buzzed over the crackle of power. *You have to admit, this isn't exactly an everyday thing. And I say this as a guy who more or less turns into a small star.*

As St. George approached, the gleaming silhouette turned in the air toward him.

Wow, said Zzzap. *They really did a number on you.*

"Who were you talking to?"

Nobody. The brilliant wraith shrugged and gestured around him. *People. On the radio.*

St. George nodded and ran his hand through the short strands of hair. "So how's it look?"

Zzzap tilted his head. *You know what's big after the Zombocalypse? Hats.*

"Seriously."

Remember when you were a little kid and your mom always made you get that pageboy-looking haircut?

"How'd you know?"

It's what every mom did.

"So it looks like that?"

Yeah, it's a little worse, said Zzzap. *It's like a blind person tried to do a pageboy with a pair of hedge clippers.*

"Great."

Zzzap shifted again. The rings crackled as he shed a few more kilowatts of power. *You still heading out?*

"Yeah. You still nervous?"

The wraith shrugged. *It's a big thing,* he said. *You and I have been over to the Valley a few times but really no one's gone there in almost two years. Hell, I think Danielle was the last one there when she came over with her Marines.*

"I don't think you're supposed to call them 'her Marines.'"

Whatever.

"We've got to go sometime," said St. George. "We've cleaned out everything we can find on this side of the hills. Now it's either the beach or the Valley, and the Valley's got a lot more resources."

I know. You have to admit, though, it's just kind of weird. I've gotten used to the Valley being "somewhere else," y'know?

He nodded. "There seems to be a lot of that going around," he said. "We're getting . . . insular, I guess. Is that the right word?"

Yeah.

"Plus I just had a talk with Billie about the Seventeens. We've got to start including them more, starting now. She's going to have one of them come out with us."

Really? Zzzap bowed his head for a moment. *You sure you don't want me coming out with you?*

St. George shook his head. "We'll be fine. This way you can keep Danielle powered up here and still make it out to us if anything goes wrong."

Assuming you have time to set off a flare.

"If we don't have time to set off a flare, there's not much you'd be able to do anyway." He held up his hand and counted off three fingers. "Remember, red is trouble, blue we need you but it's not urgent, white means we're spending the night over there."

The wraith shuddered. *Better you than me.*

"Hey, it's my last choice, too."

× × ×

Another quick flight took St. George west across the Mount to the four-story, tan-and-white office building called Roddenberry. It was named after the man who created *Star Trek*. For the past year and a half, it had served as town hall for the survivors of Los Angeles.

Stealth's office was on the top floor. She'd converted one of the large executive conference rooms into her command center. The blinds were always shut and the lights at a dim glow. It was lit by dozens of monitors she'd pulled from every office in the building, showing constant images of every street and entrance to the Mount. George wasn't sure how many of the cameras were preexisting security systems and how many she'd installed herself.

She'd also moved into another room, hidden away behind a low-profile door, which she used as a spartan living quarters. He knew it was the only place she ever took her mask off. He'd never seen the room, which meant odds were no one else had, either.

"We're heading out in a few minutes," he said. The conference room door drifted shut behind him. "I know you're here. Are you behind me?"

"No." The shadows rippled between two of the windows. The glare seeping around the blinds had hidden her right in front of him. She stepped forward. "Are you positive you wish to include a member of the Seventeens in your scavenging party?"

"News travels fast."

She rolled her shoulders and the cloak folded back away from her body. "It should not surprise you that I know such things," she said. "Please answer the question."

"Well, first off," he said, "there aren't any Seventeens in the Mount. Anyone here gave up their gang affiliation months ago. Which means they're just people."

"Very well."

"And despite that, as was just pointed out to me, we've all been hesitant about giving these folks any trust or responsibility."

"Trust must be earned."

"True," he agreed, "but if they're going to earn it they need a chance. So I think we need to start giving them chances." He shrugged. "Worst case, a bunch of people are proven right and we know some folks can't be trusted with a rifle. Best case, we've got more guards and more scavengers."

She gave a nod inside her hood. "Your logic is sound. Who will you take?"

"I tossed out a few names but I left it up to Billie Carter."

"One of your suggestions was Fernando Gomez. I would advise against him."

St. George glanced at the monitors. "Have you started hiding microphones or are you that good at lip-reading?"

"Lip-reading," she said, "although I could have deduced he would seem like a logical choice to you."

"And he isn't because . . . ?"

"He is the highest-ranked former Seventeen living here in the Mount. If your goal is to unify the two communities, you should not make your first pick the leader of one. Make it clear the person you choose is the most competent from the pool of potential candidates, regardless of their former command structure."

"And if he is the most competent?"

"Gomez once attempted to fight Gorgon while wearing a welding mask and using the name Painkiller. If he is the most competent they have to offer, this entire discussion is moot."

St. George smiled. For months the dead hero had been a sore spot everyone tried not to touch, even Stealth. They'd finally hit the point where they could remember him in a good light. "Two jokes in, what, six weeks," he said. "Once you loosen up, you turn into a regular comedian, don't you?"

"The term would be comedienne."

"Never mind, then."

"Are you still taking the Cahuenga Pass into the Valley?"

"Yeah," he said. "I've talked it over with Luke and Billie. It's narrow, but it's a lot clearer and safer than the freeway. Even if I had Cerberus with me, it'd take most of a week just to clear a path from Western to the Lankershim exit. Better to stick to the surface streets. It'll let us check some of those little shops and restaurants up at the top of the Pass, too."

Stealth gave another nod and turned her attention to the maps and charts on the conference table. "Check in with me when you return."

"That's it?" He said. "No good-luck wishes? No kiss?"

"I do not believe in luck, George. You know this."

"And the kiss?"

She didn't make a sound, but he recognized her body language.

"Okay, then," he said. "See you when I get back."

× × ×

Roddenberry to the Melrose gate was only a quick hop. A small crowd had formed, but St. George could pick out Cerberus looming by the gate and the leather-clad scavengers around *Road Warrior* as he drifted to the ground.

Road Warrior was a twenty-four-foot truck that had been used for hauling equipment out to filming locations back when the Mount was in the movie business. The scavengers had chopped the roof and most of the walls off the box and built a new frame inside it, making the vehicle into a gigantic pickup. The truck had two large reserve gas tanks, a winch, and a wedge-like steel prow that had served as a battering ram more than a few times. There were bench seats for eight people in the back with plenty of standing room, and a steel platform on the cab's roof that could hold two or three more.

Billie and Jarvis had a small handcart covered with shimmering piles of metal they were handing out to each of the scavengers. Lady Bee was there, along with Lee and Paul. He could see Ilya, Lynne, and a few other regulars in the back of the truck. Luke Reid sat on the hood of the truck. St. George saw Hector de la Vega standing a few feet away from the main group. He made a point of locking eyes with the tattooed man and giving him a nod.

They threw rough salutes to the hero. Most of them were shaking out the chain mail armor and checking sizes against themselves. None of them looked pleased.

"Trade 'em if you have to," said Billie. "They're sort of sized. Let's get everyone as close as we can."

"Did we get the sleeves?" St. George asked Jarvis.

The salt-and-pepper man shook his head. "No go, chief," he said. "He says at best he'd need another day."

St. George frowned and looked at Billie. She shrugged.

"I feel like I should be in *Lord of the Rings* or something," said Lee.

A set of chain mail armor hit the pavement like a bag of pennies. "This stuff sucks, boss," said Paul.

Lady Bee nodded in agreement. She'd gotten the nickname from her striped hair. "None of it fits right, and it weighs a ton," she said. "And I'm pretty sure I asked for a chain mail bikini."

"I asked for Bee to get a chain mail bikini, too," chimed Ilya. She blew him a kiss and everyone laughed.

St. George waved them all to silence. "Hey," he said, "anyone else with bulletproof skin, raise your hand."

Lee cleared his throat and started to put up his palm. Billie cuffed him across the back of the head.

"You need to have something out there," he continued. "It's been five months since anyone's been bitten, but we've had two close calls in the past month. If everyone kept their leathers on, it wouldn't be a problem. But it's too damned hot and once one person pulls off their jacket we all do."

They all glanced at each other. Everyone was in tank tops and T-shirts with their leathers piled up next to them. Paul prodded the chain mail with his boot. "Is this our only choice?"

"Think of it like a shark suit," said Jarvis. "They can still bite y'all, they just can't break the skin. And it's a lot cooler."

"Except it weighs twenty pounds, so we'll just get hot that way," muttered Lynne.

"Chain mail bikini would weigh a lot less," said Bee. "I'm just saying."

"Shit looks gay." They all glanced back at Hector. He scratched the back of his neck by the razor stubble that was his hairline. "I ain't wearin' it."

Billie's nostrils flared and St. George set a hand on her shoulder as she went to step forward. "It's armor, people," he said. "It's not the greatest solution, but it's what we've got. If we find something better, or it starts getting cool again, it's gone. But for now you wear it so you can all come home at the end of the day and brag about killing famous exes."

There were a few mutters. Lee worked his arm into one of the sleeves and flexed a few times. It made a metallic, rustling noise. Lady Bee raised her hand.

The hero tipped his head to her. "What's up, Bee?"

"Does this mean I'm not getting the chain mail bikini?"

"Give it up."

"I like my jokes like I like my men," she said with a wink. "Ridden to death."

Jarvis dropped the last empty box on the cart. "Who didn't get any?"

Ilya raised a hand. So did a scruffy redheaded kid and a rail-thin older woman.

St. George sighed and made a decision. "You two are out

for today," he said. "We should have enough next time we go out."

"They can have mine," called Hector.

"Ilya, can I trust you to keep your leathers on?"

The dark-haired man gave a sage nod. "You got it, boss."

"Hey, I'll keep mine on, too," said the thin woman.

St. George shook his head. "Sorry. Ilya's probably the only person I trust to sweat it out." He looked at the group. "Everybody else, let's get ready to move out."

Luke stood up on the hood of *Road Warrior* and swung himself through the cab's window. Billie slapped her hands together. "You heard the man," she bellowed. "Armor up, gear up, load up." She pointed a stern finger at Hector. "You, too, de la Vega, or it's back to the mushroom farm."

St. George walked toward the tall archway and the sound of chattering teeth to stand next to Cerberus. The titan was staring out at Melrose Avenue. The gates were mobbed with exes, as always. Since last fall's battle with the Seventeens, it felt like there were always a few more than there had been before.

Two years in and most people still said exes rather than zombies. Thinking of them as ex-humans made it easier somehow. They reached between the bars and flailed at the two heroes with slow, clumsy limbs. Their eyes were pale and cloudy. St. George knew from experience they were dry to the touch. All their flesh was chalky gray, colored with dark purple bruises where blood pooled up beneath the skin.

Most of the exes at the gate carried some injury that would've been fatal if they were still alive. Several of them had gunshot wounds. More than a few were missing fingers or hands. A dead woman close to the hinge had scraped two ruts in her forehead, right down to the bone, swaying back and forth against the gate. Another one was charred to the point of being featureless. An elderly woman in a bathrobe was missing both eyes. A few bodies back, away from the gate, the hero saw a male ex with a samurai sword through its chest.

Here and there, though, were a few of the worse ones. The ones who still looked human. A little boy with dark hair, a Pikachu shirt, and chalky eyes. An older man with a beard who could've just spilled a few drops of wine on his shirt. A well-curved blonde with alabaster skin and full lips. Being in the plastic surgery capital of the world made for some very well-preserved dead people.

All of them worked their jaws up and down, snapping teeth together again and again. The chattering never let up. A few of them had turned their mouths into a mess of gore and shattered enamel, but kept clicking the jagged stumps against each other.

Cerberus stared past all of them. It was easy enough for her to look right over the mob of exes to the bone-white cross on the other side of the intersection. It stood as tall as the battlesuit and was marked with three bold words, each carved into the wood and painted black.

NIKOLAI BARTAMIAN
GORGON

They'd salvaged what parts of his uniform they could. The body armor. The duster. The goggles. What was left of him, what hadn't been chewed apart, they burned. They'd found his last requests sitting out in his grungy apartment.

"This was a lot easier when I used to go out with you," she said.

St. George glanced up at the armored head. "You never liked doing it."

"Never said I did. I just said it used to be easier." Cerberus shrugged her massive shoulders and looked away from the cross. "Let's get it over with."

A few of the guards pulled the additional support legs from the bars. Two others, Derek and Makana, flexed their hands inside heavy gloves and stood ready to grab the steel pipe that rested across the two halves of the gate. The exes reached for them, and each man batted dead fingers away.

St. George glanced back at *Road Warrior*. The truck's engine idled and Luke flashed the headlights at him. The hero gave the driver a thumbs-up and shot into the air.

He sailed up and over the tall arch of the gateway. He kicked a few exes as he landed in the wide intersection and they pinwheeled away, knocking down others as they went. The hungry dead turned toward him and stumbled away from the gate.

St. George let them get close. They tried to drag him down and broke teeth on his stone-hard skin. He batted them away with a sweep of his arm and they flew back to crash through the horde. He threw punches and felt skulls shatter under his knuckles. He grabbed a body by the shoulder and swung it around, battering even more exes to the ground. His boots came down to smash their heads. Within two minutes of landing he'd cleared two dozen of them.

The gate squeaked open behind him, and he heard the deep thump of heavy footsteps. Cerberus strode out, her three-fingered hands letting off arcs of power. Exes couldn't feel pain, but the nerves were still there. A 200,000-volt blast along those nerves would cripple their muscles long enough to drop them. The titan swept her hubcap-sized palms across the mob by the gate, and they dropped at her touch. They were struggling back to their feet when she marched over them and waved *Road Warrior* out behind her. The truck rolled forward and crushed exes beneath its thick dually tires. She gestured it past her and it rolled up to the intersection.

St. George leaped back over the truck, landing next to Cerberus. From the back, Jarvis tossed a long pike down to him. "Get going," the hero said. "I'll catch up."

Road Warrior revved its engines and turned onto Melrose. Some of the scavengers saluted St. George and Cerberus as they pulled out, and a few waves came from the guards walking the walls.

Behind them, the hero grabbed the pike by one end and knocked down a wide swath of exes. The armored titan slammed out a punch that went through an ex's head and caved in a skull behind it. They cleared a path back to the gate, where the guards fended off exes with more pikes.

An opening appeared and Cerberus strode through it. The gate clanged shut behind her, and Derek and Makana dropped the bar back into its brackets. St. George nodded to them through the bars, batting exes away as he did. "Everyone okay?"

"Piece of cake, boss," said Derek.

"Cerberus?"

The titan turned and looked down at him. "Burned up about a fifth of my reserves with the stun fields, but no problems otherwise." The armored skull shifted, and St. George knew she was looking at the cross again.

"Okay, then. See you all tonight. Watch for flares."

A few more salutes were tossed his way and St. George flew up into the sky. The withered fingers of exes dropped away from him.

Three

NOW

ST. GEORGE CAUGHT UP with *Road Warrior* three blocks away as they were crossing Vine. Work crews had stacked cars right down the center line of the street. The Big Wall, as people called it, was still a few months from being done, but here the cars were already three high. The rare times Danielle wasn't in the Cerberus armor she worked with a few others to figure out how to build some kind of gate here at Melrose and Vine. For now it was a large opening two lanes across.

He soared above the big truck for a while, watching the road ahead for blockages or crowds of exes. The path was clear most of the way to Highland. They'd dragged most of the cars away to use in the Big Wall. A pair of zombies stumbled into the street at Ivar, and *Road Warrior* plowed over them. The hero flew a block ahead and landed at a gas station where the two big streets crossed.

Highland Avenue was one of the main thoroughfares of Hollywood. There'd been a lot of fighting here during the Zombocalypse as people trying to flee choked the street with cars. They'd been attacked either by exes or other panicked people trying to escape them. The people of the Mount had come out here more than a few times on scavenging runs.

At different times he and Cerberus had pushed cars out of the way or even double-stacked them in places. The way was clear up Highland, but it was narrow. Very narrow in some places.

St. George waited for *Road Warrior* to catch up, and a minute later the big truck pulled up alongside him. Luke grinned at him from the cab. "Need a ride, sailor?"

"I was hoping you were heading my way," said the hero. "See anything?"

The driver shook his head. "Nah, clean sailing. You taking point?"

He nodded and banged the truck's hood. "How's it holding up?"

"She's a beast," said Luke, "but she's dependable. She'll get us over the hill and back." He shook his head. "You know, there was a point when I'd make this run once or twice a day without thinking about it."

St. George smiled. "There was a time when all I worried about were muggers and car thieves."

Luke grinned and gunned the engine. *Road Warrior* swung around the corner and headed north. "Donuts," someone moaned as they passed a shop. "I still don't know if it's worth living in a world with no more donuts." It got a few chuckles.

The drive up Highland was uneventful. St. George needed to push a few cars out of the way that had tumbled from where they'd been stacked, so he balled up his leather jacket and tossed it up to Lady Bee. A handful of exes stumbled up to the truck when it slowed down and the scavengers piked them through their skulls. They came across a Prius and two electric cars, and St. George marked their roofs with a large white X of spray paint he could see from the air. Gas was still a limited resource.

"This blows," said Hector in the back of the truck. "We ever going to go over five miles an hour?"

Billie clenched her jaw and her right fist.

"It's tricky going too fast in the city," Jarvis said before she could respond. "A year or so back, there was a buncha troublemakers who left booby traps all over the place. Spike chains, deadfalls, stuff like that. Wouldn't want to hit one of those at speed and get stuck out here, would we?"

He stared at Hector. The tattooed man stared back for a moment, then blinked. "Sound like a bunch of punks to me," said Hector. The corners of his mouth curled up. "Was up to me, I would've smacked their asses down hard." He drove his pike through the head of a gore-covered girl who was clawing at the side of the truck.

Another chuckle worked its way through the scavengers.

It took them an hour to get up past Hollywood and Highland. The famous intersection was a mess of broken glass, sun-faded billboards, and dead cars. Luke inched the big vehicle between the burned-out remains of a National Guard Humvee and a pileup involving half a dozen cars and trucks. A few yards past the intersection, St. George braced his back against an eighteen-wheeler cab on half-rotted tires. He pushed it out of the way inch by inch, his boots scraping on the pavement.

The last half mile to the freeway was the worst, even when the curving road widened out to three, then four lanes. They'd been this way on scavenging runs before, but *Road Warrior* was a little wider and a little longer than their other trucks, so the going was slow. They worked their way up past the big Methodist church at Franklin and a few scavengers bowed their heads or crossed themselves.

The big truck rolled past the parking lots for the Hollywood Bowl and the long-dead marquees for the amphitheater. On the center island stood a concrete memorial to the Bowl, surrounded by long, brown grass. The electronic screens in it were smashed to bits. Lady Bee's gaze drifted over to the large marquee on her left. There were two half-eaten bodies at the base of it, gray and shriveled from the sun. Dueling vandals had rearranged the letters and numbers into Bible passages or obscenities. "Why are people always so determined to arrange numbers into six-six-six?" she asked aloud.

"Because if this is hell," said Lee, "it means things can't get any worse."

A handful of exes staggered between the mess of cars in the lot and stumbled toward the sounds of life. "Hey," said Jarvis. "One of them's in a tux." He slipped his rifle off his shoulder and into his hand.

Paul looked where the bearded man pointed. "Yeah, so?"

"Might be someone famous."

"Or it might be some poor bastard who bit it on his wedding day," said Ilya.

Jarvis pulled a small pair of binoculars from his bag. "Can't tell who it is," he muttered. He held them out to Ilya. "Check it out for me."

"No."

"If it's someone famous I need the points, man."

Ilya smirked. "If you can't tell, they're either not famous or you're out of luck."

"Bastard."

"It's nobody famous," said Paul. He was looking through a small telescope. "No one I recognize, anyway."

"Damn it," said Jarvis. "Haven't seen a good celebrity in over a month." He gestured at an alabaster statue looming over a stagnant fountain. "Is the statue supposed to be some-one famous? Would that count?"

"It's just a piece of rock," said Lady Bee. "It's nothing."

"It's not just a piece of rock. Same guy who made the Academy Award made it."

They all looked at Hector. Ilya and Paul both raised their eyebrows.

"What? I got ink so I can't read a book?" The tattooed man shook his head. "Fuck all you guys."

The truck rolled to a stop. The road split ahead of them. The right two lanes ran beneath an overpass and up onto the freeway. The left two lanes were Cahuenga Boulevard. Two roads into the Valley. The scavengers moved forward to look at the mass of concrete.

"Sailors beware," said Lynne. "Here be dragons."

St. George gave a black sports car a firm shove, knocking it into the overgrown plants on the side of the road. "Just like we planned," he called to Luke. The hero pointed up the left lanes to the Cahuenga Pass. "When I scoped it out earlier, the southbound side seemed to be clogged the least. I'll clear a path through the cars. Stay about ten yards behind me." He looked at the scavengers on the roof of the cab. "Bee, Ilya, Lee, keep me covered, but hold off shooting unless you're sure I need the help. Everyone else, watch our back, make sure we don't get blocked—"

"Watch it!" shouted Hector.

They all saw the blur coming out of the sky at St. George before he did. Rifles snapped up. He spun and raised his fists just as the ex crashed into the ground. The hero leaped into the air and gore splattered across the pavement.

"Fell off the freeway," said Hector. He pointed up at the overpass.

"You okay, boss?" called Ilya.

St. George settled back onto the pavement. "Been worse," he said. He shook a few wet clumps of meat and hair off his boots.

"You need a moment?" asked Bee with a smile.

"I'll survive," he said. "Everyone ready?"

They nodded and saluted as he turned back to the road. Luke revved the engine again. St. George took a few strides forward, wrapped his arms across the hood of a green Hyundai, and swung the car off to the side.

They headed up Cahuenga, over the hills, and into the San Fernando Valley.

× × ×

The northbound side of the road was two solid lanes packed with cars, and the south side was only marginally better. St. George shoved trucks and cars out of the way and tossed motorcycles up into the bushes and trees on the south side of the pavement. It would take him a moment to get a good grip, but he could lift the smaller cars and stack them on top of the bigger ones. Sometimes, if he had a clear shot, he stacked them on top of exes.

To their right, between the automobiles that packed the northbound side, the scavengers could look down onto all ten lanes of Highway 101. Thousands of vehicles clogged the Hollywood Freeway in both directions. Some had ended their existence in crashes. Others had been gridlocked and abandoned. They were faded and grainy, painted with over two years of dust.

Thousands of exes stumbled between the cars. Their skins were withered from months and months in the sun. In at least a quarter of the vehicles, dead things pawed at windshields or clawed the air from open doors. They'd been left prisoners of seat belts and child locks. The endless sound of teeth echoed up from the freeway.

The scavengers went forward yard by yard. The sun was high overhead when they reached the top of the pass and the road started to slope down again. Just past the crest, the burned-out remains of a garage stood behind a fire-blackened fence. The cinder-block walls had cracked from the heat. A charred corpse lay near the gate, dressed in the remains of a mechanic's coverall. St. George hopped the fence, tapped the corpse with his boot, and walked through the ruins.

Next door to the garage was a small fire station, the near side seared and blackened. The rolling door had been torn off the runners and the fire engine was gone. While St. George checked the garage, Jarvis, Paul, and Lee searched the building. It had been cleaned out either by civil servants or looters. Paul found an ex in the back and took its head off with a wide swipe of his machete.

A little farther down the road a mom-and-pop-style gas station was crammed into a tiny strip mall. There were eight cars in a line, a pathetic attempt to barricade the plaza's minuscule parking lot. Both of the pumps had been vandalized. Lady Bee pointed to the three numbers on the price signs and winked at Lee. There was a restaurant and what looked like a psychic's shop. All the windows had been used for target practice until they collapsed under their own weight. The red tile roof was shot up, too.

Road Warrior pulled up alongside the line of cars and half a dozen scavengers leaped out, their armor jingling. Billie, Ilya, and a baby-faced man named Danny moved around to check the back of the building. Jarvis, Paul, and Lady Bee headed for the mini-mart behind the gas pumps. Through the broken window they could see something tall swaying back and forth in the shadows.

St. George landed on the rooftop deck of the big truck and waited. Under his watchful eye, a scruffy guy slipped from the cab and moved to the loading ports for the station's underground tanks. He pried the metal covers off and fed a weighted line into the opening.

Lee and an older guy named Al slid out on the opposite side and took Hector with them. They watched up and down Cahuenga for movement. Hector started to line up on an ex down the road, but Lee put his hand out and guided the rifle's barrel down. "Hold off shooting outside until you have to," he said. "Noise attracts them."

"I know that," grumbled the tattooed man.

"How long since you've been out?" asked Al. He had leathery skin, dark eyes, and a few streaks of steel in his iron hair.

"Out?"

"Out of the Mount. Out from behind the walls."

"Nine months," said Hector. "Not since the war."

"You go out a lot before that?"

"On and off. When I had to."

"It'll come back to you," said Al. "Just don't get anyone killed before then."

A muffled gunshot came from the mini-mart. St. George looked over and Jarvis leaned out to give him an all clear. Billie's team returned from around the back of the building. "Two exes," she said.

"No problems?" asked the hero.

Ilya shook his head.

"There're some apartments farther back there," Billie said. "How much do you want to search?"

"Let's stay on Cahuenga," he said. "We'll have time to spread out later."

They nodded and headed for the restaurant. From the battered signage, St. George guessed it was an Italian place.

"Sweet," whistled the scruffy man. He'd moved to the second fuel tank. "There's about a foot down there. Could be as much as sixty, maybe seventy gallons." He grinned up at St. George through nicotine teeth.

The hero nodded. "We'll wait until everyone's done and then I'll make some space for Luke to pull in. Don't want to draw attention too soon."

Jarvis, Paul, and Lady Bee came back from the store shaking their heads. "Cleaned out," said Bee. "It's a mess, but there's nothing useful."

St. George sighed. "Well, we all knew there was a good chance of that. It's a main drag." He tipped his head to the next storefront. "You guys want to take the psychic?"

Lady Bee gave a too-sharp salute and clicked her heels together with a smirk.

× × ×

An ex stumbled across the road to them. It had been an older man with a wiry frame and a thin mustache. It reached out and Lee pushed it away with the tip of his rifle. "Hey, check it out."

Al and Hector glanced over at him. "What?"

"It's Vincent Price." Lee shoved it back again. "That's gotta be worth major points."

"Vincent Price is dead," said Al.

"Well, yeah. They're all dead."

"He was dead before this, fuckwit," said Hector. "Like, twenty years ago."

The other man scowled. "Are you sure? This sure looks like him."

"Sure," said the tattooed man, nodding. "He's dead."

"Maybe he came back anyway."

Al shot him a look. "How the hell would he come back anyway?"

Lee shrugged. "It's Vincent Price. If anyone was going to come back as a zombie it'd be him."

"No," said Al, "if anyone was going to come back as a zombie it'd be Bela Lugosi. But he won't, because he's dead, too." He slid a machete from the scabbard at his side and chopped through the ex's neck.

× × ×

"Well, that's something y'all don't see every day," said Jarvis.

At the center of the psychic's shop stood a round table decorated with colored scarves and cloths. Half a dozen stubby candles had been knocked over. A crystal ball had fallen from the tabletop and its dusty shards lay near one of the legs. Tarot cards were scattered and turned at all angles.

An ex sat behind the table, clacking its teeth at them. It had been a woman once, Asian by the look of it. It was in a wheelchair. With the brakes locked, it was wedged between the seat and the table. Rings shivered on its bony fingers as it reached mindlessly back and forth with its hands. Every third or fourth pass it would snag a tarot card and slide it a few inches on the tabletop.

"Either y'all want to guess how long it's been sitting there like that?"

"At least two years, looking at the dust," said Bee. "Maybe more. She could've died right at the start of the outbreak."

"Looks like she tried to give herself one last reading," said Paul. "Guess she believed this stuff." He prodded open a small fridge with his foot and recoiled from the smell he set loose.

"People believe a lot of crap when things get bad," said Jarvis. He reached out and pulled one card from the table. The ex clawed at the metal rings of his sleeve with feeble fingers. He held up the image of the black knight with a skull face. "Death," he said with a smirk. "Guess she was right on that."

"The death card doesn't mean death," said Bee. "It means a transition. A change."

Jarvis slid a bowie knife from his belt and stepped behind the ex. "Well, so she was still right," he said. He grabbed its hair, pulled its head back, and sawed through the neck. When he was done he tossed the skull in the corner. "Let's see if there's anything good in the back room."

× × ×

As St. George predicted, the rest of the small plaza was picked clean. The big score was the fifty-odd gallons of gasoline. It took half an hour to pull it all up using a small hand pump. The scavengers killed another eight exes while they waited.

Two hours later they knew the next three buildings had been stripped clean of useful materials, too. Another sixteen exes dead, five of them with their necks snapped by the hero's bare hands. The scavengers grumbled. Things had been getting tight in Hollywood proper, but it'd been a while since a mission was this unsuccessful.

At Barham Boulevard they found the remains of a National Guard roadblock. Concrete dividers were flanked with bright yellow barrels. The water that once weighted them down was long gone. The dividers blocked half the bridge that crossed over the Hollywood Freeway toward Universal City. At some point a jacked-up pickup had tried to crash through the barrier. It had wrecked a section of the roadblock but ripped up its suspension and a tire in the process. It sat a few yards onto the bridge. The paint had faded in the sun and a fine coat of dust had settled across it. Broken concrete and crumpled yellow plastic trailed behind it.

At the far end of the bridge they could see a matching roadblock and an olive-drab truck. Lady Bee stood on *Road Warrior*'s rooftop deck with her binoculars out. "I count maybe thirty exes," she said. "They've noticed us but the barricade's giving them troub—ah, two just fell over it. Nine, maybe ten bodies on this side. Looks like two or three of them are moving, but it might be heat ripples off the pavement. They look like military." She lowered the glasses and looked at St. George standing in the air over her. "Military could mean weapons and supplies."

He nodded. "Let me go check it out."

The hero shot through the air and landed on the far side of the freeway next to the truck. A few yards away the pair of exes that had fallen over the roadblock staggered to their feet. There were ten Guardsmen around the truck. Seven of them were still dead.

Both legs on one of the exes had been shredded below the knees, maybe by a grenade. The dead thing crawled clumsily on its elbows and reached for St. George's boot. He kicked it in the bridge of the nose and the skull came away from the neck. It sailed out over the freeway as the body slumped to the ground. He heard it clang on the hood of some distant car.

The other two had been a man and a woman. Their legs and arms had been eaten down to the bone before they'd come back. The woman's cheeks and lips were gone, too. Everything not covered by body armor. The dead things twitched and thrashed and stared at him with chalky eyes. He reached down, twisted each of their heads around, and they stopped moving.

All the bodies had been stripped clean of weapons and ammunition. Even the exes. Four of the bodies were missing their boots and socks. St. George took a moment to check a few supply crates and the back of the truck, but they were empty, too. He rapped a knuckle on the vehicle's gas tanks and a hollow sound echoed back.

There was a scuffling noise behind him. The pair of fallen exes had reached him, plus a third had slumped over the barricade and creeped headfirst toward the ground. He grabbed the one in the stained security outfit as it leaned into him and hurled the dead thing out over the freeway. It sailed through the air for a few hundred feet, bounced on the top of a minivan, and off the side of a white truck, and vanished between two compacts.

The other ex wrapped its arms around him and sank its teeth into his bare shoulder. Incisors, canines, and molars crumbled away against his skin, but it kept gnawing with the jagged stumps. He reached up, pushed his thumb into its mouth, and pressed up against its palate. The bone creaked but held long enough for him to swing the dead thing up and over his shoulder. He brought the ex down onto the pavement hard enough to pulverize its bones. It collapsed into mush.

He focused and whisked himself back through the air. Lady Bee scanned back and forth on Cahuenga with her binoculars. Ilya and a broad-shouldered woman, Keri, stood by while Paul went through the back of the wrecked pickup. A trio of scavengers at each end of *Road Warrior* kept an eye on the street and the exes that drifted along it.

"Nothing," St. George told them. "Anything here?"

"Looks like this guy was doing our work for us, boss," said Ilya. Paul handed a sack of canned goods down to Keri. She ferried them to Lee standing on the liftgate of their truck. "Five bags of nonperishables, three more that look like they came from a CVS. No weapons, but there was a box of nine millimeter in the glove compartment with thirty rounds left in it."

"Any sign of the driver?"

"Some blood on the seat and the steering wheel," said Paul.

Ilya pointed at the spider-webbed windshield. "Bullet hole," he said. "I bet· they got shot running the roadblock, crashed, and then . . ."

"Then walked away from it, one way or the other," the hero finished.

"The other," said Lady Bee from the top of the cab. "If they were alive, they wouldn't've left everything behind."

Paul handed down a final bag and hopped out of the truck.

"Moving on, then," said St. George. A few yards down the road he could see another, larger gas station with a shot-out sign. He could remember driving past it a few times back in the before days, back when he was just a college maintenance guy moonlighting as a superhero in a thriving Los Angeles, but he couldn't remember if it had been an Arco or a Mobil or what.

Hector stepped up onto *Road Warrior*'s liftgate and paused. He looked back and forth up the street. "What is that? Is that . . . flies?"

Lynne cocked her head to the side. "It's not flies. Bees, maybe, or hornets?"

"It's not insects," said St. George with a shake of his head. "Too steady. It almost sounds like . . ."

He rocketed thirty feet into the air. "Grab the flare gun!" he shouted down at them. "Red flare, fast!"

Jarvis fumbled in his pack. "What the hell is it?"

"No way," said Lady Bee. Her eyes were wide and she smiled as the droning sound grew louder. "No way!"

"It's a plane!" shouted St. George, going higher into the sky.

Signing Up
THEN

IF YOUR PARENTS gave you a name like Augustus Phillip Hancock, you'd've joined the Army, too. Trust me. When I turned eighteen, I wanted to be anywhere but Little Rock, so when Eddie said he was going to sign up I did, too.

Now, I ain't supposed to tell anyone about this. When I got pulled into Project Krypton last year, still a fuzzy right out of boot camp, they had us sign a bunch of waivers and security paperwork. Nobody with wives or kids. Nobody who was an only child. Then they shipped us off to Yuma, which I can say is dead center in the middle of nowhere. A woman from Broadsword Company said she'd heard the whole project used to be based at Natick, like you'd expect, but it'd gotten so big they had to set up a whole sub-base out at Yuma for it. One of the fellas said the little base should be called Kandor, and two or three fellas thought that was really funny, but I didn't get the joke.

One of the fellas in Broadsword also said all the paperwork we'd filled out was the same stuff they use for suicide missions, but I think that's bullshit. Although, looking back at it, maybe it ain't.

I was one of the lucky ones. Turns out my company, Greyhound, was the control group. We were eating sugar pills and getting shots of saline water. Apparently they can just stick that in you and it doesn't do much of anything.

So, yeah, Greyhound was lucky. Angel and Devil Companies, too. Well, kind of. They're all getting dialysis or something for a few weeks. They weren't getting sugar pills and saline.

Broadsword are the fellas that got screwed. Their company had the biggest concentration of the stuff the old doc was giving us. It didn't go over well. I've heard them talking about all the stuff Angel and Devil are getting, plus marrow transplants and hormone therapy and stuff. None of them are complaining though. We all know what happened to Lucas and Jacobs, and ain't nobody wants to go through that.

Well, none of us know officially. But we were all there for the start of it, and Eddie works in the medical wing. He saw how they ended up. So we all know.

At first it seemed great. All of Broadsword Company was bulking up, getting stronger, just like the old doc wanted. Then they all started getting cramps. And they were . . . swelling. You know those fellas who get crazy ripped? The ones who hit the gym every day and do contests and stuff? It was like that. Their arms and legs were getting bigger, and stretching their skin so it was creepy tight and their veins stood out. And they weren't even working out much.

It hit Jacobs first. He just got itchy. He tried to be a good soldier, suck it up and not let it get to him, but it kept getting worse. After two days his eyes were watering. Not crying, just watering bad.

Third day we told him he had to go see the doc. He was pissed at us and kept saying no and to mind our own beeswax. Yeah, he's one of those Southern weirdos who say beeswax. But First Sergeant Paine had been specific about reporting any symptoms and I wasn't going to disobey the first sergeant. Finally Jacobs got up off his bunk, went to grab his shirt, and when he reached up his arm split open. There was a pop and his skin broke open like a hot dog popping on the grill. There was just too much muscle packed in there. It didn't even bleed much because it was pulled so tight.

We got him down to the infirmary and Lucas came along, too, 'cause he'd started to feel itchy, and now he was worried the same thing was gonna happen to him. The docs were cutting him out of his wifebeater and it turned out his skin had split, too, right across the shoulders. They started calling for the old doc after that and we all got hustled out. But Eddie was still there. We heard it all from him later.

Apparently the old doc's serum didn't work like he hoped. Remember how I talked about the crazy ripped fellas? You ever see them when they're so big they can't put their arms down? I think that's what they mean by muscle-bound. Well, that's what was happening to Lucas and Jacobs. Their muscles were growing out of control. Four days after we took them down there, Eddie told us they couldn't even move anymore. Their arms and legs were just big sausages of muscle. They looked fat because their abs were getting so big, and they couldn't lie flat because their glutes and shoulders were twisting their backs up. And their skin was still splitting. It couldn't grow as fast as the muscles were, so they were getting some kind of sharkskin grafts or something.

On the fifth day they started screaming. We heard it all over the base. Turns out their bones were growing, too, but they weren't growing fast enough, either. They kept getting crushed between muscles or stretched apart as the muscles kept getting bigger and thicker. "It's like their bodies've turned into torture racks," Eddie said one night when he got back to the barracks. "They're being pulled apart by their own muscles."

They screamed for three days straight. Eddie told me over chow they'd gotten so big it took huge doses of painkillers just to make them stop screaming. The whole thing was freaking him out. He'd snuck his phone in and showed me a picture of this swollen red thing that looked like a fat grub. He said it was Jacobs, and that his skull'd been pushed off his neck by all the muscles, but he was still alive 'cause it hadn't actually broken his spinal cord yet. "If they can fix him," Eddie said, "he's still gonna be a cripple for the rest of his life."

On day nine they stopped screaming. All at once. On day ten we were told Jacobs and Lucas had died in the line of duty. They'd be given full honors. And the old doc was gone. Eddie said he'd heard Colonel Shelly and the higher brass were furious, and the doc had pretty much fled from the base.

Anyway, we all figured that was it for Project Krypton. Three-fourths of us out of commission one way or the other. One company left. We got three days to wonder about it and then we met the new doc at a big briefing. There was this young fella with him in a dark suit, Smith from Homeland, and he smiled a lot and gave this little speech and introduced us all to Dr. Sorensen.

The new doc's the flipside of the old doc. The old doc was actually a young fella, not much older than any of us. He was some hotshot scientist, and kind of an asshole, to be honest. The new doc's an older fella who feels like he should be a cool uncle or something. He's got a big gray beard and glasses and he talks like a teacher.

They were redoing Krypton from the ground up. Nothing was going to be the same but the name. It was going to be a whole new process. That made a lot of people rumble. But Sorensen stopped that real quick before the first sergeant could bark at us.

"These are not going to be experiments," he told us. "I will not be putting any of you brave men and women at risk. These are all established procedures, using tested drugs and chemicals. With some of you the treatments will take and with some they will not. But there will be no risk of . . . of what happened before I got here."

Then the first sergeant got up. He told us we'd done our duty and everyone here had carried out the requirements we'd signed up for. Even though they were keeping the number, as far as the Army was concerned this was going to be something new and the 456th was being disbanded. If we wanted out, we'd be debriefed and reassigned. We had until tomorrow morning to decide. He dismissed us.

The young fella, Smith, started working the crowd. He was shaking hands, asking questions, kissing asses. He shook mine and asked if I was going to stick around and I told him, yeah, I probably was. I said probably but I think even then I knew I was going to be part of Project Krypton for the long haul. It just felt like I belonged there.

I moved to the front of the room and realized a few fellas from Greyhound were behind me. I think we'd all been ready to get a new assignment. Yuma was boring as hell, and we'd all joined up to go overseas and kick some al-Qaeda ass. If Smith hadn't said anything, I think we all would've walked out of the room and started packing. Now it was almost a pride thing to finish what we started.

Colonel Shelly was having a talk up front with the new doc. If it was anyone else, I'd say an argument, but I knew the colonel didn't do arguments. Or excuses.

First Sergeant Paine was there. He locked eyes with me and I knew enough to stop where I was and stand at attention. I heard the fellas lock up behind me, too. A couple fellas call him First Sergeant Bring-the-Paine, but not if he's anywhere nearby. So we stood there for a few minutes while they talked and didn't do anything except listen.

"You can't just throw him out," the new doc was saying. "He was in the Broadsword trials for four months."

"And now he's out of them, doctor," Colonel Shelly said, "just like everyone else."

"It's not that simple. The drugs and artificial hormones that idiot was filling them with are all through his system. They're stored up in his fat cells waiting for him to have a flashback."

"You said he was clean. You also said if they never had any reaction during the testing, odds are they never would."

"In theory yes, but there're always going to be residual traces in his kidneys, his skin, his fat cells. His tests said he was clean, but like anyone with a history of drug use, weight loss could cause a flashback and then it's all back in his system again."

"Well, hypothetically, what's the worst that can happen?"

"I don't know," said Sorensen. "I'm still not sure what caused the reaction in Jacobs and Lucas. There're a dozen possible triggers. Stress. Adrenaline. A disease that strains his system. Potentially, any of it could cause spurts of muscle and bone growth."

"And what are the odds?"

"It could happen, isn't that enough?"

"Could it?" said Colonel Shelly. "Could it really?"

"The chances are slim I admit, but—"

"Slim is fine by me. He's insubordinate, he struck an officer, and he's out. He can go home and the LAPD can deal with him. If he has a reaction, it'll kill him and then no one has to deal with him." The colonel turned and walked away.

The new doc shook his head and followed him. "I still think it's a mistake," he said as he walked away.

"Specialist," First Sergeant Paine said. He was giving me that look. "What's your purpose here?"

"First sergeant," I said, still at attention, "I request to keep this duty assignment."

Five

NOW

ST. GEORGE PUSHED down against gravity and launched himself higher into the sky. He was a good three hundred feet above the Hollywood Freeway now. He spun in the air as he tried to spot the source of the low drone echoing across the Valley. The chattering of thousands of teeth had almost hidden the sound. If Los Angeles hadn't been a ghost town, they never would've heard it.

A line of fire shot past him and burst into a red star trailing crimson smoke. Between the flare and the sun, looking west was tough now, but he was pretty sure a prop-engine plane wouldn't be coming in from the Pacific. He could still hear the faint sound, but he thought it was getting fainter.

There was another flash, this time white light, and the air crackled and danced on his skin as the sonic boom ruffled his hair and clothes. Zzzap floated next to him in the sky.

Can you hear that?!

"Yeah," said St. George. "Can you spot it? Radar or engine heat or anything?"

Zzzap spun around once. *Right there*, he said. *Looks like it's following 101. It's transmitting a tight signal back thataway.* He pointed to the east.

"What's it saying?"

The wraith tilted his head as if listening. It was one of a dozen habits he kept when he was in his energy form. *Doesn't sound like talking*, he said. *I think it's a video feed. And I'm pretty sure this is military encryption.*

"Yeah?"

I saw a lot of it during the outbreak. Looks like the same kind of patterns. It's confusing at first, but once you get used to it it's like reading a ransom note, one of those ones where all the letters are cut out of different magazines.

"Can we catch up with it and signal the pilot?"

Zzzap nodded. *Shouldn't be too hard. He's only moving about eighty-five, ninety miles an hour and he's heading right at us. Been ignoring my signals, though.*

The two heroes flew higher into the sky. Zzzap moved in short hops so St. George could keep up. Five minutes later they were a thousand feet up. The air was crisp even though the sun was harsh. The gleaming wraith pointed at their target. It was a few hundred yards away and closing. They fell in next to it as it passed and kept a dozen yards between them.

The plane was about thirty feet long, if St. George judged it right, with maybe a fifty-foot wingspan. It was hard to tell with nothing to compare it to. The shape of it reminded him of a dragonfly, heavier in the front with a slimmer body. A basketball-sized blister peppered with lenses hung below the dragonfly's "head" and the tail was two large vanes pointing down at rakish angles instead of up. The propeller was mounted behind the tail. He sailed above the aircraft and looked down at the phallic front. There was no cockpit.

Zzzap flitted up to the plane. He hung in the air alongside the craft and pointed to the blue and white star crest on the slim body. *Told you it was military.*

"What the hell is it?" St. George had to shout over the propeller and slid a few more yards away from it.

Zzzap followed him over. *Seriously? Didn't you ever watch the Learning Channel or Discovery or any of those?*

"I dumped cable two years before I became a superhero. Too expensive."

So you never even saw the special they did about me?

"Barry!"

I'm pretty sure it's a Predator drone.

St. George looked at the plane roaring alongside them. "The robot planes they used in Iraq?"

Yeah. And it's not so much a robot as remote controlled. Which means somebody east of here is flying this thing.

"And watching us," said the hero. He pointed at the lenses on the metal basketball. "They can see us through those, right?"

Technically, yeah, but I've been jamming its transmissions since we got close to it. We don't know who's on the other end of this thing.

St. George glanced at his friend. "What makes you say that?"

The wraith pointed east. *I can see their transmitter over there. It's about four hundred miles away. Danielle could probably back me up on this, but I don't think the military controls Predators by straight radio anymore. It's all done by satellite to increase range.*

"You're assuming whoever's driving this thing still has access to a satellite."

The glowing figure shrugged.

St. George felt himself dropping behind the drone and pushed himself faster. "You think there's a chance it's just on automatic or something?"

Zzzap shook his head. *Nah. Somebody launched this thing.*

"You think the military's looking for us?"

Took them long enough, if they are. But, yeah, if someone sent one of these things to Los Angeles they're looking for something.

They sailed along with the Predator for a few more miles. St. George glanced down. He could see an airport and a big park below him, which meant they were over Van Nuys at this point.

The plane began to make a slow turn toward the south. *New search orders coming in,* said Zzzap. The wraith circled the drone a few times, so fast the aircraft could've been hovering in the air. *What do you want to do?*

"I'm thinking," he said. "This should be a no-brainer, but . . . I don't know. After all this time, to have this thing show up out of nowhere just feels weird."

With good reason, said Zzzap. *Pretty much every zombie movie ever made tells us that anyone who's part of the U.S. Armed Forces must be insane by now. They probably want to kill our men and take our women. And when I say take, I mean—*

"You're not helping."

Sorry, said Zzzap. *Whoops. Definitely being controlled. Someone's finally noticed they've lost the feed from this baby. They're sending a couple reboot protocols.*

"You letting them through?"

Yeah, why not? Doesn't do any harm and we've still got a couple more minutes before they realize they're being actively blocked.

They flew on for another mile. St. George twisted in the air and looked behind them. "They've seen the Mount already, haven't they? And the Big Wall?"

Zzzap looked back as well. *Probably, yeah. Might not realize we're all live people yet, though.*

"Can you send them a message? Override their signal and send a cautious 'hello' or something?"

The wraith nodded. *Piece of cake. Anything in particular?*

"Make sure they know we're here, but be a little vague about who 'we' are."

Zzzap soared above the drone for a few moments and then bent his head close to it. *Ahhh*, he said. *Yeah, I think I've got something that'll work.*

"What are you sending?"

What you asked for.

"You're doing something stupid, aren't you?"

He held up a white-hot hand. *Don't distract me. I've got to have this in my head just right or it won't transmit properly.*

"Barry . . ."

Trust me, George, said the wraith. *If we're going to reestablish contact with the world, we want it to be memorable. Like that.* He raised his head and flitted away from the plane.

"Please tell me you didn't send something stupid."

Zzzap shook his head. *I thought about it, but no. What now?*

The engine pitched higher and the drone banked toward them. Both heroes twisted to avoid the wings as they cut through the air. The Predator dropped down, leveled out, and accelerated.

I think we got their attention.

St. George paused in the air. "Where's it going?"

Home, I think. Zzzap looked at the radio waves hanging in the air. *Yeah, it's getting called home.*

"Could you follow it?"

I can beat it there. He tipped his head to the east. *If I've got the distance figured right, twenty minutes, tops.*

"Can you be subtle?"

The wraith looked up. *There's still a lot of sun in the sky. If I'm careful I can hide myself in front of it, take a quick look around.*

"Do it. I'll see you back at the Mount later."

Zzzap gave him a thumbs-up and vanished like a bolt of

lightning. St. George looked down, picked out a few big land-marks, and worked his way back toward the Cahuenga Pass.

× × ×

The scavengers still sat just south of the Barham Bridge. Jarvis, Hector, and Lynne stood watch on one end of *Road Warrior*. Lee, Danny, and Al monitored the other end. They'd killed about a dozen exes while St. George chased the Predator, and half a dozen more stumbled toward the big truck.

"Was it a plane?" Lynne shouted up to him. "Who was it?"

"Hey!" he snapped as his boots clanged on the truck's roof platform next to Lady Bee. "In case you forgot, we're still outside in infested territory. Keep it down."

She cringed. "Sorry. But was it a plane?"

"Sort of," he said.

Al frowned. "How is something 'sort of' a plane?"

"Helicopter?" asked Paul from the truck's bed.

"Was it one of those motorized hang glider things?"

"Ultralight?"

St. George shook his head and held up a hand. "Two things for now, okay."

They settled down.

"The thing that was up there, we're not sure whose it was. We want to take it easy. For all we know, these people could be another group like the Seventeens, just trying to find other survivors to steal their supplies."

Hector twisted his lip, but said nothing.

"Second thing is this. Let's not give people a bunch of false hope. Zzzap is backtracking it to its source and we should know more by tonight or tomorrow morning. But I'd prefer if you all kept this to yourselves for now, okay? We don't want to get people excited over nothing, so let's wait until we know what it is."

He could feel their enthusiasm drop. A few shoulders sagged. Lynne looked at him. "So . . . now what?"

"We get back to work," said St. George. "There's another big gas station down there. Let's see if we can make it there before we call it a day and head back." He leaped from the roof platform and sailed down to the ground in front of the truck. The hero set his hands against a dark SUV, pushed it against a sedan, and shoved both vehicles a few feet off the road.

Most of the scavengers climbed back into the truck. Billie walked up to him. "You look tired."

"Kind of, yeah," said St. George. "I don't do much high-speed flying."

She glanced past him and raised her voice. "Danny, watch your back."

They all turned. A blond ex wearing stained sweats and a tank top had worked its way across the road. Lee and Al stepped forward as the dead thing bit down on Danny's shoulder. His chain mail blunted the rotted teeth. He yelped and twisted back. The dead woman stumbled after him, its teeth chattering. He gave it a shove and it snapped at his fingers.

"The chain mail works," deadpanned Al.

"Hell, yeah," stammered Danny. He took a few deep breaths.

"See, this is what I'm talking about," St. George said. "Stay focused, people. Maybe there is someone else out there, but we'll never know if we all get killed, will we?"

"They won't kill *you*," said Hector dryly.

"Yeah, but Stealth gets really annoyed when I go out with fourteen people and come home alone."

Danny held the ex away with his rifle. "Hey," he said, "does she look familiar to anyone else?"

Keri peered at the ex and shook her head. "Nope."

"They're all getting so shriveled it's hard to tell," said Al.

"That one's not shriveled," said Lynne with a grin. "Silicone stays bouncy forever."

The ex clacked its teeth and took another swipe at Danny. He gave it a shove to keep it off balance. "Final decisions? Famous or not?"

St. George tilted his head and pointed. "What's on its arm?"

"Ink," said Hector. "Roses. She had some nice work done."

Ilya snapped his fingers. "She's a porn star."

Lee gave the ex another look. "You think so?"

"Blond hair, fake tits, one very tattooed arm, kind of familiar."

Paul pointed his rifle down the road. "Isn't there a big porn headquarters right down the street?"

"I don't think all the porn stars lived there."

"Hey, I'm just saying it's there."

Billie looked back to St. George and spoke in a low voice. "Was it a Predator?"

He blinked and dropped his own volume. "Yeah. Good guess."

"Prop engine, sort of a plane, doesn't sound like there was a pilot." She shrugged. "I was only in Afghanistan for eighteen months, but I saw a couple of them."

Lady Bee laughed. "Oh my God, I think he's right. That was Brooke-something."

"Aren't there ten or twenty Brookes?"

"No, she's a big one," said Ilya. "Damn, what was her last name?"

"I think that's enough to say she counts as a celebrity. Jarvis?"

The bearded man sighed and nodded. "Yeah, sure. I ain't never catching up, anyway."

Billie watched Danny try to trip the ex, but spoke in the same low tones. "Why are you so cautious if it's one of ours?"

"We don't know it's one of ours," said St. George. "For all we know it's a bunch of redneck survivalists who logged a lot of time playing flight simulator games. Until we know for sure, I think it's better to be cautious."

"Fair enough."

Danny kicked one of the ex's legs out from under it and the dead thing tumbled to the ground. Ilya tossed him a pike from the back of *Road Warrior* and he caught it one-handed. He took a good grip on the weapon, drove the spiked tip down through the ex's mouth, and watched a puddle form behind its head.

Six

NOW

"**IT'S A MILITARY BASE**," said Barry. He'd been home from his recon mission since sundown, changed back from the energy form, and eaten two peanut-butter sandwiches on the way from Four to Roddenberry. He was working on the third. It had apple slices in it that crunched whenever he took a bite.

They were in Stealth's conference room. The cloaked woman had spread another map across the table, this one showing most of the American Southwest. The thought flitted through St. George's mind that he had no idea where she got all her maps from. Maybe she'd looted a travel store at some point before they founded the Mount.

Barry placed his hands on the edge of the table and heaved himself up out of his wheelchair. "Army, if I remember my camo patterns and stuff," he continued, "but I'm pretty sure I saw Air Force there, too, and maybe a couple of Marines."

"All working together on one base?" said St. George. "Isn't that a little odd?"

"Unusual, but not unheard of," said Stealth. Her black-gloved finger traced out an area in southwest Arizona. "The most likely candidate is the Yuma Proving Ground."

"Didn't seem that big," said Barry. "This was just two or three little places and a small airstrip, none of them much bigger than the Mount." He took another bite of his sandwich.

"There are a lot of sub-bases in the proving ground," said Danielle. She reached up and brushed a stringy lock of strawberry-blond hair away from her freckled face, then swiped at it again when it dropped back down. The only way she could attend was to take off the Cerberus armor, and she was fidgeting. It had taken St. George an hour to convince her to take it off. "I did a quick trip out there once to test the mount for the arm cannons. As a whole it might be overrun, but it wouldn't surprise me if there was still a functioning base or two there somewhere."

Barry studied the map while he chewed. "I think it was around here," he said, twiddling his fingers at part of the map. "There was a pretty decent-sized area with a triple-fence where most of the activity was. A couple hundred exes outside. Forty or fifty buildings, a helipad, and a power substation pulling from somewhere off-base. And there was an airstrip twenty or so miles from there where the Predator was docked or parked or whatever you say. It looked pretty clean and ex-free, too."

"How many people?"

He shrugged. "Not sure. Looked like a lot less than us. I mean, the original us. Skeleton crew guarding the walls. A lot of buildings, but it didn't look overcrowded. You know how we've got tents on rooftops and all that? There's none of that."

St. George looked at the distance between the proving grounds and the city of Yuma. "Any civilians?"

Barry shook his head. "If there were, I didn't see them."

Stealth shook her head. "It is unlikely a military base would have large numbers of civilian refugees."

Danielle frowned. "It's not like the movies, you know," she said. "In a real crisis protecting civilians would be a top priority."

"It is unfortunate, then, that the ex-virus was not recognized as a real crisis sooner," said the hooded woman.

St. George let out a slow breath and a wisp of dark smoke curled from his nostrils. "So this is real," he said. "The military's still up and running and they're looking for us."

"There is the possibility the base and its resources are being used by other survivors," said Stealth, "but the logical assumption is this is a functioning base staffed by the U.S. Army."

They all stared at the map for a few moments.

"Look, I hate to be the serious one here," said Barry, "but are we sure this is a good thing?"

They looked at him. Danielle frowned again. "What's that supposed to mean?"

"These guys have been on their own at least as long as we have," he said. "We don't know what kind of shape they're in, physically or mentally."

St. George's lips twisted into a thin smile. "Still worried about a crazy military?"

"A little, yeah." He shrugged again. "I just think we should be a bit cautious before we go running up to hug a bunch of heavily armed guys who've been standing out in the sun for two years."

"There's the other side of that coin," said Danielle. "We don't know they're alone. For all we know there are military installations and population centers all over the country that are connected."

"We have seen no evidence of such a thing," said Stealth.

"And I've never heard it," said Barry, waving his half-sandwich in the air. "Even if they were all on the East Coast, I'd see something in the air now and then."

"I'm just saying it could be," insisted the redhead. "Let's not convince ourselves this is a bad thing before we have more evidence."

"Let's not forget something else," said St. George. "They know we're out here now. We sent them a message through their Predator."

Barry nodded. "That we did."

"It seems safe to say they didn't know what they'd find when they sent the drones," St. George said. "Now they know we're out here. I think we should wait and see what they do. Let them make the next move."

Stealth tilted her head at him. "And if they do not make a move?"

"Then we can send Barry to check them out again. But for now, let's play it cool."

Barry grinned. "Don't want to call too soon after our first date?"

"Don't want them thinking we're a threat," said St. George. "They're probably as freaked out by us as we are by them. And like you said, they've got a lot more guns. Let's wait a couple days and see if the Predator comes back."

Danielle nodded. "When they do, we can use my call sign and codes. Even if they can't verify it, they should be able to recognize it as our military without too much trouble."

Stealth gave a slow nod. "A sound plan for the present."

"There's one other thing, though," said St. George. "What do we tell everyone?"

"What do you mean?" asked Danielle.

"Everyone here at the Mount. Inside the Big Wall. Do we keep quiet? Do we tell them the military's coming to save the day?"

"I am sure that decision has been made for you, George," said Stealth.

He looked at her. "How so?"

"Besides the four of us, fourteen scavengers know of the Predator drone. I find it unlikely all of them have remained silent on this matter. I would estimate at least two hundred people have been told the news during the course of this meeting."

St. George sighed.

"Oh, joy," said Barry. "That won't cause any headaches."

"I would suggest we advise citizens against any premature assumptions as to the nature of this incident. Perhaps we can protect them from potential disillusionment and the corresponding blow to morale."

"Assuming, of course," said Danielle, "there's going to be a reason to be disillusioned."

The lights flickered. "That's my cue," said Barry. He swallowed the last crust of his sandwich. "Batteries are running low. I need to get back to the chair."

"They're not lasting any time at all now," muttered the redhead.

"We're supplying six times as many people," said St. George. "We need to figure out a better way to do this."

"You're telling me," said Barry. He swung himself off the table and into his wheelchair. "You know it's been three weeks since I slept in a bed?"

"Come on," said the hero, scooping up his patchwork leather jacket. "Let's get you over to Four."

"Cerberus," said Stealth, "if you could escort Zzzap back

to the electric chair, I would like to speak with St. George for a few more minutes. Alone."

"Somebody's in trou-ble," sang Barry with a grin.

The redhead took in a quick breath. "Will you be long? I was hoping to get the armor back on tonight."

"Take the rest of the night off," St. George told her. "We'll get you suited back up in the morning."

"Oh, sure," said Barry. "She gets to sleep in a bed."

"Someone needs to check the gates, though," said Danielle. "If you two are going to be here for a while—"

"I will check the gates once our meeting is done," said Stealth. "Will you see Zzzap back to Four, please?"

Her elbows pulled in closer to her body. "Sure," she said. "No problem." She wheeled Barry around and out of the conference room doors.

St. George dropped his jacket back on the table and looked at the cloaked woman. "What's up?"

"How did the new chain mail armor perform?"

"Nobody likes it, but Danny Foe let an ex get the drop on him and it stopped the bite. Not much past that. Everyone was on their game today."

"Is there anything else to report from your mission?"

He leaned back against the table. "Pretty much just what we expected to find in the Valley," he said. "Exes seem more numerous but spread out more. Most everything's looted along Cahuenga, but it's hard to tell when, so it doesn't help us figure out if there are other survivors out there."

"Did you listen?"

"What?"

"You launched a flare that would have been visible throughout most of the southern San Fernando Valley. If survivors saw it, there is a reasonable chance they would have made an effort to attract your attention."

He sagged a little. "I didn't even think of that. I was so excited about the plane."

"The fault is mine," she said. "I became focused on the flare as a signal for our own purposes. I did not consider the possibility it would serve as an indirect beacon to others until after you had left."

"It's not your responsibility to think of all this stuff."

"Someone must be responsible," she said, "and I am the best suited to the task."

"Well," he said, "maybe it won't be for much longer. If it really is the Army we're all off the hook. Someone else will be in charge."

She tilted her head at him. "I did not realize you were eager to be relieved of your responsibilities."

"Aren't you? I mean, let's face it. There's got to be people better qualified than us to rebuild civilization."

"Perhaps," she said. "Perhaps not. To my eyes, you are eminently qualified."

They looked at each other for a few moments, then a few more, and then she turned and moved to the bank of monitors. St. George picked up his jacket. The doors were closed behind him when he realized he'd missed another opportune moment.

× × ×

"So," said Barry as the wheelchair rolled along the garden, "you want to hang out for a bit? It's boring as hell just sitting in the chair all the time. I've got tons of movies."

He felt Danielle shake her head behind him. "I've got to get back," she said. "A couple things to do."

"Like what?"

"What?"

"What do you have to do?"

"Just . . . stuff. You know. I spend so much time in the armor a lot of stuff gets neglected."

"So you're doing laundry? Please tell me you're doing laundry, because it's way overdue." He gestured to the open street as they turned onto 3rd. "Hey, use the center of the lane. It's smoother. Easier on the chair and my butt."

"Whatever."

She leaned and the wheelchair worked its way out into the center of the road. "Yeah," he said. "Much better."

Danielle gave a grunt. To their south was the Melrose gate. They could hear the distant chattering of teeth in hundreds of mouths.

"So no movie, eh?"

"No, sorry."

"I've got a couple games, too. Finally figured out how to run an optical mouse remote, so I can use a laptop."

"I told you, I've got to get back to my place."

"Well, if you want you can swing by my place and take all the cushions off the couch. Keep 'em if you like. I'm never there."

"What?"

"I just figured you'd want to build yourself a little fort to sleep in."

She stopped pushing the chair. "Fuck you."

"If only someone would," he sighed. He spun his chair so he faced her. Without the handles to hold on to, her arms pulled in close to her body. "But let's talk about you. How long were you in the armor for this time?"

"As long as I needed to be."

"How long?"

She sighed. "Four days. More or less."

"More or less?"

"Almost five."

Barry looked at her. "It's only built for three, right?"

"It can do more if it needs to."

"No wonder you stink. Have you even eaten?"

"I can stand to lose some weight."

"Yeah, you and all the other fat people running around after the apocalypse."

"The suit's getting tight in the legs."

"Whatever," he said. "Look, you know you're safe in here, right? They can't get you."

She glanced over her shoulder toward the gate. Toward the big white cross.

"I've got your back," said Barry. "George and Stealth have it. Hell, most people here love you."

She smirked. "Not everyone."

"Well, there're a few idiots in every crowd," he said. "Point is, you've got to stop hiding in the damned suit."

"Mr. Burke," called someone behind him. Barry rolled his eyes at the sound of the voice and Danielle winced.

"Christian," said Barry, turning his wheelchair. "We were just talking about you. What's up?"

Christian Nguyen had been an LA councilwoman and had hung on to her small amount of power when society began to rebuild itself inside the Mount. Now she was district leader for Southeast and all of Raleigh, and some people thought she had a good chance of being mayor if everyone could agree on a fair way to do elections. She was also "super-phobic," as some called it, and made no effort to hide her feelings.

Danielle kept it simple and called her a bitch.

Christian marched across the cobblestones with a half dozen or so people behind her. She stopped in front of the wheelchair and glared down at Barry. "What's this about a helicopter flying over the Valley?"

"It was a Predator," he said. "Not a helicopter."

"Don't try to dodge," she snapped. "Why weren't we told about it?"

"If you weren't told about it, how do you know about it?"

"Everyone knows," she said. "What I want to know is why nothing official's been said."

"Well," said Barry, "Stealth figured you'd all find out in a few hours—like you did—so there was no need to make some proclamation from on high."

Christian's lips twisted into a smug smile. "What you mean is St. George ordered people not to talk and Stealth realized they would anyway."

Barry felt a faint tremor as Danielle took hold of the wheelchair's handles again. Part of him hoped she was going to ram the chair into Christian's shins. "Yet again," he said, "you know it all."

"Are you going to tell us what the pilot said?"

"The pilot?"

"The helicopter pilot."

He sighed. He made sure it was a loud sigh. "One, it wasn't a helicopter, it was a Predator drone, and b, a Predator doesn't have a pilot."

"What do you mean, it doesn't have a pilot?"

"It's a drone, Christian. A robot."

"A robot plane? How stupid do you think I am?"

One of her followers, a scrawny man, stepped forward and muttered something to her. She glared down at the man in the wheelchair.

"Did you want me to answer that last one," said Barry, "or was it rhetorical?"

"I think you need to start being a bit more respectful," she snapped. "Whatever it was, it was a symbol of the American government."

"It was a drone," interrupted Danielle. "Nobody knows who was controlling it. Could've been anyone."

Barry nodded.

Christian's scowl turned into a smirk. "Oh, you'd like that, wouldn't you? To convince everyone help isn't on the way. That the rest of the world isn't pulling itself out of the godless state Los Angeles has been left in." She threw back her shoulders and tossed a glance to her entourage. "The days of Stealth's little dictatorship are numbered," she said. "Your power over all of us is coming to an end and you'll make up any lie you can to hang on to it."

"Seriously," said Barry, "why wouldn't we want that? You think I like spending seven days a week in a metal ball so you can read at night?"

She waved off his comments and pushed her hand at his face. He felt the chair shift on the cobblestones and he was sure Danielle was about to ram it forward. "Things are getting back to normal," Christian said. "We'll see where that leaves all of you."

A murmur of consent rose from the followers. She tossed her head back, glared at Barry and Danielle in turn, and stalked off with her minions.

Barry took in a breath to shout something after her and settled for giving the finger with both barrels.

"What a bitch," muttered Danielle.

"What are you complaining about? You got off easy."

"She doesn't know who I am," said the redhead. "Most people think I'm always nine feet tall and fifteen hundred pounds. They see a skinny, helpless woman and I'm just a face in the crowd."

He twisted around to look at her. "You're not helpless."

"We're all helpless, Barry," she said. "As long as things stay like this, we're all screwed."

Daughter of Liberty
THEN

THE LAST THING I could remember was trying not to shiver with all of them standing around me. I've got no problem with airdrops, live-fire training, even being under enemy fire. I've been caught in two explosions in my six years of service, and still have scars and a Purple Heart from one of them. But lying on an operating table, wearing nothing but a paper smock and underwear while they pumped tranquilizers into my arm, that freaked me out.

I'm not supposed to freak out. Girls freak out. I'm a soldier before I'm a girl. I was born to be a soldier. It was what Dad wanted. His dad had been in the Army, and his dad before him, and his dad before him, and his before him. A line of Kennedys serving their country all the way back to the Civil War, long before someone else with our name became president.

Mom says having three girls was murder on him. He loved us, don't get me wrong. He was the greatest dad in the world and he spent every minute he could with us, but it was rough on him not to have a son to keep up the military tradition. It killed him when Ellie, my oldest sister, decided to be a kindergarten teacher and Abby announced she was going to school to be a lawyer.

I was the youngest. And the tomboy. As soon as I was old enough to understand Dad's quiet disappointment, I knew what I was going to do with my life. I just wish he'd lived long enough to see me make sergeant. To see how good a soldier I'd become.

So of course I jumped up when they offered to make me an even better soldier. Out of about 500 volunteers, 108 made the final cut, two large companies' worth. A month of shots and now some surgery. Dr. Sorensen tried to explain it to us but it was a lot of high-end words none of us understood. He told us it would be easier to explain after the operation.

I woke up in a hospital bed. Sorensen was sitting next to me, reading a letter covered with flowery, teen-girl writing. I found out later, talking with the rest of my squad, he was there when everyone woke up. No idea how he timed that out.

His monkey-boy was hovering in the background, trying not to look like he was reading over the doc's shoulder. I blinked a few times, tried to move my arm and found out how stiff it was. When I winced I discovered how bad the headache was.

"Ahhh," said Sorensen. "Awake at last. Get her some water, John." He said that last bit without even looking back at monkey-boy.

"I'm sore," I said.

"You've been unconscious for almost twenty hours, sergeant," he told me. "It's normal." He folded up his letter.

I met his eyes. "Any problems, sir?"

"Just my daughter," he said. He slipped the papers into his

coat pocket. "She's starting to pick colleges and everyone in the family has different ideas where she should apply."

I smiled. "I meant with the surgery."

He gave me a wink and a penlight slipped out of the same pocket. "I don't think so," he said, "but we'll know for sure in a few moments." He flicked the light back and forth across my eyes. "Focus on my finger."

I followed his index finger as he moved it around my face, then up and down in front of his own chest. No problems. Monkey-boy came back with a paper cup of water. I reached for it and my wrist clanked. I was handcuffed to the hospital bed's railing.

"Just a safety precaution," said Sorensen. "People can be disoriented after surgery and we didn't want you wandering off and hurting yourself."

"What if I need to use the latrine?"

"Do you?"

"No."

"We'll have you out in a few minutes anyway. Make a fist with your left hand. Good. Now, your right. Good. Hold this pencil as tight as you can."

It was a cheap pencil. It snapped into three pieces. He smiled at that.

The more tests he did, the more I realized I felt fine. Aside from a splitting headache and stiff limbs, I couldn't sense anything wrong with me. And that made me suspicious, because this wasn't the first time I'd woken up from surgery in my life. My appendix when I was fifteen and a torn meniscus in my knee four weeks after Basic ended. I knew some part of me should hurt more than everything else.

"No dizziness?" asked Sorensen. "No funny tastes in your mouth?"

"No, sir. Just really dry." I sipped the water.

"It's a side effect of the anesthesia. You were in surgery for sixteen hours."

I let my eyes slide down to my bare arms. Handcuff on one. Basic IV on the other. No stitches. No butterflies. Nothing. "Did something go wrong, sir? Why didn't they complete the surgery?"

"Do you know why my predecessor's attempts at this project failed, Sergeant Kennedy?"

I shrugged. The handcuffs jingled.

"He thought you had to force the body to achieve the performance levels we're hoping for. He spent weeks pumping soldiers full of myostatin blockers and somatotropin and other things that made a mess of their biochemistry."

I shook my head. "I don't know what any of that means."

"Of course. Sorry. Let me explain it to you like this. When you were very young, did you play a lot?"

"What do you mean, sir?"

"Play. Run around, jump, chase other children, that sort of thing."

"I was a tomboy, sir. I did all that and fought with boys, too."

"Did you ever do so much you collapsed?"

"Probably. I mean, didn't everyone?"

"Everyone did," he agreed. He paused to brush a piece of lint off his pants. "We ran and lifted things and burned through a day's worth of calories in just a few hours. We pushed our bodies to their full potential. Except . . ."

He paused again, as if he was searching for the right word. It was a lecture, I know that now. At this point he'd already given this speech a dozen times to other candidates as they woke up.

" . . . we made ourselves sick," he continued. "We got hurt. Maybe we even hurt one or two of our friends by accident. We learned it wasn't always good to operate on those levels unless it was absolutely necessary, and often not even then. You see, everyone on Earth carries the seeds of superhuman ability within them."

I took another sip of water and flexed my feet back and forth under the bedsheet. No tightness or sore spots on my legs that I could feel. "You mean like mutant genes or something?"

He shook his head. "No, I mean the things you've heard about your whole life." He ticked off examples on his fingers. "People who lift cars with their bare hands to rescue loved ones. People who run their first marathon with no training or who can swim underwater for three minutes without taking a breath. Children who fall off ten-story buildings and only get scratched. Did you know a woman once fell almost two miles from an exploding plane and received only minor injuries?"

I thought I'd heard the story before, so I nodded.

"The human body is an amazing machine," said Sorensen. "It's powerful and durable all on its own, without much help from us. We rarely see that, though, because we all learned early on not to use our bodies to their full potential. Even professional athletes who train constantly are working under a system of automatic restraint. We hold back. We don't push ourselves to our maximum limits because we instinctively understand how dangerous it can be, to others and to ourselves. And as we got older our bodies responded, getting slower and weaker because we weren't pushing them to be their best. I'm sure you've heard stories of addicts on phencyclidine—PCP—who can fight half a dozen men or punch through walls."

I nodded again.

"A similar principle. The drug high bypasses all those self-imposed safeguards. Of course, it also disables pain receptors, so it's not uncommon for them to come down and realize they've broken several bones in their hands."

Inside the paper smock, I rolled my abs and shifted my hips and clenched a few female muscles. "So . . . you're giving us PCP?" Nothing. Not even a numb spot where they'd given me a local. Just a bit stiff from lack of use.

"No, they tried that before," he said, crossing his legs. "It didn't work for the reasons I just mentioned and no one could ever get any definitive results. It also doesn't solve the real problem. We want to make you superhuman, not dependent on drugs that make you superhuman. You've felt jittery these past weeks, haven't you?"

I had. In fact, this was the first time I hadn't felt on edge in days. I'd've noticed sooner if not for the headache and sore muscles.

"The injections you've been getting for the past few weeks have boosted several processes in your body. It's a compound called GW501516 paired with AICAR, which activates a metabolic—" He paused again and smiled. "I won't bore you with all the technical terms. Your muscle tissues are developing faster. So are your skin and bone cells, which also means more red blood cells carrying more oxygen."

I frowned. "Isn't that the same drug dependency, though, sir?"

"Normally, yes. If we stopped the supplements your body chemistry would go back to normal in a few days. Which brings us back to restraint. What we've done is disable those safeguards. If you made a serious effort you'd create new pathways and learn to keep the body in check again. For now, though, you're going to run at those optimum performance levels. Your mind isn't going to tell your body to hold back. This is going to be your new normal, so to speak, and we've given your body a kick-start so it will change to keep up."

I drank some more water. My mouth was feeling better and flexing random muscles was helping the stiffness. As far as I could tell all I needed was a couple Advil for the headache and I'd be good to go.

My splitting, painful headache.

It must've shown in my eyes, because Sorensen was about to say something and stopped. Monkey-boy took a step back. They were both watching me.

My free hand, the hand that wasn't chained to the bed, reached up. The back of my head had been shaved. I brushed the wet threads in my scalp and winced. I put a bit of pressure on the raw skin and felt part of my skull shift underneath.

"What did you do?"

"It's a shock at first, I know," said Sorensen. "I'm cer—"

"WHAT DID YOU DO TO MY BRAIN?!?"

Looking back on it, I admit I lost it for a minute. Which I think he planned on. I lunged out of the bed. Monkey-boy tried to grab me and I knocked him halfway across the recovery room. I heaved the doctor out of the chair and his glasses fell off.

"What did you do to me?!"

Sorensen was very calm, even though I had his coat wrapped up in my fists. "That's not the important question, Staff Sergeant Kennedy."

Name and rank was good. Chilled me down, made me stop. I almost cried, but girls cry. I'm a soldier.

"The important question," said Sorensen, "is how did you get out of the bed?"

It took a moment to sink in. I looked away from his eyes, down to my wrists. One had a piece of surgical tape and some blood where the IV had torn loose. The other one had a single handcuff with two links of stainless-steel chain dangling from it. The last link was twisted apart. I could see a bruise forming where the cuff had bitten into my wrist.

I looked over my shoulder. The hospital bed's railing was bent a good four inches out of line toward me. The other handcuff swung back and forth in a deep gouge. Its last link was broken and stretched long. It looked more like a thick hook than a piece of chain.

Oh, hell yeah. Look at me now, Dad.

Eight

NOW

"HEY, ST. GEORGE," someone called out. "You got a minute now?"

A skinny man trotted toward Roddenberry, waving his hand. St. George settled back down to the ground and swung his jacket over his shoulder. It took a moment to recognize the young man at night. He'd never noticed how few lights there were around the central building and garden. "Cesar, right?"

"Right." They shook hands. "Look, I really need to . . . ummmm, confess something."

"You still haven't killed anyone, right?"

"No, dude, this is serious."

"Okay," he said, "what's up?"

Cesar glanced around. "Can we walk or something?"

"Why?"

"Just feel kinda nervous standing right here, y'know? In front of her building? Especially at night."

St. George felt the corners of his mouth twitch. "Yeah, I know what you mean," he said. "A walk around the garden work?"

"Yeah," he said, "that'd be cool."

He led them across the north edge of the garden. A few years earlier, when the Mount had been a film studio, the garden had been a gigantic pool that could be filled with water for movie shoots. The north edge was a huge mural called the Blue Sky. They walked along the narrow path between the base of the mural and the garden.

Cesar took a breath and steeled himself. "Probably should've told you or Cerberus or one of you guys months ago, but . . ." The former Seventeen looked left to right and back, never meeting the hero's eyes. "I'm the Driver."

St. George cocked his head and waited. "The what?"

"The Driver." He gripped an invisible steering wheel in the air before him, and the hero realized the young man's fingerless handgear was a pair of cheap driving gloves.

"The driver of what?"

Cesar sighed. "D'you remember there were a bunch of car-jackings and smash-and-grabs a couple years back? About a year before the exes showed up?"

St. George nodded. "Down in the Wilshire District? Yeah, I always meant to look into those."

"That was me."

The hero raised his eyebrows and smiled. "As I remember, the cops caught the guy," he said. "A big, fat white guy. Blew out the tires of his Mustang with a spike strip. He tried to run and the police laughed themselves silly."

"Yeah, right," said Cesar, nodding. They turned the corner of the garden and started heading south. "Wayne. He was my partner."

"Partner?"

"Look, what if I just show you, 'kay?"

St. George shrugged. "Okay."

Cesar jogged ahead a few yards. The garden had a thick wall protecting it on the east side, and there was a small parking lot where they kept the scavenger trucks. *Mean Green. Road Warrior.* The twins were *Big Red* and *Big Blue.* Off to the side, against the back corner of the Zukor hospital, stood a few stacks of spare tires. Luke's people had pulled them off other trucks on the lot, plus some they'd found in the other studios.

The young man took a few more quick steps to put himself in front of *Mean Green*'s grille. He waited for St. George to catch up and gestured the hero to the side. "No one in the cab, right?"

"Nope."

"No keys, right?"

St. George pulled the door open and glanced under the steering column. "Nope. Should be in Luke's office."

"'Kay, then. Watch this."

The young man pulled off his glove and held up his bare hand. The palm was covered with a flurry of half-faded scars. He pressed his fingers against *Mean Green*'s grille and the metal sparked. The flashes grew into long arcs that wrapped around his hand and twisted up his arm with electric crackles.

Cesar vanished in a flash of light and *Mean Green*'s engine roared to life. A wisp of smoke spun in the air for a moment, and then it was sucked into the grille by the truck's fan. *Mean Green*'s headlights came on. The engine revved three times in a row.

St. George dropped his jacket. His eyes flitted between the empty space and the growling truck. "You're kidding me."

The horn let out two quick blasts. The headlights flashed

back and forth like winking eyes. The engine growled again and the truck's front wheels shifted left to right. The hero took a few steps back and *Mean Green* rolled a few feet forward. He walked to the left and the truck turned after him.

"Okay," he said, "I believe you."

There was another crackle of electricity, a flash, and the engine cut out. The headlights faded and Cesar stood between the hero and *Mean Green*, his hand pressed against the grill. The young man swayed for a moment, shook his head, and grinned. "What you think of that?"

"So," said St. George. "The Driver."

"Damn straight."

"You possess cars?"

"Not just cars," said Cesar proudly. "Big rigs, jeeps, SUVs, anything that's self-powered, y'know? I did a generator once on a bounce house. And a golf cart. Motorcycles are tough because I can't balance that good in 'em."

"What about a walkie-talkie or a radio or something?"

He shook his head. "Too small. I get . . . I dunno, cramped. I can't fit inside."

St. George studied the young man. He didn't have a scrap of green on him, but most of the former Seventeens went out of their way not to wear the old gang color. The ornate *17* on his left shoulder was the only sign he'd been one of the bad guys less than a year ago. "How long have you been able to do this?"

He shrugged. "About four years."

"You've been part of the Mount for eight months now. Why didn't you say something before?"

"Dude, we were on opposite sides." Cesar shook his head. "Even when I moved in here after Peasey was dead, who knows what Stealth would've done if she found out there was another Seventeen who had powers. Besides"—he jerked his head at the truck—"that was the first time I've done it since the night they grabbed Wayne."

"Your partner."

"Yeah."

"If you're the one with the powers, why'd you need him?"

The young man shrugged. "I needed somebody who could grab the cash. I'm in a car, it's just a lot easier to stay there. Takes a lot out of me, switching back and forth."

"Okay," said St. George, "so if he was willing to sit behind the wheel for a smash-and-grab, why'd he need you?"

Cesar grinned. "Dude, d'you ever read *Lowrider* or *Car and Driver*? Fucking loved *Car and Driver*."

"Once or twice. In waiting rooms."

"Saw this phrase once—'the car outperforms the driver.' When you get those sweet, high-end cars with tons of torque that can turn on a dime. Rich jerks crash 'em all the time because the car is so much better than them. Moves faster'n they think it can, reacts quicker'n they think it will. Tweak the wheel *this* much and you're doing barrel rolls down the freeway, y'know?"

"Yeah, okay."

"Well, not when I'm inside," said Cesar. "When I'm inside, the car's my body. Know every inch of it, what it can do, how well it can do it. If the car can do it, I can do it, and better than anyone sitting at the wheel ever could. I'm the greatest getaway-guy stunt driver in the world. I'm like ten times the fucking Transporter times Knight Rider."

"So how'd they catch your buddy?"

He held up his hand again and showed the scars. "Like you said, man. Spike strip, right across Olympic." He pulled the glove from his waistband and tugged it back on. "Cops arrested Wayne, took the Mustang to impound. I got out, my hands and feet were all messed up something bad. Limped home and Mama took me to the emergency room. Man, that sucked. Six hours in the waiting room at Hollywood Presbyterian."

St. George picked up his jacket and batted some dust off it. He looked at the truck again, then back to the young man. "How'd you get this? Were you born with it?"

Cesar shook his head. "My cousin Tony, he was a gearhead," explained the young man. "Worked on all the cars for the Seventeens. Tune-ups, rims, nitrous, whatever you needed. One day right after my sixteenth birthday I was helping him out, trading out an alternator and . . ."

"And what?"

"I got struck by lightning," said Cesar. From his tone, St. George could tell he'd defended this point before. "Right there in the driveway, sunny day with clear skies. Burned my hair off and fried the alternator."

St. George drummed his fingers on *Mean Green*'s side. "You got struck by lightning while you were working on a car?"

"Yeah."

"That has got to be the dumbest thing I've ever heard."

Cesar glared at him. "What, how'd you get your powers? D'you get bit by a radioactive dragon or something?"

"No," said the hero, "I got . . . well, I got hit by a meteorite. And doused in some experimental chemicals."

The young man smirked. "And you're making fun of me?"

"There had to be something else to it. Thousands of people have been struck by lightning. It doesn't give you superpowers."

"Yeah, but it did."

"But it can't."

"But it did. Look, man, the important thing is, I want to join the team."

"What?"

"You know," said Cesar. "Start doing stuff for good and all that. I want to contribute something to the community."

"How?"

The other man's smile faltered. "What d'you mean?"

"I mean how," said St. George. "I'm glad you came clean and told me about your powers, yeah, but . . . well, what can you do for us? It's not like we have tons of open road to go speeding around on."

"Well, yeah, but—"

"And at regular speed, well, Luke's got half a dozen drivers for each truck past himself. Do the cars get better somehow when you're in them? Do they stop using gas or . . . I don't know, heal or something?"

Cesar shifted his feet. "No."

The hero shrugged.

"You saying I can't join up?"

St. George paused. "Look, Cesar, if things were back to normal, I'd say sure thing. But, honestly, what can you do that can't be done by half the people in the Mount?"

"But . . ." He looked confused. "But I'm the Driver."

"Yeah," said St. George, "and there's nowhere left to drive."

× × ×

He reached the top of the stairs and saw her sitting Indian-style across from his door.

"I've been waiting for you," said Lady Bee. She wore the same black tank she'd had on while they were in the Valley. Electric-blue bra straps peeked out from underneath it.

St. George nodded from the stairwell. "So I see."

"The secret superhero meeting run late?"

"Not exactly." He shook his head. "You're not here to tell me you've secretly had superpowers all this time, are you?

She smiled. "Why?"

"I just had to tell a kid his dream of being Optimus Prime was never going to come true. He took it hard."

"What?"

"You wouldn't believe me if I told you. What's up?"

Bee stood up. "I was in the neighborhood. Figured I'd swing by and say hi."

"And camp outside my door?"

"I've only been here ten minutes. None of the neighbors saw me."

He put his back against the door. "Seriously," he said, "what's up, Bee?"

She gave a lopsided shrug and one of the bra straps slipped off her shoulder. "I was just wondering if you wanted to hang out and watch a movie or something?"

"Or something?"

Her smile became a grin. "Well, I don't know about you," she said, dancing her fingers on his chest, "but I haven't had a really good 'or something' in months now. We could skip the movie and go right to that. I wouldn't have any complaints."

He took her hand. "We agreed we weren't going to do this anymore."

"Yeah, and we haven't," she said. "But it's been ages and we had an exciting day. I'm horny, I'm wearing the underwear you like, and you're here instead of being . . ." She paused and looked him in the eyes. "With someone else."

"Maybe this is my one night a week to sleep alone."

"You're a shitty liar."

"Maybe I'm not up for it."

"The George I knew was always up for it." She peeled the tank off in one quick movement and slung it around his neck. "What do you say? Two or three times for old time's sake?"

He reached up for her arms, grabbed her wrists. "Bee . . ."

"It'll be our little secret."

She pulled his head down, pressed herself against his body, and kissed him. For a second he let her, and then he straightened up and away. "We both know there aren't any secrets from her."

Lady Bee sighed. "Well," she said, "looks like that moment's passed, then." She pulled the tank off his neck and wrestled it back over her striped hair. "You know you're wasting your time, right?"

"What's that supposed to mean?"

She pushed her arms through and jerked the tank over her flat belly. "You're never going to have any kind of relationship with her. Nothing normal and healthy, anyway."

"That's a little—"

"She's the empress of all ice queens. If the exes vanished tomorrow she would, too. Back to her batcave, never to be seen again. And you know it."

"You're wrong."

Bee shook her head. "She's just like every other frigid bitch, holding the nice guy at arm's length and getting him to do whatever she wants." She gave him a peck on the cheek and headed for the stairs. "Good night, George."

"G'night."

"Maybe you'll get lucky and I'll try again in a few months."

Nine

NOW

DANIELLE HAD PULLED the mattress off her bed months ago and set it against the wall under the all-purpose table. Once she'd blocked one side of the table with a small dresser, she could get something close to a good night's sleep. She woke up aching from the concrete floor, but it beat lying awake in the cot all night and hearing imaginary teeth chattering in the corners of her workshop.

This morning someone was nudging her, and in her slumbering mind she wondered if it was a version of the dream where Nikolai was still alive and had gotten over his dead girlfriend. Then the nudges became prods, and after a few prods someone grabbed her exposed shoulder and shook. For a moment, in her half-awake state, she saw the looming dark form and thought an ex had latched on to her. She lashed out and the figure grabbed her clumsy backhand.

"Get dressed," said Stealth. She released Danielle's wrist. "We are needed at Four."

Danielle threw off her covers. Even in the sweltering heat of a Los Angeles summer, she needed to feel a certain amount of weight over her to sleep. She crawled out from under the table and stood next to the hooded woman. "Where's my crew?"

"I do not need your assistants. I need you at Four."

"George, then? Someone's got to help me get into the armor." She nodded through the doorway at the half-assembled battlesuit standing in the workshop. "I can't do it alone."

"You do not need the Cerberus armor to come with me," said Stealth. "Please put on whatever clothing you feel necessary. Time is of the essence."

"Necessary for what?"

"Danielle, in one minute I am leaving," said the cloaked woman. "You will be coming with me. What you are wearing at that point is of no consequence to me."

Sixty seconds later Danielle tugged her shirt on as Stealth dragged her out of the workshop. The cloaked woman was like the villain in a slasher movie. Her pace never approached a run, or even a jog, but Danielle struggled to keep up.

It was barely dawn. A few last stars twinkled and faded in the steel-blue sky. "What the hell's going on?" asked Danielle as she buttoned up her shirt.

"The Predator has returned," said Stealth.

"Already?"

"An hour and a half ago."

"What?" She brushed her hair out of her face. "Why didn't Barry spot it sooner?"

"I do not know."

"What did it do? Were they looking for us again?"

"This is why we are going to Four," Stealth said.

There was a rush of wind and St. George landed just ahead of them at the entrance to Four. He wore full combat leathers with his sunglasses pushed up on his forehead.

"Oh, sure," muttered Danielle, "you give him time to get into uniform."

"It doesn't take me an hour," he said.

Zzzap lit up the inside of the converted stage from inside the electric chair. *Took you people long enough,* he said. *This is why I keep insisting we need bat-poles.*

Stealth walked to the cage. "Is it still circling the Mount?"

The brilliant wraith shook his head. *It took off about fifteen minutes ago. It's still in the area but I think it's about fifty or sixty miles away.*

"What were they doing?" asked St. George.

I checked out the information it was sending back to their base. Straight low-light video plus infrared imagery. Oh, right, yeah. And it listened in on a few walkie conversations. It had a good hour of watching us altogether.

"Are you sure of this?"

Pretty sure, yeah.

"Why did it take you so long to notice it?"

Well, they are passive scans and it kept a really high altitude this time. There wasn't much to hear until it was right on top of us.

"Which was, by your estimates, seventy-five minutes ago."

Yeah, sorry. I guess I was distracted.

St. George frowned. "Distracted by what?"

I was talking with someone. As I've mentioned several times, it's boring as hell sitting in this ball all the time. Even with the awesome DVD collection.

"I was not aware of anyone else in Four this evening," said the cloaked woman.

"Is it doing anything else?" asked Danielle. "The Predator?"

Nope. Nothing but navigational commands and some quick looks through the nose camera.

The heroes looked at each other. "Well," said St. George, "I guess they've made their move."

Stealth bowed her head. "Do you agree we should send Zzzap to investigate further?"

He nodded. So did Danielle. "We should wait until sunup, though," said St. George. "That way you've got something to hide in front of."

Lucky me.

"Sunrise is in twenty-three minutes," said Stealth. "I will get the generator crews prepared. It may be wise to warn the guards, as well."

"You want to do that?" asked Danielle. "If it is the military, they're not going to like a bunch of nervous civilians taking potshots at them."

"If it is not the military, I would prefer to be ready."

Guys?

"Fine. There's enough time to get me back in the armor, then," she said.

"I'll help with that," said St. George.

"Good. I don't think anyone on my crew wakes up before nine."

Guys, said Zzzap, *you don't have time.*

Stealth looked at him, then up. In the dead silence of the morning, they all heard the noise.

Four, maybe five helicopters. They just broke radio silence. Army, by their encryption.

× × ×

People woke up and dashed out of their homes at the thunderous sound of rotors. They clogged the streets and rooftops, pointing at a sight they thought they'd never see again. Some cheered. Some shrieked in fear.

St. George launched himself into the sky, fumbling his earpiece into place. He keyed the mic as he spun in the air. "Who's with me?"

"I'm here," said Zzzap.

"Danielle?"

"Cerberus is searching for her assistants," said Stealth. "She does not have a radio."

"Who's on the wall?" called St. George.

"This is Makana," came the voice. "What the hell's going on, boss?"

"Just stay calm, make sure none of your people have their fingers on the trigger," ordered the hero. "We don't want anyone shooting at a rescue party."

"Copy that."

Hanging in the air two hundred feet above the Mount, St. George counted five olive-drab helicopters coming toward him in a V formation. They were fast, tilted forward with rotors aimed in his direction. Three of them had huge miniguns mounted on their noses. He was bulletproof, but wasn't sure if his skin could take a full-speed helicopter blade.

The hero waited until the last moment and then shifted in the air. He caught a quick glimpse of one of the pilots staring at him in dumbfounded amazement and the minigun turned to follow the stare. Then the roar of rotors pummeled him as the choppers thundered past on either side.

His ears rang for a few seconds and he realized Stealth was talking to him on his earpiece. He shook his head and keyed the mic. "What was that again?"

"Two UH-60A Black Hawk transports and three Apache gunships. Are you unharmed?"

He glanced down. She was already on the peak of the water tower, staring up at him. "Yeah, they missed me. I could use an aspirin, though."

× × ×

"Son of a bitch, that was close," said Makana. He stared up at the predawn speck that was St. George. So did most of the gate guards. The helicopters weren't the bright red-and-white rescue machines he'd dreamed of before coming to work. These were dark, vicious hunters.

One of the men on duty, a skinny guy named Matt, split his attention. He reached through the gate with his pike and jabbed an ex in the shoulder. "Doesn't this guy look familiar to you?" It was a tall man with dark hair and a square jaw. The flesh was missing from one side of his skull and the coat sleeve on that side was frayed and shredded, as if the dead thing had been dragged along some coarse surface for miles.

They glanced at him. "Dude," said a heavyset man with blond dreadlocks. "You're thinking about points? Now?"

"I'm just saying," said Matt, "I think this is somebody famous."

"So what?" snapped Makana. He'd grabbed a set of binoculars from the guard shack and was trying to focus on the flying hero.

"If it's someone famous, one of you guys needs to vouch for me."

"Get your priorities straight," said a skinny woman. She snatched the binoculars from Makana.

× × ×

Danielle dashed through the workshop door just as the helicopters blasted through the air above the Mount. The Cerberus Battle Armor System still stood in the center of the floor, soaking up power through a thick cable. Its arms and back rested in special foam molds on the oversized work tables, and the armored head glared at her from its own spot.

None of her crew was there.

"Come ON!" she snarled. She yanked off her shirt and kicked her pants away. She ran to the suit and up the short ladder standing behind it. Her hands gripped the armored shoulders and she lowered her own legs down into the titan's. She leaned forward into position and felt the tiny pricks and tingles of the sensors as they settled against her body.

Any instant now, she knew, her six hand-picked, trained assistants would rush through the door. They would put her arms in place, seal her in the armor, and she'd be strong again. When they were in top form, they could do it in just over an hour.

No one came through the door.

Danielle shouted out a stream of curses that echoed around the workshop.

When they faded she was still alone.

"Goddammit," she yelled, "somebody help me get back in the armor."

She was so close to being safe she almost cried.

× × ×

In the dim light St. George could just see the helicopters up over the Hollywood sign, swinging around to the east. "I think they're coming around for another pass. Do you want me to—"

"No," said Stealth.

"They just—"

"No one has been injured. That was not an attempted attack. They were caught off guard by the sight of you."

"It's not like they didn't know we were out here."

"It is one thing to know a flying man exists," said Stealth. "It is quite a different thing to see him in person."

"Put me in, coach," said Barry's voice. "I can do more good up there."

"No."

"But I can—"

"If the power were to go out just as a squadron of military helicopters arrived, it would cause chaos throughout the Mount. Maintain your position."

The helicopters roared forward again. This time St. George stood his ground in the air, arms crossed over his chest. They crossed the miles between them in seconds. He was tensing in the air when they pulled up to hover a hundred or so yards away from him.

A full minute passed as the hero and the helicopters stared at each other two hundred feet above the Mount.

"They're all talking about you," said Barry over the earpiece. "Three of them are pretty sure you're the Mighty Dragon and two think you're somebody new. They're not quite sure what to do."

"Well," said St. George, "let's make sure they know who they're dealing with, then." He took in a quick breath and tasted a familiar sizzle at the back of his throat. He turned his head to the side and puffed it out as a fireball the size of a Volkswagen.

It made his point. Four of the helicopters split off. Three of them were the Apaches with miniguns. They circled in the air and fell back half a mile or so. St. George squinted down at the dark shape on top of the water tower. "Any idea what's going on?"

"You would need to confirm from your position," said Stealth, "but I believe they have retreated to just beyond the Big Wall."

He looked down and tried to pick out streets in the predawn gloom. She was right. He could see the rough, uneven line of stacked cars running up Vine and across Beverly. "Good call," he said. "Any idea why?"

"They are respecting our airspace," she said.

"Our what?"

"ARE YOU THE MIGHTY DRAGON?"

The amplified voice echoed in the air for a moment. The lone Black Hawk had turned its side to St. George. A young-looking man in a dark suit waved to him from the open cabin door. He wore a bulky headset with cables that ran back into the helicopter.

"If someone asks if you're a god," said Barry's voice, "you say yes."

"It is a test of trust," said Stealth. "You have demonstrated who you are. They wish you to confirm their beliefs."

"You don't have to talk me into it," he told them. He cupped his hands to his mouth and tried shouting back, but he was pretty sure the people in the Black Hawk couldn't hear him over the rotors. After a second attempt he gave an exaggerated nod. The man in the suit smiled.

"WITH YOUR PERMISSION, WE'D LIKE TO LAND AND SPEAK WITH YOU."

He glanced down at the tower again. Stealth had vanished. "Thoughts?"

"Direct them to the Plaza parking lot," said her voice in his ear. "I shall meet you there."

St. George looked behind him and to the left. The Plaza lot was right by the Melrose gate, separated by a line of shrubs in heavy planters and some fencing. Because it was so close to the outside it had never been populated with tents or shanties like so many other spaces. He drifted through the air toward it and pointed down at the open expanse.

The helicopter shifted in the air. "WE'RE GOING TO CALL IN THE OTHER BLACK HAWK TO SERVE AS A GUARD," said the man in the suit. "JUST THE ONE. IS THAT OKAY WITH YOU?"

St. George gave another big nod. The man gave him another smile and a thumbs-up. The hero dropped down a hundred feet or so and glided over to hover near the lot. The helicopter swung in a low arc to place itself over the wide square of pavement. The air thumped as another craft moved forward to hang high above the landing zone. St. George saw a handful of soldiers in full battle gear looking at him from the second Black Hawk's cabin doors.

He drifted down to meet the man in the suit.

× × ×

"I'm telling you," said Matt, "it's that guy from that space cowboy show that was on a couple of years ago." He jabbed the dead man again. "You can't see that?"

The other gate guards ignored him. Even the exes at the gate seemed distracted by the roar of the landing helicopter. Some of them were reaching up, as if their bony fingers could pluck the vehicle from the air.

The rail-thin woman glanced at Makana. "Who do you think it is?"

He shrugged. "Army, maybe. Or the Marines."

"It's the Army," said Matt, glancing back from the gate. "Check out the markings."

Makana shrugged again. "If you say so."

"Is anyone going to look at this ex? I'm telling you, it's whatshisface. Nathan something."

"Dude, whatever," said the dreadlocked man. He gave the zombie a quick look. "Yeah, it's probably him."

"Sweet."

They all turned their attention back to the helicopter as it settled on the pavement. Behind them, Matt pulled out his pistol. He took it in both hands and lined up his shot.

× × ×

The Black Hawk cut its engines. The noise level dropped as the long rotors slowed their relentless slashing at the air.

St. George dropped to the ground on the far side of the lot. Two soldiers on board trained their rifles on him and two more looked out the far door. Their weapons were huge things with dictionary-sized boxes mounted on them.

The man in the suit wrestled with his harness. Then he fought with it. One of the soldiers reached over and flicked something. The straps dropped away and the man almost fell out of his seat. He caught himself and made it look as if he was climbing down.

The two soldiers facing St. George tensed and he saw one of the gun barrels shift off to his left. "U.S. Army," said Stealth. She was a few steps behind him. "Their weapons appear to be M240Bs with a modified ammunition case and larger heat shields."

"Yeah," said St. George. He cleared his throat. "I thought they looked different."

"It is classified as an infantry medium machine gun," she said. "It is unusual for an entire squad to be armed with it because of its weight. Each one weighs over thirty pounds with ammunition."

"They don't seem to be having any trouble with them."

"Hello," shouted the man in the suit. He stood on the pavement by the Black Hawk. The soldiers had moved forward, still sheltered by the helicopter's armor but still flanking the man. "I'm John. It's good to see you."

"You too," called back St. George.

"Mind if I come a little closer?"

"Not at all."

"What if we meet halfway?"

St. George gave a nod. "That'd be fine."

He could feel Stealth's glare on him. "You do not need to agree to his every request," she said.

"Take it easy," he said, taking a few steps forward.

The gunshot rang out and echoed between the buildings.

One of the soldiers lunged at the man named John and carried him to the ground. The other one dropped to his knee and focused his oversized weapon at St. George. Two more soldiers had appeared, weapons aimed at the heroes. They shouted short, clipped orders back and forth through the helicopter's open doors.

"What did you guys do out there?" Barry asked over the earpiece. "Is someone shooting?"

St. George looked back at Melrose. Makana and one of

the other guards were wrestling a skinny man to the ground. The hero knew what had happened. "Screwup," he said. "Big screwup."

"How are they responding?" said Stealth. She swept her cloak back to expose her holsters but didn't draw yet.

"They're saying something about . . . they're deploying Captain Freedom," Barry told them. "That's not military code for a big-ass bomb or something, is it?"

Brute Force

THEN

FUCKING BITCH. I cannot believe this. She's going to do it again.

It's supposed to be a man's Army. That was what I got beaten into me growing up. Be a man, Kurt. Nine more years and you're the Army's problem. You better cry now because there'll be no crying then. They'll make a man out of you, yes they will.

And what's up with the rest of the squad cheering her on? Stupid bitch'll start to think she belongs here. She's only doing six-forty. All of us can do six-forty at this point. We're all fucking Olympic supermen.

She's just like all those dumb cunts in school I had to put up with for years. They all thought they belonged. They thought they were special. Giggling at me in the back of class. Yelling for their friends. Crying to the teachers. Kurt Taylor's staring at me again. Kurt, don't do that. Kurt, stop it. They wouldn't know a real man if one came up and punched them in their stupid Barbie faces.

Finally get out of high school and the U.S. Army's waiting for me just like the old man said. I get in and what do I find? Tons of bitches who all think they're as good as me. Better than me. My fucking platoon sergeant is some dyke bitch. Jesus, Mary, and fucking Joseph.

Wally Monroe slaps my arm. "Taylor, dude," he says to me. He points at Sergeant Kennedy, on her back with her tits in the air, pumping away. Gus is spotting her. "I think the sarge's going to beat your record."

"Yeah, great," I say. I think about adding "Who the fuck cares?" but he's a smart guy for a grunt. He figures it out.

So I sign up for Project Krypton thinking this'll take care of everything. No more questions who's supposed to be top dog, A-number-one around here. It'll separate the men from the boys and leave the girls in the dirt. They can wise up and go back to popping out more little soldiers for the U.S. of A. like God wanted.

And what the fuck do I find? A month after surgery three-quarters of the program's washed out and there're still three bitches here. And they're doing better than me. They've got the fucking dyke balls to keep trying to make me look bad. Always faster. Always stronger.

My arm's still sore. Got our last shots this morning. I hate needles. Hate 'em. There are air guns now that don't use needles, but they're still shots. Doc Sorensen says from here on in it's up to us. No more shots, just a few tests every other day. Our bodies will keep up or not.

The money's on not for most of us. There're only thirty-eight soldiers left. Orders came down and Shelly pulled us all together into one company. Sorensen said he expects the dropouts are done. There should be enough of us left to make a solid platoon or two.

One of the bitches is already looking sick. Or maybe she's just on the rag. Stick a cork in it, sister, this is a man's

Army. If you can't hack it go back to blowing jocks under the bleachers for a dollar.

They all applaud and Gus and Monroe each throw another plate on either side of the bar. Seven hundred ninety pounds. If the bitch does ten reps she'll tie my record. Monroe shoots me a smile. They're all cheering for her again.

I was the first one to break seven-fifty. Me. I'm the strongest, you fuckers.

While I'm waiting my turn I grab a pair of free weights. I'm curling one-fifty with no problem these days. Never guess it looking at any of us, especially the chicks. Sorensen says it has to do with muscle density and fast-twitch fiber or something. I've gained fifty-eight pounds of muscle, but I've only gone up one shirt size.

I'm getting antsy just hanging around the base, too. Should be thankful, though. Signed up thinking I'd get to go kill towelheads in Iraq or Affuckistan or somewhere. Then they sent me out here to Arizona and I found out how much I hate the fucking desert. I'm sunburned half the time, sweating all the time. Iraq or Affuckistan or Ari-fucking-zona, they all suck. Maybe I'll fake sick and see if I can get reassigned.

I do twenty reps while the bitch ties my record. She sits up for a moment, shoots me a wink, and gives Gus a look and a nod. "No way," he said, grinning.

"Do it," she says. She's sweating and grinning like a bitch in heat. "Two more."

The squad hollers. Sergeant Kennedy's going to do nine-forty. She's going to beat me. Fucking bitch cunt whore.

Gus and Monroe are scrounging up two more seventy-five-pound plates across the gym when Ryan Polk comes in.

He's working as one of Colonel Shelly's staff when he's not here with the rest of us. Let him make corporal. "News from the outside," he says as he pulls off his jacket. "It's getting worse."

Nobody has to ask what. About four weeks ago, in mid March, we started hearing news stories about an epidemic. First couple cases were in Los Angeles, but then we heard about outbreaks in Vegas and New York and Boston. There was a news story about someone getting sick in London and then Colonel Shelly clamped down on all of it. That told us how bad it was. One of the MPs told me they clamp down on big bad news so no one does anything stupid and runs home or something.

The other bitch, Britney, goes up to him. Yeah, we've got a fucking cunt soldier named Britney in our squad. "What'd you hear?"

Ryan grabs a set of free weights and starts doing curls, too. Our muscles get stiff fast if we don't keep using them. "I heard Colonel Shelly say they're deploying the National Guard in nineteen cities," he says. "They're talking about martial law."

I can't believe that. Not here in the U.S. of A. "No fucking way," I say.

"That's what they were saying. It hasn't happened yet but they think they're going to have to."

"Does the Guard even have that many people left in country?" asks Eddie. "Most of them are in Iraq, aren't they?"

Ryan shrugs in between curls.

Kennedy wipes some sweat off her forehead. "Is it getting that bad? Are people looting or something?"

Gus slaps his plate on the bar and shakes his head. "I

heard it's not like a regular flu, whatever it is. People get sick but they keep walking around and infecting people."

Monroe taps his plate into place. "I heard it was turning people into zombies."

"Fuck that," I say. "That's bullshit."

"My brother's in Queens. He says he's seen people wandering around biting other people."

Kennedy leans back on the bench. "Hate to agree with Taylor," she says, "but that sounds like bullshit." She grabs the bar and takes in a few deep breaths. Her arms tighten and the bar comes off the stands. Nine-forty. Fucking cunt.

"What I want to know," says Eddie, "is why aren't they sending us out?"

"Because we're not in the National Guard," I say.

"Yeah, fuck that. If they're locking down the base it means things are bad. People need help out there and it sounds like they need everyone they can get."

"You want to go haul that flu virus off to Guantanamo?" says Britney with a grin.

"I don't like sitting here on my ass," Eddie tells her.

"Yeah, your ass looks well sat-on," grunts Kennedy between presses. Most of them chuckle. She's telling jokes. The bitch is *telling jokes* while she breaks my record. I want to throw one of my dumbbells at her head and see what happens.

It gets the attention back on her, which is what she wanted. Seven reps. Eight. Nine. Ten. Ten reps of 940 pounds. The bar clangs onto the stand and almost bounces off before Gus grabs it.

They're all pounding her back and congratulating her. She's got wide eyes. Runner's high. I drop the dumbbells back on the rack with a clang. It's my turn. Time to get my record back and—

And she flops back onto the bench. She's staring up at the bar, and I swear to fucking God if she says what I think she's going to say I will kill this bitch.

"Do it," she says. "Two more."

Fucking cocksucker bitch cunt *whore!*

They all stop talking and stare at her. It already looks like a cartoon barbell, there's so much weight on it. There's about three inches clear at either end. Just enough to fit one more plate.

"Sarge," says Monroe, "you sure? That's—"

"One thousand ninety," she says. She nods. "Sorensen says we should be able to break a thousand. So let's break it."

There's another moment of quiet and then they're all hollering and stomping. Kennedy the she-bitch is still staring at the bar. Gus and Monroe trek across the gym, grab the last seventy-five-pound plates, and lug them back. One plate is nothing to any of us these days. They're carrying them one-handed. She's got seven on each side of the bar now.

I've gotta admit, I'm pissed but I want to see if she can do it.

She swings her legs up, crosses her ankles, and we can all see her abs tighten. Her arms spread a bit and her fingers wrap around the bar. Gus and Monroe are standing on either side. That's a fuckload of weight for one guy to spot. Even for us.

She takes in a deep breath. Then another. Her arms tense up and the barbell comes off the stands. The bar's wobbling, there's so much fucking weight on it.

It goes down real slow. She's sucking in air while it comes

down on her tits. Just brushes her nipples. Fucking little cocktease.

She breathes out hard and the bar goes up. One thousand and ninety pounds. Over half a ton.

The first rep is a little slow, but then the bitch does a second. And a third. And a fourth. She almost gets the fifth one up but her arms start shaking. Gus and Monroe lean in and she barks at them to back off. Sweat's pouring off her. You can hear it hitting the floor. And she forces the bar up. Five reps of more than half a ton each.

She rolls up off the bench and the whole squad is hollering and pounding her back and hugging her. She's the fucking bitch hero of the moment. She goes through and punches everyone in the shoulder one by one. Her knuckles land right where Monroe slapped me, right where I got my shot. Fucking cunt probably did it on purpose.

There's a rattle down at the far end of the gym, and we all turn to look. A bald black guy is using the other bench down there. A big guy. Six-eight, maybe six-ten, easy, and built like a fucking linebacker. He's just hoisted his own barbell off the rests. We've got every big plate in the gym, so he's loaded up his bar with thirty-fives. After so much time in the gym, we can all tell the plates apart on sight. He's got three-twenty on there and he starts doing these clean, precise reps, one after another.

Britney looks at him, already getting her panties wet. "Who's that?"

"Our new CO," says Ryan. "Just transferred in. He's in the program now, too."

"Kind of late in the game, isn't he?" says Eddie. "Take him forever to catch up to Sergeant Kennedy."

They chuckle and punch her in the shoulder. She bats their arms away, stuck-up bitch. I take the fucking high road, 'cause I'm such a nice guy and this guy looks like a real man. "Wasn't that long ago we were all proud doing three hundred," I say. "I bet by the time he's done with his shots he'll be blowing her out of the fucking water. No offense, Sarge."

"None taken," she says. "He's welcome to try." And you can see in her eyes the bitch is looking forward to the fight.

Ryan looks at her, then at me. "You guys don't know?"

"Know what?"

Ryan grins. A big shit-eating grin. "He hasn't started yet."

Sergeant Kennedy looks over at the big officer, pumping out rep after rep like a machine. He's done twenty-five now, and it doesn't look like he's going to be slowing down anytime soon. "Hasn't started what?"

"The process. Sorensen hasn't done anything to him yet."

We all watch him for a moment. He's up to thirty reps, easy.

"All of us guinea pigs are already obsolete," says Ryan. "You're looking at the next generation of super-soldier."

He drops the barbell back on the stand at thirty-five reps. Thirty-five fucking reps of three-twenty. And he's not enhanced yet. He sits up and looks at all of us, and that fucking look lets us know he could take any of us grunts right now, shots or no shots.

No fucking way.

Eleven
NOW

BARRY'S WORDS WERE still echoing in St. George's ear when the second Black Hawk dropped a belay line. The rope hadn't even uncoiled before a soldier slid down fast. He was halfway down when the end of the line swung free, a good hundred feet over the Plaza lot.

"It's too short," said St. George, stepping forward. He focused, started to rise, and the soldier kneeling by the first helicopter opened fire with his rifle. The rounds hit hard. He imagined it was a lot like getting blasted by a fire hose would be for normal people. The hero dropped back to the ground. He glanced up and the man on the belay line shot past the end and fell.

The soldier ended his hundred-foot drop and hit the ground like a falling tree. The pavement cracked out from the impact point and kicked up the two years' worth of dust the first helicopter had swept into small drifts. Bits of gravel and dirt pitter-pattered down across the area.

St. George was back on his feet, taking in a breath to shout for medical help. In those few instants the dust cleared and he froze. The man hadn't fallen from the line.

He'd jumped.

The soldier straightened up from the crouch he'd landed in, a move that reminded St. George of Arnold Schwarzenegger traveling from the future in the *Terminator* movies. He was a black man, at least nine inches taller than the hero, and a good foot wider. He focused on St. George with shining green eyes in a face shadowed by his helmet There were two black bars on his chest, and stitched across the left side of his digital-patterned camos was one word.

FREEDOM

He pulled the biggest pistol St. George had ever seen from a thigh holster. It had a drum like an old tommy gun and venting on the barrel. The muzzle came to bear on him as the huge officer barked out a command.

"Stand down, sir," said Freedom, stepping forward. "Get on your knees with your hands on your head."

"Hey," said St. George. "There's no need for this. It's just a simple misunderstanding."

"On your knees!" The captain grabbed the hero by the shoulder with his left hand and shoved down. St. George brushed the hand aside.

"I think you need to take a few deep breaths and calm—"

There was a sound like a sledgehammer hitting concrete as Freedom's knuckles caught him under the chin. A shrub whipped St. George from behind and the wall of the gatehouse hit him in the back. He felt it crumble. The soldier marched forward, holstered his oversized pistol, and dragged the hero back to his feet by the lapels of his leather jacket. The man spun on his heel and threw St. George half a block down to 3rd Street.

The hero hit the pavement and skidded into one of the oversized planters. The concrete cracked and soil spilled out over him. He cleared his head with a quick shake and pushed himself back to his feet.

Freedom marched forward again. "Sir, stay on your knees and put your hands on your head," said the huge soldier. "This is your last warn—"

St. George leaped up, grabbed the officer's swollen biceps, and shot into the air.

When they were a hundred feet over the Mount he held the larger man up at eye level. "Unless you want to make that drop again," he said, "I suggest you—"

Freedom slammed his helmet into the bridge of St. George's nose. When the hero didn't release him, he did it again.

Smoke curled up from St. George's nostrils. He glared at the soldier for a moment and opened his hands.

The other man dropped six feet and grabbed hold of the hero's boot with iron fingers.

"Oh, come on!" snapped St. George.

× × ×

The soldier who'd taken the man named John to the ground dragged him back to the helicopter. The others shouted until the gate guards dropped their weapons, walked closer to the Black Hawk, and fell to their knees. Then they took up defensive positions around the chopper. Two of the soldiers kept the guards at gunpoint. Two others watched the nearby buildings for opposition.

One of the last two, a specialist with TRUMAN on his jacket, looked all around. "Where'd the woman go?"

"What woman?" The other soldier, labeled FRANKLIN, had been one of the last to disembark.

"With the black cape. Where'd she go? She was right here before the captain deployed."

All six of them scanned the area around the helicopter. There was ten feet of open space in every direction. Where the woman had been standing, on the far side of Freedom's impact crater, there was twice that distance to the nearest piece of cover. And most of that cover had been destroyed when the captain had punched the guy claiming to be the Mighty Dragon.

One of the civilian guards, a beefy man with dreadlocks, chuckled. He kept his hands on his head and raised his voice so they could hear him across the distance. "You guys might as well give up now," he said.

"Keep it quiet," snapped one of the soldiers watching him. "I'll tape your mouth if I have to."

He laughed again. "You guys are so seriously out of your league here."

The five soldiers exchanged a quick set of looks. Then they looked at each other again. "Hey," said Franklin, "where the hell did Mike go?"

× × ×

At Four, Zzzap searched the air for information. Telemetry danced around him from all five helicopters, and here and there a terse command from the troops on the ground. He knew their call sign was Unbreakable and it sounded like another squad from the same platoon was getting ready to deploy. On the Mount's frequencies the Melrose gate had gone silent, but many of the spotters on the wall stepped on each other in their rush to report in. The soldiers had taken the Melrose guards prisoner. Three people reported gunfire but weren't sure from what or at who. And they'd seen St. George carry someone into the air and start to wrestle with him.

He sent a pulse out to Stealth. He knew it reached her cowl radio, but she didn't respond. Which meant she was fighting the other soldiers. It shouldn't be too hard for her. If he'd gotten the numbers right, there were six or seven on the ground and maybe that many more getting ready to deploy. A ridiculously small amount, from his limited experience with the military. The sun was almost up but there were still a ton of shadows. With home-court advantage, Stealth would probably have the soldiers disarmed and hogtied before the—

Zzzap had an ugly thought. There was no reason for it, but a lot of things made sense if he was right. Maybe whoever gave this platoon of soldiers their call sign was as big a movie fan as he was. Which would explain why they didn't need to put that many soldiers on the ground. And why one of them was trading punches with St. George.

Keep an eye on things here, he said to no one in particular. *I think they might need some extra help out there.*

× × ×

St. George tried to shake the larger man loose, but Freedom's grip couldn't be broken. He kicked the huge soldier in the wrist again but it didn't seem to have any effect. The hero finally dove down toward 12th Street in the middle of the North-by-Northwest residential area. He pulled up at the last minute and slammed the other man against the ground, confident it wasn't a lethal tactic. At this point he wondered if it would even slow the soldier down.

Freedom tumbled across the pavement and rolled to his feet next to the capsized truck that blocked the North Gower gate. His helmet skittered loose across the street. He drew his oversized sidearm and squeezed off four thundering bursts at St. George. Over a dozen slugs hit like punches. They pattered off the hero's chest and shoulder and chimed on the ground with the spent shells from the pistol.

St. George glanced over his shoulder, but it looked like most of the stray rounds had just taken chunks out of Thirty-One's outer wall. "Look," he said, "isn't this a little clichéd? I'm one of the good guys. I'm pretty sure you're one of the good guys. Let's pull our heads out of our asses before either side does something stu—"

The four guards from Gower gate lunged forward with pikes and weapons drawn. One of them howled a battle cry. A pike got close to Freedom and he grabbed it by the end and snapped the tip off. He blasted the ground by their feet. "Drop your weapons," he bellowed.

The guards smiled. One pointed behind him.

He turned and St. George's fist cracked across his jaw. The soldier shook it off and a second punch knocked him back against the truck. He swung a roundhouse with his free hand but the hero leaped away and up.

Freedom holstered his weapon and charged across the pavement. He leaped up and tackled St. George in midair. The hero's concentration faltered and they slammed into the ground.

The huge soldier drove three quick punches into St. George's face with the distinct sound of large stones being slammed together. Each one drove the smaller man's skull down into the pavement until the surface cracked. "You will stand down, sir," said Freedom. "I'm not going to tell you ag—"

St. George slammed his palm up. Hard. It caught Freedom in the breastbone and knocked him a dozen feet into the air. The soldier hit the ground running and threw himself back at the hero before he could finish getting to his feet. The two slid across the road and into the side of Thirty.

Freedom brought his knee up and St. George folded over with an all-too-human pain. The huge man drove his fist into the hero's gut twice, then grabbed his collar and threw him back out into the street. St. George coughed out some smoke and a few tongues of flame.

At which point the gate guards opened fire.

A dozen rounds struck Freedom in the back. He turned and caught a dozen more in the chest and arms. He lunged forward, far too fast for a man his size, and three of the guards had been disarmed and knocked down before the fourth had time to re-aim. The soldier took another burst to the chest before snapping the edge of his palm against the guard's temple. The man dropped like an empty set of clothes.

St. George grabbed Freedom by the neck and hurled him away from the gate. The soldier was charging forward again before the hero could finish turning. They traded blows that echoed in the tall canyons of North-by-Northwest. Then Freedom blocked a roundhouse punch and slammed his fist up into St. George's gut. The impact sent him sailing into the air. He soared up and over the spiked top of the Gower gate.

He landed outside the Mount.

"Son of a bitch," muttered St. George as the exes swarmed over him.

× × ×

Stealth's arm swung around and delivered a fast strike to Specialist Truman's throat before she dragged him between the potted shrubs. One blow to paralyze the voice box and give her time to incapacitate him. The man let out a faint hiss of air. It was a weak noise under ideal conditions. With the Black Hawk's rotors still making a last few circles in the air, he was effectively silenced.

The soldiers were each carrying an M240B as a standard weapon and a complete set of body armor with no apparent effort. It indicated great strength, bordering on superhuman. It was more time-consuming, but she delivered a series of strikes across Truman's body. Biceps, armpits, pectorals. Each one hit a nerve cluster, the end result being two arms numb from the shoulders down.

When he still rolled up and grabbed for her she realized how dense his muscle tissue must be. She frowned beneath her featureless mask and drove a punch into his forehead, right where his eyebrows met. He dropped.

Nine seconds to stop one man. Too long. The others had noticed he was missing. She heard one of them call out for him. A change in tactics was required. The soldiers had already demonstrated one weak point. It was somewhat distasteful, but she would have to exploit it.

She jumped up, kicked off the concrete planter, and flipped through the hedges.

× × ×

On an average day, there were anywhere from a hundred to two hundred ex-humans milling around on the street outside the Gower gate. A decent amount of noise could draw another hundred on top of that. St. George put the mob of exes he'd fallen into at about one-fifty with another hundred or so close by.

They fell on him with hungry teeth that broke on his skin. Withered lips and fingers worked their way over his arms and shoulders and legs. The only good thing about two years of the undead in Los Angeles was most of them had dried out by now.

He pushed down against gravity and rose up through the mob, carrying half a dozen chattering exes with him. They dropped off as he rotated in the air, some of them knocking down other dead things as they fell. He turned back to the Mount and the first rounds hit him.

The drum-fed monster that Freedom carried spat out ten rounds in a two-second burst, and each one hit like one of his punches. The soldier had leaped to the top of the white truck that blocked the gate. "Please stand down, sir," he called out. "I don't enjoy doing this."

St. George faltered in the air as a second burst caught him in the chest. He dipped low enough for thin fingers to grab at his boots again.

Freedom lined up a third shot when he heard the air sizzle behind him and saw how dark his shadow had gotten. He spun and fired off another burst. There was a hiss as the rounds vaporized inches from Zzzap. The captain wasted some more ammunition. There was a hollow clang from his oversized pistol.

Well, said the wraith. He held his hand up. The air in front of his palm twisted and rippled from the heat. *That was all pretty impressive until the part where you got here.*

"You would be Zzzap, correct, sir?"

Thank God someone knows me. I'm sick and tired of being mistaken for Stealth.

"Give it a rest," said St. George. He shook off the last ex and drifted over to hang a few yards above the soldier. Smoke was billowing out his nostrils and between his teeth. "So, feel like having that calm talk, now?"

The huge officer looked at each of the heroes in turn and then dropped his oversized pistol. It clattered on the roof of the truck as he raised his hands. "I choose to decline at this time, sir," he said.

What about name, rank, and all that stuff?

"Captain Freedom, sir," he said. "Alpha 456th Unbreakables, first U.S. Army super-soldier company."

There was a long pause.

Oh, that is too cool, said Zzzap.

× × ×

The woman in black came over the hedge. She spun in the air and her cloak spread like a huge set of wings. It blotted out the sky as she came down at Franklin and the squad's sergeant, Monroe. Their weapons came up and twin bursts ripped into the darkness. Her descent didn't shift in the slightest and shadows raced on the ground below her. The sergeant fired another burst as Franklin dove to the side. She came down on the sergeant. He fought for a moment, a thrashing shape beneath the cloak, and then he tossed the fabric aside.

"Nothing," said Monroe. "Just her cape. She's gone."

"She was there," said Franklin. "We saw her."

"Excuse me, gentlemen," said the man in the suit. He was still in the helicopter's crew compartment.

"Not now, sir," said Monroe. "We've got a hostile in the area."

"Yeah," said the man. "I'm very aware of that at the moment."

The sergeant shot a look over his shoulder. John was sitting very still. His arms were at his sides and his head was tilted back. Monroe gave his eyes a moment to adjust to the shadows inside the Black Hawk and saw the harness straps pulled tight across the man's arms and body. His collar and tie sat funny, and another second of light-adjustment let the sergeant pick out the black chrome bar pressed against the man's throat.

Monroe blinked. It had only been a few seconds since he turned his head, but now he could see the very feminine shadow behind John. She gave a slight dip of her head, an acknowledgment he'd spotted her. Then she pulled herself closer to the man named John. On either side of the helicopter soldiers raised their weapons.

"The M240B has a prodigious rate of fire," she said in a clear voice. "Seven hundred fifty rounds per minute at its lowest setting. It is not a weapon designed for pinpoint accuracy, however. Firing into an enclosed space will almost guarantee you hit your civilian advisor."

The weapons stayed up.

No one moved.

"You know what I think?" said the man in the suit. "I think we should all take a moment here and relax. Wouldn't that be good? Let's all stop and calm down for a moment before this gets any more out of hand."

Twelve

NOW

A HUGE CROWD gathered a little before noon to watch the second Black Hawk land in the Pickford lot on the other side of the Melrose gate. Thousands of people packed the streets and rooftops. A few of them glared at the helicopter as it settled down and the wind whipped up clouds of dirt and dust, but most of them stared in amazement. Some applauded.

St. George and Stealth stood on 3rd Street with the crowds behind them. She had slipped back into her cloak and the bullet holes vanished in its folds and gathers. Every now and then a shaft of light would slip through one of the dime-sized holes and St. George would feel his jaw tighten.

Barry sat in his wheelchair next to them. He'd powered down as a concession to Freedom's people shouldering their weapons. Danielle lurked behind the chair. She'd given up on anyone helping her with the armor and stood with her head bowed and her arms crossed.

Freedom was a few yards away with his soldiers standing at ease behind him in a loose circle around their helicopter. The man in the suit was inside the circle. They'd insisted on separating him until they could have more troops on the ground.

The Black Hawk had barely settled when a second group of soldiers leaped out and loped across the pavement. Each of them carried the same oversized rifle with the bulky ammo box. They formed their own loose circle around their helicopter.

"Supporting units," said Stealth. "Each positioned to keep us in line of sight."

A woman with a collection of chevrons on her jacket gave a set of hand signals across the way to Freedom. He looked back at the man in the suit and gave a nod. The young man called John whispered a few words to the captain, and then made his way across the space to the heroes. Freedom followed a few paces behind. The man in the suit beamed a broad smile. "Let's try this again, shall we?"

"Sure," said St. George.

"The Mighty Dragon," said the young man. "This is a real honor. Wow." His smile got broader. "Can I shake your hand?"

St. George was caught off guard. He held his hand out without thinking and the man pumped it five or six times. People cheered and applauded. "I'm going by St. George these days."

The smile shifted. "St. George," he echoed. "Clever. I like it. And you must be Stealth," the suit continued. He stepped past St. George to stand before the cloaked woman. "You're just as formidable as I've always heard. I'd love to shake your hand, too, if that's okay? No hard feelings?"

It was so unexpected; she held her hand out. There were more cheers and applause.

"It's just amazing," he continued. "You've saved so many people. People talk about superheroes and you think about fighting monsters and supervillains and stuff. You don't think about things like this."

"I'm sorry," interrupted St. George. "I didn't catch your name."

The young man's smile faltered and in that instant the hero realized the man in the suit was probably older than he was. "Sorry," he said. "Caught up in the moment. This is just . . . It's so rare we find survivors, let alone such a huge group with, well, people like you." He straightened his tie. "I'm John Smith. Department of Homeland Security, seconded to DARPA and working with Project Krypton as . . . well . . ." He shrugged. "These days I just try to help out wherever I can, like most people."

He took a few steps back until he stood near the soldiers. "Good job, Captain Freedom," he said. "You and your people did great considering the opposition. I'll make sure the colonel and Dr. Sorensen know."

The huge officer gave a sharp dip of his head. "Thank you, sir."

"St. George, Stealth," said Smith, turning back to the heroes, "I believe you've already met our super-forces commander."

"Captain Freedom," said St. George with a smile. He rubbed his jaw and held out his hand. "So that's the best name they could come up with, huh?"

"Captain John Carter Freedom, sir," he said. He took the hand, gripped it hard, and gave a single shake.

"Ahhh. Sorry."

The crowd, not hearing any of it, applauded again.

Smith broke up the awkward moment with more babbling. It was like nervous hero worship. "You can imagine our surprise," he said to St. George, "when our sentries looked west on the Fourth of July and saw fireworks out over Los Angeles. Sixty miles over, as far as we could tell."

"Yeah, I bet that was a bit of a shock."

"Of course, we sent out a Predator to investigate," he continued. "It was a little more disturbing when it stopped sending back telemetry and started pounding out 'Radio Nowhere' by Bruce Springsteen."

Barry cleared his throat. "Told you it'd be memorable," he said to St. George.

"That was you?" said Smith. "You're Zzzap, yes?"

"Yes."

The suit pumped Barry's hand three or four times. "This is just such a great day. People are going to be going crazy back at Yuma when we report in. I mean, we had some wild hopes of what we might find out here in Los Angeles but . . ."

Smith stopped talking. Even the crowd sensed it and grew quiet. He stared at Danielle, his mouth open.

After a moment she registered the silence and raised her head to see what was going on. She glanced around, shrunk when she saw everyone staring, and finally noticed the man in front of her. She blinked and opened her eyes wide.

"John?"

He lunged past the wheelchair and hugged her. "We thought you were dead," he said. "Everyone thought you died years ago."

She pulled away and stared at him with a look that was half amazement, half anger.

"Oh, come on," he said. "After all that's happened, you're not going to say you're glad to see me?"

Danielle smiled and bear-hugged him back. "I am glad to see you," she said.

Barry inched his chair out of the way. "Soooooo," he said, "you two know each other?"

She released the man in the suit. "We . . . kind of dated," she said with a smile.

This time Smith pulled back to look at her but also didn't let go. "Dated? We were living together for six months."

She pulled him back. The embrace lasted for another few moments and then his manic energy took over again. "This is . . . This is unbelievable," he said. "We got the news your plane was diverting to Van Nuys and then no one ever heard anything from your team again. Not to sound morbid but, well, we all assumed you were dead and the battlesuit was a rusting statue somewhere."

"The suit's fine," she said. She turned her head and pointed over at the scenery mill she'd converted to her workshop. "It's right over there. I'd be wearing it right now but . . ." She shrugged. "You remember what it was like putting it on."

"The suit's here?" He blinked. "And it still works?"

"I built it to last." She looked at the others. "John was my first liaison with the DOD. We met while I was building Cerberus."

"I think most of us figured that out," said St. George.

"We need to get you back to Yuma," said Smith. He looked around. "All of you are welcome, of course. Captain, can we arrange to get some kind of cargo transport out here?"

Freedom glanced at Sergeant Monroe. The man took a look around the Plaza lot and nodded. "Yes, sir," the captain said.

"One moment," said Stealth.

Her voice cut across the festive mood. They all paused. The cloaked woman had moved, taking a position between Smith and the workshop.

"You are planning to take the Cerberus suit?"

Smith shifted his gaze from Danielle to Stealth. "Well, I just figured Dan . . . Dr. Morris would want to come back with us," he said. "We've got better facilities, machine shops, and . . . well . . ." He looked at the redhead again. "You know."

"I do not," said Stealth. "Cerberus is an essential part of both our community and our defensive measures."

Danielle's brow furrowed. "Are you telling me I can't leave?"

"I am saying—"

"Okay, let's all stop for a second," said St. George. He could feel the icy glare Stealth gave him through her mask. "Big day, a lot to take in, everyone's a little overstimulated. Not to mention"—he tilted his head at the crowd—"there're a lot of people here who've been waiting for a day like this for some time now."

"I agree," said Smith. "We can talk about all this later. Captain Freedom, would your people like to say hello to the crowd?"

"Yes, sir," said the huge officer. He turned to the soldiers. "Unbreakables," he snapped, "dismissed."

Their salutes shook the air. Then they moved to the crowd, shaking hands and hugging strangers. Some even posed for photos. St. George saw Billie Carter exchange salutes with one and the two began to speak at length about something.

Danielle dropped her voice. "What the hell are you talking about?" She looked at Smith. "Both of you, for that matter."

"We should discuss this matter in private," said Stealth. "It is not good for the civilians to see us argue amongst ourselves."

"We're not arguing," said St. George. "We're just talking."

"I'm ready to argue," said Danielle.

"Look," said Smith, "I'm sorry if I spoke out of turn. I just got excited. This is like winning the lottery three times on the same day."

"You were so excited to find us here," said Stealth, "yet your first response was an assault."

"Standard operating procedure, ma'am," said Freedom. He loomed behind Smith and made the suited man look even less like an adult. "In an unknown situation, when you hear gunfire, your first duty is to protect your people and take control of the situation. I'm sure you can understand."

"So you attacked us," said St. George.

"Because you resisted our attempt to control the situation."

"We resisted because you attacked us. Welcome to the real—"

"This country is under martial law," said Freedom. "My authority here is absolute unless otherwise ordered by Colonel Shelly or the president himself."

There was a moment of silence. His words reached some of the closer edges of the crowd and nervous whispers began to work their way through the people gathered to see the soldiers.

"Martial law?" said Danielle. She raised an eyebrow.

Smith cleared his throat. "As of July 2009, the country's been under martial law. It still is. Nobody's thrilled by it, but the fact is the military's in charge. As the only known ranking officer in the American Southwest, Colonel Shelly is the man running things."

Stealth shifted her stance again. "What are you implying, Mr. Smith?"

"I'm not trying to imply anything," he said. "I just think we all need to be aware of where things stand, with no confusion or illusions."

"So the Mount is now under the Army's control?"

"Technically, unless you seceded from the United States at some point in the past two years . . . yeah."

"Which United States are you referring to?"

The question froze Smith and Freedom. It jarred the others, too. The man in the suit coughed once. "I . . . I'm not sure I understand your question."

Stealth crossed her arms. "Which states are still united? California has not had a functioning state government for twenty-two months now. There are no social services in effect. No taxes levied or laws enforced. Its borders and lands are not maintained. As a state, California has ceased to exist by any possible definition. From our own limited reconnaissance, I can say with some certainty it is not alone in this respect. Alaska. Arizona. Florida. Hawaii. Massachusetts. Nevada. New York. Oregon. Texas. Washington." She paused for a moment, then added, "The District of Columbia."

Smith shifted his feet.

"So I ask," she continued, "which states are still running and operating to the extent they can form a united nation, one that you and these soldiers can represent?"

"Captain," said Smith, "perhaps you could field this one?"

"Ma'am," said Freedom, "it's good that you're reluctant to hand over everything you've saved. But let me assure you, we are here as representatives of the government of the United States. Our commanding officer is in regular contact with the president, who is still in office in principle if not the actual building. We represent one of dozens of military outposts that are trying to reestablish local governments and provide services."

"Why has it taken you two years to do this?"

"Because, ma'am, believe it or not, you're not the only people who've taken heavy losses."

Smith cleared his throat. "Can I just say one more thing?"

St. George glanced between Stealth and Smith. Stealth nodded.

"I can't really speak for the Army," the man in the suit said, glancing over his shoulder at Freedom. "I'm a loose liaison at best. But I can tell you this is going to be good for you. We've got a lot to offer and I know the Army is going to want to offer it. We're here to help. We're not going to take everything you've got and leave you helpless like . . ." He shrugged and gave a smile. "Well, if you'll pardon me saying it, like the military would in some bad zombie movie."

Barry let out a loud cough and shot St. George a look.

"If Dr. Morris decides to come out to Yuma for a while," Smith continued, "we'll supplement your defenses with troops, weapons, whatever you need that we can supply."

Stealth still hadn't moved. "What do you propose?"

Something tugged at Danielle's leg as Smith replied. Barry gave her a look. She bent her head to his. "What?"

"Seriously," he said. "This guy?"

"What about him?"

"You and him? He looks like he's barely out of high school and he acts like Burke in *Aliens*."

Her lips pulled into a faint smile. "It was convenient, I guess," she said. "We barely had anything in common, and he put his job above everything else."

"I'm old enough," said Barry. "You can just say it was for the sex."

"Honestly, I don't even remember the sex being that great. We were together for a few months while I was building the suit and then he moved out, left me with a drawer full of shirts he didn't want, and that was it."

"He didn't even show up to end it? Not even a phone call?"

"Nope. We traded a few e-mails later. Guess we both knew it wasn't working."

"Want me to blast him for you?"

She laughed. It was the first time Barry had heard her laugh in months. The others glanced over and she waved them off. "You know what's the worst?" she whispered to Barry. "I swore for ages I'd kick his ass the next time I saw him. Now it's just so damned great to see someone from . . . from before all this. Someone from the real world. Even if it's him. Does that make sense?"

The man in the chair nodded.

"I can have another Black Hawk out here tomorrow," Smith told St. George. "Two days, tops. It'll take Dr. Morris and the Cerberus suit, plus anyone else who wants to come. You can meet Colonel Shelly, our CO, and we can all shake hands and talk about what we can do for each other." He looked at Danielle. "We've got full machine shops out there and even some manufacturing facilities. There's no way you can tell me the suit doesn't need a full strip-down and cleaning."

Stealth was a statue.

"Look," said Smith, "they want to help. It's their job, remember? Protect American civilians. You've got nothing to worry about." He shrugged. "Do you want a tour of the Krypton base first? I'm sure I could set something up."

"That might not be a bad idea," said St. George with a glance at Stealth.

Smith nodded. "Okay. Do you want to do it yourself or have somebody else go?" He looked at Barry. "Didn't I see on a television special or something that you can fly at the speed of light? You could be there and back before lunch, right?"

"I'm not that fast, but I could."

Smith's head bobbed again and he looked from the heroes to Freedom. "So how's this sound? We send the three Apaches away so everyone feels a little more relaxed. We get another Black Hawk out here tomorrow morning. While we're getting the Cerberus suit loaded and stowed, Zzzap flies out to Krypton, looks around, gives a yes or no. If it's a no, he's back here to say so before we're even ready to leave. Does that work for everyone?"

They all agreed. Even Stealth gave a slow nod. "I always wanted to fly to Krypton," said Barry with a smile.

"Great." Smith turned back to the huge officer. "Freedom, could you have someone report in and check on a helicopter for tomorrow morning?"

Freedom turned and barked out an order to Monroe. Monroe relayed it to someone else and a soldier broke from the crowd and headed for the Black Hawk. When Freedom turned back, Barry was in front of him.

"Have you ever thought of a shield?" Barry mimed something circular on his arm. "Maybe in a patriotic color scheme? It could really work for you."

"If it helps," said Danielle, "we ignore half of what he says, too."

Stealth had vanished. St. George realized she was probably halfway back to her office by now. He wasn't sure if this was a good thing or a bad thing. When he saw her next time he'd have to ask.

"This is amazing," said Smith. The man had moved to stand near St. George as they looked at the celebrating crowds. "Sorry to sound like a broken record, but it is. We've checked so many places and if we found twenty or thirty survivors it was a miracle."

"I didn't think we were special," said the hero. "I figured

every city had a few thousand survivors holed up some-where."

Smith shook his head. "I wish. Phoenix is a ghost town, same with Scottsdale, Mesa, Tucson. We've never been able to raise anyone at White Sands or Camp Pendleton." He shook his head again. "You must have every living person in south-ern California here."

"No," said St. George. "There's a group of about two hun-dred people down in Beverly Hills. They're what's left of a street gang called the South Seventeens. Real die hards who refused to join us here in the Mount." He shrugged. "We check in on them once a week or so, make sure they're doing okay. And we still find a few survivors here and there who've managed to make it this long on their own, although . . ." He looked past the helicopters to the gate. "It's been a while since we found anyone."

"Hey," said the younger man. "I know it's been tough, but this isn't the day to be getting morose. This is the day it all gets better. You saved all these people. You brought them through hell and got them home."

St. George looked at Freedom talking with Danielle and Barry, the Black Hawks flanking the Melrose gate, and the crowd mobbing the soldiers. "I guess we did," he said.

"Hell, yeah, you did." Smith gave him a punch in the arm. "Welcome back to the United States of America."

The Spirit of Freedom
THEN

MY GREAT-GREAT-GRANDFATHER was born a slave. On his fourth birthday he and everyone he knew became free citizens of the United States. When he was eighteen, he changed our family name to what he thought was the greatest word in the English language. I never met him, but my father did. It's a powerful thing, to think how short a time that was.

Now there's a black man in the White House. And a black man was selected to be the symbol of the new American military. It was a long process for both of us.

My first posting as an officer was Iraq. December 2003. I'd been there for eight weeks, a freshly minted second lieutenant, when a soldier in my section, Private First Class Adam James, found a well-constructed IED on a patrol. He was killed instantly. From what I was told later, the two soldiers on either side of him were dead within the hour. They were lucky never to regain consciousness. Sergeant James Cole lost his left leg and three fingers off his left hand. I was thrown fifteen feet into the side of our Humvee.

Three men dead. One crippled for life. I suffered a concussion, a broken arm that needed two pins, five fractured ribs that got wire supports, and eleven pieces of shrapnel that needed to be surgically removed. One of the doctors said they took out as much metal as they put in. I know some men and women who save such things as trophies. I didn't want to be reminded of failing the people under my command.

I spent three months in a hospital in Germany, received a Purple Heart, and was put back in the field. I always prefer to be in the field, and those days an officer who went into the field willingly was considered an asset.

Six years later I was standing in front of the colonel's desk at Project Krypton, asking to be assigned to the field. It was May 14, 2009. I recall thinking later we should mark it as the day the world ended, but that kind of negative thinking was bad for morale.

"They're mindless things," Shelly told me. "This virus turns people into walking vegetables. No real threat at all unless they're in large numbers. The media's just blowing things out of proportion again."

I hadn't served under the colonel for long. I don't think I even knew if he was married or not at that point. I did know he was a horrible liar. Lying is a politician's game, not a soldier's. All good soldiers are bad liars. The best ones are horrible at it.

Shelly was lying. There were uprisings in every major city. Even Yuma proper had reported a few dozen wandering the streets. If there were dozens wandering the street in a state where more than half the citizens carried firearms on a regular basis, it didn't bode well for anywhere else. But he was a good soldier, and his orders told him it wasn't a crisis and we weren't needed.

"Be that as it may, sir," I said, "I'm requesting deployment into one of the hot spots. The Unbreakables are ready to go."

"It's still too soon for active deployment," Shelly said.

"Sorensen thinks all of you need another month or so of observation. Especially you, captain. It's been three weeks since
you finished your treatments."

"And I feel excellent, sir. Better than excellent."

The corners of his mouth twitched. It was what passed for
a polite smile in the colonel's office. "The official decision,
captain, is you and your men would just be overkill."

The Unbreakables had only been my men for a month.
But I knew they were good soldiers. When I was first introduced to them, Shelly and Sorensen assured me they weren't
picked just for their names. I think the doctor found something funny about it. I'm sure similar coincidences have happened in every branch of the service at one time or another.

Besides, I've taken enough good-natured ribbing about
my name over the years. I can't say anything about anyone
else's. According to my mother, I was named after her father
and the sitting president when I was born. As my father tells
it, I was named for his boyhood hero, a man of honor and the
greatest soldier of two worlds. I've often sided with my father
when the topic has come up.

"From what I've heard, sir," I said, "the actual heroes are
trying to pitch in and not having much luck. We'd hardly be
overkill."

"Really?" said Shelly. His voice was dry. "What exactly
have you heard, captain?"

"Through official sources, sir, I've heard they've deployed
the Cerberus exoskeleton in Washington, D.C."

"Official sources is Agent Smith shooting his mouth off
again, correct?"

"Yes, sir."

"What else have you heard?"

The base was locked down, but rumors still made their

way in. A few sources said the heroes were kicking zombie butt everywhere they went, but most of them told me the heroes were making no headway at all. They were slowing the spread of the infection at best. And there were a few stories that some of them had died. Even one or two claims they'd come back, and there were superpowered zombies overwhelming the police in some cities. It did occur to me that no one could name which heroes had died.

"Nothing else, sir," I said.

He nodded. I was sure there was nothing I'd heard that he hadn't. "Is that all, captain?"

"Sir," I said, "permission to speak freely?"

"Granted."

"As I understand it, sir, all of B Company is being pulled out of Yuma and redeployed in civilian centers."

"Yes," he said, "they are. There's still more than enough forces stateside to deal with this epidemic, especially with a few platoons of regular Army backing them up."

"Regardless, sir, isn't this just what the Unbreakables were created for? If our control group is gone, any testing has to be over. If the testing is over, there's no reason for us not to be doing our jobs."

Colonel Shelly considered my words and a red drop swelled up under his nose. In the desert climate, nosebleeds aren't uncommon. First Sergeant Paine tells me two or three of the soldiers in A Company get them. I opened my mouth to say something and the drop hit the bursting point, too big to support its own weight. It became a red line across the colonel's lips. A few drops hit his paperwork.

"Damn it." He pinched his nose and tilted his head back.

"Can I get you anything, sir?"

"Thank you, no," he sighed. "Captain, for the time being

you and your men are not needed in this action. You will remain assigned to the proving ground. Those are your orders. Is that clear?"

"Yes, sir."

That was that. He took his hand away from his nose and returned my salute. His attention went back to the paperwork on his desk. He yanked a Kleenex from a drawer to dab at it. I'd reached the door when he called out to me.

"Captain Freedom."

"Yes, sir?"

He held out the blood-streaked warning order he'd been working on. "Take the Unbreakables toward Yuma tomorrow morning and see if you can find any civilians in need of assistance. Bring three transports with you in case you need to evacuate anyone. Deal with any infected you encounter."

"Yes, sir. Thank you, sir."

I left his office and got a quick salute from his staff sergeant, who was talking with First Sergeant Paine. Paine fell in next to me as we headed out into the hall. Walking side by side we filled the hallway. "Orders, sir?"

"Orders," I said. "Finally." I handed Paine the warning order. "Get first platoon prepared. We head out at oh-six-thirty. Any questions?"

He skimmed the paper. "None, sir." He gave a sharp salute and reversed direction. I walked around the corner and almost flattened Dr. Sorensen. He glanced up at me.

"Captain," he said.

"Doctor."

"How are you feeling?"

"Fine, sir," I said.

"What did you lift in the gym last night?"

"I'm up to twenty-two-fifty on the bench press, sir," I told him. "I'm limited now by what can fit on the bar."

He gave a nod. "I should've thought of that sooner," he said. He reached out and pressed on my biceps with two fingers. His hand moved up and he tried to drive his thumb into the spot where my pecs ran into my shoulders. "Any muscle pain?"

"None at all, sir. Not even aches from exercising."

"Excellent." He peered over his glasses into my eyes. "How's your appetite? Still good?"

"I'm on double servings, sir, but I think I'm burning most of it off."

"Converting most of it straight to muscle and bone mass is more likely. Have you weighed yourself today?"

I'd started weighing myself every day while I was at West Point. For a man my size it's important to keep off extra pounds. Since beginning Sorensen's process I'd been gaining weight steadily. "Three hundred and twenty-nine pounds," I told him.

"Measured yourself?"

"Sir?"

"Your jacket seems a bit tight. I think you may have grown another inch."

"It's possible, sir."

"Remind me to check during our next exam."

"Yes, sir. If you'll pardon me, sir, I need to prepare."

His brows went up. "What for?"

"Nothing to worry about, sir. Standard recon in Yuma, looking for refugees and infected."

"I see," he said. He let it hang in the air. "Colonel Shelly is in, then?"

"I believe he is, sir. I just spoke with him a moment ago."

"Thank you, captain."

"Thank you, sir."

The doctor had been distracted these past weeks. His family was back on the East Coast. A wife and daughter, as I understood it. As the situation across the country had been getting worse he'd been debating if they should come out to join him at Krypton.

I was two yards down the hall when he called out to me. "Don't exert yourself if you can avoid it," he said. "Stop if you feel any pain at all."

Asking if I was feeling any pain had almost become a joke with Dr. Sorensen. Once I'd been accepted into the program he'd explained most of the process to me. The hormone and steroid shots. The surgeries. I glazed over most of it, to be honest. It wasn't anything I needed to understand, and I got the sense he was saying it the same way some officers will work through a prepared speech whether it's still relevant or not. He had stressed how much it was going to hurt when my muscles started to develop. I remember Colonel Shelly had given another of his subtle smiles at that.

I'd been serving in Afghanistan for seven months when, on a fine Wednesday morning in 2005, my squad was pinned down in a village between Farah and Shindand. One man was shot in the throat. Two took body shots in the sides that slipped past their armor. Another got shot in the thigh. It was deliberate. It forced us to leave him crippled and in the open, or to go after him. When a second round struck him in the shoulder I told the squad to lay down cover fire.

I'm big, but I'd surprised people with how fast I could move long before I went through Sorensen's process. That surprise and the cover fire threw off the snipers' first three shots. The fourth one didn't miss, and I felt a kick in the middle of my back that told me my body armor had saved my life.

I never felt the fifth shot. In his report, Staff Sergeant Drake said there'd been a sound like a huge egg breaking and my helmet exploded on my head. I'd dropped in the dust, my head covered with blood, right next to the soldier I was trying to save. The rest of the squad fought off the snipers, lost two more men, and left me there for an hour before someone decided to make an obligatory check for my pulse.

There are just so many times you can be "one of the only survivors" before people begin to feel uneasy around you.

If I was a superstitious man, I'd've resigned my commission at the end of my Afghanistan tour. The thought did cross my mind, and I was going to be finishing that tour in the hospital anyway. But I knew better. The Army was where I was supposed to be and I was going to serve until I died. I had a duty to serve my country. The United States had fought a war against itself, spilled its own blood, so my great-great-grandfather could be free. So I could have this proud name.

Could I do any less for my country?

Fourteen

NOW

THEY BROUGHT CERBERUS out in pieces. Each component was sealed in heavy wooden crates. A team of volunteers lugged them out with hand trucks and furniture dollies and rolled them down Avenue E to the Plaza lot. Danielle stood at the intersection of E and 3rd, reacting to every bump or rattle with a flurry of curses.

"Ease up," said St. George. "It's packed solid. It's not going to get damaged by any of this."

"I know, I know," she sighed. "Sorry," she shouted to the two men, who acknowledged it with a wave. Two soldiers joined them and they hefted the crate up into the Black Hawk. An olive-drab case replaced it on the furniture dolly. The second wave of soldiers had brought medical supplies, some ammunition, and a variety of odds and ends. St. George had seen one case that seemed to be nothing more than boxes of candy bars.

"You sure you want to do this?"

"Yeah," she said. "If they've got half the resources John says they do out there, I'll be able to give the armor a major overhaul. Implement a couple of ideas I've had."

He looked down E and saw Cesar and Lee bringing out

one of the smaller crates. HELMET was stenciled on it in blue letters. The younger man shot him a sullen gaze as they got closer. "And?"

"And what?"

He tipped his head back toward the helicopter. "Are you coming back?"

She followed his gaze. "Maybe," she said. "I don't know. I was talking with John last night. He thinks they might want the suit to stay with them. If it stays, I stay."

St. George's forehead wrinkled at the news.

"He's not sure," she added. "From what I gather the military's spread so thin they'll probably ask most of us to keep doing what we've been doing out here. You might be stuck with me."

He smiled. "It hasn't been that bad so far."

"You haven't been paying attention, then," she said. Her eyes snapped to the soldiers as they took the crate from Lee and Cesar. "Hey," she called out. "Be gentle! That helmet cost more than that helicopter."

St. George laughed.

"Hey," said Smith. He walked over to them. Captain Freedom loomed behind him. "Did I miss something funny?"

They shook their heads.

"So," Smith continued, "it looks like everything's moving along. Did you guys decide who's coming with us?"

"I shall be accompanying you back to Yuma," said Stealth. She'd appeared behind them in the shadows. "Your Colonel Shelly and I have much to discuss."

Smith nodded. "Excellent. I'm glad to have you with us."

"I am not with you yet," said Stealth. "That is one of the points we shall be discussing. I dislike the idea of removing one of our most powerful assets from the Mount."

"The colonel isn't about to leave you with weak defenses, ma'am," said Freedom. "We'll work something out."

Smith turned his gaze to St. George. "I wish you were coming with us."

"We've got a run scheduled for this afternoon," said the hero. "We're going down into Larchmont to clean out a bunch of the fruit trees people had in their yards. I'll go with them and catch up with you later tonight."

Freedom glanced over at the scavengers loading a truck on the far side of the garden. "You're making the civilians search for supplies, sir?"

"We are not making them do anything," said Stealth.

"You're at no risk," the officer said to St. George. "Wouldn't it make more sense for you to go alone?"

He looked up at Freedom and gave a faint smile. "It would if there was some way for me to bring four or five hundred pounds of fruit back on my own," he said. "It's not like I can throw it all in a few grocery bags and carry two in each arm."

"I was led to believe you could carry at least three in each arm, sir." Freedom's expression didn't change, but there was a faint glimmer in his eye as he said it.

"Believe me," said St. George, "no one goes out who doesn't want to and we minimize risks wherever we can."

"So they'd like you to believe."

Christian stood a few feet away with her fists on her hips. Danielle recognized it as Gorgon's sheriff pose. The councilwoman ignored the heroes and spoke directly to Smith. "These people have endangered our lives again and again and refused to give us any voice in how we govern our lives here. It's been a fascist dictatorship, and I wanted to make sure the proper authorities knew about it."

St. George caught most of the sigh before it slipped out, but a wisp of smoke spiraled up from his nostrils. Danielle's hands clenched into fists. Stealth grew very still, which he knew was a bad sign.

Smith stepped forward and pulled Christian's hand into his. "Agent Smith, Department of Homeland Security," he said. "I'm helping the Army out as a government liaison. You must be one of the local community leaders. It's a pleasure to meet you."

She returned the handshake after a moment of awkwardness and straightened up even more as she processed the torrent of words. "Christian Nguyen. I've been elected by a majority here to speak for the people of the Mount."

"A majority of the people in your districts doesn't mean the majority of the people here," scoffed Danielle.

"Since your overlords refuse to hold democratic elections, we all have to make do," said the older woman.

"I'm very sorry to hear you've been having problems," said Smith. He led her a few steps away from the heroes. "We expected to hear about some problems when we encountered survivors, but we'll be wanting a full account of everything that's been going on for the past few years."

"I'll be glad to give one," she said. "Under oath, even."

"I'm sure that won't be necessary."

She shot a suspicious glance back at the heroes. "I just want to make sure it's clear who's been doing what."

He nodded. "I'm glad to know there are people like you here in the Mount. People we'll be able to depend on even when things are tough." He paused. "I can depend on you when things get tough, can't I, Christian?"

She smiled. It crossed St. George's mind it was the first

honest, happy smile he'd ever seen on the woman's face. "Of course you can," she said. "I'm always honored to serve the people."

"Excellent," he said. He had his practiced smile up again. "I'll be in touch on my next trip out here. Do you mind if we finish making our arrangements for this trip? There are a few things we still need to iron out."

"Of course, Agent Smith."

He took her hand again and gave it a single shake. "Please, just call me John."

Christian beamed, and her eyes flashed with triumph. "Of course, John." She squeezed his hand back and walked away.

"I take it back," St. George murmured to Danielle. "Maybe he's not bad to have around after all."

A soldier stepped forward and gave Freedom a salute. "Ready to move out, sir."

"Excellent." He gestured them all toward the helicopter.

"Time for us to get strapped in," said Smith.

Danielle pulled St. George aside. "Are you sure you're okay with this? All of us heading off and leaving the Mount like this?"

"It's not all of us," he said. "You guys are going now. I'll be here for another few hours, and Barry'll probably be back before I leave. If all goes as planned, even if you decide to stay, Stealth and I will be back tomorrow night."

"And she's okay with this?"

"Yeah. Kind of weird, I know, but . . ." He shrugged.

"Just feels strange," she said. "It's been a long time since we've had to say any good-byes."

He smiled and pushed her toward the Black Hawk. "Unless you guys run into Zzzap on the way," he said, "or I see him here before I head out, I'll see all of you out there later tonight."

Smith strapped himself in with some help from one of the soldiers. He twisted his head over to look out the cabin door and up at the sky. "I wonder if he's made it out to Krypton yet?"

"He left about half an hour ago," said St. George, "so, yeah, everyone there's probably sick of him by now."

× × ×

People of Krypton, shouted Zzzap in a deep, buzzing voice, *I tell you our world is doomed. We must take refuge in the Phantom Zone!*

"Hard as it may be to believe, sir," said the colonel, "we've heard all the Superman jokes you can think of." Shelly was in his mid-to-late forties, and in great shape whatever age he was.

Dammit, said the glowing figure. He hung in the air a good thirty feet above the helipad. Close to a dozen soldiers stood around the slab of concrete. *What about the classics? Mysterious figure arrives at the Army base in the desert?* The hum of his voice dropped an octave again. *I come in peace. Take me to your leader.*

"Are you done, sir?"

Tough crowd, he sighed. *Yeah, I'm done. Thanks for humoring me.*

"Of course. On behalf of the United States Army and Project Krypton, I'd like to welcome you to the Yuma Proving Ground, sir. I'm Colonel Russell Shelly."

I'm Zzzap, but you probably knew that already. How do you want to do this?

"We can do a tour around the base," said Shelly. "Show

you the perimeter, our supplies, anything you'd like to see, sir, that's not classified or restricted for safety reasons. I thought you might like a late breakfast first. Nothing special, I'm afraid. I think we've got scrambled eggs and bacon, maybe some French toast. The coffee's not too bad, though."

Did you say you have bacon and coffee? Colonel, you may have just become my favorite person on Earth.

Shelly gave a polite smile. "Right this way, then, sir. I've got clothes and your other equipment waiting by my office."

It's okay to say "wheelchair." It won't come as a big surprise to me, really.

"Sorry. I have to be honest, it caught me off guard when Smith told me."

Oh, believe me, the irony's not lost on this end, either.

A pair of soldiers waited for them by the building. Their eyes went wide at the sight of the gleaming wraith. They had a basic wheelchair with a seat made of faded leather. One held a pair of boots in his hand and a set of camos draped over his arm.

Zzzap flitted down and tilted his head to the ground. *I don't suppose you have a blanket or something?*

The colonel glanced at the wide-eyed men. "We could get one. Is it important?"

He sighed. *Not really. I just hate crawling naked on hot pavement.*

"If we swing around to the other side of the building, sir, there's a small lawn. It's not much, but it's—"

Don't worry about it. Can you set the clothes down there?

The soldier did as asked. Zzzap settled closer to the ground, spreading his arms and legs wide. The brilliant wraith dimmed, the air settled, and the dry sound of a vacuum being filled echoed between the buildings. Barry dropped to the steaming tarmac with a thump.

"Sonofabitch!"

"Are you okay?"

He rolled onto his side and reached for the clothes. "Scraped my hand," he said. "Nothing I haven't done before." He dragged the pants across the ground and twisted his legs into them. He wrestled the sand-colored T-shirt over his head, waved off the boots, and hand-walked himself over to the wheelchair. The soldiers stepped forward and lifted him in a fireman's carry for the last few feet, setting him down in the leather seat. One of them handed him the coat. It had been stripped of rank, but the name ZZZAP was on a Velcro strip above the heart. He smiled.

"Good, sir?"

"Yeah," he said. "Thanks for the assist. Nice jacket." He draped it across his lap.

"Will you need an escort, sir?"

It took him a moment to understand they were offering to push the wheelchair. "That'd be nice, thanks."

They went up the ramp into the office building. It was spotless, and the scent of cleaning chemicals hung in the air. More than half the lights were out. Colonel Shelly pulled off his cap, revealing a wire-brush scalp. He followed Barry's eyes up to the ceiling. "Power conservation," he said. "We try to run as few lights as possible, even at night."

"Gotcha."

"I appreciate your trusting us like this, sir," he said.

"We've all got to start somewhere," said Barry. "And could you not use 'sir'? It always makes me feel like my dad's leaning over my shoulder."

"Force of habit, but I'll do my best. What do you prefer?"

"Barry. Mr. Burke if that's too casual for you."

"I can make do with Mr. Burke. Agent Smith tells us you've got almost twenty-four thousand people out in Los Angeles."

"More or less."

An older man was waiting for them in the officers' mess. His uncombed beard was a tangle of gray and silver, and it looked like he'd slept in his clothes for a while. He ran a finger back and forth across the tabletop, like a blind man reading a braille headline again and again.

"This is Dr. Sorensen," said Shelly. "He's the scientific head of Project Krypton. Captain Freedom and the rest of the Unbreakables are the result of his work."

Barry held out his hand. "You must be very proud. They're pretty amazing, from what I've seen. Not a lot of people can take on St. George *mano a mano,* y'know?"

Sorensen looked up from the table. His watery eyes met Barry's and he reached out to take the hand. He moved in slow motion, as if every action needed hours of rehearsal time he hadn't been given. "Hello," he mumbled.

"Pleased to meet you."

The older man moved his mouth a few times, starting half a dozen words, and then went back to examining the tablecloth.

There was a small buffet set up for them. Bacon and eggs in one chafing dish, English muffins and French toast in another. Two large pots of coffee. The soldier guided the wheelchair along the table while Barry overfilled a plate. He shoved some food in his mouth while they moved.

"Oh my God," Barry said. "You don't know how much you miss bacon until after the zombie apocalypse."

"We're spoiled, I guess," said Shelly. He and Sorensen followed behind the wheelchair with plates of their own. "The Army keeps these places well stocked, and even with the rationing we've set there's still enough food here and in Yuma for another twenty-eight months or so."

They took places at a table. Shelly paused to say a silent grace and nodded for them to begin. Barry ate with his usual gusto while the colonel took quick, precise bites.

Sorensen had a single scoop of scrambled eggs on his plate. He pushed them back and forth with the fork, still in slow motion. Every third or fourth push one of the tines would scrape like fingernails on a chalkboard. Barry glanced from the doctor to the colonel. The officer didn't seem to register the older man's behavior.

"How long did it take you to get out here, Mr. Burke?" Colonel Shelly asked after a few minutes of eating. "You caused a sonic boom, didn't you?"

"About twenty minutes," said Barry. He crunched down on another piece of bacon and let it sit on his tongue for a moment. "The sonic boom's a bit of a trick, though."

"How so?"

Sorensen interrupted by dropping his silverware. "Is your energy output related to caloric intake? Does your body begin to cannibalize its own muscle and bone mass after a certain point?"

"Yes and yes."

The doctor began to tap the fingers of his left hand against his thumb. "Is it dangerous," he said, "for you to come in contact with other objects?"

Barry folded a piece of French toast in quarters, ate it in two bites, and washed it down with a mouthful of coffee. "How do you mean?"

"I would assume proximity to you would excite molecules

to some degree. Some things may incinerate or covalent bonds could break down. Perhaps even . . ." He stopped tapping his fingers and mimed an explosion with his hands.

"I've had things go bang, yeah," said Barry. "I feel really queasy if I come in contact with too much solid matter. I think it may be some kind of psychosomatic warning or something." He shoved another piece of bacon in his mouth and paused to yawn. "Sorry. Minor food coma setting in. It's been a while since I got to gorge myself like this."

Shelly sipped his coffee. "Are you short on supplies out in Los Angeles?"

"Not short, but we definitely don't have tons of excess. Ammunition's running low, so our scavengers are using knives and machetes a lot more these days. We've managed to set up a decent-sized garden in the Mount, and we're breeding chickens in one of the other lots, so there's meat and eggs."

The colonel dabbed his mouth with a napkin. "Where did you find chickens in the middle of Los Angeles?"

"There were a bunch of families from Mexico and South America who kept them in their backyards. Lots in Chinatown and Little Tokyo, too. Some of them found shelter with a group calling themselves the Seventeens."

"The Seventeens?"

"They were a street gang that survived. They saw the Zombocalypse as a chance to go all *Road Warrior* and start their own little kingdom. When a bunch of them came to live with us, they brought about fifty chickens with them."

"If I may," said the doctor. His voice trailed off as he twisted his napkin once or twice. He set it back down next to his plate and smoothed out each wrinkle with his finger. "Ummmm, how did you acquire your abilities?"

Barry took another sip of coffee and cleared his throat.

"There was an accident involving a particle accelerator, a liquid lunch, and a pair of rubber bands."

Shelly smiled. The doctor looked up. For the first time in the course of the meal it seemed like he'd noticed Barry sitting there. "What did you say?" His eyes were wide.

"It was a joke. Didn't you ever read *Life, the Universe, and Everything?*"

"Was that Carl Sagan?"

"Douglas Adams," he said, yawning again. "Is it really warm in here?"

The doctor and the colonel exchanged a look. "It's always a little warm during the day," said Shelly. "The curse of being in the desert. You get used to it after a while."

Barry glanced up at the air vent. Little strips of colored paper fluttered in the breeze pumping out of it. He took in a deep breath and stopped himself before he yawned a third time.

Shelly and Sorensen looked at him. Sorensen's eyes flitted to the coffee mug.

"You fuckers," Barry said.

He focused inside himself, reached for the trigger in his cells that would turn him back into Zzzap, and the yawn pushed its way out. He tried to shove the wheelchair away from the table but his hands slipped and his head dropped. He heaved his chin back up, clenched his eyes shut, and tried to force the change. The trigger stayed just out of reach, and he realized he couldn't pry his eyes back open.

He heard a clatter and felt something warm on his forehead. His last clear thought was that he'd collapsed in his scrambled eggs and it was a waste of perfectly good bacon.

There were voices he couldn't understand, a sense of movement, and his final shreds of consciousness faded to black.

Fifteen

NOW

SMITH HELPED DANIELLE out of the Black Hawk and guided her out from under the slowing rotors. Freedom held out a hand for Stealth, but she ignored him and walked after Smith. The wash from the helicopter blades whipped her cloak around her like a bonfire of black flames.

Project Krypton was a collection of brick buildings painted milky white in the middle of miles of sand and rocky hills. At first glance the base didn't look that different from the dozen or so colleges or corporate campuses Danielle had spent time on, just with more lava rocks than grass. It wasn't until she registered that everyone's clothing was tan that it started to seem "military" to her.

A sergeant waved Smith over and he left Danielle standing on her own. The redhead looked at the open yard, the sprawling space between structures, and on the other side of the buildings, just a few hundred feet to the west, the three chain-link walls with gaunt figures pushing against the outside fence. Even with the huge open space, the sound of clicking teeth danced on the edge of her hearing.

Her arms pulled in tight around her. She turned to check

on the armor, wondering how soon before she could get it back on, and saw Stealth a few feet away.

"It's strange," Danielle said, "being outside without the suit on. Outside somewhere else, y'know?"

The cloaked woman looked across the tarmac at Smith, then at one of the nearby buildings. "Perhaps we can arrange for you to wait indoors while they finish unloading."

She shook her head. "I'll wait until they finish."

"I shall remain with you, in that case."

"I'm okay," said the redhead.

"You spend every waking moment in the Cerberus armor," said Stealth, "and you sleep in a corner under your kitchen table. I am certain these exposed conditions are causing you no small amount of stress."

"I said I'm okay," Danielle repeated. "Stop trying to be nice. It's creepy."

A lieutenant with a white armband approached, flanked by two other soldiers. "Ma'am," he said to Stealth, "I'm going to have to ask you to please surrender your sidearms while you're on base."

She turned her head to him. "I will not."

The MP's hand settled on his own weapon, and his partners raised their rifles a few inches. Danielle saw Stealth's pose shift. "This isn't a request, ma'am," said the officer. "Hand over both of your sidearms."

"John," called Danielle. "We've got a problem."

Smith jogged back over. "What's going on?"

"This woman refuses to surrender her weapons, sir."

Smith looked at Stealth's elaborate double holsters and back to the MP. "She's a guest of the colonel, Lieutenant . . . Furber," he said with a clumsy glance at the officer's name. "I don't think this is necessary."

The soldier's hand was still at his pistol.

Smith turned to Stealth. "Look, you know how the military works. This guy's willing to let you pummel him just so he doesn't have to break procedure and disobey an order he got six months ago. Just let it slide for now and I'm sure we'll get it sorted out in less than an hour."

The cloaked woman stayed focused on the MP. "I will not."

"Can you just do it for now? I swear, Colonel Shelly will get this all resolved in no time at all."

The blank face of her mask turned to Smith, then back to Furber.

When her hands moved, it was too fast to see. The pistols were drawn and held out to the soldier, butt first, before any of them could register it. One of the other MPs jerked his rifle up out of instinct, a few moments too late.

"Jesus," muttered Danielle.

Furber took a slow breath and retrieved both of the weapons. "Glock 18C," he said. "Nice. I didn't think you could get these in America."

"I did not," said Stealth.

"Ammunition?"

She pulled two extended magazines from alongside each of the thigh-mounted holsters and four more stored in a pair of rigid pouches on either side of her waist. Furber looked up and down her skintight uniform. "Do you have anything else you'd like to declare before—"

"If you attempt to search my person, I will break both of your thumbs."

Smith stepped between them. "I think we're good, don't you?" He gave the MP a smile. "I'm sure the colonel will agree you've done your duty. Thank you, Lieutenant."

"Yes, sir," said Furber. He and his squad made a quick retreat.

"So, the colonel's running a couple minutes behind," said Smith. "He should be here by the time we've got everything unloaded, and then we can see about getting you those back." He squeezed Danielle's shoulder and headed back over to the helicopter.

Stealth examined the triple line of chain-link fence a hundred yards away. Danielle watched the cloaked woman turn her head to follow the barricade. "Something bugging you? Besides being unarmed?"

"I am never unarmed, Danielle," said Stealth. "You should know that. I count twenty-eight sentries along this section of the perimeter alone. There are another four in the towers and ten patrolling between the fences."

Danielle shrugged and watched the soldiers give one of the Cerberus crates a nudge to make sure it was secure on their cart. "Not many more than we've got on the wall most of the time."

The cloaked woman turned to examine the fence line to the east, almost half a mile away. "It would appear these numbers are consistent along their entire perimeter."

"What's your point?"

"When Zzzap did his reconnaissance, he indicated the base had limited personnel. His exact words were 'a skeleton crew.'"

Danielle looked at the distant fence and tried not to think about all the open space. "Maybe they put everyone on just to impress us."

"If they had the manpower to put such numbers on their perimeter, why would they choose not to do so on a regular basis?"

The redhead shrugged. "I'm sure they've got their reasons," she said. "Besides, there're only, what, thirty or forty exes out there. Hardly a threat against four dozen well-armed soldiers."

"Yes," said Stealth, "I had noticed the low numbers."

"Once the full scope of the epidemic was clear, the Army took much more aggressive measures toward controlling it," said Freedom. He'd moved up behind them. A few yards back, a pair of soldiers pushed the heavy cart laden with the Cerberus crates. Danielle walked over to inspect their loading job. "There were attempts to contain them, at first," continued the huge officer, "but it came down to killing them. We used a backhoe to dig a few mass graves out there by the hills, and burned most of the ones we'd already contained."

"Of course," said Stealth with a faint nod.

"It took a little over a year, but we cleared out a good chunk of the surrounding region. We've even made some headway into Yuma." He looked down at her. "To be honest, ma'am, I'm surprised you haven't accomplished more at your base."

Danielle looked up from the crates. "What's that supposed to mean?"

"No offense meant, ma'am," he said. "I just thought, well, with your combined abilities I'd think Los Angeles would be a lot further on by now. It looked like there were a thousand exes just gathered around your base."

"We estimate fifteen hundred on an average day."

"Again," said Freedom, "no offense meant, ma'am, but why haven't you done anything about them?"

The cloaked woman stared at him. Danielle recognized the look and could guess what was coming next.

"We are at a sub-base on the Yuma Proving Grounds, correct? The city of Yuma is fifty-nine miles south-southwest of our current position."

Freedom paused just for a moment. The corners of his mouth twitched with grudging respect. "That's correct, ma'am."

"So the area you 'cleared out' with your superior numbers and weaponry consists of the mostly empty proving ground and the outskirts of a small city, population ninety thousand, less than fifty thousand of which would have transitioned according to all known statistics regarding the ex-virus."

The smile flattened out. "Correct again. Ma'am."

"There are over five million ex-humans within the city limits of Los Angeles," said Stealth. "This is one hundred times the numbers you have dealt with, and does not include the greater Los Angeles County area. If we had killed one hundred exes a day, every day, for the past nineteen months, we would have only eliminated one percent of the undead population of the city." She paused to let the numbers sink in. "We have better uses for our time and resources."

"I apologize, ma'am."

"Why did you say most of them?"

Freedom blinked. "Ma'am?"

"When you were explaining the Army's aggressive stance, you said you burned most of the ones you had contained. What did you do with the ones you did not burn?"

He set his mouth in a line and stared at her blank mask. When she didn't budge, the huge officer leaned back on his heels. "The project director, Dr. Sorensen, asked us to get him some live specimens, so to speak."

"What did he require these specimens for?"

Freedom straightened up to his full height. "The doctor's

a genius in the fields of neurology and biochemistry, ma'am. He was trying to determine the nature of the ex-virus and determine if anything could be done for the people who'd been afflicted."

"And what did he determine?"

"I couldn't say, ma'am. I'm a soldier, not a doctor."

"This is everything, right?" interrupted Smith. He'd wandered back and was looking over the cart. "Nine crates altogether. Looks like we didn't lose one between Los Angeles and here."

No one returned his broad smile.

Danielle checked the boxes and gave a nod. "Everything looks good."

"And here's the colonel," said Smith. He waved to a quartet of men. Freedom's back went stiff and he delivered a sharp salute, as did the soldiers around him.

"As you were," said the officer. He held out his hand. "Colonel Russell Shelly, commander of Project Krypton. On behalf of the United States Army, I'm honored to welcome you both to the Yuma Proving Ground."

Danielle shook his hand. Stealth ignored it.

"You just missed your companion, Zzzap," said Shelly. "He left about fifteen minutes ago. Did you get his messages?"

"If he had a full stomach he probably forgot to send them," scoffed Danielle.

"Well," said Shelly, "why don't we get out of the sun? We could have lunch if you like. Or we've got a shop set up for you, Dr. Morris. Want to take a look and see if it meets with your approval?"

Smith cleared his throat. "Sir, there's a matter of some

weapons and ammunition. Miss . . . Stealth had her guns confiscated when we arrived."

The colonel looked at her and his eyes dropped to her empty holsters. "Very sorry about that, ma'am. Standard procedure for wartime, you understand. My people are just as antsy about armed strangers as yours are."

"Since she is a guest," said Smith, "in the interest of diplomacy, I told her we'd get them back to her. Would that be okay, sir?"

He nodded. "Of course. Sergeant, find the officer on duty," he said to one of his staff. "As soon as those weapons are processed at the armory, have them unprocessed and returned to our guest."

"Yes, sir." The soldier saluted and headed off.

"Why don't we go look at the workshop," said Danielle. "That'll let me open the crates and check on the armor."

"If you like," said the colonel. He gestured them down a dusty concrete road. "It's about a ten-minute walk if you don't mind conserving some gasoline. Mr. Smith gave us a list of what he thought you'd need. We got the last of it set up this morning."

The cart with the crates caught on a rock and jammed to a stop. The two soldiers wrestled with it for a moment. Danielle stepped back to make sure none of the boxes had shifted.

"Not all of your soldiers have enhanced abilities," said Stealth.

"That's correct, ma'am," Shelly said. "The ex-virus caught us in the middle of the program. When the president declared a national state of emergency, we barely had fifty soldiers through the process, plus Captain Freedom. We had a hundred and fifty or so washouts, plus another hundred and eight who were serving as our control group. In the time since, we've lost about half of those numbers."

"Yet it would appear you have more than that serving here on base."

"Some of them are survivors from other sub-bases, like Lieutenant Gibbs here." He gestured at a man walking with them in digital camos with a tiger-stripe pattern. "There're just over thirteen thousand square miles to get lost on here at Yuma. When things got bad, everyone locked down where they could. A lot of them couldn't. We were lucky Krypton had been built to be secure and self-contained. Once the situation stabilized, we started to expand, secure other areas, and find other units that had holed up. At the moment, I seem to be the senior officer left alive, so people from all branches are under my command."

"And civilians?"

"There aren't many civilians left, ma'am," said the colonel. "We saved about eleven hundred people from Yuma."

Danielle coughed. "That's it?"

"Unfortunately, yes. There were a lot of folks who felt they were safer in their homes with a shotgun and a few pistols than putting themselves under military control. With our own limited manpower, it came down to picking our battles. We could rescue three or four willing families in the time it took to get one irrational resister out of their home. So we did what we had to do, even if it meant some people got left behind."

Stealth moved her head left to right. "Where are these civilians now?"

"Right here, ma'am." Shelly nodded at the soldiers pushing the cart. "It was around New Year's last year that we realized the solution to both of our problems. We were short on manpower. We had over a thousand civilians who needed organization and a way to contribute. Two birds with one stone."

Danielle blinked and looked at the soldiers. "You drafted them all?"

Shelly shook his head. "No one was drafted. We had Smith explain the situation so no one would feel coerced. He made the offer and seven hundred of them signed up. We ran four separate boot camps."

"I would think the majority of the civilians would not have been viable candidates," said Stealth.

"Not normally, no, but these aren't normal times. We took anyone over sixteen and under forty-five." He coughed. "Between you and me, more than a few of them did it just to get in shape. Here we are."

The building was an oversized garage, first in a row of near-identical structures. Smith stepped forward and tapped a code on the keypad next to the main door and it began to roll open. "I used all your old codes," he said to Danielle. "Do you still remember them?"

"Some," she said. "It's been a while since I needed to use a confirmation code for anything not related to the suit."

He nodded. "Do you still have all the same passwords?"

She tried to look at Stealth out of the corner of her eye. "No," said Danielle. "I changed a lot of them a year or so back."

Shelly's gaze shifted between the two women. "Why was that?"

Danielle shrugged. "I was bored. I was defragging the system one day and just switched the passwords for the heck of it."

"For now," said Stealth, "perhaps it is best if those passwords remain secret."

Smith's smile wrinkled and the colonel gave her a hard look. "Ma'am," said Shelly, "I understand the past twenty-two months have not been easy for anyone, and they've forced us all into patterns of behavior we wouldn't have in a peacetime situation. But I can't help feeling like you're one of those civilians who feel they're a lot safer at home with their shotgun and pistols."

"If that were the case, colonel," said Stealth, "would I run the risk of being left behind?"

There was a brief silence. Then the door clanged open.

The space was large, as big as the scenery shop Danielle had turned into a workspace back at the Mount. The ceiling was dotted with half a dozen sunroofs, filling the area with natural light. A trio of large, rolling toolboxes stood in the center of the room near a few work platforms. Along the wall were some larger tools and tanks of gas for a welding setup. "Very nice," she said.

"If you need anything else, we can try to get it for you. Any special tables or racks for the armor can be constructed to your specifications."

"Well, this is a good start," she said. "I can use the foam molds in the crates for now." She found a pry bar in one of the toolboxes and opened the smallest crate. It was the helmet. Her shoulders loosened at the sight of it.

Colonel Shelly looked down at the armored head and met its gaze. "Would you be up for a demonstration, Dr. Morris? Mr. Smith has been singing the praises of your armor for a few years now. I've seen some videos, but I'd love to see it in action.".

She looked at Stealth. The cloaked woman gave a slight nod from within her hood. "I'd need some help," Danielle said. "Maybe half a dozen people with some electronics experience. Or at least some brute muscle that can follow orders."

Shelly looked at Freedom and the huge officer gave a wry smile. "I believe specialists Wilson and Garfield fit that description," he said. "I'll put in a call. We should have a team for you in ten minutes, ma'am," he told the redhead.

"Do you want a place to change into the undersuit?" asked Smith. "There's an office and bathrooms over there."

"No need," said Danielle. Her fingers danced down the buttons of her shirt and pulled it open. Underneath was the skintight black Lycra mesh, studded with gleaming micro-contacts. She tossed the shirt aside.

Freedom smiled. "You wear your costume under your civilian clothes, ma'am?"

"It's more convenient," she said. "And it's kind of a security blanket."

They had half the crates open by the time the group of soldiers arrived. Four of them set up the legs while Danielle worked with Lieutenant Gibbs to assemble the codpiece. She found a ladder, lowered herself into the legs, and Freedom's two super-soldiers got the torso locked together around her. The left arm went on without a problem, but there was some trouble with the right. By this point there was too much armor around Danielle for her to see the problem, so she tried calling out instructions.

"Wow," said Smith. He ran his fingers across the twisted metal on the battlesuit's forearm. "What happened here?"

"A few months ago I got in a fight with another super-human called Peasy," said Danielle. "He ripped that M2 off and used it to club me in the head a couple of times.

Wrecked the gun and the mounting, almost broke some of the optics, too."

Stealth examined the damaged assembly. "What about this made it impossible to repair at the Mount?"

"Not much," said Danielle. She tried to shrug, but buried in the inactive armor her tiny head just seemed to twitch. "Nothing. It just seemed like a waste of time to rebuild it after Peasy ripped off the old one. The barrel was bent, we didn't have any more ammo for the guns, and . . ."

Smith looked up at her. "And . . . ?"

She shrugged. "It felt like giving up," she said. "If I was going to build things under half-assed conditions with iffy material, it meant I was accepting things were going to stay like this."

The arm locked into place and they tightened down the bolts. One of the super-soldiers, Hancock, got the helmet balanced on a ladder while Gibbs made the final connections. He met Danielle's eyes. "Is that all of it?"

She nodded. "Get the collar bolts done and stand back."

The armored skull settled over her and the soldiers spun their Allen wrenches. Hancock hopped off the ladder and pulled it away. The titan hummed with power and dozens of small hatches snapped shut across the armor, concealing the bolts. The collar slid together and the battlesuit's eyes flared to life.

Cerberus flexed her fingers. "Much better," she said. She made a point of looking down at Freedom. Then she stomped out into the sunlight. Colonel Shelly followed the battlesuit outside. All the soldiers marched behind him except for Freedom. The oversized captain stood like a statue across from the cloaked woman.

"After you, ma'am," he said.

Her cloak swirled around her as she strode out of the workshop.

Cerberus was holding a jeep in front of her at arm's length. She set it down on the ground. "I've made a few adjustments, but at the last recorded test the suit could deadlift 19.4 tons. The armor can deflect sustained fifty-caliber fire and can survive a direct RPG hit with minimal damage to the suit or the pilot."

"Amazing," said Colonel Shelly. He ran his eyes over the battlesuit's armored plates. "Imagine if this suit had gone into production. Do you know what a company of these things could've done in Iraq or Afghanistan?"

"And this is still the Mark One system," said the titan. "We'd planned out a few improvements for the Mark Two that we—"

"What is stored in that building?"

They all looked at Stealth. Her arm was pointing at the third structure in line after the workshop.

Smith's smile appeared. "I'm not sure what you're talking—"

"You have exchanged three glances with Colonel Shelly at times when Cerberus has turned toward that building. The first time you both looked at the building afterward. At least one of you has looked at it each time since. What is stored there you are worried we will discover?"

"Ma'am, we're less than an hour into this visit," said Shelly. "You can't expect us to be open—"

"Cerberus," snapped Stealth.

Inside the suit Danielle shifted though her lenses. "It's cooled to the point that I can't make out any heat signatures inside," said the titan. "I can hear some movement, though."

"Open it," ordered the cloaked woman.

The battlesuit took two steps forward and Freedom was in front of it. He set his huge hand against the armored chest. "Ma'am, I suggest you stand down."

"Suggestion noted," said Cerberus, brushing him away. Freedom tensed to fight but Shelly waved him down.

When the keypad didn't respond to her codes the armored titan grabbed the edge of the door in her football-sized hands. The huge panels slid open with a groan of metal. Cold air washed out of the dark warehouse.

Over a hundred figures shuffled and turned toward the door. None of them blinked at the brilliant afternoon sun as it spilled over their dead eyes. They swayed for a brief moment and then the exes stumbled toward Cerberus.

Common Sense

THEN

PLEASE CONSIDER THIS as an addendum to my original report, and I ask now for anyone reviewing this to excuse my
informal language. I cite extenuating circumstances.

I think this mission was the one that finally made me
wonder if Captain Freedom really was a death-magnet. I was
aware of his record when he was recruited for the project and
I became his First. It's a bullcrap superstition. But with the
way things turned out, you have to wonder.

Yuma was overrun. We'd gotten word of different groups
of survivors holed up throughout the city. There was a big
group down on the south side. Colonel Shelly had run the
numbers and was sending us to get them. We'd expected to
find a few dozen exes at a time. Maybe as many as two hundred. It would be a good mission for the Unbreakables, a
chance to flex our collective muscles and burn off some rest-
lessness.

We moved out of the Proving Grounds in one long convoy
as planned. Three sections from the Unbreakables were in
the front carriers, backed up by equal numbers of norms. Behind us were a dozen Humvees. Captain Freedom was in the
lead with Section Eleven. I was with him. He likes to be in the

front, setting an example and sharing in the threat with his soldiers. More than a few people think he has a death wish.

To be clear, Freedom's a good man for an officer. Like most people, brass tend to be fifty-fifty. Half of them think they're superior to any enlisted man, no matter how many years of experience you've got over what they learned in a classroom. Freedom's in the other half. He's decisive and confident, but he's not so chock-full of ego it makes him stupid. He listens to his intel. He listens to his First. He listens to his gut. And he makes great calls because of it. He'd seen Colonel Shelly's warning order and heard the S2 directives culled from intel coming in from all over the country. No body shots. No grenades. No intimidation. Just head shots.

If I may make an observation, though, there's a point where this becomes useless. That's what the brass never gets. You can't spend years training a soldier to do *A* and then expect him to switch to *B* in a day just because some intel told him to. Oh, he'll get it right during that week of drills, but once he's on mission those years of training are going to kick back in and override that week.

I know training. I was a drill sergeant for seven years before I joined Project Krypton. There's something special when a fuzzy hears he's been assigned to Sergeant Paine. You can see the dread on their faces before you even start talking. So I knew—I know now—we were overconfident and our brains were filled with the wrong kind of training. We went into Yuma and all that training kicked back in.

Yeah, even for me, too. I was a former drill sergeant who could throw a refrigerator fifteen feet. Damn straight I was well trained and overconfident.

The convoy went forward down Freeway 95, the long stretch when the road runs east–west but before the locals start calling it County. The first exes were sighted at approximately oh-nine-forty-five hours. They crawled out from behind cars or staggered out of ditches. You could hear their teeth clicking before you saw them. They were put down.

All the Unbreakables were carrying M240 Bravos. One of those will put a trio of rounds through a skull with no problem. The downside to the Bravo is it's damn loud. We knew sound attracted the exes. Rather than four or five targets at a time, we'd have a dozen or so staggering at us at one mile an hour. We didn't think it'd be a big deal. Even if one got close, all the Unbreakables were wearing the newest ACUs. They still had pockets for knee and elbow pads, but were also triple layered at the shoulder, forearms, and calves—all the major bite points.

We found our first large cluster of about ten exes close to ten-fifteen hours. They were heading our way, stumbling down 95, bouncing off abandoned cars and trucks. Freedom already had Sections Eleven and Thirty-one flanking them when he saw the movement. I think I saw it at the same time, but I'm not sure.

There was another cluster just a few yards behind the first one, maybe as many as fifteen of them. They were almost close enough to be one big group. And there were two or three lone exes stumbling along either side of the street. Freedom pulled in Twelve and also brought up two sections from Charlie Platoon for support. Charlie's most of the washouts from the program, and Delta's the only control platoon left at Krypton. They've started calling themselves the Real Men. It's probably going to stick.

Section Twelve and the Real Men started at the back and worked in. It took about two minutes to put down all the exes with head shots. I remember I saw a few rounds punch through chests and barked an order down the line to confirm targets. Looking back, I should've seen where it was going right then.

Captain Freedom made a point of grabbing the last ex and twisting its head off with his bare hands. It was a heavy man with long hair and a thick mustache. He tossed the head underarm, letting it roll up the street like a bowling ball. A couple soldiers chuckled at that. It was a good morale boost. We needed it. The road was getting too clogged for the Humvees.

By ten-thirty-five the convoy had gone another mile and a half and killed another three dozen exes. Sections Twelve and Thirty-three dropped back to reload. The other downside to the Bravo, for us, is it eats ammo like candy. The spare ammo boxes were awkward things for a soldier to carry. Even for a soldier who can bench nine hundred pounds.

We'd also found four survivors in a mobile home. Family of three and the son's girlfriend. We loaded them in one of the last Humvees. We had three with us just for potential survivors.

From here we could see the intersection of 95 and East County 9½ a hundred yards or so ahead. It had a gas station and a Circle K. Everyone stops there if you're taking the long way back to the proving grounds after a night in Yuma.

There were a lot of cars there. I couldn't tell if it was a huge fender-bender or everyone in this part of the city decided to drive out and all abandon their cars at the same place. There were two or three big trucks as well, including one semi stretched right across most of the intersection. We could see a few exes milling around the vehicles. Nine, maybe ten. One or two of them had seen us or heard our weapons.

We moved up nice and slow. Another four exes stumbled

out from between the cars while we did. They were finding a path through the pileup. We got close enough to hear their teeth clacking together.

But there was a lot of clacking. Too much for the exes we were seeing.

Two or three looks, a couple of gestures, and Freedom had Twelve and Thirty-one flanking either side of the intersection. Sections Twenty-two and Thirty-three dropped back to watch our rear. The Humvees were about fifty yards behind us now. Section Twenty-one moved forward toward the baker's dozen of exes.

By now, most of us knew how strong and fast we are. There was a period of broken doorknobs, torn shirts, and lots and lots of snapped bootlaces. We went through bootlaces like you wouldn't believe. But that was long past. Section Twenty-one flitted across the open space and eliminated the exes. They grabbed skulls, twisted, and moved on to the next one before any of the dead guys could raise their arms. You can only get two or three that way, but six people doing two or three each is a lot of damage in less than ten seconds. Not one shot fired.

The last ex hit the pavement and Twenty-one leaped up into the air one by one like it was the most natural thing in the world. A fifteen-foot vertical jump. They came down on top of the semi.

"Oh, screw me," said Taylor. We could hear him forty feet away. He didn't say "screw." I see no need to use his exact phrase, even in an informal report.

A voice crackled over my radio. Sergeant Harrison, Twenty-one's leader. "Unbreakable Seven," he said. "This is Unbreakable Twenty-one."

"Unbreakable Twenty-one, this is Seven," I answered.

"Seven, this is Twenty-one. Six is going to want to take a look at this, sir."

Captain Freedom took three steps and leaped into the air. Thirty-five feet from pretty much standing still, the magnificent bastard. I had to run more, but I ended up landing on the semi just after him. The rest of Eleven was right behind me.

A sea of dead things. I'd read that phrase in a few reports. Once in a book someone loaned me at the start of the outbreaks, some horror-sci-fi thing about the Grim Reaper hunting zombies. It always struck me as a crap phrase. Something people said to avoid being exact. I'd dealt with hundreds of soldiers in boot camp and never had trouble keeping them separate. I'd been at ceremonies with over two thousand men and women present and it never seemed like a sea.

There was a frigging *ocean* of dead things on the other side of the pileup. It's one thing to read reports about the walking dead, to hear how many of them there were. Seeing it is like getting dropped in ice water. Seven, maybe eight thousand exes. Maybe more. After one of the first briefings we attended together, Freedom told me the human mind can't comprehend numbers over one hundred. As the previous paragraph might indicate, at the time I thought it was bullcrap. Now I'm not so sure.

They'd been drawn this way by the sound of our engines and our weapons, stumbling in our direction for an hour now from all over the city. The semi across the road was acting like a floodgate. They just piled up against it, stretching back a mile down the double-wide road. I couldn't see pavement anywhere. The chattering from their teeth was like static. It went on and on and you knew it wasn't ever going to end. It just hung in the air like flies over garbage.

The ones closest to the semi saw us and surged forward. They clawed at the sides of the box. Most of them still looked like people. I saw one that looked like it'd been set on fire. I couldn't tell if it'd been a man or a woman. Another one looked like its arm had been shot off. There was a woman with dark hair like my sister. Her jaw had been blown off. There were strings of muscle and skin hanging off her upper teeth. The strings twitched as the dead woman tried to clack her missing teeth together.

"Screw me," Taylor said again. "Screw me."

"Shut it right now, specialist," I snapped.

"Yes, sir." He stopped making noise but his lips kept moving.

Right there. Taylor was an arrogant jackass but he knew to keep his mouth shut when told to. Seeing all these things was throwing him. Heck, it was throwing me. I should've said something.

A message came in from Twelve. Enough of the exes were making it around the pile of cars that they needed to take action. Freedom gave the word and I relayed. There was a roar as Twelve's Bravos cut down the dead things. Section Thirty-one joined in a moment later.

It was gas on a fire. More exes started staggering toward the sound. By the time the echo of the gunshots faded another three dozen, easy, had made it through the maze of cars. They were finding their way just by raw numbers.

"Wait here," said Freedom.

A few quick steps along the roof of the semi and he launched himself over to the roof of the Circle K, another five or ten feet up. Some of the exes in the crowd shifted to follow him through the air. They clawed the front of the store. One of them fell through a broken window into the building.

The captain got his bearings before looking east with a pair of binoculars. Looked at the church and the homes about three-quarters of a mile down the road. The road we couldn't even see under all the exes. He shook his head. He knew what I knew. Even if every single round in every weapon we had took out a zombie, we didn't have enough. Not enough ammo. Not enough time to use it if we had it.

I looked at my watch. It was eleven-hundred hours on the nose. I knew right then we weren't going to be reaching those possible survivors on the south side of the city. They were going to have to hold out for a few more days.

Credit where credit's due, like I said before, the captain's got a brain in that head of his. Some officers will bury their soldiers rather than admit they need to change tactics. Not many, but enough of them. Freedom's willing to toss a plan on the spot if common sense tells him things have to be done different.

I'll also go on record and say he made the right call. If anyone reading this has any doubts, Captain Freedom made a difficult choice, but the only viable one. I would've made the same one if I'd been in command.

He dropped back down onto the semi. We all felt the roof tremble. He was a big guy. "First Sergeant Paine," he told me, "let's fall back and regroup with the transport. Tell Twenty-two and Thirty-one to hold and give us cover until we're back on the ground and clear of this traffic jam. Everyone else moves now."

"Yes, sir," I said. I sent the order down the lines and got back a drumroll of confirmations. Across the intersection Sergeant Pierce with Twenty-two gestured his understanding and his team's readiness.

The exes were thick around the semi-trailer now. They

were flowing between the cars, like water finding the path of least resistance. The bodies Twenty-one had dropped to get up here were being mashed under hundreds of stumbling feet. The captain could've jumped clear to safety, but no way the rest of us could.

"The cars," he said. "Don't jump for the ground, jump for the tops of the cars. It's too high up for them to reach us." He pointed out a path, from an SUV to a battered station wagon to a minivan to another minivan to another SUV to a shiny Lexus and hitting the pavement right near Section Twenty-two. "Once we go, we go as fast as we can. Don't stop or they'll have time to grab you and overwhelm you."

Again, training kicks in. Discussing tactics right in front of the enemy in a loud voice. It feels wrong. It's hard to take it seriously.

"Section Twenty-one then Eleven," I told them. "You heard the captain. Hop, skip, and a jump. Line up and make it snappy."

Another burst of gunfire from the ground. Section Thirty-one had a steady stream of exes coming at them from two directions. Their support section of Real Men moved in and laid down more fire. Some of the dead things shifted course for the sound. Most of them kept heading for Twenty-two and the sections falling back.

Hayes, Polk, and Taylor moved bang, bang, bang. SUV, station wagon, minivan, minivan, SUV, Lexus. All three were safe and some of the exes were still raising their arms. Too slow to get them, too slow to shift targets. Sergeant Harrison gave them a moment to make sure they were clear. Then he moved.

Franklin, Truman, and Jefferson from Twenty-one were next. Truman's foot slipped on the second SUV and he stumbled for a moment. In that moment I pictured Jefferson slamming into him from behind and both of them falling down into a crowd of exes. I don't think I was the only one picturing it. Truman went with it, though. Threw himself forward again with the stumble. He pretty much hit the Lexus on all fours and pushed himself off as hard and fast as he could. Shoved himself back into the air with his arms. Right there, super-strength paying for itself with one life. He hit the ground by Twenty-two face-first and rolled away before Jefferson landed on him. Sergeant Monroe hit the ground a few seconds later.

It left me, Captain Freedom, and Unbreakable Seventeen—Platoon Sergeant Kennedy—on top of the truck. She's another damn fine soldier. "Ladies first," I told her.

Her lips twisted from a scowl to a tight grin. "With all due respect," she said, "screw you, first sergeant."

"Noted," I said. "Get yourself down there."

"Nosebleed." I gave her a blank look. She mimed wiping her upper lip and pointed the finger at me. "You're leaking, Top."

My glove came back red when I wiped it across the bottom of my nose. I didn't remember getting hit or bumping anything. Damn air's so dry out here. I wiped it again and pointed Kennedy off the truck.

She jumped down to the first SUV. It was a little tougher for her. The exes were already gathered around the cars, already had their hands up. And there were a lot more of them making their way through the pileup. She was fast, though. Bang, bang, bang. They reached for her. They grabbed air every time.

"After you, Paine," said Freedom.

"After you, sir."

"It's getting tight. You should go next."

"Sir," I told him, "don't make me push you."

He gave me a look and launched himself into the air. The truck's shocks squealed as it rocked. He hit the pavement right next to Monroe.

Freedom turned to check on me. I saw his face shift. I looked to see what he was seeing.

The exes had figured out the way around the wall of cars. That's too generous. Don't want to overestimate the enemy. They'd figured out a way around the same way water figures out how to get out of the sink when you leave the tap running. They just started spilling off the road and into the fields on the south side of the road. It had been a couple dozen when I first looked. It was a hundred, easy, already. Just like a sink.

Section Thirty-one was closest to that flank. They were laying down fire while Twelve moved back in to give them some support. I could see a couple of them twitching and called out a stand-your-ground to Sergeant Boyle of Thirty-one.

Then someone in the section flipped their rifle to burst. I saw the chest of one dead man ripple just below its neck. The next burst came a moment later. It was a little higher and tore through the corpse's neck. Its head hung by a flap of skin and muscle for a few seconds and then tore loose. The zombie fell over.

"Unbreakable Thirty-one," I said, "this is Seven. Controlled burst only."

Another burst of fire from Thirty-one. And another. Section Twelve was in position and now they were firing big, long bursts from their Bravos.

"Unbreakables Thirty-one and Twelve, this is Seven. Single shot only. Boyle, Washington, get your soldiers under control." I tried to map another path across the abandoned cars, then saw Freedom was already heading that way with most of Eleven.

Then I made my mistake. I jumped for the SUV, then to the station wagon. At the second minivan, though, I switched course. I cut across to a pickup. Then up onto a different SUV. From there to a Volkswagen. I needed to get back to Freedom before he did anything foolish. Officers are good at that sometimes. No offense to any officers reading this.

I shouldn't've changed the plan. I don't know what made me do it. Deciding to change objectives in the middle of the plan is stupid. It gets people killed.

A hand grabbed my ankle on the Volkswagen. I yanked out of instinct. Out of training. It threw me off. My next leap landed me right in the middle of a good-sized group of exes. They were so focused on Twelve they didn't notice me. I was on my feet and pushing through them in a second.

Then they grabbed me from behind.

I slogged forward, trying to get as far away from those dead things as I could. Their skin's like old paper. Gives me the creeps. Two of them dropped off while I ran. One hung on and ran straight into the butt of Sergeant Washington's Bravo. The front of its skull just caved in.

Exes were overwhelming our flank. Section Thirty-one had gotten it under control with Freedom there, but they'd let the corpses get too close. It was turning into a close-quarters fight, and that's not where you want to be with these things.

I charged in to get by the captain. He'd pulled out Lady Liberty, that monster sidearm he'd made from an AA-12, and was turning skulls into mush. Washington's soldiers were using their Bravos like clubs. I saw a few heads go flying.

Someone from Thirty-one screamed. Specialist Richards. One of the last ones to wash out of the program. She'd been bitten on the hand, right through her glove. A corporal reached to pull her back. He got grabbed himself. Half a dozen hands latched on and pulled him into the crowd of exes. I couldn't see him, but I could hear him screaming. Freedom fought his way there. By the time he made it he was too late.

I shattered an ex's knee with my boot and broke its neck as it spun to the ground. Lady Liberty's drum was empty, so Freedom was using those big hams he called fists, throwing punches that'd put any prizefighter to shame. He broke necks and cracked skulls with every one.

A call came from Unbreakable Twenty-seven, Sergeant Johnson. All other squads had embarked and they were pulling up transport for us. Five minutes of fighting later and we were all in or on a Humvee.

We'd barely made it a mile past the city limits. We'd lost eleven soldiers. Eight Real Men, three supers. Half our ammo was gone. Freedom called the retreat and it killed him to say it. You could see it on his face.

Of course, we weren't even halfway back and I started feeling sick. Tried to ignore it but Freedom took a good look at me and called up Franklin, the medic from Eleven. He gave me a good once-over. He found the scrape on the back of my neck, right between the collar and the back of my helmet. Teeth marks. Shallow ones. Just deep enough to draw blood. I'd been so amped up I hadn't felt a thing.

It was my own fault. I must be clear on this point, again, for the record. I was disobeying orders by deviating from the path Captain Freedom had laid out for us. He is in no way to blame for any of this.

Freedom gave me the news himself. They'd counted over

thirty different infections in my blood. Spread all through me because of this awesome, over-muscled heart I've got. If they treat all of them, the cures will kill me. If they pick and choose, there's a good chance I'll end up crippled or useless. Or dead anyway.

I've had tubes in me for nine days now. Got caught up on all my paperwork. Three days ago my hands started shaking too much to write with a pen. Sorensen's man dug around and found me a laptop no one was using. Wanted to make sure he couldn't get me anything else.

Yesterday, I had to start taking breaks while I used the laptop. I've been working on this last report since oh-six-hundred and it's dinnertime now. I'm nauseous and tired all the time, even though they switched out my bags. And my nose is bleeding nonstop now. My ears, too. All this stuff they've done to us, but no one here can stop a nosebleed.

This is a siege now. I saw the fences when we drove in. Heck, they gave me a bed near a window. I can't see out, but I can hear them. I can hear their teeth.

I know I'm never getting out of this bed. I'm going to lie here and use up resources until I croak. So the real question is, how long am I going to be the weak link? How long will I hold back the company and eat up supplies they're going to need?

I've had a few visitors. Most of them are polite and for-mal. One of them was good enough to get what I need from my quarters. I haven't checked, but I can tell by the weight it doesn't have a full magazine.

That's okay.

Seventeen

NOW

THE EXES STAGGERED FORWARD. Cerberus swept aside the first wave and the air crackled around her fists as the stun fields ignited. She shouted over her shoulder, "Those of you with weapons, forward! Everyone else, get back!"

One of the first exes, a young man with a gaping hole in his cheek, stumbled over the battlesuit's toes and fell headfirst against the armored shin. Cerberus grabbed a dead man's shoulder and threw the ex back through the mob. It knocked over a dozen other shambling forms before slamming into the back wall of the garage. Next to the titan, Stealth had already broken two skulls with her batons.

"Hold position," shouted Freedom. His voice echoed between the buildings.

The exes stopped. A few of them were off balance in mid-stride and fell over. They lay still on the ground.

A few seconds later they still weren't moving.

"What the hell just happened?" growled Cerberus.

"They're programmed to move out when the door to their Tomb opens," said Shelly. "They just needed a counter-order."

Stealth still had her batons up. "Programmed?"

He nodded. "Yes, ma'am."

The armored titan took a step back. "These are, what . . . domesticated exes?"

Freedom gave her a nod. "More or less, Dr. Morris."

"Cerberus."

"Sorry, ma'am." The huge officer stepped forward, lifted a fallen ex by the scruff of its neck, and set it down on its feet. It made no attempt to grab him. It didn't do anything.

"They are not moving their jaws," said Stealth.

Smith nodded. "It's one of the first behaviors Dr. Sorensen eliminated," he said. "No more chattering teeth. Also helps us tell ours from the feral ones."

The exes were dressed in Army uniforms. A few had tan T-shirts or tanks. On the ones with ACU jackets, the ranks were stripped off, leaving fuzzy patches of exposed Velcro. Now that they weren't moving, Cerberus could see they were standing in loose rows and columns. There were a hundred and fifty of them here, all standing immobile. They were shaved bald, no matter what their gender had been. A few had bristle across their scalps, and she remembered reading somewhere that hair and nails kept growing for a few days after death. She'd never considered if it applied to exes or not.

"You called this a Tomb," she said.

Freedom nodded. "Where we keep all our unknown soldiers."

Above the left ear, each of them had a green plastic housing the size of a box of cigarettes. There was dried blood where the screws went into the skull. A bundle of thin wires spread out from the housing to a handful of sockets across the bare scalp.

The crackling stun fields deactivated. The armored titan took a step forward and looked at the closest ex, the one

Freedom had placed back on its feet. Stealth was already there. They could see its teeth through the gaping hole in its cheek.

The cloaked woman reached up and squeezed the edges of the green box. The front panel popped off in her hand, revealing an array of circuitry and LEDs.

"Careful," said Shelly. "Damage that and you'll have a killer on your hands."

"Perhaps these components should not be in an unsealed housing," said Stealth.

"Not much to it," said Cerberus. The titan had dropped to one knee and bent close to the dead man. "A few flash memory cards, micro-transistors, batteries . . ." The thick metal finger traced wires for a few moments before the armored skull turned to Freedom. "This thing lets you control them?"

"Sir," Smith said to the colonel, "perhaps I should see if Dr. Sorensen can spare some time away from his current work?"

"Please do, Mr. Smith. The captain and I will answer as best we can in the meantime."

Smith adjusted his tie, gave a quick smile up at the Cerberus armor, and headed out the door. One of the sergeants followed him.

"Company," called Freedom. "About face."

There was a pause, and the undead shifted with a thump of boots.

"Five paces, march."

The exes took five stumbling steps and stopped again.

"About face."

Stealth stiffened. Even with the armor, Danielle's reaction was apparent. The colonel glanced at them. "Something wrong?"

"Last time we saw a bunch of exes moving in sync," said the titan, "it didn't . . . it didn't work out well for one of our friends."

"You've seen them act like this before?"

"The same superhuman who damaged the Cerberus armor," said Stealth, "also had an ability to control ex-humans."

"Where's this person now?" asked Shelly.

"What's left of him's at Melrose and Gower," said Cerberus. "I burned all the big pieces."

"Sir," said Freedom to the colonel, "if you'll pardon me I have a drill in ten."

"Of course, captain. Dismissed." The two men exchanged salutes, and Freedom bowed his head to Stealth and Cerberus.

"The immediate question," said the cloaked woman, "is why?"

"Why?"

"Why have you developed a method of controlling the exes?"

"Why wouldn't we?" countered the colonel. "If we can't contain the ex-virus, we need a way to control it."

"But why use them as soldiers?"

"We were short-staffed," Shelly said. "At the start of the year we were down to nine hundred soldiers, and over six hundred of those were our barely trained civilian recruits. They've come a long way since then, but it still left us with a lot less than a base like this needs. Dr. Sorensen's work is going to be a huge benefit to the United States."

"It would seem the risk of losing control would cancel any possible benefits."

"There's no risk," he said. "Besides, at the moment we're only using them for low-pressure jobs like sentry duty."

"Of course," said Stealth. "The large numbers at your perimeter."

"That explains why Zzzap didn't see anyone," muttered the titan. She looked back at the rows of silent exes. "I'd love to get a better look at those control boxes."

"Shouldn't be a problem," said Shelly. "I'm sure you'll have plenty of time to go over all the specs with Dr. Sorensen once you're set up. We could even move your lab into the main building near his."

"It's better if I stay out here so the suit has easy access," she said.

The colonel gave her a look. "Well, that won't be your concern, though, will it?"

"Sir?"

"Dr. Morris, you were never intended to be the pilot of the Cerberus suit," said Shelly. "We both know that. If it hadn't been such a time-intensive, crisis situation you never would've worn it into battle." He shook his head. "Now we can get you back in the lab and working on improvements to the system. That's what you want, too, isn't it?"

"But . . ." the armored giant looked at Shelly, then over at Stealth. "It will take months to get anyone up to my level of proficiency. It's better to have Cerberus out on the front lines, isn't it?"

"Of course, and Lieutenant Gibbs has been studying the suit's specs for some time. We even got him a working copy of the simulator you designed."

The Air Force lieutenant stepped forward. "I've logged over fifteen hundred hours, ma'am," he said. "You've built an amazing weapons system."

"I didn't think the simulator was ever built."

The colonel smiled. "Some of our tech boys have had a lot of time on their hands. I think you'll find Gibbs is qualified and ready to take over as the Cerberus pilot."

"If," said Stealth, "we decide to leave the armor with you."

Shelly took in a breath to respond and bit his tongue. "Yes," he said. "If that's what we all decide."

Her head tilted inside her hood. "It strikes me as suspicious this point has not come up before, colonel."

"Is it, ma'am?" He looked up at the armor. "If I recall, Dr. Morris, the only reason you agreed to put on the suit and fight during the outbreak was because you were worried someone else might damage Cerberus, correct?"

"Well, yes, but I wanted to help—"

"You weren't expecting to be the one using it when you built it, were you?"

"No, but I was the only one who knew how to use it to its full potential."

"Before you were deployed in Washington, had you ever been in a fight?"

"I've had several fights over the requirements for—"

"Not arguments, doctor," he interrupted. "Fights. Had you ever come to blows with someone? Did you ever once throw a punch?"

"I'd fired over ten thousand rounds through the suit's M2s on the firing range."

"At wooden targets," he said. "Did you receive any training at all as to how to deal with combat situations? Basic tactics? Target priority? Anything?"

A rasping hiss came from the armor. A sigh. "No."

"So," said Shelly, turning back to Stealth, "the most so-phisticated weapons platform on the planet has spent the past two years in the hands of an untrained civilian who didn't want to be using it in the first place, and you think it's suspicious I want to put an experienced soldier behind the controls?"

"I find it suspicious," said Stealth, "the matter was not brought up until we were here and disarmed."

The colonel looked up at the nine-foot battlesuit. "You call that disarmed? I think if Dr. Morris disagreed with me, there wouldn't be much anyone could do to stop her, would there?"

× × ×

"It's very simple," said Sorensen. He peered at the elbow joint of the Cerberus armor. It was at his eye level, and he'd pushed his glasses up onto his head to squint at it. "We couldn't train them because they'd died."

"No wonder you're a doctor," murmured Cerberus.

Sorensen stepped away from the battlesuit and moved to one of the exes standing at attention. It was a dead woman with a square jaw. "It takes three to four hours for a corpse to make the transition to ex-humanity," he said. "Lack of oxygen destroys the mind and memories, leaving only core survival patterns like eating, basic motions, and reaction to raw stimuli like sound or movement." He set his glasses back on his nose and rapped the dead woman on the forehead. "There's nothing there to train. It'd be easier to teach a grass-hopper how to type."

Then he went silent, staring into space.

"Doctor," said the colonel.

"Madelyn had a baby bib with a grasshopper on it," said Sorensen. He looked at Shelly. "Eva and I saved it. I'm sure it's still boxed up in the attic at our house."

"The exes, doctor."

"Yes," the older man muttered. "The exes." He glared at them for a moment, then poked the dead woman in the forehead again. The ex rocked back and forth. "The physical structure of the brain still exists," he said. "Just like a computer processor without power. The Nest restores electrical activity to key areas, allowing simple memories to form and reflexes to be redeveloped."

Stealth interrupted him. "The Nest?"

Sorensen turned the dead woman's head to the side before pointing at the green box. "Neural stimulator," he explained. He looked annoyed by the question. "It took almost a year to find precisely the right regions of the brain, the correct amperage and voltage."

"I would think decay within the brain would prevent such a device from functioning for long."

The doctor shook his head. "No, no, no," he said. "Yes, there's initial decay. We have to give each subject several EEGs to make sure it's still viable. But once the ex-virus takes hold the level of decay drops to almost nothing, so our largest worry is dehydration."

Stealth tilted her head at Sorensen. "According to our research, the dead continue to decay, just at a decreased rate."

He shook his head. "Your research is wrong. A lot of work was done before . . . before . . ." The doctor was lost in thought for a moment. "Before things went bad," he said. "One of the last things they established about the ex-virus was that it's lethal."

Stealth shook her head. "It is harmless," she said. "Individuals die from secondary infections, not from the virus itself."

"Humans," he said, nodding. "That's not the problem. The ex-virus is a lethal bacteriophage. It attacks necrotic bacteria and uses them to reproduce. All necrotic bacteria. An ex's decay rate drops by eighty-seven-point-eight percent."

"They smell like they're rotting," said Cerberus.

"Material in their digestive tract or on their clothes," the doctor said. "You notice none of these exes have the scent of decay on them. Once they've been cleaned, they tend to just smell like . . . well, clean skin. When you calculate in the resilience the virus creates in cellular membranes and the lower core temperatures in the afflicted—"

"Exes could remain active for years," Stealth said.

"Almost eleven," said Shelly, "by the last estimates we formulated here."

"It's a magnificent freak of evolution," said Sorensen. "I've never heard of any organism in nature so perfectly suited to keeping its host alive. Or as close to life as possible, I suppose." He shrugged and began to examine the Velcro fuzz on the female ex's shoulder.

Cerberus shot a glance at Stealth while moving a metal palm back and forth before one of the exes. "Do they remember anything? About, you know, who they were."

Sorensen glanced up from the Velcro and shook his head again. "That was my first hope, but no. They're blank slates. Not a scrap of individuality or independent thought left in them. In fact, every time a battery pack dies, they lose any training we've given them and it's back to square one."

"You're sure? What if they're . . . comatose or something?"

"Positive. We've done numerous EEGs and MRIs. No

activity at all in either the Broca's or limbic regions, which means minimal language and emotion. I'd put their IQ below a lab rat at best."

"A rat cannot be trained to follow complex commands," said Stealth.

"Neither can the exes," said Sorensen. "You can only issue one command at a time, and it must be an order they've been trained to follow. The most complex thing they grasp is a priority scale, that some commands can supersede others."

"Priority?"

"On a few occasions we've gotten them to acknowledge soldiers over civilians, officers over enlisted men. There's more work needed. Speaking of which"—he turned to Shelly—"if I may get back to my lab, colonel? I was in the middle of something."

"Of course, doctor. Thank you for your time."

"Shall I, sir?" said Smith. When the colonel nodded, the younger man guided Sorensen out of the Tomb.

"He's a bit off," said Colonel Shelly, "but believe me, he's brilliant."

Stealth was examining a Nest unit again. "Who is Madelyn?"

"His daughter," said Shelly. "He lost his family at the start of the outbreak. We tried to evacuate them here to Krypton, but there was an accident. His wife and daughter were both killed."

Stealth's head tilted inside her hood. "Killed?"

"What would you rather hear, ma'am? Eaten alive? When he got the news it shattered him. He was in shock for months, and he's still in denial. It's not unusual to just find him sitting in a corner in his lab. He probably could've gotten the

Nest done seven or eight months sooner but he has trouble focusing."

The cloaked woman turned from the exes and walked out into the sun.

"If you don't mind my saying, Dr. Morris, your companion isn't very social."

"No, she isn't," said Cerberus. The titan turned and followed Stealth outside.

The cloaked woman was a pillar of black in the sun-bleached road. "Are you going to give them the battlesuit?"

Another metallic sigh rasped from the armor's speakers. "I haven't decided yet."

"They filmed the assembly procedure," said Stealth. "There are four cameras in your work space. Two visible, two concealed. I would assume the office is monitored as well."

"I'll remember to be careful in the bathroom, too," said the titan. "Look, they already know how to assemble the suit. That lieutenant said they've got all my records. They didn't get anything from me they wouldn't've figured out after doing it one or two times themselves."

"Cerberus may have once been just a weapons platform," said the cloaked woman, "and you were once just an engineer. But that is no longer the case. You have become a symbol to the people of Los Angeles. A hero. If you give the battlesuit away, that will go away as well. It will be just a weapons platform. You will be just an engineer."

The huge lenses looked down at her. "Maybe that wouldn't be such a bad thing."

Eighteen
NOW

THE SUN HIT the horizon just as St. George crossed the Krypton fence line. He'd circled the base once to make sure they knew he was there. A group of soldiers waited for him. They didn't aim their weapons at him as he landed, but they didn't make a point of aiming them away, either.

"Hey," he said, pushing the biker goggles away from his eyes. "I think you were expecting me. I'm St. George."

One soldier stepped forward. He was about the same age as the hero and wore a single chevron on his chest. "Sir," he said, "we weren't expecting you until later this evening."

"I got done early in Los Angeles. Decided to see if I could race the sun."

None of them relaxed. "Do you have any ID on you, sir?"

St. George blinked. "Seriously? Are there a lot of people trying to get onto the base who can fly?"

"Standard procedure, sir," said the soldier. "If you don't have ID someone here on base will have to vouch for you."

Twin lines of smoke curled out of St. George's nostrils. "Well," he said, "I forgot my wallet about a year and a half ago, so I guess somebody'll have to vouch for me. Is Freedom around?"

"*Captain* Freedom is in a meeting," said another soldier. This one was pushing fifty and had a fair amount of gray in his hair. Again, the hero saw only one chevron. If memory served, it meant the man was a private.

"Look," St. George said. "Can I be blunt?"

They shuffled on their feet.

"I just flew close to four hundred miles at top speed. I'm tired, I'm hungry, and none of you is carrying anything that would even slow me down if I decided to walk into that building over there." He pointed at a random office. "So could somebody please find Captain Freedom or Agent Smith?"

They exchanged glances and mouthed a few silent words. The gray-haired soldier stepped away and turned his attention to his radio. The first soldier gave St. George a polite bow of his head. "It'll just be a moment, sir."

"Thank you."

He shoved his hands in the pockets of his flight jacket and looked around. He'd never been on a military base before, but Krypton looked a lot like what he expected from watching movies. Most of the buildings looked like they were designed for function more than form, and they all felt just a few years out of date.

Of course, everything was starting to get a few years out of date.

St. George turned his head and noticed one of the soldiers, the youngest one, was staring at his forehead. He reached up and tapped the goggles. "For flying," he said. "It can't hurt me, but getting a bug in your eye at a hundred and fifty miles an hour is still pretty gross."

All of them grinned. "It wasn't that, sir," said the private. He was nineteen, tops.

"What, then?"

"I just . . . nothing."

"What?"

The private shrugged. "Well . . . I always thought you were green. With a big fin on your head."

St. George smiled. "That's the Savage Dragon. I was the Mighty Dragon."

"Was he your partner or something?"

"No, he's a comic book character. I'm real."

"St. George? That's like, a knight, right?" One of the other soldiers gestured with his chin. "Is that why you've kinda got one of those pageboy haircuts?"

He sighed. "No, we just don't have any good barbers left back in Los—"

"St. George," called Freedom. The officer strode out of a building, towering over the woman who followed him. The hero recognized her from the Mount.

The soldiers around St. George stepped away and fell into a line. The officer crossed the gap in a few quick strides and grabbed the hero's hand in a grip that would've cracked bones in a normal man. "It's good to see you again, sir."

"Good to see you, captain." He tried to return the grip and realized Freedom had done that damned macho-leverage thing to lock St. George's fingers.

"Your people are waiting for you at Dr. Morris's new workshop," said Freedom, releasing the hand. "It's about a ten-minute walk from here if you're up for it."

"Sure. Good to stretch the legs after all that flying."

"As you were," Freedom told the soldiers. They snapped off a set of salutes and he turned to the woman. "I'll meet you back at the office, first sergeant."

She handed him the bundle she'd been carrying. Then she

gave a salute of her own and a quick bow of her head to the hero.

"I'm never quite sure how things line up between officers and enlisted," said St. George. "Is she your assistant or something like that?"

"First Sergeant Kennedy?" He shook his head and gestured in a direction to walk. "Easiest way to think of it is I'm the one in charge of the Unbreakables, but she's the one who runs everything."

"Okay."

"I've got a small welcome gift for you," said Freedom. He handed over the bundle. "I noticed your jacket was a little ragged. This is the newest Army Combat Uniform coat. Reinforced with a triple-layer Kevlar weave. A bit more durable than what you've been wearing."

The hero shook out the coat. "Thanks." It was a blur of tiny squares. Someone had stitched up a Velcro name tag that said DRAGON in bold letters.

"Let me know if it doesn't fit. Sergeant Johnson estimated your size." They walked in silence for a few yards before Freedom spoke again. "I also hope you'll accept my apology, sir, for our hasty actions back in Los Angeles. It wasn't our intention—definitely not mine—to start our association by throwing punches."

"Tense times," said St. George. "I guess it wouldn't've been that out of the question for someone to take a shot in a situation like that."

"You have no idea," the huge officer said. "Regardless, I am sorry, sir. We were all on edge, and it doesn't help it was the first serious action any of my soldiers had seen in close to six months. It sets a bad first impression."

"Not a lot going on out here?"

"Oh, there's lots to do," said Freedom. "The proving ground is the largest military test facility in the world. We've barely reclaimed a third of the sub-bases and stations here. Even discovered two no one knew were out here. But it does get a little . . ."

"Monotonous?"

He grinned. "I think that would be the word, sir." He raised his huge hands and flexed them into fists. "Dr. Sorensen's enhancements feel like a waste when we don't get the chance to do anything with them."

"Yeah," said St. George. "I know that feeling."

They walked for a few more yards. The white brick buildings gave way to a series of more industrial-looking structures. St. George caught a glimpse of the distant fence line between two and saw sentries plodding back and forth.

"Would you mind if I asked a question, sir?"

"I guess that depends."

Freedom had his fingers laced behind his back again. His eyes dropped below St. George's chin. "What's with the tooth? I noticed it in Los Angeles."

He glanced down at his lapel. "Oh, that." He ran his finger along the length of ivory. "Believe it or not, that's a demon fang."

"Come again?"

"A fang. From a demon. Honest."

The corner of Freedom's mouth twitched. "Pardon my language, sir, but bullcrap."

"Hey, I don't blame you. If I hadn't been there I wouldn't believe it, either." St. George pushed up the sleeve of his jacket, revealing a line of ragged scars. "That's where it bit me. The tooth broke off in my arm."

The captain stopped walking. "Are you serious?"

"You ever hear of a hero called Cairax?"

"The monster man? Yes."

"Demon man, not monster."

"I thought Cairax was a hero."

He stopped walking and looked up at the officer. "Are you a religious man, captain?"

"Why do you ask, sir?"

"Because I've tried talking about Cairax with a few religious people and it doesn't always go well. We can leave it at 'monster' if you like."

"I'm comfortable with my faith, sir."

"Okay," said St. George with a nod. "Max, the guy inside the demon, was a sorcerer. An honest-to-God, Harry Potter sorcerer. As he explained it to me, he trapped the demon with a special medallion he made. Or in the medallion." The hero shrugged. "I wasn't clear on that part. Anyway, sometimes demons possess people and make them do evil things. He figured out a way to possess a demon and force it to do good things."

They started walking again while Freedom mulled over the facts. "He died near the end of the outbreak, didn't he, sir?"

"Yeah, he did. But we all know dying doesn't mean what it used to. His ex was part of the group that attacked the Mount last fall. Which is how I got this." He tapped the five-inch fang again.

"So he was . . . what, a zombie demon?"

"Yeah. Sounds silly, I know."

"You beat him?"

St. George shrugged. "I cheated a bit, but yeah."

"And the medallion, sir? What happened to that?"

He studied Freedom's face. It was a firm face, but an honest one. "Destroyed," said St. George. "I crushed it myself. The demon's gone for good. So's Max."

The captain nodded. "Let's hope so."

The hero looked at him again.

"As you said, sir, dying doesn't mean what it used to. Your friends are in here."

They'd reached an oversized garage. Or maybe a small hangar. St. George held out his hand again. "Thanks for the escort."

"Of course, sir. I believe the colonel arranged dinner with Dr. Morris and Stealth at twenty-thirty hours. I'm sure you're invited as well."

He batted some dust from the sleeve of his flight jacket. "I don't think I'm dinner-ready."

Freedom smiled. "Good thing you've got a new coat, then, sir," he said. "Wash up, shake the dust out, you'll be fine."

"Thanks again."

"One other thing. Your friends have some news for you. We agreed it's best they tell you, but I hope you'll see where we were coming from."

"Okay," said St. George. He looked at the honest face again. "That doesn't sound too ominous at all."

× × ×

St. George hefted the three-hundred-pound array of armored plates. "And you say they've got over a thousand of these . . . what, ex-soldiers?"

"At least," Danielle said from inside the half-disassembled armor. "I did a sweep before we came back inside. Four other buildings in this section of the base have the same overpowered cooling units, and I saw two more near the far side. At a hundred and fifty per building . . ." She turned her head back to him and raised her eyebrows. "That's a lot of exes on this side of the fence."

He set the back section of the armor down on the work platform, nestling it into the foam cradle. "And this Nest thing makes them docile?"

"It activates enough of their brain to dominate the core behaviors that manifest, yes," said Stealth. "Or so Sorensen claims." She was sketching out circuit diagrams.

"If he's lying he did a great job convincing the exes to fake it for him," said Danielle.

St. George drifted into the air behind the armor and hooked his arms under Danielle's shoulders. He lifted her out of the battlesuit and floated down to the ground. She shook out her legs and arms and took a few unsteady steps.

"You okay?"

"Yeah," she said. "I was only in there a few hours. Barely had time to adjust." She hobbled across the workshop in her bodysuit, each step more confident, and grabbed a thick power cable. She leaned into it, dragged it back with her, and plugged it into a hidden socket above the armor's hip. "This is going to suck without Barry here. No quick recharges."

"Another point for you to consider," said Stealth. She didn't look up from her notepad.

"Where are your pistols?"

The cloaked woman shifted her head inside her hood. St. George was looking at her. He pointed at the empty holsters.

"They were seized upon our arrival," she said. "Standard military protocol for civilian guests, and by their definitions we are civilians."

"It doesn't bother you? Being unarmed?"

"It does not. Why do you ask?"

"I ask because I would've expected not having them to drive you into a rampage."

She turned her attention back to her sketch. "Colonel Shelly asked for them to be returned to me. I am satisfied."

He looked at Danielle. The redhead glanced up from the armored helmet and shrugged. St. George returned the shrug and nodded at the cable. "Where are they getting their power?"

"A large solar farm, three miles to the north-northwest," said Stealth. She pointed her left hand without looking up from the diagram. "It was visible during our approach in the Black Hawk. No doubt an Armed Forces renewable resource project. I would estimate it provides the base with six to seven times the electricity of our own solar resources."

"For less than a thousand people," said St. George. "Not bad."

"But twice the equipment and resources, at least," said Danielle. She ran a second cable from the battlesuit's helmet to her laptop. "It's not bad, but not good. Definitely not great." A third cable ran out from the laptop to the armored spine on the back section of the torso. The redhead's fingers danced across the laptop's keyboard.

St. George peered over Stealth's shoulder. "Almost done?"

"I believe so," she said.

"You did all that from memory?"

"Of course."

"That's kind of amazing."

"Thank you, George." The cloaked woman set the diagram in front of Danielle.

The redhead stopped typing. "Did you just thank him?"

Stealth straightened up. "Yes. What of it?"

"What's going on with you? You've never thanked me for anything."

"You have never paid me a compliment."

"Oh. Yeah, fair enough." She shrugged and traced the circuit patterns with her eyes. "Like I said before, it's pretty simple. Just a monitored power source for the organic components."

"From the slight variations in the two we saw," said Stealth, "I would reason the Nest units are individually assembled."

"Makes sense," said Danielle. "They've got raw materials and tools, but not much in the way of actual manufacturing facilities."

St. George glanced at the diagram. "So what's bugging you two about this? Isn't this a good thing?"

"Perhaps," said the cloaked woman. "However, Cerberus and I were both struck by how simple this technology appears to be."

"Is that bad?"

"Maybe," said Danielle. "It's not like these things do miracles, but they're right on that edge of being *too* simple. I'm not skeptical it works because, well . . ." She jerked her head at the door and the Tombs across the road. ". . . it does. It's just hard to believe something so small could do so much. I mean, have you ever seen anything brain-related in a hospital that didn't need its own cart, at least? Usually its own room?"

Her laptop sang a few bars of Wagner at her. She muttered to herself and slid her fingertip back and forth across the mouse pad.

Stealth's head tilted inside her hood. "Is there a problem?"

Danielle shook her head. "The sensors got a little sluggish after I picked up that jeep. The response time was just off enough that I could feel the lag, but the diagnostics are coming up clean."

St. George glanced at the legs and half-torso standing on the other side of the work platform. "Do you want to keep working on it?"

"No," she said, "I want to get some food. Let's go to this dinner. Might as well thank our saviors and enjoy our first meal as U.S. citizens in ages." She grabbed her jeans and pulled them up over the Lycra bodysuit.

"Aren't you going to be hot like that?"

"I'll be fine."

"Were you wearing it under your clothes when you left this morning?"

"George," she said, "focus." She buttoned the pants and reached for her shirt. "You know, I just figured out what bugged me about all those exes."

"What was that?"

"Well, it's just..." Danielle stopped buttoning and flapped the edges of her shirt. "They were all wearing fatigues, right?"

"That is standard for military personnel under these conditions," said Stealth.

"Yeah, that's my point. Did you find it kind of creepy that every single one of them is wearing an Army uniform?"

"They probably dressed them like that," said St. George. "Y'know, to make them look ... well, uniform."

Danielle adjusted her collar. "Are you sure?"

"Sure of what?"

"That they got dressed like that after they were bitten?"

× × ×

Barry woke up with a splitting headache. Which, he supposed, was better than waking up with his face in a plate of scrambled eggs. And they'd been crap powdered eggs, now that he thought about it. He'd just been so excited about the bacon he hadn't noticed.

Definitely better than not waking up at all.

Wherever he was, the curved ceiling was concrete with steel plates. Some fluorescent lights glared down at him from recessed sockets. One had a flickering tube.

He sat up and shook the last bit of blurriness from his eyes. He was on a simple wooden cot with a passable mattress and fresh white sheets. Military corners, he noticed. He was still wearing the pants and T-shirt they'd given him outside. There was no sign of the coat. Or the wheelchair.

"Bastards," he muttered.

He let his mind settle, focused, and reached the trigger with no problem. He held off using it for now. Good enough to know he could reach it if he needed it.

The room was a huge dome, over a hundred feet across and a little over half that high. It was all concrete. In front of him was a long window, curved to match the wall. The room on the other side was dark. Way off to his left was a massive door that looked like a bank vault. The wrong side of a bank vault.

It was familiar, but he couldn't put his finger on why.

He grabbed his legs and swung them off the cot. Getting off the flimsy bed was a challenge, but he managed to do it without tipping it or himself onto the floor. He paused for a quick breather and looked around again.

Part of the concrete, a large circle around the cot, was fresh and clean. The other stuff was older. He saw a few clusters of rust-colored spots where bolts had been cut off and ground flat against the floor. There'd been something here in the center that had been taken out, and new concrete poured to make a flat floor.

Just as he realized where he was, the lights flickered on in the other room.

"Oh, sure," he called out. "Wait until I'm down on the floor. Real classy."

Three men and a woman walked into the room from a door he couldn't see. The first man and the woman were in Army uniforms. He couldn't make out any ranks or names from where he sat. He didn't recognize either of them.

The third man was Sorensen, followed by Smith.

Sorensen issued a few orders Barry couldn't hear, then leaned forward to a microphone. "Good evening, Mr. Burke," he said. His tinny voice echoed out of speakers hidden around the window. "I hope you slept well."

There was a long pause and Barry realized the doctor was waiting for an answer. "Great," he said. "Like a baby."

"Wonderful. I don't know if you remember me. I'm Dr. Emil Sorensen. We met at breakfast. I believe you already know Agent Smith from Homeland Security. I want to assure you you're somewhere safe."

"Well, thank God for that," said Barry. "Last thing I remember some nutcase had drugged my food."

"I apologize for that. The duty sergeant thought a Taser would be better, but I was afraid a surge of electricity in your nervous system would trigger the change."

"Yeah, and we wouldn't want that."

"Precisely," said the older man with a nod.

"I was being ironic."

"Actually, you were being facetious," said Sorensen. "But I was ignoring it, regardless. May I ask you a few questions?"

"This is an old reactor, isn't it?" said Barry. "You've got me locked up in the core chamber."

The doctor nodded. "One of the many projects the Armed Forces was working on. It was a breeder reactor, built beneath the proving ground to keep it isolated in case something went wrong. There's no danger of radiation. The core never even reached the testing stage."

"Radiation isn't a big worry for me," said Barry. "It was an accidental overdose of gamma radiation that altered my body chemistry and caused this startling metamorphosis to occur."

"Really?" Sorensen picked up a clipboard. "Not the rubber band thing you mentioned earlier?"

Barry sighed.

Smith put his hand over the microphone and leaned forward to speak in the doctor's ear. There was a brief pantomime between them. The government man stepped back and Sorensen glowered through the window. "Must you always speak with so many pop culture references?"

"I must, yes, but no one's making pop culture anymore, so I'm starting to feel dated. I haven't seen a new movie in two years. And you know what else I just realized?"

The doctor stared at him.

"I'm never going to find out what the hell was going on with *Lost*. I mean, was it just sheer coincidence their plane crashed on the island or was it this Jacob guy pulling the strings all along? And how did most of them end up back in the 1970s with the Dharma people?"

"Mr. Burke," said Smith, stepping forward again. With the tinny effect of the intercom, his young voice sounded like a cartoon. "I know this is frustrating for you. Probably a bit scary, too. I'm sorry we had to do it this way, but if you work with us I think you'll find we all want the same things here."

Barry pursed his lips and nodded. "Can I be honest with you, John?"

"Of course, Mr. Burke. Can I call you Barry?"

"Please do. The thing is, John, Danielle thought sex with you was mediocre at best. She told me so herself right after you showed up."

Smith's smile became a tight line. He put his hand over the microphone again. The few words Barry could lip-read made him smile.

"Well," said Sorensen once Smith had stepped away. "Perhaps it would be better if we just went to the questions."

"You mean the interrogation?"

"Are you the same Barry Burke who worked on the Pulsed Power Program at Sandia Labs in New Mexico from July 2002 to January 2008?"

"Guilty as charged."

"How did you get your abilities? Was it a deliberate process or an accident?"

"I'm afraid that's need-to-know information."

"Well," said Sorensen, "I need to know so I can—"

"Pass. Next question."

"Stop acting so childish, Mr. Burke."

"Or what? You'll drug my dinner, too? Pardon me if I don't feel like playing your little game." Barry looked at Smith. The younger man was rubbing his temples.

"Madelyn loves games," said the doctor.

"What?"

He was looking past Barry at the back wall of the reactor core. "My daughter, Madelyn. She's very competitive. Loves games. My wife, Eva, thinks it's amazing we get along so well, even though we're so different."

Barry looked at the older man. Sorensen's face had gone slack, a body on autopilot. "Where are they now? Your wife and daughter. Are they here at Krypton?"

"I brought them out here to save them. I'm always trying to protect her, even when her mother tells me not to. I keep doing things to keep her safe."

Smith put his hand over the microphone again. The two of them talked and Sorensen's face became solid again. He leaned into the microphone and glared at Barry. "I would appreciate it," said the doctor, "if you left my personal life out of this."

"Ummm, you were the one—"

"Just answer the questions," snapped Sorensen. "How much energy can you put out?"

Barry drummed his fingers on his thigh. "In ambient heat or as directed bursts?"

"Both."

"Ambient, a lot. Directed, a real lot."

Sorensen made a fist around his pen.

"Hey, here's a thought," Barry said. "How about a demonstration?"

He flipped the switch in his mind.

Light blasted through the window and Sorensen and Smith both flinched back. The cot was incinerated and the concrete floor burned. The window flared again as Zzzap hurled a blast of energy at the massive door and a deafening hiss of static boomed from the intercom. He threw another burst and it sizzled against the steel.

Son of a bitch, the gleaming wraith said. *That is a big door.*

"As you yourself pointed out," Sorensen said, "you are in a reactor core. It's extremely heat and radiation resistant."

Well, I had to try.

"It was foolish."

Hey, do you have any idea how much damage those bolts can do? One of my small blasts is three or four times more raw power than a bolt of lightning.

"One-point-twenty-one gigawatts," said Smith with a faint smile.

Points for the reference, but like I said, it's a bit more than that.

"At breakfast you implied your focused energy was derived from your own mass," said Sorensen. The doctor paused to tap his fingers against his thumb. He twisted his head back to look at Smith. "Remind me to check his follicles and nails when he reverts to human form. Why not shoot smaller bolts, then, and conserve your resources?"

Doesn't work that way. It's like a fire hose. It's on or it's off, and you do not want to be in front of it when it's on. There's no "light mist" option. The wraith drifted over in front of the window. *Quid pro quo, Clarice. What's the point of all this?*

"I would think that's obvious," the doctor said. Even through the glass, he managed to look down his nose at Zzzap. "You're the most powerful superhuman in the world, Mr. Burke. If I can figure out how to duplicate your abilities it could mean a rebirth for this world. Clean, limitless energy for America and its allies."

Yeah, said Zzzap. *And you'll figure this out how? I mean, considering it's already stumped a lot of really smart people?*

"The usual methods. Examination. Physiological and neurological testing. If all else fails, we've been authorized for more invasive procedures. I'm sure we won't need to go that far, though."

The burning wraith hung in front of the window for a moment. *Okay, then*, he said. *I think it's time I was leaving. Thanks for the bacon and the massive dose of sedatives. Let's not do it again anytime soon.*

"You seem to be forgetting something," said Sorensen, rapping his knuckles on the window between them. "You're in a decommissioned nuclear reactor. This whole chamber was designed to contain energies like yours. You could spend the next six—"

Not like mine.

The doctor paused. "Sorry?"

Zzzap moved his head to the left, then to the right. *This is a fission reactor*, he said. *In this state, I'm a whole different scale of magnitude. Thousands of times more powerful. It's like saying a pair of sunglasses can protect you from the visible light output of a hydrogen bomb.*

"I stand corrected," said Sorensen. "As I was—"

I mean, I could just let 'er rip and burn a hole straight up and out.

"You could," said Sorensen, "except for all the soldiers."

What soldiers?

"There is a military base above us with close to a thousand men and women. There could be a barracks right above that chamber. Or a mess hall. Perhaps a fuel depot that could explode and injure or kill dozens of people."

Zzzap focused his attention on the ceiling. *Maybe nothing.*

"You can't be sure, though, can you? The reactor shielding screens any X-rays or infrared that would tell you what's above you."

Yeah, you got me there. Not that it matters.

The doctor paused again, his mouth open.

You keep thinking of me in terms of a man. As matter. I'm pure energy.

"What do you mean?"

Look at all this. The wraith waved his arm around himself. *The big door. The walls. You set this up thinking you needed to hold a physical person who lets off a lot of energy.*

Smith pushed his way to the microphone. "I . . . I'm not sure we follow you."

I don't blame you. It's a hard thing to wrap your head around. I'm not physical. I'm a few bazillion trillion joules of energy bound into a human shape by my consciousness. Heck, the only reason you can even hear me is I learned how to excite air molecules to create sound waves.

There was a long moment while they stared at each other through the glass.

"You're lying," said Sorensen. "I have twenty-three con-firmed reports of you causing sonic booms in my files. You did it just this morning when you arrived. You can't cause a sonic boom without mass to displace air."

Unless I'm displacing the air by some other means. He held up the gleaming arm again and wiggled the fingers. *Inside the visible area of the energy form is a little over nine hundred and fifty degrees Celsius. I keep all that energy contained, but air still comes near me, gets heated, and pushes away. That's where the sonic booms come from. I'm not solid, but the atmosphere acts as if I am.*

The doctor stroked his beard. "Assuming I believe you, Mr. Burke, what are you getting at with all this?"

What I'm getting at, Emil—Can I call you Emil? What I'm get-ting at is that to a being of pure energy, a big pane of clear glass is the same thing as an open door.

The shadows vanished as Zzzap flitted through the ob-servation window.

Sorensen and Smith stumbled back. The soldiers drew

sidearms. Zzzap raised his hand and the temperature shot up by twenty degrees. *Don't do anything dumb*, he said to them. *You can't hurt me and I don't want to hurt you.*

Sorensen pulled off his glasses and stared at the wraith with wide eyes. "You could've done that at any time."

Yup.

"Then why spend so much time talking?"

Because I wanted to hear what you had to say about all this. And I hate to be the one to break it to you, doctor, but your own personal Elvis has left the building, if you get my drift. Now, if you'll all excuse me, I think my friends are somewhere nearby and they need to hear that you people are a bunch of nutjobs.

He shot toward the door and there was a deafening crack. Zzzap flailed in the air, then rushed the door again. There was a second report, and the wraith was hurled away a second time. His outline blurred for a moment, then pulled back to a crisp silhouette.

The doctor polished his glasses on his shirt sleeve and balanced them back on his nose. "I'm sure you're familiar with the concept of a Faraday cage, Mr. Burke," he said. "They were very popular with scientists and espionage agencies because they block out all outside signals and interference. One as well built as the one around this chamber can block any type of electromagnetic signal. Cell phones, television, radio waves—it can keep all of it out."

The rumpled old man smiled at the gleaming wraith.

"Which also means it can keep anything in."

Smith cleared his throat. "I know you don't want to hurt anyone," he said. "But I'd guess just hanging out in an enclosed space like this with you isn't . . . well, it's probably not healthy for any of us mere mortals in the long term." He nodded at the soldiers. "Definitely not for these two who are going to be here monitoring you. Maybe you should go back into the core?"

Sorensen was still smiling. Zzzap glared at him. He didn't have eyes, but they all sensed the glare. He drifted toward the window.

"If it makes you feel any better," said Smith, "I just lost a bet with Colonel Shelly. I was sure you'd get out."

Yeah, thanks. That makes it all much better.

Sad Songs
THEN

I DIDN'T EVEN want to be in the Army. I wanted to be in a jazz band. Get out of college, make a little money giving kids horn lessons, and spend my nights playing trumpet somewhere down in the Gaslamp district as Harry Harrison and the Starlighters or something like that. That was my real dream.

Yeah, I know. There was a writer named Harry Harrison, too. Only about ten thousand people have told me that, thank you.

Then the White House had to start this stupid war in the Middle East while I was in high school and it looked like I might get drafted. People were talking about the draft, can you believe it? That was what I heard all through college. There hadn't been a draft in forty years, and the last time was for a stupid, pointless war, too. If the Repugs stayed in power after the election, everyone on campus knew they'd keep the war going.

Dad sat me down. He'd done a stint in the Navy right out of high school and he explained why. If there's a draft, they decide where you go. If you enlist on your own, you get a lot more say in where you go. He spent Vietnam on board the

Will Rogers, slept in a warm bunk almost every night, and never got shot at once.

So I went to the recruiting office just before I graduated college and the Army officer told me there was an Army band. They'd actually pay me to play trumpet for four years. I signed up and told Dad it was one of the best decisions I'd ever made.

Yeah, I joined Krypton right after I made sergeant. What better way to stay off the front line than to volunteer for a stateside experiment? And there was a decent chance I'd end up in the control group, so I wouldn't even have to deal with side effects or anything, right?

Little did I know.

I made the cut. The surgery took. Three weeks later I raised my horn to lips, took a firm grip, and dented the outer cylinders. Gus and Wilson thought it was funny as hell. Wilson dug up a bugle for me a few days later, left it on my bunk.

Fucktards.

Of course, all this was kind of moot. Turns out no one's just a musician when there's a war going on. First it was in the Middle East, but then it was everywhere. The main instrument I had to play was my rifle, and since the exes showed up I'd gotten very proficient with it. Solos, duets, I even led a few six-piece numbers that got rave reviews under the name Staff Sergeant Harry Harrison and the Unbreakable Twenty-ones.

When it all went really crazy, it had been six weeks since our first attempt into Yuma. Four weeks since First Sergeant Paine blew his own head off and most lines of communication went dead. The last one said the feds had flown some super-robot out to Los Angeles, and that made Captain Freedom furious. He'd been arguing we should be on the front line all along, and Project Krypton had just been lost in the chaos of the Zombocalypse.

Yeah, Zombocalypse. Neat, huh? Gus told me that one.

Thirteen days since the first of a small army of exes staggered across a few miles of desert to pile against our fence line and fill the air with the staccato chatter of enamel and ivory.

Hard as it may be to believe, that wasn't our biggest problem at the time. It was part of the problem, yeah, but the real issue was how we could work around it. The big problem was Doc Sorensen. The doc was crazy worried about his family. Turns out he had a wife and a teenage daughter back home. We caught him twice trying to steal a Humvee so he could go get them. Freedom pointed out to the old guy there was no way he'd make it over a thousand miles and back, but the doc didn't care. He argued they couldn't order a civilian around and threatened to quit the program.

That was when Smith stepped in. The monkey-boy finally started carrying his own weight. God knows how, but he'd pulled some strings and gotten Sorensen's family on a plane heading out here. Only problem was we didn't have an airstrip on the Krypton base. There are seven here at the proving ground, including one nobody's supposed to know about, and the closest one's about nineteen miles west and north of us.

Unlike Krypton, it wasn't fenced off. There were exes all over it. A lot of them were wearing tiger-stripe camo and flight suits. I knew it was on a list of priority areas to reclaim as soon as things stabilized. Thing is, we needed it now.

The captain came up with a plan. A pretty solid one. We were going to coordinate landing time with a mobile unit.

Unbreakable Twelve under Sergeant Washington was going to drive a Guardian armored vehicle to the airstrip and hit the runway at the same time as the plane. They collect the doc's wife, daughter, and the pilot as soon as they touch down, then bring them back to Krypton safe and sound.

This was the other problem, because going off-base meant we had to open all three gates. Twice. And we hadn't opened them since the wall of exes got here.

Most of us were on the gates. My section, Twenty-two, and Thirty-two were inside the first ring of fences. Captain Freedom had issued us all M16s on single-shot. They felt like toys after carrying a Bravo for months. Too light and too small. Their volume didn't even go to eight, let alone eleven. All we were going to do was walk back and forth, stick our rifles through the fence, and pop exes as they headed for the gates. The catch was we only had two magazines each. The quarter-master was already rationing ammo, just to be safe. So one for the exit, one for the return.

Sections Eleven and Thirty-three had the second ring. When the gates opened they formed a single lane into the base. They were in charge of any exes that slipped in there. Sergeant Monroe, the new platoon sergeant, was with Eleven and itching for a chance to take out some of the dead.

And above us all, in one of the watchtowers, the captain was conducting the orchestra with an Mk 19 grenade launcher. They'd stripped off the vehicle mount and he had three or four cans of ammo with him. He could almost use the damned thing as a pistol. He was going to make a lot of noise away from the base. In theory, the exes would follow.

Colonel Shelly wasn't too keen on any of this, but he and Smith had a talk and monkey-boy convinced him taking care of Sorensen was in all our best interests. Maybe there was still final testing to be done and if the doc left we were all going to explode or something. Smith talked with the soldiers from Twelve for half an hour, too, impressing the importance of this on them, asking them again and again if they were sure they were up for it, if they knew how to handle different things that might happen. I think in the end they were ready to smack him.

Actually, I know they were ready to smack him. Britney told me so when we met up for a good-luck fuck in the armory before she left. Yeah, it's frowned on, but believe me, once you've had superhuman sex or enhanced sex or whatever you want to call it . . . well, we weren't going to give it up until they ordered us to. Besides, at the time I was pretty sure First Sergeant Kennedy didn't know. She was serious about her new rank, and I'm sure she would've had us both over the coals. I found out a little later that she did know, and it was an awful way to find out.

Squad Twelve left with no problem. It all went smooth and by the numbers. Captain Freedom dropped a cluster of grenades about a hundred yards from the fence and half the exes wandered off to see what was making all the noise. They were halfway there and he dropped another cluster to keep their attention.

Yeah, I know what you're thinking. Why didn't he just use the grenades on the exes? I asked that, too, when we were going over the plan. Kennedy smacked me upside the head and reminded me the dead things were already dead (her exact words). The blast might mangle them, might even destroy one if it got caught just right, but odds are it'd just be wasting grenades. A mashed-up, slashed-up torso will kill a person pretty quick, but all it does is slow down exes.

In five minutes our teams in the outer ring had picked

off about two hundred exes that wouldn't leave the fence. The posts on the gates got pulled and Twelve got escorted out. They had one of the base's five Guardians and Adams was behind the wheel. He floored it and kicked up a fan of dirt and dust as they shot across the desert. In theory they'd reach the airstrip in about thirty minutes, just as the plane was touching down.

Two hours passed. A long intermission.

We still had radio contact, and Kennedy made sure we got the updates she thought we needed. The plane had been twenty minutes late. Enough time for the armored vehicle at the airstrip to attract a lot of undead attention. It took a lot of close-quarters fire to get Mrs. Sorensen and not-yet-legal Sorensen into the Guardian. Sergeant Grant didn't make it. Neither did the pilot. Another Twelve had been bitten hard and was bleeding, but we didn't know who. But they had the package and they were heading home.

Sorensen was about halfway between the gates and the helipad. I could see him through the fences. His hair was pretty thin on the top and I remember wondering if he had any sunscreen on. When Kennedy told him the news he applauded.

About fifteen minutes later we saw the cloud of dust where the Guardian was coming across the desert to us. Everyone took their places. Squads Twenty-one, Twenty-two, and Thirty-two loaded fresh mags in our rifles. The two inside gates opened.

In the past two hours, most of the exes had wandered back to the fence. They were pretty determined to get in, what with all these tasty soldiers standing right on the other side. Freedom sent another volley of grenades out across the desert, about ninety degrees off from where the Guardian was coming in. A bunch of the exes at the back of the crowd turned and staggered toward the noise. Not as many as last time, but still a good chunk of them. He sent his second cluster and it attracted a few more.

Then the Guardian stopped. It was still a good two hundred yards from the outside gate. We heard the engine cough and give up under the clicking teeth. It was against protocol, but I switched over to the command channel.

"It's got a fifty-gallon tank," snapped Kennedy's voice. "How the hell are you out of gas?"

"Seven, this is Twelve. I don't know," said Britney. Sergeant Washington. I remember that, too. Forcing some distance between us right at that moment. Her voice was stressed. "We're bone dry. The tank must have taken a hit or something."

"A hit from what?" I looked up at Kennedy, standing near Freedom on the tower. I could almost see her grinding her teeth.

"I don't know, first sergeant!"

There were voices in the background when she talked. I could hear somebody muttering, and another woman. Sorensen's wife, wanting to know why they'd stopped. There was an edge to her voice.

A tiny figure leaped from the passenger side of the Guardian. There was a spare gas can on the roof. You wouldn't carry one in combat, but it's not like the exes had snipers hiding on rooftops. He looked around for a moment then dove back inside and slammed the door.

The exes saw him moving. They heard the door. They started to veer away from the captain's grenade show and stumble toward the armored vehicle. A few by the fence turned and we shot them in the back of the head.

Washington came back on the radio. "Seven, this is Twelve. There's no gas."

"Twelve, this is Seven. Explain."

"Seven, this is Twelve. There are no spare cans. We have no gasoline."

I saw Kennedy shoot a glare down at Gus and Wilson. I'd be the first to think they fucked up, except I saw them loading two cans on the Guardian an hour before the mission. They should've been there.

Freedom set off another wave of explosions away from the carrier. A few exes paused, but most of them kept heading for the Guardian. Movement trumps sound in their tiny brains.

The grenades didn't help things in the carrier, either. Civilians don't do well with explosions that aren't on television. Washington came back on the radio and a girl's voice was shrieking in the background. "Start the engine," she was yelling. "Please start the engine."

"Seven, this is Twelve," said Washington, "how should we proceed?"

The first of the exes had reached the Guardian. They could see the people inside through the narrow windows. They started clawing at the sides of the vehicle.

"Twelve, this is Seven, hold your position," said Kennedy. "We're going to figure a way to get you out of there."

"Seven, this is Twelve. The Sorensens are not dealing well with this." The muffled sound of teeth clicking together came over the radio with her voice.

"Twelve, this is Seven, understood," she said. "Hold your position."

There were about twenty exes around the armored vehicle. In five minutes there were going to be twice as many. "Twelve to Seven. Copy."

"Don't make me run for it," said Adams in the background of the Guardian. I never thought he'd be one to panic. First-night jitters, I guess. "Please don't make me run."

"What's going on?" Sorensen was next to me. "Why did they stop out there?"

Freedom dropped a few grenades on the exes heading for the transport. It pulped some of them, but once the haze cleared I could see things with no legs dragging themselves toward the armored carrier. One of them had a hole in its stomach that daylight shined through.

Adams snapped. He kicked open the door of the Guardian, knocked a few exes back, and tried to run. He was an Unbreakable, after all. He had a chance. Not much of one, but a chance.

Then he yanked open the back door and pulled the girl out after him. Sorensen's daughter. He was still going to try to get her to the base. Blood was gushing out of his nose where she'd tried to fight him off or something.

The doc pressed himself against the gate. I pulled him back so the exes wouldn't chew his fingers off. "What's he doing?" shouted Sorensen. "What's he doing?"

Adams knocked down a bunch of exes. Hit them with his shoulder one after another. Even opened up on a few with his Bravo. He was maybe thirty yards from the Guardian, dragging the wailing girl behind him, when he stumbled. Stumble's not the best word. He just jerked to a stop. At first I thought he slipped up on some zombie-mush from the barrage. Eddie Franklin had a better view and he told me later it was like one of his legs cramped up or something in the middle of the stride. A few people in the towers tried to give him cover fire, but it wasn't enough.

The girl was screaming for her father. He heard her. We all heard her.

The exes swarmed over them. Even this far out we saw flashes of red from the girl. Adams fought for a few moments, even after his ACUs turned red. They were hidden by a press of exes, so we didn't see them die. But I'm pretty sure we heard it, even over all the chattering teeth.

Sorensen started howling. No other word for it. Just this raw sound coming out of him.

Someone tried to pull the rear door shut on the Guardian and got dragged out. Three or four dead things were forcing their way through the driver's door at the same time. I remember I heard screaming through the radio and the same screams off in the distance. It was a creepy stereo effect that made my stomach churn. Screams and gunfire and teeth.

I kept waiting for Washington—for Britney—to leap out of the transport and up onto the relative safety of the roof. She could last for an hour or two up there. Long enough for us to get another Guardian or a Humvee or something out there.

Sorensen was wailing in my arms. "Do something!" He looked at me and shouted up at Freedom. "Why aren't you helping them?"

Somebody yanked my radio out of my ear. Kennedy was standing next to me. She'd leaped down from the tower. "Sergeant Harrison," she told me, "escort the doctor away from the fence."

Sorensen grabbed her sleeve. "You have to help them," he screamed. He was crying so much his beard had two wet streaks in it. "You have to do something!"

"I'll lead the recovery team," I said. "Twenty-one can be out there in ten min—"

"Sergeant," snapped Kennedy, "I am ordering you to escort the doctor out of sight of the fence and into that building. Clear?" She pointed over my shoulder.

"Yes, first sergeant." That's when I knew Britney was dead. They were all dead. "Clear."

I dragged the doctor away. I could bench-press over nine hundred pounds, but he was twisting and flailing and shrieking and trying to get to the gate. If you've ever tried to hold a really determined four-year-old, that's what I was dealing with. I didn't look back. My radio was dangling around my neck and I could still hear the screams. There were less of them, but one of them was a woman's.

I kicked open the doors of the admin building, broke one of the hinges, and dropped Sorensen into a lobby chair. He was just gone. He wasn't moving. There was a vacant look in his eyes I remember from a few guys after their first live-fire test. He couldn't process what was happening. Who could blame him? He'd just seen his daughter taken down in front of him.

I thought about Britney. Three hours ago she'd been alive. I was very cold all of a sudden. Cold and empty, like everything in my belly had just vanished and left me hollow. I thought about sitting down, but I had a feeling I wouldn't get back up if I did. I leaned against the wall.

Britney was dead. Everyone in Twelve was dead. There was never going to be an Army Band again. No horn lessons for kids. No nights playing jazz down in the Gaslamp. Nothing.

"Sergeant Harrison?" The doctor's voice was small and reedy. He was hoarse from screaming.

"Yes, sir?"

He looked up at me. It was like locking eyes with a sad dog. He was calling me by name, but I don't think he really knew who I was.

"Are they . . ." he started. He coughed, cleared his throat, and whispered, "Are they going out soon to rescue Eva and Madelyn?"

Twenty

NOW

ST. GEORGE PUSHED the last bit of toast into his mouth. He couldn't remember how long it had been since he had butter. He almost felt guilty for eating it.

Across from him, Stealth sat before an empty plate with her arms crossed. She hadn't made a sound since they'd been led to the officers' mess for breakfast and sat down alone.

He pushed the plate a few inches away. "Are you going to eat anything?"

"No."

"You didn't eat anything last night, either."

"As usual, George, your attention to detail is beyond compare."

"You should eat something to keep your strength up. Might make you less grouchy, too."

Her head tilted inside the hood. "You are making a joke at my expense."

"In a good-natured way. You do need to eat."

"I ate last night in my assigned quarters."

"Ate what?"

"Food from the dinner with Colonel Shelly."

"You smuggled food back to your room?"

"I did."

"Weren't you worried about someone watching you eat with all these cameras?"

"There are three in my quarters," she said. "I disabled the two visible ones and allowed them to think I had not discovered the one concealed in the air vent. I ate with my back to it."

"And then what? Slept in your uniform?"

"Of course."

St. George stood up and stretched. "So you still don't trust them?"

"I maintain a healthy skepticism, yes."

A sergeant marched into the mess hall. "Good morning, ma'am, sir," he said. "I have messages for you. Colonel Shelly has asked for a meeting with you at eleven-thirty hours to discuss reintegrating Los Angeles into controlled territory. Also Dr. Morris asked if you could join her in D Lab once you're done eating."

"Where is that?"

"The far side of the complex, ma'am. East side, heading north. It's the only tall building without satellite dishes on the roof." He held a folded piece of paper out to her. "We also received a message from your people at the Mount. The colonel asked that you get any such communications as soon as possible."

Stealth glanced at the sheet of paper and handed it off to St. George.

Just checking in. Hope things are going good with our new friends. Dark clouds here since last night, might even rain. Otherwise all good.

                                        —Hiram Eggplant Jarvis

"When was this received?" she asked.

"About twenty minutes ago, I think, ma'am."

"Thank you, sergeant."

He gave her a polite bow of his head and left.

The blank planes of her mask shifted. "We have a problem, George."

"I kind of gathered." He held up the paper. "Unless eggplant is Jarvis's middle name, I'm guessing it's a code?"

"It is, as I am sure the military has already deduced."

"And it means . . . ?"

"The message is authentic. Jarvis was to use the name of a vegetable we do not grow in the main garden as his middle name, rotating in a new name for each communication. Zzzap did not return to the Mount." She strode out of the mess hall.

He took a few quick steps to catch up with her. "What?"

"Before we left I instructed Jarvis in a series of phrases and compromise words to use in any communications. References to the weather deal with us. The mention of the sun, or lack thereof, tells me Zzzap has gone missing."

"I think you might be overreacting just a bit."

"The message indicates he has been absent since last night. We were told on our arrival he had just left to return to the Mount. Since you did not see him there, the logical assumption is he went missing sometime after leaving Krypton Base. Assuming he did leave the base."

They pushed open a double set of doors and stepped out into the morning sun. Stealth looked even more like a walking shadow in the brilliant light.

"Assuming he didn't just go sightseeing or something," said St. George. "He's gone off flitting around the world before. You know what he told me the morning after the

Fourth? He's been thinking of flying to the Moon. Just to check it out. He was pretty sure he could make it there in under an hour."

"He has always made a point of telling us where he was going and for how long."

"Telling us, yeah. It might not occur to him to tell anyone else. Not until he gets back, anyway. You've got to admit, Barry can get a little absentminded at times."

She stopped walking and turned to him. "You do not find this disturbing?"

"A little bit, yeah," he said. He glanced around and dropped his voice. "But I'm not going to declare war on the U. S. Army just because I feel a little disturbed. Do I disagree with some of their choices? Yes. Are they doing some weird things with the exes? Hell, yes. But it's still America we're talking about. From what Shelly was saying last night it sounds like the president might even still be alive and holed up at NORAD or something."

"NORAD could be as much a trap as a safe haven if a single infected person was inside. Besides, Shelly did not say the president was still alive."

"Yeah, but he also didn't say he was dead, and he did say he was still getting orders from above."

"I hope you are right, George. But there are too many people depending on us to not make contingency plans."

× × ×

"I don't know," said Danielle. She glanced up from the circuits she was soldering. "Maybe he's just off checking out other cities or something again."

St. George threw his head back and sighed with relief. "That's what I said."

The redhead bent to her work again. "Besides, what could they even do to him? He's probably invulnerable to everything they've got on this base, even with all the super-soldiers."

"Zzzap is," said Stealth. "Barry is not."

"Look," said St. George, "we'll ask the colonel about it again at this meeting. Until then, I think we need to let this drop. I don't want to mess anything up with accusations and then have Barry show up half an hour later bragging he spent the night racing between Hubble and the space station. Okay?"

Stealth gave him a look he could sense through her mask. The one that meant she thought he was being foolish. "Very well, George," she said. "If you feel this is the correct path, I shall defer to your judgment."

Danielle finished her work on the circuit board, blew on it, and removed it from the small clamps. She lowered it into a box that resembled a small metal coffin and reached in with a screwdriver to fasten the board in place. "In happier news," she said, "I realized something."

"Please," said St. George, "share the happier news."

The redhead glanced at Stealth. "You know what I said yesterday about not wanting to do all these repairs and up-grades because I thought it'd feel like giving up?"

The cloaked woman gave a single nod.

"Well, starting this last night didn't feel like giving up," said Danielle. "It made me feel guilty."

St. George tilted his head. "Guilty?"

"I should've been doing all this stuff months ago. It's easy work. I had enough of the parts." She glanced up from her work again. "And people were depending on me. That's been stuck in the back of my mind all morning."

Danielle pulled the screwdriver away and picked up a studded metal plate the size of a hardcover book. It had a shaft on the back that slotted into something inside the little coffin. There was a loud clack as it settled into place.

"Shelly was right," she said. "I wasn't supposed to be the one in the suit. But I volunteered for it. I wanted to be Cerberus, and that's who I am now. And I think I'm needed at the Mount a lot more than here."

"I am pleased to hear your decision," said Stealth.

St. George rapped a knuckle on the steel box. "So what is this, anyway?"

The redhead gave a wicked grin. "It's a new weapons mount to replace the one Peasy tore off. I've been playing with this thing in my head and on paper for almost two years. I might be able to have another one built and both installed by tomorrow."

St. George smiled. "Just in time to go home?"

"Yeah," she said. "I think so."

× × ×

"Colonel Shelly got tied up with some administrative things," said Smith. Today's suit was charcoal gray with a crimson tie. "He asked if I could go over things with you in his place."

Stealth crossed her arms. "This meeting is such a low priority he could neither attend himself nor send one of his staff?"

"Is that a problem?"

Stealth glared at the young man for a moment. Her head shifted in the hood as she glanced at St. George. He could see the effort it took her to relax. "No," she said. "It is not."

"Good," said Smith. "Thank you."

"We've got a couple questions, too," said St. George. "A few things we want to double-check with you."

"Do you mind if we do these first?" Smith held up a clipboard covered with scrawled phrases and sentences. "I'll answer anything you want afterward. I've just got a lot of this fresh in my mind and I don't want to miss anything."

A twist of gray smoke curled out of the hero's nose. "I suppose so."

"Thanks." Smith looked at his notes. "Now, what's going to happen over the next few weeks is an assessment, just like I mentioned back at the Mount. The Army's going to look at your defenses and make sure they're adequate for the threat we're facing. If they are, great. If not, they'll help improve them. Odds are they'll just leave you to keep running things the way you have. You're doing fine, so why mess with something that's not broken, right?"

St. George gave Stealth a cautious glance. "Okay," he said.

"Can we depend on the Army for medical supplies and ammunition?"

"Resources gets more complicated," Smith told her, "but medical supplies are a definite yes. That includes some food and vitamin supplements, as well. The military will do an inventory and see what you already have. They're going to give you supplies for the Mount, but they're also going to need some things in return, just so you know."

Stealth shifted in her chair. "Such as?"

"Well, people for starters. They're going to have a recruitment drive, just like they had when they rescued people from Yuma. The Army needs soldiers right now, and odds are there are a few thousand eligible people in your Los Angeles population."

"Eligible," repeated Stealth. "Are you initiating a draft?"

"No," said Smith. "Sorry. Poor word choice on my part. It's completely voluntary. But you figure even if ten percent of your people decide they want to sign up, that's over two thousand people."

"A generous estimate."

"Actually, going off how the survivors from Yuma reacted, it might be low. I also understand from one of your security people, Sergeant Billie Carter, there are a number of Marines living in the Mount and the surrounding complexes."

"Yeah," said St. George. "About a dozen of them, counting her. Their platoon flew out to L.A. with Cerberus and stayed with us because . . . well, they didn't have anywhere else to go. A few have died since then. We've also got seventeen National Guardsmen, two Navy guys, and a retired Air Force general."

"Didn't know about those last ones," muttered Smith, checking over his list. He scribbled a note in the margin. "Anyway, point is they're all going to be called back to active duty and returned to military command. It's a stop-loss situation."

"The stop-loss provision applies only to currently active personnel," said Stealth, "and can only be enacted by the president."

He shook his head. "Special provisions. They can pull back anyone who ever served if the situation calls for it. When martial law was declared, it went into effect automatically."

"Unpleasant, but not surprising," said Stealth. "Continue."

Smith tapped a finger on the edge of the clipboard. "Okay,

like I said, they don't have any trouble leaving you in charge, but they want to make sure everything's on the up-and-up."

St. George sighed. "Is this about Christian Nguyen?"

"Sort of. The Army's lawyers are going to go over how you've been running things, look at this government you're putting together, and make sure it doesn't violate anyone's rights."

"The Army has lawyers?"

"Oh, yeah. Tons of them. There're three here on Krypton. They're also going to take custody of any prisoners you have and give them a trial under the military justice system."

"No."

St. George looked at Stealth, and then his own shoulders tensed. "Yeah," he said, "there might be a problem with that. Some of our prisoners are . . . special cases."

"It's not an optional thing," said Smith.

"It is not," agreed the cloaked woman. "Prisoners shall be released on a case-by-case basis. This is not up for debate."

He reached up and gave his tie a small tweak. "I'll have to talk with Colonel Shelly about that." Smith flipped to another page of notes. "I think it's also understandable that they want the Cerberus system."

"Yeah, about that," said St. George. "Thing is, we were just talking with Danielle and she—"

"She has decided to return to Los Angeles with us," said Stealth. "And with Cerberus."

"Ahhh," said Smith. "That's . . . that's unfortunate."

"Why?" Stealth shifted her hips and her shoulders tensed.

He took the clipboard in both hands. "The Cerberus Battle Armor System was developed under a DARPA contract, paid for with military funds. It's government property. It stays here."

Stealth took a step forward. Smith stepped back, bumping against the conference table. St. George set a hand on the cloaked woman's shoulder.

"I'm sorry," Smith said. "I know you won't believe me, but I didn't want to play this card. I even went to bat for you guys. But the colonel's firm on this. He wants the suit here and he wants her building more of them."

"You might get the suit," said St. George, "but not her. Danielle wants to come back to the Mount. She's a private citizen. You can't stop her."

"Actually," said Smith, "we can. She's been a government employee since 2006. She's been stop-lossed, too."

"The stop-loss act applies to military personnel," said Stealth.

"Thanks to a little clause in the Patriot Act, it applies to any government employee above a certain security level. The same badge that let her peek at all those other exoskeleton projects while she was building Cerberus is keeping her here and under Colonel Shelly's command."

"This is bullshit," said St. George.

"It is also entrapment," said Stealth. "We were brought out here under false pretenses for the sole purpose of seizing the Cerberus suit." Her head tilted toward St. George. "As I tried to tell you."

"Look, guys," said Smith. "Guy and gal. You have to believe me, I didn't think we'd ever need to talk about any of this. I thought Danielle would want to stay here at Yuma. I didn't want to bring any of this up because I knew how you'd react."

"We'll fight you on this," said St. George.

"You can't. If you resist they'll slap the 'traitor' label on you and have a court-martial."

"They can't court-martial us. We're civilians."

"Martial law," said Smith. "What do you think it means? The Army is the law right now. They're judge, jury, and executioner in any legal matters."

"I'd like to see them try."

"Look, I know this seems like a bad thing at first, but you don't need Cerberus in Los Angeles if you've got a platoon or three of soldiers stationed there. Heck, they could rotate in a squad of Freedom's men and they'd probably be even more effective than the battlesuit."

"Cerberus isn't really the issue," said St. George. "Danielle's our friend. We're not going to abandon her."

"I'm sorry. I wish there was more I could do to help, but the colonel's not going to bend on these points. I think you should—"

"What else is there?"

Smith glanced at her. "I don't know what—"

"Your body language indicates continued reluctance. You have more to tell us."

He sighed. "Yeah, there is. The other thing they want, the big thing really, is . . ." Smith rolled his shoulders and studied his shoes for a few moments.

"Yes?"

"Well . . . they want your power supply."

There was a moment of silence. Then Smith felt the floor drop away from under his feet and the wall whirled around to slam into his back. The clipboard clattered away. His clothes were painfully tight. St. George had wrapped shirt, tie, and coat into his fist when he grabbed the smaller man.

"Where is he?"

"Hey, hey, hey!" Smith raised his arms as best he could in the twisted coat. He waved his palms. "I can't . . . I'm not at liberty to say."

"What's that supposed to mean?" Ripples of heat and smoke flowed out of St. George's mouth.

"I'm under orders not to tell you."

"We are giving you new orders," said Stealth.

"Look, it's not that simple. I don't like it either, but you need to see the big picture. You've got to calm down and listen if we're going to work together, okay? You want to work with me, right?"

St. George loosened his grip and Smith slid down to the floor. "I'm listening."

"Thank you." He brushed the bigger wrinkles out of his shirt, adjusted his tie, and picked up his notes. "I'd like to help you. I would. But it pretty much amounts to treason, and treason can get you shot around here."

"Are citizens being executed?" asked Stealth.

"No, of course not. Hell, the stockade's full of people who probably should've been executed for the crap they've done. But that's bad for morale. That's how you end up with a rebellion. And none of that helps rebuild America."

St. George cracked his knuckles. "Where is Zzzap?"

Smith sighed. "The important thing is he's fine and he's safe. No one's going to hurt him. But he's way too valuable to the military. He's a walking reactor, for Christ's sake, and if these people are going to rebuild America they need power."

Stealth crossed her arms. "Has he also been stop-lossed?"

"No," said Smith. "They're detaining him as a person of interest."

"Oh, come on," snapped St. George. "This is ridiculous."

"Colonel Shelly must realize if we decide to free Zzzap, there is little his forces can do to stop us."

"I wouldn't be too sure of that," Smith said to her. "He's got a full brigade of soldiers, plus Captain Freedom and his company of super-soldiers. Heck, there're two tanks here somewhere."

"It would not be enough to stop us," said Stealth.

"Okay, think for a minute. Think about what happens if you *did* get him and get away. Los Angeles gets branded hostile territory. No food, no medical supplies, nothing. And once they gather enough forces they'll just come in and take over anyway. Then we're back to courts-martial." Smith shook his head. "You have to play ball."

"Like you have?" asked Stealth.

"Yeah," he said, "just like I have. You have to understand. America's in pieces and these guys are the glue. They're trying to save the country they swore to protect. It's nothing personal." He sighed and tossed his clipboard on the table. "Your best bet is just to go with it. Tomorrow the two of you will go home to Los Angeles. Everyone there will still think you're heroes."

× × ×

St. George stalked along the fence line. A halo of dark smoke surrounded his head as he clenched his fists. "I should've let you beat it out of him," he said. "If we knew where they were holding Barry, we could just break in there and set him free. The three of us could level this place. How could I be so damned stupid?"

Stealth walked alongside him. She'd said nothing since they left the conference room.

"You were right," he said to her. "We shouldn't've trusted them. Hell, Barry was right. The military always turns evil during a zombie apocalypse."

"They are not evil," she announced. "They are doing what

they believe is right, in a way consistent with the training and orders they have received. I once held many of the same views myself. Over the past two years you have convinced me otherwise."

"They've got Barry locked up somewhere and you don't think that's evil?"

"Is it so different from what we do? At the Mount he is often trapped in the electric chair for eighteen hours at a time."

St. George shook his head. "He volunteers for that."

"He volunteers because we have placed him in a position of unavoidable responsibility. By eating an apple and staying in the chair he can provide power to over twenty thousand citizens of Los Angeles for lights, security, cooking, entertainment, and more. If he leaves the chair, they will have none of these things."

"It's not the same."

"It is, George," she said. "It is why I had the chair built. Once it existed, I knew he would not fail us."

"But that's different. We're on the fringes. We're just trying to survive. This isn't what it was supposed to be like. I thought . . ." He sighed and let another mouthful of smoke out into the air.

"What?"

He kicked at a rock and it skittered through the chainlink to hit an ex-soldier's boot. "I guess I was like Danielle," St. George said. "I always figured someday everything would go back to normal. Someone would drive up outside the gates and tell us everything was okay, we could all go home. I could go back to being a maintenance guy who got Thai food from the place on the corner and dressed up in a costume to fight muggers. You could go back to . . . whatever it was you did for a living."

"I was a retired fashion model with multiple athletic championships and doctoral degrees," said Stealth. "By most standards I was independently wealthy."

"Wow," he said after a moment. "You really are Batman, aren't you?"

"You are avoiding the subject, George. What do we do now?"

"What do you mean?"

"We must free Zzzap and also ensure Danielle and the Cerberus suit return with us to Los Angeles. How will we do this?"

He stopped walking and looked at her. "We can't," he sighed. "I don't like it either, but like you said, they're not evil. They're the good guys."

"They seek to undo much of our work at the Mount and to bring a sizable part of our population under their direct control."

St. George glanced around. They were a few dozen yards from the closest guard tower. There was one soldier in it, half watching them.

"It would appear we are between shifts," she said. "There are minimal human guards on patrol to hear our discussion, and I have guided us away from the perimeter cameras and microphones."

"Look," he said in a lower tone of voice, "this isn't some movie supervillain or something. It's the United States Army, acting under orders of the president. It's like Smith said, we'd be committing treason."

"Would we? We cannot be traitors to a nonexistent country. Are we still living within the United States?"

"Of course we are."

"Geographically, perhaps, but a nation is defined by more

than mere borders." She turned to the fence and looked out at the dirt and scrub of the proving ground. Three exes were stumbling toward them out of the desert. "All this land was once Native American territory, correct?"

He shrugged. "I guess."

"Suppose an individual came to you claiming to be the representative of that territory. If they demanded you follow their laws and obey their commands, would you?"

"Are we on a reservation or something?"

"No."

"Then I'd probably be as polite as possible but keep following the current laws as best I could."

She nodded. "Just as you have at the Mount."

They looked out at the sand for a few minutes. A trio of exes pawed at the outer fence. One was a topless woman with clotted filth in her hair. Another, an elderly man with one arm, had a pair of spectacles hanging around his neck by a chain.

"I feel sick."

"It is understandable. You have spent the past two years awaiting the arrival of the authorities. Of someone who would relieve you of responsibility for the Mount. You have just realized no one is coming. You are the authorities. You are and always will be responsible for the people of Los Angeles."

"And this isn't freaking you out?"

"I have told you before, George, I am not an optimist. I have never expected us to be saved or relieved of duty. I accepted this responsibility two years ago."

She turned and continued along the inside of the fence. St. George took a few quick steps to catch up with her. "You've already got a plan, don't you?"

"You will go back to Danielle and get her to the work-shop where Cerberus is being stored. In turn, she can direct you to Sorensen. I am certain he knows where Zzzap is being held. Once Danielle is back in the armor, we shall demand transport back to Los Angeles. If they refuse, we may have to steal it."

"That'd be great if any of us knew how to fly a Black Hawk helicopter."

"I do," she said, "but I believe a basic M35 cargo truck will get us back to Los Angeles in four days at the most."

"Okay," he said, "what are you going to be doing during all this?"

"I shall give Colonel Shelly a final chance to present evidence of his claims that the federal government is still functioning and to convince me that his plan represents our best option. Barring that, I shall convince him to allow us to leave without incident."

"Just to be clear," said St. George, "when you say 'convince him' are you talking about attacking a U.S. military officer?"

"Of course not," said Stealth.

"That wasn't very convincing."

"George, we do not have time for this. It is twelve-forty-three. You must endeavor to have Danielle at her workshop and Zzzap freed by one-thirty." Her head turned to him within her hood. "Are you comfortable with this? I do not want to influence your decision."

"You influence most of my decisions," he said with a half-hearted smile. He took a slow breath. "No, I don't feel comfortable about this at all, but sometimes the right thing to do isn't the comfortable thing. And this feels right."

"Then it must be so," she said.

"How can you be so sure?"

She stopped and turned to him. "Because you think it is, and you are the only person I have ever known who always does the right thing."

They looked at each other, and George realized an opportune moment had just slipped past him again. He cleared his throat and tried to brush it aside. "I hope so," he said. "Six months from now I don't want any of our people walking between fences like Bub there." He gestured at an ex staggering along on patrol.

"Bub?"

He nodded at the ex-soldier with the dangling rifle. "Barry makes me watch a George Romero movie every other month. The zombie with the gun is named Bub."

"I do not understand."

"Don't worry about it."

Twenty-One

NOW

THE SOLDIERS MARCHED down the dim hall with an easy, even stride. They were two of the older recruits, both in their thirties and specialists. A year of guard duty with nothing more challenging than a handful of exes had relaxed them, but they still paused when they turned the corner and saw the darkened hallway.

One of the fluorescent tubes flickered for a moment, then went black again.

"Dead light," said one soldier. He nodded at the office door. "The colonel'll be pissed the next time he works late. Remember to tell maintenance."

"You remember."

"It's your turn to write up reports."

"Asshole."

"Hey, you lost fair and square."

They turned the corner, still trying to pass off their paperwork, and Stealth dropped down from the ceiling.

The colonel's office was locked with a Medeco3 dead bolt, but she had seen schematics of the tumbler mechanism at a seminar in Las Vegas several years earlier. Six minutes of work and she was inside the reception area of Shelly's office.

The door closed behind her without a sound and she reengaged the lock.

Her fingers skimmed the adjutant's desk. She looked at letterheads and printed e-mails, paged through the appointment book and the desk calendar. She considered the computer. Based on the personal items on the desk and in the drawers, she was confident she could break the adjutant's password in less than ten attempts. However, there was little chance the materials she needed were on his hard drive.

The inner office door was not locked. She paused to listen for overt movement or heavy breathing, signs of someone working or even sleeping. If there was anyone in the office, they were making a point of being as quiet as her.

She opened the door and slipped inside.

Colonel Shelly sat behind his desk, facedown on a set of disciplinary reports. Red lines ran from his nostrils, his ears, and his left eye. Enough of it had pooled on the desk to start spreading out past his skull.

There was a faint rustle of hair on linen from behind her. The low hiss of a seat cushion shifting.

"What happened to him?" Stealth asked in a clear voice.

"If I had to guess," murmured Sorensen, "I would say he suffered a massive cerebral hemorrhage. Three or four blood vessels all bursting at once. He never knew what happened. It was just like flipping a switch. Alive. Dead."

The doctor sat in a chair against the far wall, half hidden in shadows. It wasn't clear to her if he was relaxed or stunned. He stared at the corpse.

"Believe it or not, it may have saved him from the exvirus," Sorensen continued. "If certain key parts of his brain were destroyed by the hemorrhaging, there won't be enough left for the virus to reanimate."

Stealth slid behind the desk and examined the body. It was still warm. Dead within the past two hours. There were no visible bullet wounds in the head, and the doctor didn't appear to be armed, but she did not rule out the possibility of a low-caliber shot in the mouth.

"What are you doing here, doctor?"

His eyes flicked up to her for a moment, looking over the edge of his glasses. "I was going to ask if they'd found Eva and Madelyn yet."

She moved in front of him. "Your wife and daughter?"

He bobbed his head up and down.

"We were told your family was killed by exes during a recovery mission."

Sorensen turned his head and glared at her. "Captain Freedom never recovered their bodies," he said, "so they must have gotten away."

"It is far more likely they were devoured or dismembered to a point where they were not recog—"

"They got away!" snapped Sorensen.

He leaped up and Stealth shifted her weight to her back leg for a kick.

"Colonel Shelly was sending out patrols to look for them. He promised me. Madelyn's a smart, special girl. She got away." The doctor tilted his head. "The real question is what are *you* doing here?"

"I was hoping to speak to the colonel about his claims of contact with a governing body. Why do you believe he suffered from a hemorrhage?"

"He's not the first," said the doctor. He walked to the desk. "Three people have died the same way. They all had too much on their minds. Very conflicted, just like the colonel."

"Conflicted?"

"He didn't want any of you out here. He just wanted to establish contact, make sure you were doing a good job, make sure you were all safe . . ." His voice trailed off again and he ran his fingers back and forth on the desk. The tips passed just a few inches from the puddle of blood.

"Doctor?"

"And then he changed his mind," said the older man. He drummed the fingers of his other hand against his thumb. "Between breakfast and lunch. Just like someone flipping a switch."

Stealth stared at him as he traced lines on the desk. "Did you have something to do with this, doctor?"

"No, no, no." He stopped tracing lines and glared at her for a moment like an angry child. Then his face went slack. "I didn't mean for it to happen like this," he whispered through his fingers. "Any of it. I just wanted them to leave me alone."

"Who?"

"The dead. The dead keep talking to me. I just want to be left alone and everyone keeps talking to me."

She heard the footsteps and spun. A trio of soldiers stood at the door. Each wore the patch that marked them as supersoldiers. The closest one was a staff sergeant named PIERCE. He looked at the body. The other two looked at her.

"So sorry," said Sorensen. He sank back into his chair. "It wasn't supposed to be like this."

Stealth threw a punch at the soldier next to Pierce and the man blocked most of it. He was too fast, she realized, and they were ready for her. She swung her heel around in a wide kick. They dodged again but it gave her time to grab the ASP batons stored across her back.

She brought the weapons up and Pierce and the other man, Hancock, grabbed her arms. Her legs kicked up, caught the third soldier under the chin with her boot, and let her flip up and over. The movement surprised them enough for her to twist free.

The third man stumbled back. She spun and drove a kick into Hancock's stomach as she snapped the batons open and fractured Pierce's wrist. She swung her leg back to Pierce and—

Hancock had her leg. The kick had winded him but he'd grabbed hold. She could free herself, but it disrupted her timing. Just for an instant.

The third soldier was back on his feet. She freed her leg and snapped two kicks into Hancock's face.

Pierce's fist struck just under her armpit and she felt the jolt travel down her arm. It was like being hit with a baseball bat. She knew that from experience.

He pulled back his good hand and punched the same arm square in the bicep. Her hand went numb but she forced her fingers to stay closed on the baton. She brought her other arm around, struck the third man, and Pierce's knuckles hit her in the side of the head. She heard the ASP hit the floor.

× × ×

It was a little after thirteen hundred hours when Freedom entered Shelly's office. "Is it true, sir?"

Smith stood at the desk, looking at the dark puddle. "Yeah," he said. "I just talked to Sorensen. He walked in on the woman, Stealth, beating Colonel Shelly to a pulp. He was lucky there were three of your men nearby who heard them."

Freedom stood ramrod straight. "What's the colonel's condition, sir?"

"I haven't seen him, but Sorensen says it's critical. There

may be . . ." Smith took a slow breath. "There may be brain damage. She beat his skull with those metal batons of hers."

Freedom said nothing, but his jaw got tight and his knuckles whitened around his patrol cap.

"There's a good chance he won't make it," said Smith. "You'll forgive me for saying so, captain, but either way this means you're in charge."

"I'm aware of that, sir." Freedom took in a slow breath of his own. "Do we have any idea why she did it?"

"If I had to guess . . . I don't know, maybe she was angry we were going to be keeping Dr. Morris and the Cerberus suit here at Krypton. Maybe she thought she could kill him and they could all slip away in the confusion." He shrugged. "I don't know, does that even sound plausible to you?"

"More than plausible," said the huge officer. His face twisted into a scowl. "She's in custody?"

"Pierce and Hancock delivered her to the stockade five minutes ago."

"Excellent," said Freedom. "Then let's get the rest of them."

× × ×

"Damn," said St. George as the sirens started up. "I think those are for us. I guess Stealth's talk with Colonel Shelly didn't go too well."

"Well, she's such a fantastic diplomat," muttered Danielle.

They ran between the buildings. He'd offered to fly them, but she pointed out they'd be exposed. So they were on foot and trying to stay out of sight.

They came to a wider intersection where the roads were paved. "This is it," Danielle said, pointing left. "From what they told me, Sorensen's lab is that way. Building nineteen, on the fourth floor. The building's got the same layout as mine, his lab is right above where mine would be. Think you can find it?"

"I'll manage. You sure you can make it to the workshop on your own?"

She fingered the collar of her camo jacket. "Doesn't look like there are many soldiers out yet. I'll blend in enough with my hair under the cap. Cerberus will be ready to go by the time you get there with Barry."

"It better be," he said. "I think we're running out of time."

"Have I ever been slow about getting back in the suit?"

"I'll see you in an hour or sooner, then."

She tugged her cap down, gave him a ragged salute, and marched down the road with her arms tight to her sides. St. George kept an eye on her until she'd passed two buildings, then headed in the opposite direction.

He could move faster on his own. If he focused on the spot between his shoulder blades he could feel gravity get weak. It let him move in quick, long strides. He crouched behind a parked truck as a Humvee sped down the road.

Building nineteen had a security keypad. St. George kicked himself for not asking if he'd need a code or something. He was sure he could force the door open, and just as sure it would set off an alarm if he did. Then he kicked himself again for being dumb.

The lock popped off as he pried the window open. As he suspected, the Army contractors hadn't bothered to put alarms on the fourth-floor windows. He slid it open the rest of the way, spun in the air, and slipped into the building.

He couldn't hear much in the building. The faint rumble of air conditioning. A phosphorescent tube crackled somewhere. As far as he could tell, there were no voices, ringing phones, or any of the other sounds of life one would expect from a populated building. St. George slipped into the empty hall.

It took him about ten minutes to find Sorensen's lab. It had his name on a small plate, along with three long words the hero couldn't pronounce—two *bio*s and a *neuro*. It also had another security keypad. He considered skimming around the outside of the building until he found a window into the lab, then realized Danielle was probably already at her workshop. If her numbers were right, she'd have the suit ready to assemble in twenty minutes.

He braced his feet, put his palm just above the latch, and pushed. The metal frame let out a little groan. The latch leaned in toward his hand and wrinkles appeared in the painted steel around his fingers. There were four quick pops from the hinges, a squeal of metal, and the door flew into the lab.

St. George half expected the room to be filled with bubbling chemicals and a Tesla coil. It was mostly computers, including a huge screen he knew Stealth would never admit to wanting. A few brains floated in small tanks near diagrams and cross sections of their structure.

Five exes were fastened down on tilted gurneys, each pushed up against the back wall. The row of almost-vertical figures reminded him of a carnival ride, one of the ones that spun people around. Four of them had nylon straps across their foreheads and were gagged with what looked like pieces of a broomstick. The fifth's head was free and it swiveled back and forth, snapping its teeth at the air.

Sorensen sat in the middle of the lab on a tall stool. He looked over his shoulder at the hero. "It's open," he said. "I haven't locked it in months."

"Where's Zzzap?"

"Somewhere safe."

St. George soared across the room and lifted the doctor by his collar. "No games," he said. Hot smoke streamed out of his nostrils and mouth. "You're going to take me to him now and you're going to release him."

"He's much safer where he is," said Sorensen. "They can't get to him in there."

"I said no games."

"You can put me down," said the doctor. "I won't run. If it's what you want, I'll take you to your friend. But he is safer where he is."

"Forgive me if I don't believe you."

The doctor tried to shrug, but hanging in St. George's hand he just swung in his coat. "I'll need to get the blue flash drive from my desk."

"What for?"

"It's a code key. Mr. Burke's held behind an interwoven trio of Faraday cages. It's what's keeps him there. The key shuts them off."

"That's it?"

"There's a matching key one of the soldiers on duty will have. In theory we need both. I'm sure you could destroy all three cages if you needed to, though."

St. George set the older man down on the ground. The doctor's shoes clacked on the linoleum, a softer noise than the clicking teeth. "You're awfully helpful all of a sudden."

Sorensen shrugged again and adjusted his glasses. Then he tried to flatten the hundreds of wrinkles in his clothes. "It doesn't matter anymore. None of it."

"What are you talking about?"

"It's all over now. With Colonel Shelly dead there's going

to be confusion. They've got no reason to keep pretending. Especially with you here."

"Wait," said the hero. "Back up. How did Shelly die? What happened?"

"Too much pressure on his mind," said Sorensen. "That's one of the bad things out here. These are good people. Good, brave people. There's just too much on their minds."

"Pressure on their minds? Wait a minute. Is this . . . Does this have something to do with the Nest?"

The doctor shook his head. "No, of course not," he said with a sigh. "The Nest doesn't even work."

St. George looked at the older man and followed his eyes to the oversized diagram on the big screen. He recognized it from Stealth's sketch the day before. The neural stimulator.

"That was the deal, you see," Sorensen said. "I made a deal with the dead. I wouldn't say anything if any of you came here. If they found you and you came here, I couldn't say anything. Especially to her."

St. George tilted his head. "Her who?"

"Her. Dr. Morris. That was the deal. The dead would follow commands, they'd act just like the Nest was working. But I couldn't warn the one who'd killed him."

"What are you talking ab—oh, shit."

Across the room, the fifth ex had stopped clicking its teeth together. It stared at St. George. It grinned.

× × ×

Danielle was stuck across the road from her workshop, hiding by the Tomb. Just as she'd reached the building a jeep had pulled up. Now two soldiers were searching inside her shop. Two more waited outside and did a weak job of looking around. They were some of the new recruit soldiers. One of them was seventeen, tops. The other looked closer to fifty.

After what felt like ages the searchers trotted out and shook their heads. They gave a last glance around the corners of the building and the sergeant typed something into the keypad. All four of them piled back into the jeep and roared off to another part of the base.

In the same situation, she figured Stealth would wait at least three minutes before stepping into the open. Danielle waited twice that. And then two more minutes just to be safe, even though she desperately wanted to get inside.

There was no sign of other soldiers. She couldn't even hear another jeep.

She scampered across the street, bent low even though she was in plain sight and she knew it couldn't hide her. Her cap slipped and she yanked it off, letting her hair spill down. Once she was by her workshop she tried to squeeze into one of the shrinking shadows as the morning sun got higher in the sky.

She waited another minute and then slipped around to the keypad. As near as she could tell, nothing had changed. It looked like the soldier had just reset the locks and security system.

If they'd reset her codes, using the keypad would alert them to her location. If not, it would get her into the shop and still alert them to her location. But if they hadn't changed her codes, maybe it hadn't occurred to them yet to track her with them. Unless they'd left the codes active just for that reason.

Her fingers danced on the keypad. The door clicked open. No sirens went off.

She pulled the door shut behind her and breathed a sigh

of relief as it separated her from the outside world. Then she turned and bit back a scream.

A ring of twenty exes circled the tables where the Cerberus suit was spread out, lit by the high skylight. Four more stood at the center by the upright legs and torso section. All of them were in piecemeal ACUs. Each of them held an M16 rifle across its chest.

None of them moved.

Danielle took a moment to steady her breathing and took a step forward. She made a point of setting her sneaker down hard and scuffing it on the concrete floor. The sound echoed in the workshop.

They didn't react.

She took a few more cautious steps forward, dragging her feet on each one. If they started to move, she was sure she could beat them to the door. Of course, if they were even fair shots, they didn't need to be that fast.

Her laptop was just outside the ring of dead soldiers. The cables ran between two of them to the helmet and the armor's spine. She could see the suit was still hooked up and charged. No one had touched it. They'd just stationed guards.

She was five feet from the ring when the two closest exes took a step forward. Their shoulders bumped as they blocked her path. Danielle hopped back and they stopped advancing.

Her codes were still active. Shelly had said the programmed exes could take simple orders. And sometimes they understood priority.

Danielle took in a breath and looked at the closest ex. It was a man, shaved bald, in a sand-colored T-shirt with a bullet hole in the chest. No blood. She cleared her throat. "Soldier," she said, "I order you to let me pass."

The ex didn't move. She inched forward and it took another lumbering step toward her. Its hands shifted on the rifle.

"I *order* you to let me pass," she repeated.

It didn't move. It also didn't change its grip on the M16. The ex stared past her with blank eyes.

"I repeat, this is a direct order from Cerberus three-zero-three-alpha."

The dead thing started to move but shuddered to a halt. The withered head turned and locked eyes with her. It knotted its brow.

"I said, this is a—"

The M16 clattered to the ground. The dead thing lashed out with an arm that moved too fast and grabbed her throat. It glared at the redhead and marched her back, off balance, until the worktable hit the small of her back. The arm bent her over and she fell back next to the laptop. Her feet swung inches above the ground.

Cracked lips pulled away from the teeth. "Fucking *puta*," it growled. "Not so tough without your fucking armor, are you?"

She flailed at the arm, but she was weak. Just weak skin and bones.

The dead soldiers took in a dry, shuddering breath and spoke as one.

"IF I'D KNOWN IT WAS YOU," said the chorus of exes, "I'D'VE RIPPED *YOUR* HEAD OFF YESTERDAY!"

Ghost in the Machine

THEN

THINKING IS BAD. That's the lesson of the past year. I don't want to think anymore.

Captain Freedom told me the most fascinating story a while ago. He was very careful about telling it. He knew it was still a touchy subject at the time. Thin ice, as they say.

It's been fifteen months, seven days, two and a half hours since Eva and Madelyn went missing during the rescue attempt. I still look at clocks and assign mental labels to every date. One month since they vanished. Ten weeks since they were lost. Six months since they were lost. One year since they—

I mentioned it to John the other day and he said he did the same thing for almost two years when his father passed away.

Two years? How can I live like this for another year? I still feel cold and empty all the time. Will it be twice as long because I don't know what happened to either of them? I can't take four years of this.

Freedom came to see me. It was almost a year ago, now that I think of it. Three months since they'd gone missing. He had a puzzle, of sorts. They had gone out that morning to get the armored vehicle, the Guardian, he called it. It had been sitting out there all that time. Ever since they were—

They—

I need to get more work done. I still haven't managed to get the Nest working and reboot the exes. They're needed more than ever now. I need to focus on that. Must stop my mind from wandering so much. They weren't here in the lab before, so it shouldn't be hard to work now that they're—

Now that they're—

Madelyn Sorensen. Everyone said we were so cruel to give her rhyming names. That we were bad parents. Did she think I was a bad father? Did she blame me? God, I hope she knows how hard I tried. I wanted to go to them. I wanted to be with them.

Freedom said they were going to tow the Guardian in but they didn't have to. It still had half a tank of fuel. Sitting there in the sun for months and still over twenty gallons of diesel in it. There was no reason it should've stopped.

I remember at first I was very happy, because if the armored carrier still had gas, perhaps it meant Eva and Madelyn hadn't . . . that the whole thing had been a mistake. Perhaps they were still back at the airstrip. Maybe they never even got on the plane.

Freedom was very good about calming me down. He was a good man. He still is, I think. I don't see him that often. They leave me alone. They all have a lot on their minds.

The puzzle had been that half his soldiers still insisted the tank was empty. He had a dozen of them look at the gauge and only five of them saw the needle above E. Even when they drove it in, some of them still said there was no gasoline. Nothing the captain did could convince them otherwise. A few of them couldn't even start the engine.

He'd wanted to know about hallucinations. If they were a side effect to the process I didn't warn the Army about.

He hadn't reported it yet, but he was very firm his soldiers couldn't be put at risk. "I don't want anyone else to die," he told me.

I think it was a year ago today he was here. It may have been a year ago yesterday. No, it was two days ago. When I was talking with Freedom it had been exactly ninety-nine days since they went missing. Since one of the super-soldiers I created tried to bring my little Madelyn across half a mile of sand and was attacked by an army of exes that tore him apart. Since they crawled into the armored carrier and they—

I need to work. I need to think of other things. That's all I need these days. To work and be left alone.

On the other side of the lab there were six exes strapped down on gurneys. They were also handcuffed to the rails and gagged with a wooden bit. One of the soldiers trained as a field medic, Franklin, I think, came up with the clever idea of using back boards and head restraints to keep them immobile.

All my attempts to return the brain to a cogitative state had failed. This set of exes had new contacts in place. I think they were in place. I remember I was drilling placement holes in skulls when Captain Freedom came to talk to me. He had a problem he was trying to work out. That was day ninety-nine. Not yet one hundred.

I attached the Nest box to the leads and it sent a new pattern of electricity down into the dead brain. Nothing. No response at all. I checked each of the six subjects. Their EEGs were all flat.

Back to the first one. It was a young man with blond stubble and a large hole in his right cheek. I think it was a bite, but they'd all been cleaned up before they came to me. For the first six months they'd also all been male. I think that was John's doing.

I could see the young man's teeth through the hole. He didn't have a single filling on this side of his jaw. Madelyn had very good teeth, too. Freedom said he couldn't find their bodies. There was no trace left of them. Not even one of Madelyn's glittery sneakers. He was polite while he told me they were dead. He insists on seeing the evidence that way. I tried for weeks to tell him it could also mean she got away, but he wouldn't listen. Still won't.

I've had dreams about those sneakers. I see them running across the desert toward the gate. I still wake up crying most of the time.

No, no, no. Can't think like that. Must stay focused.

There was something odd about the young man's eyes. All exes have the same gray eyes. They accumulate dust because of the lack of tears and then get scratched. It's a process of refraction, the same way a scratch on clear glass looks white.

Its eyes were gray and they were odd, but I wasn't sure why they were odd. I checked one of the other exes to be sure, then I came back to the first one. I moved my head back and forth to see if it was something about the light. Something was wrong. I needed to focus on this better. I was missing something obvious.

Oh. Of course. Exes always turn their heads. They lack the fine muscle control to move their eyes. I'm still not sure they need to move their eyes, in the same way some blind people never move theirs.

The dead man with the hole in its cheek was watching me. It was following me with its eyes.

I found myself very focused. I checked the Nest again. It was still on, still sending the new pattern.

"Wehhh ahhh I?"

The ex was trying to talk. This was more than I'd ever hoped to achieve. I was so amazed I couldn't wait to tell Eva and Madelyn about it, and then I was horrified I'd forgotten they were—

How could I forget? It was only fifteen months. Since they went missing.

"Wahhh tha fugg ess thsss," said the young man. Its face had twisted into a scowl. I could see its jaws and tongue working through the hole in its cheek, trying to get the bit out.

My mind tripped over three or four different things to say. I leaned over the ex and its gray eyes focused on me. One of the irises had a small tear in it. "Can you understand me?"

"Wahhh tha fugg! Gehh diss hing owdda ma moff!"

I knew I shouldn't take out the bit. At the very least I should call for a few soldiers to stand guard. But part of me was too intrigued.

And the other part . . . the other part didn't care at all.

I unstrapped the neck brace and tossed it aside. A normal ex would be stretching its head, trying to bite me. This one just looked annoyed. I reached behind its head and tugged at the Velcro straps that kept the bit in place.

The ex started talking as soon as the wooden bar was out from between its teeth. "'Bout fucking time," it said. "What the hell is this? What you doing to me, *pinche*?"

It was looking around. It was making observations. It was thinking.

"What is . . ." I tried to think of an appropriate question. I'd never expected to have this level of success. "What is the last thing you remember?"

"I was in Hollywood," it said. "Just outside the Mount. Fighting with that metal . . ." The ex seemed to lose track of its thoughts, and for a moment I wondered if I'd made a mistake. "No," it said. "I was in the mountains. One of those ski towns."

Its tone was familiar. It was uncertain. Hesitant. I realized it sounded like me.

It also had a strong Spanish accent, which was odd for a young blond man with Anglo features.

"I was a bunch of places," it said. "Like I've been traveling, but I don't . . ."

The head lunged up, looking down at its torso. It turned to me and I yelped. Its expression was vicious. "What the hell is this? What you trying to pull?"

"I'm not sure what you mean."

"What is this? Where's my body?"

"What . . . what do you mean? I don't under—"

"This isn't me," it shouted. "Where's the rest of me? You sew my head on a new body or . . ."

Its voice trailed off. It stared at me again.

"Waitaminute," said the ex. It ran all the words together into a mishmash of English. "I know you. You're the mad doctor."

I shivered. "What do you mean?"

"You're the one who got me out. They wanted to court-martial me and shit and you gave me a clean bill. Said all those drugs and things were out of me and I was good to go."

The phrases swam in my head. I knew this should be familiar, but it was from before. The longest conversation I'd had with anyone in a year and I was freezing up.

"This is, whassit, Project Krypton, right? Some Army base?"

I blinked. "Yes. You . . . you're that private. Casares. The one from the previous trials."

"Yeah. What day is it?"

"Tuesday."

"No, *stupido*, I mean what's the number? The date?"

"The fourteenth," I said. "Of December." As I said it, I realized I hadn't done any shopping, and Eva and Madelyn would be so upset. I'm a very good gift-buyer. And then I remembered I didn't have to buy gifts this year, either. And there still wasn't anywhere to buy them. And they probably both hated me.

I must stay focused on work.

He growled. "A month," he muttered. "My boys prolly fell apart without me."

It wasn't until that moment that I started thinking of him as a he. He was conscious. Sentient. No longer an it.

"Your mind has been reactivated," I explained to him. "There's a device on the left side of your skull that I call a Nest. It stands for neural stim—"

"Hey, *esse*," he said. "Your gizmo don't do jack shit, okay? This is one hundred percent Rodney talking, you get me? How long have I been here?"

"Your body was brought in two weeks ago with three other—"

"No, doc," he said, shaking his head. "Me. My head. Did they ship it here or something?"

"I . . . I'm afraid I don't understand."

"Get me a fucking mirror!"

There was a hand mirror in the scrub room. I used it to make sure nothing splattered on me when I had to drill. I brought it in for the ex and caught a glimpse of myself in it. I needed a haircut. And my beard needed to be trimmed. Eva always hates it when my beard gets too long, because it was short when we met in grad school.

"What the fuck," he said. The ex tilted his head left and right. It took me a few moments to realize he was looking for a different face. He turned his head and poked his tongue out through the hole in his cheek. "Guess I can get in a lot of practice for the *chicas*, eh, doc?" His mouth pulled into a grin.

It was an eerie expression for a dead thing.

I cleared my throat. "You . . . you said the Nest wasn't working?"

His eyes came away from the mirror. "What?" He squinted his left eye a few times, making the Nest unit shift on his temple. "Naw, this thing's crap. It was keepin' the brain warm, that's it. Kinda gives me a headache, too." He lifted his chin to his chest and let his eyes roam around the room. "So what is this place? You still trying to make everybody be all they can be and that shit?"

"Yes. And trying to return some of the exes like you to a semicogitative state."

"Not like me," he said. His eyes focused past me and flitted back and forth. It was as if he was speed-reading an invisible book. Or in REM sleep. "Three fences," he said. "And you're low on guards." He squinted. "Fuck me, is that Colonel Shelly? I hated that fucker."

"How did you . . ."

"I'm everywhere, doc." He looked at one of the other test subjects. "So, what, you need to get 'em all under control? That's what your thing's supposed to do?"

"Yes."

He nodded. "Well, look at this. Put your left foot in and shake it all about, eh?"

The five other exes all swung their left feet side to side.

"Or what about this. Drumroll, *mis amigos*."

One of the exes was missing a hand, but nine sets of fingers tapped against the padded gurneys. They were in perfect unison, already like a military unit. They stopped and their fingers went straight to the sides of their legs.

The dead man grinned again. "I'm gonna make a deal with you, doc," he said. "You need a bunch of exes doing what you say. I need somewhere to lay low while I figure out what I'm doing. You see where I'm goin' with this?"

I didn't.

The grin spread even wider. It pulled at the flesh around the hole in his cheek, forming an oval crater in his face. "Congrats, doc," he said. "Your gizmo works."

Now I did.

"Why?"

"Because I can," he said. "Maybe I owe you one and I don't like owing people nothing. You made me into death incarnate."

"I didn't do anything but run some tests."

"You said they could let me go. That's enough for me. I'm tryin' to do you a favor."

"It wouldn't be that simple," I said. "If he thinks it works, Colonel Shelly will expect me to have dozens of exes outfitted with the Nest. Maybe hundreds. You can't—"

The ex's grin faded. "Don't you tell me what I can't do. If I wanted, every dead thing for three miles would pick up a rock and beat their own skulls in. Or anyone else's." He glared at me with his dusty, scratched eyes.

"I don't want any—"

"I can find them for you."

He spoke with such certainty it made me shake. "What?"

"The soldiers at the fence," said the ex, "they're talking

about you and your kid. You think your girl and your old lady got away, right? That's what they're saying."

"Colonel Shelly is—"

"He's fucking stringing you along's what he's doing. You really think he's going to send his people out to look for corpses?"

"They're not dead!"

"Sure they're not, doc," he said with a smile. "And I'll help find them. I got a thousand eyes here in the desert. If I see them, I'll let you know where they are."

"You . . . you'd do that?"

"Hey, doc, *familia* is everything, you know?"

I knew it was wrong and I didn't care. I could tell he was as mad as me in his own way—in a dangerous way—and I didn't care. I just wanted to know Eva and Madelyn were safe and be done with the Nest project so they would all leave me alone and I wouldn't have to think.

I looked the dead man in the eyes. "What do you want?"

"Just tell them the thing works. Tell 'em I'm still kinda slow, so they won't expect much. Then I'll be free to move around."

"That's all?"

"We may need to iron out some details later," he said, "but that's all for now. Deal?"

His right hand bent up under the strap, ready to shake on it. A gentlemen's agreement.

I reached down and unfastened the strap.

Twenty-Three

NOW

"SO," GROWLED THE EX, "we meet again and all that shit, eh, dragon man? Bet you weren't expecting this."

St. George pushed Sorensen behind him. "How the hell did you survive?" he asked the dead man. "Cerberus killed you. We burned your body with a few hundred other corpses."

"And I got better." The ex laughed. It was a dry sound. "I'm Peasy, *esse*. Patient zero. D'you think I'd go down that easy?"

"You're not patient zero," said St. George. "You're patient zero's first victim, a street punk and a murderer who lucked out and got superpowers."

"It wasn't luck," said Sorensen. He cleaned his glasses in a halfhearted way. "He was one of the Krypton subjects before I took control of the project a few years ago. I thought we'd flushed all the synthetic hormones and steroids from his system, but when he was exposed to the ex-virus they reacted in unforeseen ways."

St. George glanced over his shoulder at the older man. "You did this to him?"

The doctor shrugged. "I didn't stop it from happening to him, if you care to make the distinction."

"Don't matter to me," said the ex. The dead man's eyes

blinked as they tried to focus. "What the hell happened to your head, dragon man? You look like a sick altar boy or something."

"So how did you survive? Where are you hiding?"

The dead thing grinned. "That's the cool thing. I'm everywhere and nowhere. I been like this since that bitch tore my head off. Hell, if I'd known that redhead was you, I'd've ripped *your* head off yesterday."

"What?"

Peasy grinned. "Got her," he said. "And believe me, I been thinking for months now about—"

× × ×

"—all the things I'm going to do to you. I don't even know where to start."

Danielle batted at the desiccated arm. "Fucking murderer," she snarled. "I'd do it again. Give me half a chance and I'll tear you to pieces."

The dead soldier leered down at her through dusty eyes. On some level she knew how vulnerable she was. All flesh in a room full of exes. He could do anything to her. Anything at all.

But all she could think of was Gorgon. About his twisted body as a monstrous giant dropped it like a used napkin. About finding it half eaten the next morning and crushing the oversized skull of the thing that killed him.

She reached up and smacked the dead man across the jaw. It laughed at her and bent her back farther over the table. She swung again and it grabbed her wrist.

"Know what I'm going to do, *puta*?" It shook her arm. "I'm gonna let them eat your hands."

A few of the exes in the circle trembled. They lowered their guns and their teeth clicked a few times. They turned to look at her.

"Gonna let them bite your fingers off one at a time. You ever see a zombie when they get someone fresh? If you're bleeding they'll sit there and suck on it. It's liquid meat to them."

All the teeth chattered. Two dozen exes. None of them moved, but they all stared at her.

"And if you start to get weak," said Peasy, "we'll just burn you. Stop the bleeding that way. Then maybe I'll let them eat your toes. You like that, bitch? Bet you're one of those toe-sucker freaks."

She twisted her arm free and screamed at him. Her hands flailed back on the table looking for a screwdriver or a pry bar. There was nothing. She tried to keep things clean and tidy.

"And when I'm bored with watching you cry," he said, "I'll just divide and conquer. Pull off your legs, your arms, and—"

× × ×

"—then her head. Maybe I'll save her skull, put it up on a mantle or some shit."

"You're with Danielle now," said St. George.

"Oh yeah. These idiots put me on guard duty around her armor. You guys pissed off the Army something harsh."

"If you hurt her," said the hero, "I'll crush your skull."

It grinned at him. "I got a hundred thousand skulls, hero. And a billion more waiting for me to move in."

"There's nowhere you'll be safe."

"Well, good for me I've been nowhere for months now," cackled the ex. "I'm the new zombie virus, dragon man. Now, you got any last words before . . . BITCH!"

× × ×

"You got any last words before—"

Her fingers closed on the laptop and she swung it over her head. The cables caught, just for a second, but then the USB connectors popped free and she brought the metal and plastic case down on the dead man's skull. The corner gouged open the flesh from the middle of his forehead across his brow ridge and forced his eye shut.

"BITCH!"

She didn't wait to see how much damage she'd done. She let the computer drop, dove under his arms, and skittered away across the floor.

He growled and all the teeth in the room stopped chattering. The exes turned as one and tracked her movement across the floor. Their arms raised in perfect sync and pointed at her. Peasy turned and snarled. His face was covered with dark, clumpy blood. He took a step, and the exes stepped forward with him.

Danielle had the M16.

She rolled over and fired. He wasn't even six feet away, bending down to grab her. The first two rounds caught him in the chest. The third in the Adam's apple. The last one punched through his nose and out the back of his skull. His face sagged and the ex collapsed in a pile.

"Don't work like that anymore," said another one of the exes. This one was a woman. Its hair was shaved short and there was a ragged bite mark on its left forearm. It sneered at her from the circle of dead soldiers. "Don't you get it, big girl? I'm the big one now. Way too big for you to kill."

She fired again. The first shot was wild, and she forced herself to take a breath and aim down the rifle's simple sights. The second round punched the talking ex in the shoulder. The third blew out its left eye and part of its cheek. It dropped to the ground.

"I'm not just one guy anymore," said another ex. A thin black man with a skull tattoo on his bare arms. "I'm all the zombies in the world."

She fired again and a black crease pulled open along the side of the ex's skull, just above the Nest. There was a clang, she adjusted, and realized the rifle hadn't chambered a new round. It was empty.

"Eight shots," he said. "They don't trust the exes with more'n that."

Danielle grabbed the hot barrel like a baseball bat and leaped up at the ex. She swung, connected, and got a grand slam. The ex fell to the ground, its skull caved in.

"You know what, though?" said another ex. "'Peasy' don't do it for me anymore. I need something—"

× × ×

"—bigger. A good name for death incarnate."

"You talking to me now?" asked St. George.

"A little out of practice," said the dead man on the stretcher. "But it's like riding a bike, y'know?"

"Good to know you're still having trouble focusing," said St. George. "It's always nice when you can beat the bad guy the same way twice in a row."

"You a church man, Dragon? My mama was, bless her soul. Made me go to church, do confession, all that. Didn't see the point, but I did it to make her happy."

"Yeah, you're a model citizen."

"You remember the story of Jesus and the pigs? That's how I always remembered it. There's a guy who's all possessed and shit, and Jesus took the demons out and they filled up a whole herd of pigs. Hundreds of them. Remember that one?"

"Yeah," said St. George. "The story of Legion."

"Legion." The ex smiled and its legs twitched beneath the gurney's straps. Left, right, left. It took the hero a moment before he realized the exes were—

× × ×

—walking toward her. They marched in lockstep like soldiers. Like Nazis in old newsreels, with their rifles across their bodies.

Danielle ran toward the door. She couldn't remember if it locked on this side or not. If it didn't open they were going to reach her before she could remember the code.

She reached for the handle and the door opened. Sunlight poured in for an instant. A figure blocked the sun, a dark shadow her eyes couldn't make out.

"On your knees," shouted the figure. "On your knees, put your hands on your head."

Another soldier moved in behind the first, and a third.

"Shoot them," Danielle shouted. "He's controlling all of them. You've got to—"

They slammed her to her knees and yanked her hands up. Way too strong for her to resist. She glanced back in a panic.

The exes stood like statues. Their weapons were up, just

as they were when she'd entered. They were back in a circle. Back on guard duty as if nothing had happened. A few gaps stood out in the formation where she'd put down the talkers.

The light from the door vanished as Freedom stepped into the workshop. "Sweep the place," he said. "Top to bottom. Make sure he isn't here, too."

Two of the soldiers moved off into the workshop, looking up into the rafters and under the tables. They passed the circle and the zombies took a clumsy step forward. One of the soldiers raised a fist and pointed.

"Stand down, soldiers," barked Freedom.

The exes lowered their weapons to their sides. Some dropped their rifles altogether. They swayed for a moment and grew still again.

"Listen to me," said Danielle. "The exes are being controlled by someone else. The superhuman we told you about, Peasy, he's—"

"Dr. Morris, I'm taking you into custody for possible involvement in the assault on Colonel Russell Shelly," said Freedom. "The MPs will be here shortly to place you under arrest and read your rights as they stand under the military code of conduct."

"Shelly was attacked?" said Danielle. "How? Is he okay?"

"*Colonel* Shelly was beaten by your associate, Stealth, almost two hours ago in an attempt to force the release of you and the Cerberus battlesuit."

She shook her head. "No way."

"We have a witness who found her standing over him."

One of the super-soldiers walked over and examined the bodies on the floor. "Damn it," said Kennedy. "She took out three of them. Sorensen's going to be pissed."

"Screw him," said Truman. "I just don't want to go catch more for him."

"Look, that's not the real problem," said the redhead. "I'm telling you, those things are not under your control."

"Building is clear, sir," called one of the soldiers. He walked back across the workshop and cut through the circle of exes. He gave one a casual whap on the back of the head, and it swayed back and forth for a moment.

"Does it look like she was able to sabotage the suit?"

Truman picked the laptop up off the floor and studied it. "Nothing visible, sir. Looks clean. Probably want to check the software before they test it, though."

"I know how this works," Danielle said. "You've got to have some sort of protocol in case the Nests fail. Just put it into effect so you'll be ready."

"The ex-soldiers have been operational without a single failure for six months now," said Kennedy. "What makes you think they're all going to stop working now?"

"I didn't say they're going to stop working," snapped Danielle. "I'm trying to tell you they've never worked. They're not working now. There's been someone else controlling them all this time."

"That's your answer to all this?" said Freedom. "There's been a supervillain here at Krypton all this time and no one's noticed?"

She looked back as they dragged her outside. One of the exes winked at her.

× × ×

"Ahhh," said the ex. "Too bad."

St. George punched through the zombie's head and the

gurney beneath it, twisting steel tubes out of the way. Dark blood and brains poured out of the ruined skull through the hole and splattered on the ground."

"Fugg yuu, yuu dumm fugg raggen maahh," another ex growled around its bit.

The hero snapped the leather band and yanked the dowel out, taking a few teeth with it. "Hope that stung," he said. "What'd you do to her?"

"Nothing," spat the ex. "She got nabbed by the man. Stealth beat up the colonel, huh?"

"What are you talking about?"

"Sounds like someone can't keep his bitches in line," laughed the dead man.

St. George turned to Sorensen. "Are you going to help me? I need to know whose side you're on."

The older man nodded. "I'll help," he sighed.

"Doc," said the ex, "you know the deal. You help them, I don't tell you where your kid is."

Sorensen looked at the dead man. "You've never looked for her." He hooked his glasses back over his ears. "Just like Shelly. None of you even looked. You all just think I'm mad."

St. George brought his fist down and shattered the ex's skull. A few steps took him to the next gurney and he moved down the line. When he'd killed the other three exes he grabbed a bright blue towel and wiped the gore from his knuckles. "Are there any more of them in here?"

The doctor shook his head. "Those were the only exes in this section of the base, as far as I know."

"Yeah," said St. George, "that's the bit that worries me. How far is it to where you're keeping Zzzap?"

Twenty-Four
NOW

THE EX PUSHED open the workshop door and looked outside. There were a few soldiers off in the distance, but none close enough to recognize it for what it was. He'd chosen the body because it was less decayed than most of the ex-soldiers, and it had the most complete uniform.

It looked back over its shoulder and had the dead soldiers around the armor adjust their feet. After a bit of shuffling, it was hard to tell one of them had walked away. By the time anyone noticed, it'd be too late.

The ex tugged his headgear down to shade his eyes, stuck his hands in his pants pockets, and tried to whistle as he crossed the road. It took too much effort, so he gave up after a few steps. A soldier at the end of the block turned his way, and he pulled out a hand and gave a quick, casual salute. The soldier gave an acknowledging salute and turned back to his duties.

Just like that, he was across the street. A zombie walking around in broad daylight. He stepped into the shrinking shade of the Tomb.

The main door was still crimped where Cerberus had forced it open the other day, but they'd beaten it back into shape enough for it to lock shut. They were idiots. Locking the door so he couldn't get out, but they'd typed in the codes right in front of him dozens of times. He knew half the codes and passwords for the whole base.

Stiff fingers tapped the keys. He opened the access door. Inside, he saw himself through one hundred and fifty sets of eyes. A company's worth of dead soldiers grinned back at him.

He'd wanted to wait a little longer. Shelly and Sorensen had planned to process another three hundred ex-soldiers in the next few months, but who knew if that would happen now. His hopes of getting a few of the super-soldiers infected were fading fast. The damned heroes were messing things up again.

He held out his hand and one of the exes gave him the wadded-up paper he'd hidden in its pocket. He crammed it into the door frame so the lock couldn't engage. They tried the door from both sides, and then he walked down the street to set more of himself free.

× × ×

The red light flashed and the door cycled. Dr. Sorensen entered the reactor observation room.

"Good afternoon, sir," said one of the soldiers. He was a twentysomething man with the name KING sewn on his jacket. Not one of the super-soldiers. "We weren't expecting you until later today."

The doctor cleared his throat and brushed at his shirt front. "I decided to shift my schedule around, Sergeant King."

"Specialist, sir."

"Yes, of course." The doctor shuffled into the room and picked up one of the clipboards. "Any problems?"

"Negative, sir," said the other man. There was a touch of silver at his temples and HARDY over his heart. "Been pretty quiet for the most part. The prisoner got a little agitated a few times, but no problems."

"He's not a prisoner," said Sorensen. "He's a guest."

"Of course. Sorry, sir."

"Agitated how?"

Hardy got up to stand next to Sorensen and they stared at Zzzap through the window. "The guest has been in his energy form the whole time," said the soldier. "He examined most of the cell. Threw a few more of those lightning bolts. One of them burned out the southern camera and microphone. We offered him lunch about an hour ago but he refused."

"Said he didn't like the taste of our sedatives," added King.

"Has he . . ." Sorensen paused to tap his fingers against his thumb. "Did he eat anything yesterday?"

"No, sir," said Hardy. "He also . . ."

Sorensen flipped the page on the clipboard. "Yes?"

The two soldiers exchanged quick looks. "He's talking to himself, sir," said King.

"What do you mean?"

Hardy looked at the glowing wraith through the window. "If we stayed at our stations for a while, sir, two or three hours, I think he'd forget we were in here. And he'd start talking."

"Talking about what?"

The soldier shrugged. "About the fact he's stuck in the cell. Things he should've done. Things he could try."

"One bit about not being able to touch anything," added King. "It's all on the tapes."

"So he's thinking out loud," said the doctor. "Not so unusual, is it?"

"It isn't like that, sir," said Hardy. "His phrasing and tone are very distinct. It's like we're hearing half a conversation he's having with someone else."

"Are you sure he isn't transmitting to someone?"

"We've left the microphone off in here as ordered, sir. He's had no contact with us, and the Faraday cage is blocking all signals in or out. We've even done a few radio checks to be sure."

King turned his head to gesture at the gauges and the door burst off its hinges. Sorensen stumbled away and covered his ears as it clanged on the floor. Hardy and King drew their sidearms.

"Sorry, doctor," said St. George. He tossed a piece of smoking circuitry the size of a cereal box on the floor. "You're taking too long and we don't have the time."

"Sir," shouted King. "Get on your knees and place your hands behind your head."

"If you start shooting," the hero said, "odds are someone's going to get hurt by a ricochet. And it won't be me. So just put your weapons down." A few streamers of smoke trailed from his nostrils for emphasis.

The soldiers didn't budge.

"Fine," said St. George. "Doctor, get behind me."

The soldiers were tensing when the shadows in the room shifted. *I thought I saw you in here*, said Zzzap. He slid the rest of the way through the observation window. *About frakking time.*

King switched his aim to cover Zzzap. The wraith brushed the pistol with a gleaming fingertip and the weapon's muzzle flared white hot. *I wouldn't fire that,* he warned. *Probably blow up in your face.*

St. George held his hand out for the other pistol. Hardy resisted for a moment, then surrendered the weapon. The hero took it in both hands, folded it in half, and tossed it back to the soldier.

So, what've I missed?

"Shelly's dead. Peasy's not. He's controlling all the exes on the base. Probably all the ones within a few miles if he's still got the same range."

There are exes on the base? said the wraith. *Really? I didn't see any.*

× × ×

They pushed Danielle down the hall. Her foot slipped, she couldn't shift her weight quick enough, and she stumbled against the wall. She'd studied kinesiology enough to know just how much being handcuffed behind the back could mess up someone's balance. She would've been fine with leaving that as textbook knowledge.

"Look," she said, "if you're going to lock me up at least listen to me first."

The MP jerked her back to her feet and propelled her forward. There were three of them. Two kept her at gunpoint and gave pushes. She recognized the one in the lead as Furber, the lieutenant who'd taken Stealth's pistols. The civility had dropped a lot since then.

"The Nest units don't work," Danielle said. "Every one of

these things is smart and they're your enemy. You're in serious trouble. We've fought this guy before and he's a murdering psychopath."

They came to a metal door and a fourth soldier entered a code. The cell slid open an inch with the clack of magnetic locks disengaging. One of the MPs twisted her arms to release the cuffs.

"You've got protocols. Follow them. Now!"

They pushed the redhead through the door of the cell and pulled it shut behind her with a clang. One of the soldiers hit the lock button and the magnets kicked back in.

Her muffled voice came though the door. "Don't I get a phone call or something?"

"Jesus," muttered one of them, holstering his pistol. "Why can't she be quiet like the other one?"

The MP across from him chuckled. "Why can't she be hot like the other one?"

"We're going to have to cut the other one out of that outfit of hers," said Furber.

"Yeah, no shit."

The lieutenant shook his head. "No, seriously." He pointed down the hall toward Stealth's cell. "We tried to strip her after they brought her in 'cause there're so many damned knives and tools in that harness of hers. We could get the belts and holsters and all the gear off her, but if there're any zippers or anything in that outfit, we couldn't find 'em. I think she might actually be sewn into it. We couldn't even get the mask and gloves off."

"Goddamn," said one of the others. "I don't know if that's hot or fucked up."

"Little of both," said another soldier with a grin.

Furber gave a sage nod.

One of the MPs swaggered two doors down the hall. "That suit of hers is so damned tight, bet you can see them tittays all nice now without the straps and shit in the way." He slid the viewing slot open and peered into the bright cell. "Shit," he muttered. He glanced at the armored door on either side. "Which one's she in again?"

"She's in five," said Furber.

"Nah, five's empty. Check the roster again."

A moment passed. Then all four men pulled their weapons.

Furber shoved the letch out of the way and peered into the cell. It was a gray concrete room with a steel cot, a steel toilet, and a pair of fluorescent tubes ten feet up behind a wire cage bolted to the ceiling. The tubes washed out everything in the cell and made it look pale.

It was empty.

The cot was placed to make hiding beneath it impossible, and the sheets were still wrapped around the thin mattress without a wrinkle on them. The toilet wasn't large enough to hide behind and was bolted in the corner, anyway. The cell wasn't much wider than the door, but he craned his neck to make sure no one was pressed into the small space on either side.

"Shit," he said. "Fuck, fuck, fuck, shit."

"Call it, Lieutenant," said one of the MPs.

He dropped his voice. "Get ready to open it," he said. "Jake, you're with me. Kenny, Greg, you're out here covering us. You see anything at all, don't hesitate. She was out cold when they brought her in but this bitch can move, believe you me."

"What if she's not in there?" said Kenny, all lecherous thoughts gone from his mind.

"Then we call it in and we all get court-martialed," said Furber.

They nodded and he tapped his code into the keypad. The locks clacked and the door fell open an inch. Four fingers tensed on four triggers.

The lieutenant inched the door open. It rolled back into the frame until it hit the full-open position with a thud. He mouthed a three-count and he and Jake swung into the tiny room.

Nothing.

He gestured for Jake to cover him and crouched by the cot. The flashlight beam swept back and forth beneath the steel frame, highlighting areas he could already see by the light of the tubes.

"Shit," Furber said again. He turned to the men in the hall to have them call in an escape and saw her over Jake's shoulder.

The woman in black was upside-down in the three-foot space above the door. Her back was pressed against the wall and her feet braced against the ceiling. She balanced on the half-inch door frame on her fingertips.

By the time he realized what he was seeing, she was already in motion.

Her legs swung down and struck Jake between the shoulders. She knocked him onto Furber and launched herself into the hall. Her arms wrapped around and under Greg's shoulders as she twisted over him. She rolled down his back, let momentum lift him off his feet, and flipped him into the far wall.

She whirled and her cloak billowed out. She grabbed the edge with a flick of her wrist and it snapped like a whip, catching Kenny across the eyes. He howled and fell back. By the time he blinked the shock away she'd disarmed him and driven strikes into both of his shoulders.

Furber and Jake untangled themselves. She grabbed Kenny by the back of the neck, yanked the nightstick from his belt, and pushed him forward. The two MPs collided and the nightstick spun through the air to knock the lieutenant's pistol from his hand. He threw himself at her, but she ducked both of his punches and batted his grab away. Furber felt the palm of her hand as it touched his jaw and knew the blow was going to knock him out cold.

She spun from the unconscious lieutenant and brought her heel up to Jake's temple. He slammed into the wall, his duty cap flew off, and he dropped. She brought the foot down and snapped a kick to the back of Kenny's head. The blow left him senseless and his face hit the floor.

Stealth retrieved their weapons, standard 9mm Beretta pistols. They would not fit well in her holsters, and she paused to wonder why she had not been more insistent about getting her own weapons back. She flipped one of the nightsticks into a defensive position against her arm.

"Stealth," shouted a muffled voice. "I know that's you out there. Open this damned door."

The nightstick smashed the face of the keypad and her fingers danced through the wires behind it. The door unlocked with a thump. "Good to see you," said Danielle.

"Where is St. George?"

"He's getting Barry. We were going to meet at my workshop." She glanced at the MPs. "Did you kill any of them?"

"Of course not," said Stealth. "They are still law enforcement officers." She handed two of the pistols to Danielle. "You will need these."

"You have no idea. You'll never guess what's going on."

Stealth gestured her down the hall. "The Nest units have never worked. Rodney Casares, also known as Peasy, is alive and controlling the exes."

"How do you always know this stuff?"

"You were very loud when they brought you in, Danielle. Did it appear as if any of the officers would heed your warnings?"

"Not a chance," scoffed the redhead as they rounded a corner. "Did you attack Shelly?"

Stealth guided them past the elevator toward a stairwell. "Colonel Shelly was dead when I found him."

"Dead? Are you sure?"

"Yes," said Stealth. She reached around the corner to grab an MP's wrist. Danielle yelped as the cloaked woman twisted the soldier's arm, slammed the nightstick into his stomach, and dumped him on the floor. She did something fast with her fingers and he was unconscious. "Does St. George know of Peasy's presence?"

Danielle shrugged. "No idea. I don't think so."

Stealth opened the stairwell door and peered out at a hallway. There was no sign of guards or other personnel. "You must keep your rendezvous at the workshop," she told Danielle. "I will try to convince Captain Freedom of the threat Krypton faces."

"I don't think he's going to listen. He's furious about Shelly."

"That may be, but we must try." She gestured them out into the hallway and turned left. "There are over a thousand people here who will be caught off guard and slaughtered when Peasy decides to attack, and it is likely revealing himself to you has forced his hand."

"What if I try speaking to John instead? He's not part of the military. He might have a cooler head about all this."

"Do you think he will listen to reason?"

"I think so, yeah. He can be a stubborn jerk, but he's not stupid."

Two soldiers stood guard in the lobby. Even with their backs turned, Danielle could tell they were both zombies. She turned to whisper a question, but Stealth was already moving.

The cloaked woman drove the tip of her nightstick into one ex's spine, right at the base of the skull. There was a sound like driftwood breaking and the dead man fell forward. The stick whirled in her hand and smashed back and forth across the other ex-soldier's jaw. She kicked its rifle into the air, dropped below its hands, and swept the legs out from under it. It landed on its back and she drove the rifle barrel through its eye, putting all her weight on it. There was a pop of breaking bone and the M16 sank into the dead man's skull. It went limp.

She turned to Danielle. "Return to your workshop," she said. "Meet with St. George and Zzzap. Apprise them of the situation. I will contact Agent Smith."

"He might be more receptive to me," she said.

"He might," said Stealth, "but you will need the time to get into the Cerberus armor."

× × ×

"Good to go, sir," said the sergeant.

Captain Creed nodded. "All right, then," he said. "This is dry run number one for the Cerberus Battle Armor System. The pilot is First Lieutenant Thomas Gibbs. What's the time?"

"Thirteen-thirty hours, sir."

"Note it. Let's see what this thing can do."

The eight-man build crew climbed down and pulled their stepladders away from the armored figure. The hum of power leveled out just as it started to echo in the workshop. The armored collar snapped tight around the base of the helmet and covered the bolts securing it in place. The titan's eyes lit up.

Creed stepped in front of the battlesuit and looked into the twin lenses. "Any problems with start-up, lieutenant?"

Inside the Cerberus armor, Gibbs checked over the multiple screens and readouts. "Negative, sir," he said. He saw the soldiers around him flinch from the suit's volume and searched until he found the control. "Seems like everything's up and running."

Gibbs took a cautious step. The reactive sensors tingled through his sock, like walking on a foot that was numb with pins and needles. He wiggled his toes and heard the plates on the armor's foot scrape on the tarmac. Another step, this one more confident.

"The simulator was good, sir," he said, "but the real thing's very different."

"Only to be expected."

"Yes, sir. I think I'm overcompensating a lot when I don't need to be."

"Let's hold off on movement for now. Do all systems check out?"

"One moment, please, sir." The lieutenant tried to scroll through menus using the optical system. The simulator had been neat and organized, but after two years of field use Dr.

Morris had personalized the Cerberus system's heads-up desktop to match her own style and needs. To him it was a mess, and he had to search for each icon and file. She'd also re-keyed it to respond to two blinks, not one, which kept throwing him off. He needed to find the system menu that would let him reset everything.

The arms stretched out to either side and the steel fingers flexed. The suit made a few quick fists and shifted its weight from one foot to the other. It looked left, then right, and then down at Creed.

"Good job, Gibbs," said Creed. "Seems like you're getting the hang of it."

"That's not me, sir," said the battlesuit.

"What was that, lieutenant?"

"It's not me sir. The armor just started moving on its own. I'm getting yanked around in here."

There was a flash from outside that was a little too much like lightning in a horror movie. The suit took three big, confident steps. It loomed over the officer and stretched again. Creed was very aware of how big the titan was. "Can it do that?"

"I didn't think so," said Gibbs. "Might be some start-up, shakedown protocol Morris created over the past two years."

"Did you see anything like that when she demonstrated it earlier?"

"No, sir, I did not."

Gibbs tried to scroll through the menus again. The system wasn't responding. The optical system was on but the cursor wasn't registering his eye movements at all. It drifted and bounced across the heads-up desktop.

A laugh echoed over the speakers and tapered off into a low whistle.

"Sorry, sir?"

"What?"

"I thought I heard something, sir."

"No one said anything, lieutenant."

"Nobody just laughed? Kind of a . . . a happy laugh?"

Creed looked up at the lenses and shook his head. "No one out here." He looked around at the build crew and saw several shaking heads and a few shrugs. "Does the suit have enhanced audio?"

"I don't believe so, sir," said Gibbs. "I might be getting some radio bleed over the speakers."

"Not exactly," said a voice. "Christ, man, this suit is so fucking awesome. Should've thought of this months ago."

The lieutenant tried to find the radio in the heads-up display. "Who is that?"

Creed raised an eyebrow. "Lieutenant?"

"An incoming transmission, sir. Voice only. It's making reference to the battlesuit."

"Dude," said the voice, "d'you have any idea what it's been like waiting for someone to put this thing back together again? Like having my arms and legs asleep, just stuck in here since yesterday." Another low whistle echoed over the speaker. "Got to be honest—almost lost it, bro."

There was another flash from outside.

"This is a restricted government channel," snapped Gibbs. He wasn't sure if he'd activated the radio or not, but it seemed like the speaker could hear him. "You will identify yourself immediately." His voice didn't echo through the external speakers. They'd been shut off. He was trapped in the armor with no communication.

"Keep your panties on, G.I. Joe. Just gotta find St. George and Stealth and those guys."

The battlesuit marched past Creed. The titan brought up its arms and tore through the doors like they were paper. It moved straight out into the sunshine and Creed followed behind with a handful of soldiers, shouting for the lieutenant to halt.

It broke into a run and Gibbs felt his arms and legs get pulled back and forth like a puppet. He had a creeping dread the battlesuit would move too far or too fast and leave him trapped inside with a bunch of broken bones. "How are you doing this?" he yelled. "Who the hell are you?"

"I'm called the Driver," said the voice, "and this, *esse*, is the coolest carjacking ever."

Twenty-Five

NOW

IT OCCURS TO ME, said Zzzap, *that someone's probably going to notice us up here.*

The two heroes hovered a few hundred feet above the grid of Krypton, Sorensen tucked safely under St. George's arm. They'd left the old reactor and leaped into the air. Now they were trying to find landmarks.

"No time for subtlety," said St. George. "Who knows how long we've got before Peasy decides to start letting the exes loose on the base."

We should've stuck to the rooftops. All good superheroes use the rooftops.

"There," said Sorensen. "I believe that's her workshop there."

"You believe?" said the hero.

Sorensen tried to shrug. He wasn't dealing well with hanging three hundred feet over the base. "That's Dust Road there with the Tombs on either side," he said, tracing the road with his finger, "and that should be Sand Street. Granted, I've never seen them from this angle before."

They sank toward the ground. No one had shouted.

St. George wasn't sure how he was going to protect Sorensen if someone started shooting. "Looks clear," he said. "This has almost been easy so far."

Too easy?

"Maybe." He looked back and forth over the empty streets. "Shouldn't there be a couple hundred people out looking for us by now?"

"The soldiers are most likely doing training exercises," said Sorensen. "They run laps each morning around the inside perimeter of the fence or spend time on the southern firing range."

I don't hear any gunshots, said Zzzap. *And still, the alarm's been raised. Why aren't they manning the towers and using searchlights and all that?*

"It's broad daylight."

I meant metaphorically. There's been an alert for over half an hour now and I don't see anyone anywhere.

"Here at the center of the base things are quite calm and peaceful. It's why the labs are near the center. I can go whole days without seeing anyone else."

St. George frowned. "Days?"

The doctor shrugged. "I keep to myself," he said. He mopped his face with a handkerchief. "Are you sure Dr. Morris will be at her workshop?"

"Unless they found her she should be there with the armor prepped. Figure maybe another forty or forty-five to get her into it. And then we'll be ready to deal with Peasy or whatever he's calling himself now."

I think it's too late for that, said Zzzap. He pointed a gleaming arm at the ground below them. *You see what I see?*

At the far end of Dust, a stream of ex-soldiers staggered

out of the last Tomb on the left, a few dozen of them so far. They shuffled and spread out like a stain on the base. The sound of chattering teeth vibrated up through the air.

"Crap," said St. George. "Think you can handle all of them?"

If you don't mind this part of the base being annihilated in the process, sure.

The hero sighed and swung over to the nearest rooftop. "Doctor, do you mind if I leave you here for a few minutes? You should be safe."

Sorensen nodded. "I understand. I'll be fine."

The two heroes zipped through the air and St. George dropped into the midst of the zombies near the open door of the Tomb. He grabbed a dead woman by the arm and swung her in a wide circle, knocking down a dozen of them. Another swing cleared a path to the door and left him holding an arm and most of a shoulder.

He tossed the limb away and an ex came through the opening at him. He shoved it back inside, knocking down a handful of bodies behind it. With the other hand he grabbed the huge door and dragged it shut. Inside, dead things clawed at his knuckles and broke their teeth on his fingers.

Once it was closed, he gave it a hard tug and yanked the oversized guide wheels off their track. Just to be safe, he stomped down on the track and twisted his heel. It wrecked his boot, but the door wouldn't open again without a few hours of work from a repair crew.

The light shifted and a hiss of superheated air came from behind him. Zzzap vaporized a baker's dozen of exes, and another handful that had been near the blast charred and crumbled into ash. *Ah, hell,* said Zzzap. *Radio ga-ga. They had*

Danielle and Stealth, but they both escaped a couple of minutes ago. There're already soldiers inside the workshop and Freedom's sending a squad to reinforce them.

"Damn it." St. George crushed a dead man's skull and brought his fist around to shatter another one. He grabbed them by their jackets and threw them over his shoulder.

Good news is it sounds like most everyone's still looking for you. They don't even know I'm out yet. Bad news is it seems like no one's noticed the exes going nuts.

"Can you let them know?"

It'll be pretty obvious I'm not locked up anymore.

St. George twisted the head of one ex-soldier and grabbed another while it dropped. "Do it."

Zzzap floated higher in the air and focused on the signals swarming around him. *Done. And they all just went very quiet.*

The other hero tossed a few more exes into the rough pile he'd made. "If they know you're out," he said, "they know we can hear anything they say." He threw one last ex-soldier. "I think that's all of them. You want to torch these?"

The wraith nodded and held out his hands. The shadows leaped away for a moment and the score of zombies were dust. *Whoa,* he said. *That took a lot out of me.*

"You okay?"

Yeah. Just haven't eaten anything in a day or so.

"What?" St. George shot a glance at Sorensen on the nearby rooftop. "Do you need to get away?"

I'll be okay.

"You sure?"

I'll be okay, he repeated. He nodded at one of the other Tombs. *Next building's empty. So's the one across the street.*

"Damn it," said St. George. "He's making his move."

They soared back up to Dr. Sorensen and St. George carried him down to ground level. Sorensen glanced around. The window panes were trembling. "Is that artillery?"

Half a block down, the Cerberus battlesuit smashed through the doors of the workshop, twisting the steel slats around itself like paper. St. George yanked Sorensen back and shielded the older man from the shards of metal scattering everywhere.

Once the suit was in the clear it broke into a run. Its armored feet left gouges in the concrete road where they hit. A few moments later it was at the end of the street and racing away.

"Was that Danielle?"

I don't know who's inside, but it isn't her. Zzzap tilted his head after the battlesuit. *Heck, was that even our giant robot? It looked different to me.*

× × ×

Sixty exes shambled across the base in what passed for tight formation. The lieutenant at the front of the line, a thin man with sunglasses and his cap pulled low, gestured them along and they followed. A few of the soldiers walking by on their own duties noticed the dead men, but the Nest had made them almost commonplace.

The lieutenant led them up to Barracks Eight. It was closest to the fence line, and the soldiers living there had earned the nickname "Gatekeepers." A few yards from the door he waved to the specialist on fire patrol. "Cleaning lady's here," joked the lieutenant.

Specialist Gorman looked at the approaching mob of

exes and shuddered even as he saluted. "Good afternoon, sir," he said. "May I ask what's going on?"

The lieutenant had turned back to the ex-soldiers as he covered the last few feet, waving them onward. It struck Gorman he'd never seen anyone guide the exes with gestures before, and he wondered if it was something new the doctor had figured out. Then the officer was in front of him and the exes were at the door.

"I told you," said the dead man in the lieutenant's jacket. "I'm here to clean the place out."

This close Gorman could see the chalk eyes behind the sunglasses. The ex slapped a leathery hand across his mouth even as two or three others pinned his arms and took away his weapons. They carried him through the doors without breaking stride, an actual wave of the dead.

The exes marched into Barracks Eight. Thirty of them marched up the four-story stairwell and split off ten-man groups at each level. The first door to the left on each floor was a small armory where the Gatekeepers kept rifles, side-arms, and ammunition. The exes stomped into each one, grabbed the soldier on duty, and chewed out his throat. On the fourth floor, Corporal Hesh got off one shot, which was muffled by the walls and the press of bodies. Only Specialist Douglas on the second floor managed a scream, but it was over as quick as the gunshot.

If anyone heard the scream, they didn't react.

The others stayed on the ground floor, and half a dozen of those ate Specialist Gorman. The dead lieutenant kept his hand over the soldier's mouth and muffled his screams for the two minutes it took him to die. They left enough of his body to be useful when it got up and grabbed his baffled

partner as she stepped out of the bathroom. The dead lieutenant sank his fingers into her upper lip and held her jaw
shut with the heel of his hand. He glared at the auburn hair
poking out from under her duty cap.

"Fucking redheads," he muttered as the exes tore open
her stomach. "All you bitches are gonna die."

According to the mailboxes in the lobby, Barracks Eight
housed 199 soldiers. At least half of them should be sleeping
until night duties began. The ten exes on the fourth floor
split into two groups of three and one of four. They opened
the first three doors after the armory and stalked in to grab
the off-duty soldiers.

All three rooms were empty. There were dusty beds and
photos covered with cobwebs. The papers on one sunlit desk
were yellow and faded. Some of the exes checked closets and
raised clouds in the air as they batted at the hanging clothes.

The next three rooms were the same. And the next three.
And the last six.

So were all the rooms on the third floor.

The top two floors were deserted. They had been for
months by the look of them. Maybe years.

"What," said the dead lieutenant, "the fuck?"

On the second floor they found a baker's dozen of soldiers
trying to sleep in warm rooms with the blinds drawn against
the brilliant day. They died, groggy and unarmed, before
most of them realized what was going on. In the carnage, the
dead lieutenant forgot the top floors.

× × ×

Smith cranked open the blinds in his office. Freedom was
confident he'd have all the heroes in custody within the hour,

but Smith wasn't so sure. Stealth had already escaped once, and he knew Danielle was a lot cleverer than anyone gave her credit for. She didn't need the battlesuit to be dangerous. Classic mistake, to assume your opponent's helpless because they don't have a weapon.

And he had no idea what they were going to do with St. George. The reinforced cells they'd built in case some of the super-soldiers got out of line wouldn't be enough. Hopefully the hero wouldn't be too resistant to what Smith had to say and they'd all be on the same side again soon.

Smith opened the other set of blinds and the last shadows became distinct shapes.

"Well," he said. He took a breath and collected his thoughts. "This is a surprise."

"It is important that I speak with you," said Stealth. She brushed her cloak back. Without her weapons and harnesses, she was just a shapely outline.

"Okay," he said. He sat down and set his hands on the desk. "Talk."

"Move your hands away from the phone."

He slid his palms over to the desk lamp. "Go ahead."

"Project Krypton is facing an imminent attack from within. The neural stimulator units do not work, and in fact have never worked. The ex-soldiers are being controlled by an individual named Rodney Casares, also known as Peasy."

Smith's brow furrowed. "The superhuman who attacked you last year in Los Angeles," he said. "I thought he was dead."

"His body was destroyed, but it appears his ability to project his consciousness into the undead has allowed him to survive. He is here and he has close to a thousand exes inside your fence line to work with. You must instruct the Army to place the base on high alert and begin the systematic destruction of all ex-soldiers."

Smith's fingers drummed the desktop. "My first instinct," he said, "would be to think you're trying to cover for leaving Colonel Shelly in a hospital bed."

"Colonel Shelly is dead," said Stealth. "Dr. Sorensen has been lying to you."

Smith looked confused for a moment, but then his practiced smile appeared. "Go on, please," he said.

"It would appear the doctor is in league with Peasy, and has known all along the Nest units do not work. He also may have manipulated several events here at Krypton to suit his purposes."

The agent shook his head. "Sorensen has trouble manipulating silverware. He's a brilliant man, don't get me wrong, but he's not pulling any strings behind the curtain." He tilted his head. "That's a mixed metaphor, isn't it?"

She heard the sound of metal on metal in the hall and turned. Harrison, Taylor, and Polk burst into the office, rifles up. Taylor and Polk kept her covered while the staff sergeant moved to Smith. "Are you okay, sir?"

"Fine, thank you, sergeant." He stood up and brushed a few wrinkles from his suit. "Excellent response time."

"Thank you, sir."

He looked at Stealth and gestured to the desk. "The panic button's in the base of the lamp, if you were wondering."

"You are making a mistake," she said.

Smith looked back at Harrison. "Can you make sure Captain Freedom knows you caught her? And that she confessed to the attack in front of you?"

"Of course, sir."

"I have done no such thing," said Stealth.

Smith's eyes went up and down her body. "Would you agree we may need to replace all the military police with super-soldiers for now? She seemed to escape with very little effort last time, didn't she?"

Harrison gave a sharp nod. "My squad can take over immediately, sir."

"Then take your prisoner into custody, sergeant."

"Agent Smith—"

"Ma'am, I suggest you say nothing else until you are read your rights," said Harrison.

"I will not—"

Taylor grabbed her upper arm and pressed his Bravo against her head. "Give me an excuse, cocktease," he said. "Just give me one fucking reason to spray your stupid cunt brains across the wall."

They heard the echo of shouting outside and all the eyes in the room flitted to the window. Less than a second. It took Smith and Harrison a few moments to understand what happened next. They saw it all, but their minds needed time to break the blur down into actual movements.

One moment Stealth was a prisoner at gunpoint. They looked back from the window and her free hand was up and Taylor's rifle was aimed over her shoulder at the wall. Her fingers stabbed out and drove four strikes into the soldier's throat one after another. On the last one her hand twisted over to grab the top of his head and yank it down as she leaped up. Her knee smashed into his face and she spun in midair, driving her heel into his chest.

Taylor crashed into Polk and collapsed to the floor. Everyone knew the soldier wouldn't be getting up anytime soon.

Then they realized, in that instant of seeing and understanding, Stealth had crossed the five yards separating the door from the desk.

She landed with one foot on Harrison's rifle and pinned it to the desk. She slammed the edge of her palm into his throat. He staggered back and she grabbed Smith's tie with her other hand. She dragged the smiling man forward.

"Stealth!" he snapped, holding up his hands. "You don't want to hurt me, do you?"

The fist froze inches from his head. It trembled for a moment as she tried to force it through the air.

"Do you?" repeated Smith. He leveled his eyes at her. He didn't blink.

"No," she said. She opened the fist and let her arm drop to her side. "I do not."

Smith brought his arms down. He adjusted his tie and smiled his broad, fake smile. "Good."

Influence Peddler
THEN

THERE'S NO SUCH thing as a smart criminal. It's a complete myth. You know why? Because if there was such a thing, you'd never know about it. Criminals people hear about get caught. Every bank robbery or liquor store holdup, those were all morons. And think about it—someone would have to be a complete idiot to put on an eye-catching costume and draw attention to himself and what he can do.

No, the smart ones would go out of their way not to be seen or heard. They'd hide in plain sight. They'd be that person barely anyone acknowledges is in the room. The real supervillains wear business suits and paisley ties with full Windsor knots.

When we first got the news some of the superheroes were alive in Los Angeles—well, superheroes or Bruce Springsteen, take your pick—I don't think the airman who brought the news even saw me. Freedom didn't. He doesn't register half the civilians he meets. He and Shelly had been talking with a few of the officers for five minutes before the colonel and I locked eyes. It always made him angry when he forgot I was there.

Especially when I made him forget.

I never got noticed, though. The middle child who didn't need much attention. The quiet kid in class who wasn't so quiet the teachers worried about him. Just the average guy with the average name, sitting there in plain sight.

I still don't know if this was something I was born with or something that was done to me. I remember the first time I did it, though. Well, it might not have been the actual first time, but it was when I knew for a fact I'd made someone do something they didn't want to do. Sophomore year of high school. I spent a week working up my nerve to ask Phoebe Bradshaw out on a date and she shot me down in front of her friends before I even got it all out. I tried to save face while they were all giggling and asked if I could get a blowjob instead. I'd heard the line in a movie and it seemed appropriate.

Three minutes later we were in an empty classroom and Phoebe was unzipping my jeans.

It has something to do with questions. It took a while, and I got slapped and punched more than a few times because of it, but I figured that out. The way your brain receives and processes a question is different from how it hears statements or instructions or music or whatever. I can't order people to do things, but I can ask them and they give me the answer I want. And they believe that answer.

The rest of high school went very well for me. I got excellent grades, great recommendations from every teacher, and slept with every cheerleader from every sports team. When I started applying to colleges, I got a full scholarship offer from anywhere that would give me an interview. College was a lot like high school, in pretty much every respect.

It was also where I learned I could push people too far. Or for too long. I mean, I'd figured out the nosebleeds, but college was the Christy incident. She was a minister's daughter who said her prayers each night and was saving herself for marriage. Until she met me, anyway. After a month or so of using her every way I could think of, I decided to have a threesome with her and her roommate. The sex was great, but the next morning Christy was dead and her brains were leaking out on her roommate's pillow. Turns out five weeks of making her mind do a complete moral one-eighty had all piled up, triple-sinful sex was the breaking point, and she had five or six aneurisms all at once. On the plus side, I guess, she never felt any pain.

It is true, by the way. Some schools give students straight A's if their roommate dies. And if I'd known what an animal her roommate would be during grief sex, Christy would've died a few weeks sooner.

Anyway, it was after the Christy incident that I started thinking a lot more about what I did and what I could do with it besides getting good grades and porn star–level sex every weekend. College wasn't going to last forever, after all. I needed a postgraduation plan. Something more than the grad school and grades of my choice. *Summa cum laude* would attract too much attention, but a solid *cum laude* would make my résumé believable without being noteworthy, wherever I ended up.

It's amazing how many people in the world make a living by backstabbing or blackmailing or screwing their way into a position of almost-power, and it's amazing how many people let them. All those clingers and hangers-on who get maximum benefits for minimum effort. The trick is just to find the most powerful people you can and latch on. In that sense, I wasn't doing anything any different than thousands of other people.

And the thing is, most people are easy-to-manipulate idiots anyway. They *want* someone to tell them what to do, no matter how much they say otherwise. Just pay attention to any election and see how often morons get convinced to vote against their own best interests. Heck, they'll cheer and sing as they screw themselves over and make someone else rich and powerful.

The White House was the obvious first choice. Too high profile, though. Plus, at best you've got eight years before someone new comes in and cleans house. These days most politicians are way too partisan to hang on to someone from the last administration's staff, even if they're doing a good job. I could make them keep me, sure, but then I'd stick out like a sore thumb. And the goal, as Monty Python says, is not to be seen.

Then there was a month checking out Fortune 500 businesses. It'd be easy to have some CEO hire me on as a personal consultant or something. Thing is, most of those guys are rich, but their power's limited to one little sphere of influence. Think about it. How many high-end movie studio executives can you name? None, right? They step outside Hollywood and they're just another schmuck in a town car.

So what did that leave me?

I was getting a guy to write a biochem paper for me senior year when I had my epiphany. I was wasting my time trying to find someone with all the right qualifications. I didn't need to find powerful people.

I needed to *make* powerful people.

One college job fair later I was recruited for the Department of Homeland Security, complete with a generous signing bonus. DHS was pretty much custom-made for me. What better place for an influential guy than a whole government agency created to lean over everyone's shoulders?

I got assigned a nice office and spent six months trying to find what I wanted. The Cerberus Battle Armor System seemed like the best place to start. I could get the project green-lit, into production, and then have a whole platoon of armored bodyguards throwing themselves in front of the guy I was already standing behind.

Plus, to be honest, I hadn't nailed a redhead in a while. Dr. Danielle Morris was rude and talked to me like I was an idiot. Her whole superior attitude made it even more fun later when she was on all fours in bed.

Of course, three months after I got myself assigned to the Cerberus project the superheroes showed up. Honest-to-God superheroes flying around, fighting crime, shooting ray beams, and all that stuff.

I admit, there was a week or two when the thought of a costume ran through my mind. I pictured myself squaring off against the Mighty Dragon or the Awesome Ape and getting them under my control. Blockbuster and Cairax both seemed pretty powerful, too. It'd be like collecting action figures or something.

Then I came to my senses. No masks. No capes. Nothing that involved revealing myself. Everybody goes after the guy they see. Nobody goes after the man behind the throne.

Maybe a month later I heard rumors about some Reagan-era program, Project Krypton. It was like the Star Wars defense system—no one expected it to work. It was just something else the Soviets would need to match our research on and drive themselves deeper into bankruptcy doing it. Except Project Krypton worked. They got some serious results before the project was mothballed at the end of the Cold War.

When all those superheroes started showing up, though, it got people thinking. Especially me. They reactivated the program. I got transferred to it.

I mean, the battlesuit is a great idea, but it's a *thing*. Things can break down. They can run out of bullets or batteries. And your power runs out with them. But if the power's something inherent, something the soldier *is*, not something they're wearing, then it can't go away.

Besides, the military was a great place for me. After knowing a few overeager ROTC students in college, I almost didn't need any power to manipulate them. Say *terrorism* and *patriotism* in the right order and half the soldiers I met would shoot their own mother without asking why. The other half . . . well, they'd do it if I asked them.

Granted, when the exes showed up it was a big wrench in my plans. Now nobody else could wash out of the program. I was still weeding through candidates, figuring which ones were easiest to influence without risking their brains bursting. Too many people die of multiple aneurisms and it starts to look suspicious. It starts to draw attention.

So I had to put a bit more thought into getting rid of the troublesome super-soldiers. The ones whose morals or sense of duty were too strong. But it wasn't that hard. After all, they'll do or believe anything I tell them. I can make them think their vehicle's going to run out of gas. Or they should run full-speed into a mob of exes when the smart thing to do is to sit tight. Or that they should put a gun in their mouth.

Now, though, it looks like I might get the best of both worlds. The heroes are alive out in Los Angeles, and they've got a pile of civilians with them. Hell, the Cerberus suit might even still be out there somewhere. At first Shelly was all for letting them stay self-governed and alone, but a quick Q & A changed his mind for him. So now a team's heading out to welcome them back to the United States of America. I'll ask if I can tag along, too. In an advisory position, of course.

After all, what do you get when you're the ultimate power behind the throne?

You get ultimate power.

Twenty-Seven
NOW

THERE WERE, by Specialist MacLeod's guesstimate, about a thousand exes around the Krypton fence. He was good at guesstimates. Not even three years ago he'd worked the produce department at the Albertsons on West 24th, where he'd amazed coworkers with the ability to put a number to avocados on an endcap or jalapenos in a bin. Since he'd signed up, he was still amazing people, but now it was spent brass on the firing range or zombies at the fence.

A thousand was more than usual, but not by a huge amount. A lot of them seemed to be stumbling across the desert these past few days and joining the mobs at the chain-link. The open space muffled their chattering teeth, but not by much.

Still, it was quieter up in a watchtower than down on the ground. Morning run around the perimeter always creeped him out. A lot of the dead things at the fence were wearing the same uniform he was, and he didn't like to see it up close. Heck, the ex-soldiers walking the perimeter were bad enough.

His watch ended at fourteen-hundred. Fifteen more minutes and he was off duty. Pulling a shift alone sucked and he couldn't wait until it was over.

He looked along the north side of the fence and gave a wave to D.B. over at the next tower. He was stuck with a solitary shift, too. The soldier waved back and MacLeod wandered across his tower's small deck to look down at the gates. Three layers of steel pipe and chain-link between him and the dead.

Movement made him glance back into the base. A figure was wobbling across the open space between the gate and the helipad. At first MacLeod thought the back-and-forth gait might mean it was First Sergeant Kennedy, but just as quick he realized it was more of a stagger than a pleasant sway. He lifted his binoculars and confirmed one of the ex-soldiers was heading for the gate.

He picked up the tower's handset and punched in the extension for the zombie handlers. "Short Bus, this is Tower Two," he said. "I think one of your kids is skipping class. You know anything about it?"

"Negative, Tower. Do we have a dead Nest?"

"Don't know. Doesn't seem to be feral, just wandering."

"Copy. Someone probably gave it a vague order and now it's trying to walk to Washington or something. I'll send somebody out to retrieve it."

"Copy that, Short Bus."

Below him the ex had smacked into the inside fence and was still trying to walk through it. The zombie tilted and slid along the chain-link. It swayed as its head and shoulders slapped the fence again and again.

MacLeod sighed and wished he had a cigarette. He looked west and saw more figures dotting the horizon. Damn, there were a lot of exes today. He wondered what made them all wander in the same direction.

Over the chatter of teeth he heard a faint beep. Then two

more. Then a fourth and fifth. He looked back down to the gate.

The lone ex was at the keypad for the gate controls. One finger from each hand stuck out. It stabbed at the keys with quick, precise movements.

It took MacLeod a few seconds to register what he was seeing. By then the red lights had started to flash. He saw movement between the fences as soldiers ran to safety. The exes outside the fence lumbered toward the gate with far too much purpose. Their teeth had stopped chattering. After two years of listening to the click-click-click of enamel he thought nothing could be more unnerving. A hiss filled the air, a sucking noise, and he realized they were breathing. A thousand exes were pulling air into their shriveled lungs.

When they spoke, it was in one voice.

"CALL ME LEGION," roared the exes, "FOR I AM MANY."

Their leathery voices echoed across the desert plains and between the buildings of Krypton and broke down into a dry laughter.

× × ×

"It's a nine-foot-tall, red-white-and-blue robot built like a linebacker," growled St. George. "Where the hell did it go?"

After watching a dozen or so soldiers file out after the battlesuit, Sorensen had asked to be left at the workshop. He seemed fine with being left behind, and said he'd try to contact Freedom or Smith through normal channels. St. George and Zzzap had returned to the skies to hunt down whoever was wearing the Cerberus battle armor.

Invisibility field? said Zzzap.

"I think if Danielle could turn invisible, she would've mentioned it before now."

Yeah, but that isn't Danielle.

Legion's roar echoed up from the base below them. The two heroes looked at each other.

"That's that," said St. George. "We're out of time."

Joy.

"Fly the perimeter, make sure there aren't any gates or openings at risk. Keep an eye out for Stealth, Danielle, or the Cerberus suit. Burn any ex you find."

On it. You?

"I'll take the main gate. I'm willing to bet he goes for the obvious choice again."

Zzzap nodded. *Grab a radio if you can find one. I'll be listening for you.*

They split up. St. George headed south for the base's entrance. He was a few hundred yards away when he saw muzzle flashes and the echo of gunshots reached him. He dropped to the ground and his boots scraped the concrete.

One man, a specialist with MACLEOD on his coat, jabbed at a control panel again and again. The ex lying at his feet was missing most of its skull. The soldier slapped the box, entered the code once more, and threw a panicked glance at the gate.

The three chain-link gates had only opened a few feet, but it was enough. Now they were crammed with bodies as exes pushed and heaved at the gate. At least a dozen blocked the innermost gate from closing, and more clogged each opening past that. The motors made a grinding noise over the chattering of teeth.

A few dozen soldiers—the less-experienced civilian ones, the hero realized—were at the gates. They beat at exes with rifle butts and tried to force them back. A few fired close-range bursts, but most of them were too panicked to aim for the head. Their bullets tore off arms and blew holes in chests. Less than half the ones that went down stayed down, and many of them fell inside the gate.

"Back off," shouted St. George. "Give yourselves room to shoot."

The hero pushed between two soldiers and put his heel through a teenage ex's skull as it crawled along the ground. He grabbed a dead man wearing a Sam's Club vest and threw the zombie up and over the fences. It cleared the first two and hooked a leg on the last one as it descended. It hung there and flailed in slow motion.

All at once the exes stopped chattering. They looked at the hero advancing on the gate and grinned. "DRAGON MAN," they said. "NOT GOING TO SAVE THE DAY THIS TIME, *ESSE*."

St. George brought his fists down like hammers and shattered two skulls, then swung them out to break two more. The dead things pushed at the fence line. Close to fifty of them threw their weight at the innermost gate.

He looked back at the soldiers. "Come on," he shouted. "Help me clear the damned gate! Line up and take your shots."

"THEY'RE TOO SCARED," said the exes. "I BEEN WATCHIN' FOR MONTHS. THESE SOLDIER BOYS ARE GREEN AND YELLOW." The dead things broke into another fit of laughter.

St. George sucked in air and sprayed flames out onto the exes. It burned hair and melted eyes. Some of the brittle clothes and skin caught fire. They flailed and stumbled back for a moment. Then their teeth started chattering again and the dead things shambled forward. He swept his arm in front of him and broke skulls, jaws, and necks.

It made enough of a gap for him to grab one side of the gate and push it two feet more closed. That got him close enough to grab the other section and yank at it. He heaved them together, crushing exes between them, and a smell reached his nose. Just beneath the scent of burned hair and flesh was metallic smoke.

The soldier by the keypad freaked out. "The motors," MacLeod yelled. "They burned out the motors for the gate!"

"I can close it," shouted St. George. "Just take down a few of them!"

Something heavy stomped up behind him, and two massive hands clanged against the pipes lining the gate. Servos hummed and Cerberus pushed the two halves of the gate together. Exes crumpled and burst between the chain-link panels.

"See?" crowed the battlesuit. "Told you I could do good stuff, St. George. You shoulda had more faith in me."

"Cesar?" St. George looked at the huge eyes looming over him. "Is that you?"

"Damn straight," said the titan. It turned and pressed itself against the gate, using its bulk to hold the two sections shut. The exes reached through the chain-link with pale fingers that scrabbled on the armor plates.

"How the hell did you get here?"

"Was easy, man," said the battlesuit. "Knew you guys would need me, 'cause everyone knows you can't trust the government, right?" He slurred the word into *goverrment*. "So I switched into the helicopter while we were loading the suit up back at the Mount. Then I snuck out of the helicopter into a jeep, and then she picked the jeep up with the suit and I was in. It was that easy. Pretty cool, huh?"

"Why didn't you say something?"

The titan shrugged and its shoulders scraped on the chain-link fence. "I was going to once we were all alone, see, but Stealth kept hanging around with Dr. Morris and then she shut the suit off and it made me, like, sedated, y'know?"

"Where the fuck are the Gatekeepers?" bellowed one of the soldiers. He looked at Barracks Eight a hundred yards away. "It's been over ten minutes since the perimeter alarms went off."

One man with sergeant's stripes and the name STEW-ART separated himself from the others. "Yates, Benton," he snapped, "go find out what the hell is taking them so long. The rest of you, take up positions. You know the drill—single shot, pick your targets, now move." He glared at St. George and whispered something into his radio.

"Hey," said the battlesuit. There was a squawk from the speakers and Cesar's next words were a metallic whisper. The armored skull nodded at the sergeant. "I can hear that guy talking in my head. They're coming for us, man. We gotta split."

× × ×

Freedom and his squad burst from the old reactor complex and double-timed it across the base. Their pace would've made Olympic sprinters jealous. It didn't feel fast enough.

"Unbreakable Twenty-two," he snapped into his radio. "This is Unbreakable Six."

"Unbreakable Six, this is Twenty-two," came the reply.

"Twenty-two, this is Six," said Freedom. "Main gate, double-time. Hostiles inside and out."

"Six, this is Twenty-two. Understood. ETA five minutes."

It was going to take him six minutes to get all the way back across the base. Smith had suggested checking on Zzzap, and sure enough the electrical man was out. Sorensen was missing, too. He was supposed to be helping the base medics take care of Shelly. According to the soldiers on guard duty at the old reactor, the doctor had sided with the heroes. He'd led St. George there and helped free the prisoner.

Freedom tried to think of himself as a rational man. It was one of his strengths as an officer. He knew hate was an irrational emotion. Nevertheless, there were things he hated. Cowardice was one. Betrayal was another. And he couldn't think of a worse form of betrayal than treason.

It was one of the few things he had in common with Smith.

The agent had delivered the bad news. Shelly was not doing well. The colonel was hanging on, but his injuries were too great. "He may end up comatose," Smith had said. "Can you believe that?"

Freedom's grip tightened on his Bravo, and he felt the comfortable weight of Lady Liberty on his hip. The super-beings from Los Angeles—he couldn't call them heroes anymore—were going to pay for what they'd done here.

× × ×

St. George leaped thirty feet and landed next to a sign warning all visitors to declare weapons and electronics. He ripped the metal signpost out of the ground. His fingers crumbled the concrete mass at the end like a lump of dried mud. "Cesar, listen to me," he said, soaring back to the fence. "You want to be part of the team, right?"

"Hell yeah!"

"Here's what I need you to do." He bent the post into a large U shape. The sign got in the way, so he broke the rivets and tore it off the post. "I need you to find Danielle," he said. "Dr. Morris. Head back to the workshop. If you find her, your job is to keep her safe. Got it?"

"Got it? What about everyone else?"

He pushed the U through one side of the gate. "If you find soldiers in trouble, help them out. If you find exes, just kill them."

The titan's head tilted. "Kill 'em? All on my own?"

St. George looked up at the armored skull as he worked the signpost around and out the other side of the gate. "While you're in that suit you've got as much armor as a tank and you can rip a Hummer apart with your bare hands. You can handle exes with no problem."

"Right," said the titan. "Okay. Still gettin' used to this. What if I see Zzzap or Stealth?"

"Tell Zzzap to make sure your batteries are good. If he asks, tell him . . ." He tried to think of a good code phrase while he twisted the signpost like an oversized garbage tie. The posts of the gate squealed and bent in until they touched. "Tell him I said you're five by five."

"What the hell does that mean?"

"It's from one of his favorite shows. He made me watch four seasons' worth of it. He'll know what it means."

"Okay. And Stealth?"

For a moment he considered telling Cesar to stay at the gate, but he knew the kid would be more useful searching the base. "Stealth can take care of herself," he said. "Don't worry about her. Find Danielle, find Zzzap, keep as many people safe as you can."

The gate was holding for now. Hopefully they wouldn't need to open it soon. Close to a hundred exes lined the inner fence, with more pouring through the open outer gates. The soldiers had fallen into a good rhythm and bodies were piling up almost as fast as they trickled in.

Almost as fast.

He banged the titan on the shoulder. "Get going."

The battlesuit gave him a thumbs-up and charged away. St. George spotted Stewart. "Sergeant," he yelled, "shouldn't you have reinforcements by now?"

The man gave him an angry glance and continued to direct the soldiers thinning out the dead.

"Hey!" St. George took a small leap and sailed down to the ground in front of the sergeant. "I know I'm not high on the chain of command, but you've got a serious problem here."

"Sir," Stewart barked, "we have things under control. Please step back." He had two inches on the hero and he knew how to use it.

St. George took a breath, counted to five, and let it slip out of his nostrils as smoke. "Have you ever seen exes talk before, sergeant?"

It shook the sergeant for a moment, but he recovered. He didn't answer.

"I have, and nothing good came of it. We lost a lot of people. Friends." He glanced over his shoulder at the base. "I don't want the same thing to happen here."

The sergeant looked at the soldiers. "There should be a hundred men here," he said. He pointed at Barracks Eight. "They're the first responders for a perimeter alarm."

"And they're not responding," nodded St. George. "How long has it been since you sent those guys to investigate? About five minutes?"

"Almost, but we haven't heard anything."

"If they didn't radio you, what would you have heard over all this?" The hero gestured at the soldiers picking targets through the fence. "I'm going to go check it out. Can you spare a radio?"

Stewart opened his mouth, then paused. "I'm supposed to keep you under observation, sir," he said.

St. George gave another nod. "Feel free to observe me heading over to that barracks, then. When Captain Freedom gets here make sure he knows where I am, too."

"Yes, sir."

He shot into the air and covered the hundred yards in seconds. Barracks Eight was silent. St. George was pretty sure someone was supposed to be standing guard duty, too. Billie Carter had called it the anti-fuckery patrol. The barracks across the street also didn't have anyone standing guard.

He stepped inside.

The lobby was covered in blood. There were three dead bodies, two men and a woman. Their throats had been ripped open to kill them fast and quiet. He could see bloody handprints on the woman's uniform where her arms had been held, and a smear across her face where they'd covered her mouth. One man's jaw had been pried open until it snapped.

There was a shuffling noise down the hall. Two ex-soldiers shambled toward him. Each one had a useless Nest device. Their teeth clacked together like a rock drummer banging his sticks before a song.

"Anyone here?" he shouted. "Anyone? Help's here."

Behind the exes the first-floor rooms were all open. He

saw blood pooling in some of the doorways. A limp hand stretched out from one room.

He counted to ten and heard nothing but the click-click-click of teeth echoing through the building. Then a noise came from behind him.

Freedom and a handful of super-soldiers stood in the main entrance. "Sergeant Pierce," said the huge officer, "take your squad and return to the main gate. Provide tactical support and hold position there."

"Sir," said the sergeant with a quick salute. A handful of men vanished back outside.

Freedom took another step forward and raised his Bravo. "St. George, get down on your knees and place your hands on your head."

"Are you serious?" The hero shook his head. He heard the awkward footsteps of the exes in the hall behind him. "All this going on and you want to fight with me?"

A Bravo roared and the zombie behind St. George was headless. Sergeant Kennedy stepped around the hero and twisted the skull of the other one. Two of the other super-soldiers, Franklin and Monroe, moved up on either side to cover her.

And also, St. George noticed, to surround him.

"There's enough to deal with in our current crisis without having rogue elements on the base," said Freedom. "Your partner is in custody. You will surrender now. Sir."

The hero's face hardened. "You've got Stealth? Where?"

"Last chance to surrender, sir." He held the Bravo out at arm's length.

"You know that can't hurt me, right?"

"I do, sir," said Freedom. "We're going to do this one the old-fashioned way."

Kennedy slammed the steel stock of her rifle between the hero's shoulder blades. The shock staggered St. George more than anything. He turned and she cracked him across the jaw with the weapon. His head snapped around and Franklin's fist smacked into his face.

The super-soldiers closed in on the hero.

Twenty-Eight
NOW

ZZZAP HAD CIRCLED the base three times. Exes were stumbling out of the hills and traipsing across miles of sand. The wide-open space made their numbers look like a lot less, but he knew he was seeing hundreds and hundreds of them. In another hour or two, at a guess, there'd be over five thousand of them surrounding the base.

There were tons of them inside, too. He'd incinerated a dozen exes (and the corner of a building) with one blast and swung down to fly straight through a group of about twenty by the base's post exchange. Most of them were left with cauterized stumps on top of their shoulders. The skull of one exploded like a grenade when he hit its cochlear implant. He shook for a minute afterward.

He also couldn't spot Danielle or Stealth anywhere. Stealth didn't surprise him, but not being able to find Danielle was bothersome. It was so rare to see her out of the armor, especially when he was Zzzap, he wasn't sure he even knew what she looked like.

And he was starving. He almost never got hunger pangs in the energy form. It didn't bode well for when he became solid again.

Yeah, I know, he said to no one in particular. The wraith stopped in midair and glared off to the east. *Look, why don't you do something useful and figure out where Danielle is?*

After a moment he let out a buzzing sigh and continued along the fence line. He rounded the northeast corner of the base and saw the Cerberus armor. It was stomping down a back alley between one of the lab buildings and the hospital. Going off its body language, the titan looked lost and annoyed.

It wasn't Danielle inside, that was for sure. The suit might look the same in visible light, but Zzzap saw a handful of things that were wrong. The heat signature was different, the reactive sensors were shimmering in an odd way, and there was a strange electromagnetic haze around every system.

He flitted down just as the battlesuit stepped out into the street that ran alongside the eastern fence. *Hey,* he said, *did you ask anyone before you took that out of your mom's closet?*

The helmet tilted up to look at him. "Bro," it cheered. "Man, am I glad to see you."

I'm sure the feeling would be mutual if I had any idea who you are. So who are you? You're not Army or they wouldn't've been chasing you.

"It's me, Cesar. From the Mount."

Who?

"Cesar Mendoza. I work on the trucks. I used to be one of the Seventeens."

The wraith flew back a few feet and raised his palm. *Not a great character reference to pull out.*

"It's okay, bro. Same team. St. George, he vouches for me."

Got anything to back that up with?

The titan nodded its huge skull. "Yep. He said I was . . .

damn, something from a television show." It reached up a hubcap-sized hand and scratched its head. "He said you guys watched a bunch of seasons together. That's how you'd know I was okay."

What show was it?

"Oh, come on, man. I don't even think he told me the name." The battlesuit snapped its fingers, a noise like a hammer hitting an anvil. "I'm five. He said to tell you I'm five. That sound right?"

It sets the stage for some IQ jokes, but that's about it.

"About time you stopped, you bastard."

Danielle half jogged out of the alley to the west. She gave the Cerberus armor a glare and looked like she might take a swing at Zzzap. "I've been chasing you for fifteen minutes now."

Hey, he said. *I've been looking for you, too.*

"So have I," chimed the battlesuit.

"Here's a tip," she panted at the gleaming wraith. "If you want someone to reach you, try moving at less than three hundred miles an hour."

Ahhh. Didn't think of that. Sorry.

She rested her hands on her knees. "I think I'm going to puke." She glanced up at the titan. "What the hell are you doing in my armor? Are you Army?"

"Nope," said the suit. "I'm the Driver. Maybe St. George told you about me?"

He said he's from the Mount.

"The Mount? How'd he get here?"

"Well, y'see, I switched into the helicopter while we were loading the suit up yesterday morning. Then I managed to—"

He's been babbling a lot. The wraith tilted his head at the armor then back to Danielle. *You want him out?*

"Hey, whoa," said the titan. The metal fingers came up, spread wide. "Same team, bro. Same team!"

"I wouldn't complain about it," she said. "Then we need to figure out how to get me in—"

"Guys, seriously," said the titan, "you don't want to do anything rash, because—"

Check this out, said Zzzap. He pushed his palm forward. There was a crackle of static, a flash of light, and Cesar flew out of the back of the suit. He hit the wall of the lab building and collapsed to the dirt. Cerberus froze up like a statue.

"Whoa!" shouted Danielle. "How the hell did you do that?"

Something I'd been playing with. Opposite charges attract, like charges repel. So all I needed to do was match his frequency and—

"No, I mean how did you throw him out of the suit?"

Oh, said Zzzap. *I thought we were on the same page. He wasn't wearing the suit, he was* in *it, like a virus or static buildup or something.*

She looked at the groggy youth. "So you've been inside the suit all this time?" Her brow furrowed. "You were in the suit while I was *wearing* it?"

"Look," said Cesar, "this is a little weird for all of us, yeah, but—"

"On your knees," bellowed the armored titan. It stomped into an offensive posture and raised its fists. Arcs of electricity raced across its knuckles as the stunners fired up. "On your knees now and put your hands behind your heads!"

"Yeah, tried to tell you," Cesar muttered from the ground. "There's another guy in there."

× × ×

They'd halted the dead at the front gate. And no one else had died. That was the best Sergeant Stewart could say.

Once St. George tied the gate shut with the signpost, they'd been able to get the exes under control. Ammunition was too low to get the upper hand, though. All the soldiers could do was break even, dropping the exes at about the same rate they were reaching the fence line.

Plus the gate was coming apart. Little by little. Under Legion's command, the exes threw their massed weight right at the gap of St. George's knot and the simple gate hinges were squeaking again and again. Once he even caught a few of the dead men and women clawing at one of the lower hinges. They were trying to pry apart the riveted metal.

When they noticed him staring, they'd all winked at him and leered.

Then Staff Sergeant Pierce had shown up with a squad of the Unbreakables to take control, and Stewart breathed a faint sigh of relief. If nothing else, the twin mantles of leadership and responsibility were lessened a bit.

The suppressive fire halted while the super-soldiers reinforced the gate with the sandbags from the machine-gun pits. They tossed the fifty-pound bags the way regular men would throw a beer to one another, even Pierce with his forearm in a splint. The bags piled up against the gate and held it steady. Withered arms clawed at them.

Then the gunfire began again and Pierce's men added their own weapons to the noise. The Bravos cut exes apart with short, vicious bursts. Bodies were falling faster than they were arriving.

Stewart heard the roar of an engine behind him, and his confidence swelled again. The truck from the armory was here with fresh ammunition. In just a few minutes things were going to be under control.

It wasn't a truck. Not even a jeep. It was one of the Guardians from the motor pool, building up speed fast. One soldier was lugging a case of ammo and was sucked under the vehicle's wheels in a windmill of surprised, broken limbs.

The armored car roared past Stewart, aimed straight at St. George's knot. He caught a quick glimpse of the driver. It was a grinning soldier with pale skin and a green box on the side of its head.

× × ×

In the lobby of Barracks Eight, Truman, Franklin, and Monroe took turns pounding on St. George with their rifle stocks. They started on his back, and when he tried to get away Jefferson grabbed his leg and flipped him over. The metal stocks were nicked and dented where they'd hit his bones. He rolled to the side to dodge one of Truman's blows. The rifle cracked the tile floor and the concrete beneath it.

Freedom had punched him once, right at the start. A big roundhouse punch in the jaw. If he'd been a regular man it would've snapped his neck. Since he'd fallen to the ground, Kennedy had kicked him once in the gut, and Monroe twice in the small of his back.

"Stay down, sir," said Freedom. "We do not have direct orders to kill you but I do have that authorization if you do not surrender."

The hero threw a punch from the ground that grazed Monroe's jaw. The man staggered back, then charged in again with an angry glare. He drove his boot into St. George's kidneys and the hero winced. "I'm not going to surrender to a bunch of bullies in uniform."

Truman's rifle hit his shoulder blade and he dropped to the floor again.

"For what it's worth, sir," said Freedom, "I wish it hadn't come to this. I had a lot of respect for you."

"Yeah, you seem really heartbroken." He got the words out just before Kennedy's knuckles connected with the back of his skull.

"I'm just following orders."

"Orders?" Another punch struck his head.

"You're to be detained, and then you and your companions will accompany us to a secure facility."

"You've got something—" He whuffed out a cloud of smoke as someone drove a kick into his stomach. "You've got something else besides Yuma?"

"That we do, sir. The Air Force's Groom Lake facility in Nevada. Agent Smith has decided it would be a safer location."

St. George tried to raise his head and winced again. "And what," he said, "you're just going to load us on a helicopter and fly us there?"

Freedom looked down at him. "That's exactly what's going to happen, sir. Stealth is already in handcuffs and there's a Black Hawk prepping."

"In that case, captain," he said, "for what it's worth, I've been—" He coughed a stream of smoke and fire as another kick connected with his gut.

"What was that, sir?"

He rolled onto his knees and brushed the rifles away with a sweep of his hand. "I said I've been faking it."

They had a moment to look confused.

And then St. George's backhand sent Truman through the far wall of the lobby.

× × ×

"Gibbs," said Danielle, "that's you in there, isn't it? We're not the enemy."

"Dr. Morris," said the battlesuit, "please keep your hands up. Until I get orders otherwise, I am treating the three of you as hostiles."

"On what grounds?"

"Hijacking," said Gibbs. The titan turned its head to Cesar. The young man stood up and dusted himself off. "I'm sure Colonel Shelly and Captain Freedom will be interested to know you brought another superpowered person with you."

We didn't bring him with us, said Zzzap, gliding forward.

"Keep your distance, sir," said the battlesuit. "This weaponry might not be able to hurt you, but I'm sure you don't want any harm to come to your friends."

"Gibbs, come on," snapped the redhead. "You must have seen the exes overrunning the base. You need to be dealing with that problem right now, not us."

"Ummmm," said Cesar, "you all hear that?"

The growl of an approaching engine came from behind the battlesuit. About half a mile down, a Humvee swung out onto Dirt Road. It took the corner so sharp the wide-bodied vehicle almost lifted onto two wheels. It roared along the fence line at close to seventy miles an hour.

In seconds it was close enough for them to see the face behind the wheel. It was a buzz-cut woman with leathery skin.

There was a gash along her forehead down to the Nest unit blinking on her temple. Legion grinned at them from behind her chalky eyes.

It took Danielle another few seconds to put it together, and Cesar dragged her out of the way, back against the lab buildings.

Zzzap summoned his strength, focused, and fired a blast that skimmed the speeding vehicle. It was close enough to ignite the gas tank and melt one of the rear tires, but the Humvee kept moving. The tire made it veer off to the side, and the hood ended up aimed right at the battlesuit.

If Danielle had been in the armor, it would've been no contest. She knew the suit and what it could do. She'd thrown cars, punched through engine blocks, and pulled apart buildings. She could've sidestepped and grabbed the Humvee as it sped by and either hurled it into the air or torn it apart.

Lieutenant Gibbs knew a simulator. He wasn't used to the armor's smooth responses. He'd already forgotten there was over a thousand pounds of battlesuit protecting him from the outside world. He acted out of instinct. A big vehicle was rushing at him. He tried to leap out of the way.

The burning transport hit the Cerberus battlesuit in the hip. The titan spun, crashed into the building a few feet from Danielle and Cesar, and collapsed in the dirt. Part of the wall crumbled, and a chunk of concrete and plaster hit the ground inches from Danielle's sneaker.

The Humvee veered off to the right, carried by its own momentum. Legion spun the wheel and kept the pedal pressed to the floor. They heard him laugh as he rushed by.

The front corner of the vehicle hit the fence and ripped through the first layer of chain-link without slowing down.

It crushed a pair of ex-soldiers wandering between the barricades and broke through the second fence. A section of chain-link twenty feet long tore loose, crumpled, and fell. One of the Humvee's tires ripped open on the stiff wires and exploded, but the vehicle lurched on and struck one of the outer poles by the watch tower. The engine roared, the tires spun in the dirt, and with its dying breath the flaming vehicle pushed the pole over.

The fence sagged on either side and knocked down the exes pressed against it. It sprang back up for a moment, then dropped to the ground with a crash of metal. Close to thirty exes were pinned under it when it fell. Twice as many moved for the opening.

Fucking son of a bitch, said Zzzap.

× × ×

Truman stumbled out of the crater in the wall, tripped over one of the dead soldiers, and crashed to the floor. By the time he hit the tiles, St. George had put down Franklin with a strike to the forehead. The hero glared at Captain Freedom across the lobby. "Did you actually think you could take me in a fist fight? Even all together?"

Kennedy tried to hit him with her rifle stock. He took the weapon away from her and broke it in half. The ammo box fell open and the belt spooled out across the floor. She drove three punches into his jaw and felt her knuckles crack on the last one.

"I mean, do you guys have any clue how far out of my league you are?" He caught Jefferson's punch against his palm and gave the knuckles a sharp twist. They all heard the bones splinter and snap along the arm. The soldier screamed and dropped back even as the hero batted away a kick from Kennedy. "A group of first graders would have a better chance of taking out Mike Tyson. If I didn't need you to monologue about where Stealth—"

Freedom's double-handed blow caught St. George across the cheek. He closed in, slammed some fast punches into the hero's stomach, and then swung his elbow up to catch him in the chin. St George staggered back into the wall. The captain moved forward and swung a backhand that sounded like a gunshot when it connected. He brought the hand back around in a punch that could dent steel.

St. George grabbed the larger man's wrist. The punch stopped dead in the air.

"Okay," said the hero, ribbons of smoke streaming from his nostrils. "That's enough." He straightened up off the wall, still holding the wrist.

Freedom stumbled back. He tried to twist his arm around, a simple break to free his hand and get control back, but the hero's fingers were like stone. The captain twisted his free arm around and threw his weight into an elbow that connected with the middle of St. George's forearm.

The arm was like stone, too.

Jefferson drew his SOCOM pistol left-handed and emptied the magazine at St. George. The rounds thudded and spun off his side and shoulders. The last three slapped his temple. The bullets clattered on the tile floor.

Stone.

Kennedy leaped onto his back. She got a chokehold across his neck and threw her weight onto her arm. He reached up with his free hand and swung her over onto Truman's unconscious form.

Freedom battered at the stone arm and threw a kick into

the hero's stomach. It was like hitting a wall, and he knocked himself off balance. He would've fallen over if not for the iron grip on his wrist. He flailed at St. George's chest for a moment and righted himself.

"I'm used to having to pull my punches with people," said St. George, "so you got in a couple good shots back at the Mount. But don't confuse catching me off guard once with being stronger than me." He moved Freedom's arm back and forth, and the huge officer was dragged back and forth after it.

"I'd never say I'm stronger," said Freedom. "Just smarter."

He made a fist around the demon fang he'd torn off St. George's lapel and slammed it into the hero's arm just behind the wrist.

× × ×

The Humvee had left an opening in the fence line almost forty feet wide. The stumbling dead worked their way over the fallen chain-link and onto the base, their teeth chattering.

"Bro," said Cesar. He rapped his knuckles on the steel forehead of the fallen battlesuit. "You still alive in there?"

The armor shifted and a metallic groan hissed through the speakers.

"Cool. No broken bones or nothing?"

"I . . . I'm good," said Gibbs. "What the hell was that?"

"Dead girl driving a Hummer," Cesar told him. "Look, you sure you're okay?"

"A little dizzy."

Danielle crouched by the helmet and looked for damage.

"Is the suit okay? No problems with monitors or the reactive sensors?"

The battlesuit flailed for a moment as the arms pushed it up to a sitting position. "Power's down to sixty-eight percent, but as far as I can tell past that, all systems read one hundred percent across the board."

"Good," said the redhead. She sighed. "I'm sorry about this, but I think your loyalties are a little too split for you to be of much use right now."

Cesar's face broke into a grin.

She glared at him. "One scratch, one circuit I need to replace, and I own you for life. Clear?"

He wrapped his arms around the armor. The air crackled as he vanished, and a few arcs of electricity danced across the helmet and chestplate. "Crystal, ma'am," said his voice from the speakers. "Cerberus, reporting for duty."

"Let's get one thing clear right now," she said as the armor clomped back to its feet. "You're a kid with a neat power. I'm Cerberus."

× × ×

The fang ripped through St. George's jacket and flesh. Its tip burst through the other side of his arm. Blood splashed out over the sleeve. The hero roared and it came out as a blast of fire that blinded everyone in the lobby. He let go of Freedom's arm and the officer twisted away from the flames.

Freedom looked back and St. George grabbed him by the throat. The fang was still buried in the hero's forearm. It was bleeding, but not enough to be fatal. Just painful as all hell. The arm stretched up and Freedom's feet left the floor.

"We're not going to surrender," grunted Freedom.

"I'm not asking you to," said St. George through gritted teeth. "Say you won if you want. I just don't want to waste any more time fighting. My friends and I want to help."

"One of your friends beat Colonel Shelly to within an inch of his life."

"I don't know what that's all about," said the hero, "but it's not the issue. There's a threat to this base we need to deal with. All of us. No one heads off in any helicopters or anything. You've got the manpower but we've got the experience with this guy. Once that's done, you and me and all our friends can sit down and figure out who did what to who."

Freedom glared at him. Out of the corner of his eye, St. George could see Kennedy struggling to her feet and Jefferson trying to reload his pistol one-handed. Franklin and Truman began to stir.

So were the dead soldiers, he realized.

Noise burst from their earpieces and the hero saw their faces shift. It woke up Franklin and Truman, and they shot glances between Kennedy and Freedom. The captain's jaw was still set, but St. George could see the conflict in his eyes.

"What's going on?"

The soldiers looked to Freedom. "The main gate just fell," he said. "Someone drove a Guardian through it. They're getting in."

St. George nodded at the waking exes and the bloody lobby. "What's it going to be, captain? Help us save everybody, or do you want to keep trying to put handcuffs on me?"

Freedom's shoulders relaxed. Just a little. "What's your plan?"

St. George let his arm drop and opened the fingers around

the officer's throat. He tried not to wince as the muscles around the fang shifted.

"Peasy—Legion, whatever he's calling himself now—he attacks on multiple sides. When he tried to take the Mount, that's how he did it. I'll bet he's going to do the same thing here if he hasn't already."

Freedom and the other soldiers nodded. "Ask and you shall receive," said Kennedy, pressing a finger to her ear. "The same thing happened at Tower Nine. The whole fence line is gone between Nine and Eight." She glanced at St. George. "Sounds like your people are already there. Zzzap and the robot."

"Exes?" asked Freedom.

"About a hundred with as many closing in."

St. George pursed his lips. "Anyone got a radio?"

The teeth of one of the corpses clicked together and Truman's boot lashed out to shatter its skull. The specialist pulled the radio from the headless body's belt and stripped off the headset and mic. He tossed it to St. George. Catching it made the pain in his forearm flare again.

"Zzzap, you out there?"

"Hey, fearless leader," said the radio. "We're in hell. How are things with you?"

"He sounds normal," said Kennedy. "Is that him?"

"It's because you're not hearing him, you're hearing him broadcast his voice." He held up the radio. "What's going on?"

"Our boy Peasy brought down the fence at the northwest corner of the base. We've got a gap about thirty-five, forty feet across."

"So I've heard," said St. George. "Under control?"

"The soldiers and Cerberus—sorry, the Driver—are keeping them at bay so far."

"Copy. Is Danielle with you?"

"Yep."

"Good. I'm going to see if we can get some people there to assist. If you think you can spare a minute, meet me here."

"Gotcha."

The hero shoved the radio into the pocket of his flight jacket. Jefferson tilted his head up from the crude splint Franklin was building around his arm. "How's he know where you are?"

"Because he could see where the signal was coming from," said St. George. He looked at Freedom. "Where's Stealth being held?"

"She's probably still in the brig. Last I heard Smith had all of squad Twenty-one guarding her."

"We need her."

Freedom's jaw locked up again. "She attacked Colonel Shelly."

"Later, captain. Right now she's the smartest, best fighter within about a hundred miles and she needs to be helping us."

They could hear Freedom grinding his teeth but he reached for his radio. "Unbreakable Twenty-one, this is Unbreakable Six."

"Unbreakable Six, this is Unbreakable Twenty-one."

"Twenty-one, this is Six. You are to release the prisoner named Stealth. Escort her to the main gate. We'll meet you there. Be advised this is a combat situation and you are entering a hot zone."

× × ×

Staff Sergeant Harrison furrowed his brow and shot a look to Taylor and Polk. "Six, this is Twenty-one," he said. "Could you repeat, please?"

"Twenty-one, this is Six," said Freedom's voice. "Release the prisoner and escort her to the main gate immediately. Be advised this is a combat situation and you are entering a hot zone."

"Six, this is Twenty-one," said Harrison. "Sir, Mr. Smith was very precise with his orders on the prisoner. He believes she'll be good leverage against the—"

"Twenty-one, this is Six," barked Freedom. "You are not taking orders from *Mr.* Smith, you are taking them from me. Is that clear?"

The super-soldiers shot a few confused looks back and forth. They looked at the cell Stealth was in. Then they looked at the man in the good suit sitting on the desk across from them.

Smith opened his eyes wide, as if something had just occurred to him. "They couldn't be forcing him to say all that, could they?"

Their eyes opened wide, too. "St. George," said Polk, "the Mighty Dragon, he's probably strong enough to force the captain into something."

"That fucker," said Taylor. He wiped another thread of blood from his nose. It was still going from when the bitch kneed him in the face.

"But . . ." Harrison blinked and shook his head. What Smith said made perfect sense, but there was something wrong with it. Something nagging at the back of his mind. "Compromise words," he said. "Why isn't the captain using the compromise codes?"

Taylor frowned. "What's today's word?"

"Chocolate, I think," said Polk.

"Six, this is Twenty-one," Harrison said. "Things that bad, sir? You said this mission was going to be all cake and ice cream, remember?"

"Twenty-one, this is Six. Understood and negative. Release the prisoner and get your legs in gear."

Smith shook his head. "Could they have learned the codes somehow? Or maybe they've got some of his people at gunpoint. He'd lie to keep them safe, wouldn't he?"

"Fuck, yeah he would," said Taylor.

Harrison stared into space and tried to work his brain around something. His own nose was bleeding, and he couldn't remember if Stealth's vicious attack had caused it or not.

Smith looked at him. "Staff Sergeant Harrison?"

He blinked twice. "Yes, sir?"

"I think we need to get the prisoner to the helipad and prepare to leave, don't you?"

"Of course, sir," said Harrison.

Smith shook his head as they moved to Stealth's cell. "She was telling the truth about the zombie supervillain. I did not see that coming."

× × ×

"They've gone silent," said Kennedy.

Freedom's brow wrinkled.

"We'll deal with it," said St. George. He gritted his teeth and pulled out the fang. It was red and slick. More blood splattered out onto the floor. He dropped the fang in his pocket and squeezed his palm over the wound. "I think everyone in this building is dead. Maybe the next building over, too. How much does that hurt you, number-wise?"

Freedom glanced at Kennedy. "If they're all dead," she said, "it's almost a quarter of our troops gone."

"Can you still mount a defense? You must've planned for something like this, right?"

Freedom gave a sharp nod. "It'll be difficult, but not impossible. First sergeant," he said to Kennedy, "Operation Red Sand is in effect."

"Yes, sir."

"Make sure your people understand they're not fighting regular exes," said St. George. "They're fighting Legion. He'll make plans of his own and react to what your people do. Or what they don't do."

Kennedy nodded and began to bark commands into her microphone.

Freedom looked at the hero and gave a quick nod to Franklin. "What else can you tell us about this Legion?"

"We beat him before by splitting his attention. He wasn't experienced with his powers, so fighting on multiple fronts made him lose control and then we just focused on the man himself. It looks like his control may have gotten better, though."

"Great," muttered Franklin. He pushed up St. George's sleeve.

"Stow it, sergeant."

"Yes, sir." He pulled some disinfectant from a pouch and wiped the blood away from the wound. It was a ragged hole the size of a dime. "Shouldn't've pulled that tooth out," he muttered.

"The big problem, though," said St. George, "is the ex-soldiers. Since he's controlling them, he's effectively got a thousand people on the base already. Double agents, guerrillas, saboteurs, whatever you want to call them. He's got a lot of them, but I bet they're all going for simple goals. Even if he's gotten better, he probably won't risk splitting himself onto too many complex fronts."

"Probably?"

The hero shrugged. "He's still just a guy, and not a terribly bright one."

Franklin mashed gauze on the bloody holes and wrapped the arm with white tape.

"Sergeant Monroe," said Freedom, "take the rest of Eleven and clean out this building. We don't want any surprises two or three hours from now. If it's down, make sure it's staying down."

"Sir, yes, sir." He bent down to the other twitching corpse and twisted its head around to face the floor. The body went limp.

"Jefferson, you're with me. We need to secure the armory and make sure the perimeter holds," continued the captain. "It's going to be getting dark in about five hours and this situation needs to be stabilized before then."

Sunlight poured in through the barracks door and blinded them all for a moment. *So,* said Zzzap, *how are things on this side of the giant military deathtrap?*

Freedom and a few of the soldiers glared at him.

"I want you to go with them to the armory," said St. George. "Stay there and make sure they get everything they need."

And then?

"We get the weapons, stop the exes, and then we go after Smith."

Smith?

"He's got Stealth. He's trying to get away to a more secure base. She's going to be his hostage to keep us all in line."

Smith took her *as a hostage?* said Zzzap. *Wow, talk about making a poor—*

He froze and hung in the air for a moment, like a statue of light.

"Barry?"

I just want to be clear on this, said Zzzap. *We need to get guns— lots of guns—and then rescue our ultra-calm leader who's been captured by Agent Smith?*

St. George sighed.

Oh, this is so *going to rock!*

Twenty-Nine
NOW

IN THE DISTANCE they could see the opening in the fence and the flash of weapons. The clatter of dead teeth echoed in the air, closer than it had been.

"I'll help at the gate," said St. George. "You get to the armory and do what you need to do."

"We'll join you there in ten minutes," said Freedom. "Tell Staff Sergeant Pierce you've got my approval. If he asks, say you're five by five. He'll know what it means."

Zzzap let out a buzzing laugh. St. George tried not to grin. "Got it."

Freedom gave him a quick nod and sprinted off with Kennedy and Jefferson. The three of them were damned fast, the hero had to admit, even the one with the broken arm. It took them seconds to cover a hundred yards and vanish around a corner.

Watch your back, said Zzzap. *Buffy references aside, I still don't trust any of these guys.*

"It's not like your movies."

Yeah, it's going a lot worse so far. He flitted away after the soldiers.

St. George leaped into the air and came down in a cluster of exes stumbling through the middle fence. A sweep of his arms sent half of them sprawling and he snapped out a backhand that collapsed the skull of one more. Dozens of them shifted their awkward march, heading for him instead of into the base.

He grabbed a dead woman in tiger-striped camos and swung her into the crowd like a flail, battering one body against several. Her boots crushed a handful of chattering skulls before the shoulder he was holding pulled apart. He let the body's momentum carry it off into the crowd. It knocked down another half-dozen exes as it soared away.

Off to his left, the head of an ex burst with the whine of a high-velocity round. The gunfire trailed off, and he heard shouts from behind him. He glanced over his shoulder and saw the soldiers looking at him.

"Don't stop firing," he shouted. "Don't worry about me, just keep firing!"

An ex latched on to his wrist and tried to bury its teeth in his bicep. He flexed and cracked its jaw, then swung his elbow up to send it sprawling. Another one fell onto his back and he shrugged it off.

The snap and crack of bullets rose in the air around him again, matching the clack of teeth. One ex in a plaid shirt reached out for him and dropped when the top of its head vanished. The teeth of a dead man with a thick mustache snapped twice and then splintered away as a round tore through its mouth and out the top of its spine. A woman in a waitress uniform collapsed to the ground after the back of her head burst in a baseball-sized exit wound.

St. George spread his arms, caught a half-dozen exes, and marched away from the soldiers. The half dozen caught four more, and another six got tangled in with those ten. By the time he reached the outer fence he was pushing close to forty of them. They flailed at his arms and neck and shoulders. Their fingers ran through his hair and over his scalp. One tried to snap its teeth on his cheek and pulled three of its incisors loose.

Just outside the fence line was a tall armored vehicle with a boatlike hull. It had part of the chain-link gate twisted beneath it. He got outside the boundary and threw the exes at the Guardian. Some of them crashed into the vehicle, others just stumbled back before they fell to the ground. More of the walking dead staggered around the vehicle and tripped over their fallen comrades.

The hero kicked a few bodies out of the way and managed to drag the outer gate about two-thirds shut. The chain drive on it snarled the whole way. He thought about forcing it farther but didn't want to risk tearing the chain-link panel. He leaped back and did the same with the middle gate, but this one only went halfway.

"Guess we're lucky those were already open," said Pierce from behind him, "or that Guardian would've torn down all of them." The sergeant had led the super-soldiers into the fence-line area while the rest of the men covered them. They moved through the bodies and paused at each one to ensure they were down for good.

St. George punched an ex making its way through the opening and it flew back into a steel post. "If this is the best luck we're going to have, we're in real trouble."

They fell back into the base as the dead resumed their relentless march forward. The sergeant nodded at the exes. "Can't you burn them all?"

"If we're willing to wait the two or three hours it'll take

them to burn, sure. We need something to block this opening with, like a truck or something big."

"Sergeant Stewart," shouted Pierce. "Get hold of the motor pool and get us a truck or the dragon wagon over here pronto. Don't worry about a full tank, just move it."

St. George grabbed a dead man in a Marine uniform and hurled him underhand into the crowd like a bowling ball. "How long will it take them to get something here?"

"Three or four minutes if someone's there," said Pierce. "Maybe ten or fifteen if we send a runner. That's if I send one of mine."

"I'd do it if I were you."

The staff sergeant nodded. "Guess until then it's still a shooting gallery," he said. He hefted his Bravo and hooked a new box of ammo onto it.

× × ×

Danielle crouched behind the soldiers with her back against the wall. An undermanned squad had shown up and made a passable fire line, especially with the lone men in either tower picking off exes with sniper shots. She had the pistols Stealth had given her, but she couldn't stretch her arm out to aim them.

There was so much open space around her. Open space and undead.

At the fence gap, the Driver did a fine job dealing with the exes one on one. She had to admit, the battlesuit moved in a fluid, natural way she didn't even think was possible. It crushed skulls and batted exes away with a casual grace. It looked alive.

Just as the thought crossed her mind, the armored figure turned and stomped back to the fire line. Two of the soldiers dove out of the way to avoid being trampled. It stopped in front of her like an oversized puppy.

"Ummmm, hey," said the titan. "Big crowd of zombies coming. You got any tips?"

It pointed back at the hole in the fence. Fifty or sixty yards away, a thick mob of exes shambled forward. There were at least two hundred of them, with dozens of stragglers all around the main cluster. The soldiers saw the mob, too, and a palpable wave of unease washed over the line.

"Use the stunners," said Danielle. "That'll give these guys more time to make their shots."

The armored skull tilted to the side. "The what?"

"The stunners. The Taser fields built into the fists," she said. "They'll put an ex down for a few seconds, long enough to give us an advantage."

The dry rasp of wind filled the air as the exes sucked in a breath. "COMING TO GET YOU, BITCH," they shouted. Dozens of arms pointed across the open space at Danielle. "GONNA STICK YOUR HEAD ON A FLAGPOLE AND CARRY IT EVERYWHERE!"

The titan looked over its shoulder and back at her. "That's him, isn't it? Peasy's still alive."

"Yeah," she said. There was nothing between her and the zombies. She tried to sound calm. "Looks like he is."

The battlesuit froze for a moment. "Okay, stunners," it said. "How do I do that?"

"I thought you were controlling the suit?"

"Yeah, but that doesn't mean I know everything it does. It's like getting a new car, y'know? I know how to do the basics, but none of the special features."

"Great," muttered Danielle. "Okay, let me talk you through it . . ."

✕ ✕ ✕

Zzzap hung over the door to the armory as Freedom's group caught up to him. At first glance it looked like any other building. With his own unique eyesight, Zzzap had seen the metal door and the double-thick concrete.

Behind them, three clusters of ex-soldiers came together to form a decent-sized mob. They staggered forward, their teeth snapping together again and again with a sound like wooden hail. Some of them still had the straps of their rifles tangled in their arms.

Awwwww, you found some friends, said the wraith. *Good for you.*

Kennedy was in the lead. She ran to the door and yanked open a panel that covered the keypad. Jefferson hit the wall next to her and twisted up his face as his arm slapped the concrete. Freedom let off two more bursts from his Bravo before it ran empty. He slung the rifle over his shoulder and pulled Lady Liberty from her holster. The modified shotgun bellowed and a trio of heads vanished in a spray of blood and gore.

"A little help would be appreciated," the captain called up to the glowing figure. Lady Liberty roared again and the closest ex came apart into half a dozen pieces.

Kennedy tapped out a code. The keypad flashed red and she swore.

The wraith sighed and floated forward, putting himself between the soldiers and the undead. *Watch your eyes.* He held out his palms, took a deep mental breath, and focused.

There was a blast of light, a howl of superheated air, and the exes vanished in a cloud of fire and ash. So did a parked jeep, a large swath of pavement, and the gravel beneath it.

Zzzap slumped in the air for a moment while the desert breeze scattered the new dust. "Are you doing okay, sir?" Jefferson squinted at the gleaming figure. He could almost see through it at points. "You look . . . pale."

Don't give me that "sir" crap, said the wraith. *A few hours ago you people were happy having me locked up in a box.*

"I didn't know anything about that," said Freedom. He pushed past Kennedy and tapped the code into the keypad.

Sure you didn't.

"I didn't, and if I had I wouldn't've stood for it. The president has been very firm on the treatment of prison—"

Yeah, whatever. You're a real American hero. Go get your guns. He shook his head as the door locks clanged open. Then he snapped, *I'm fine. Don't you start in on me, too.*

Sergeant Kennedy glanced up as she dragged the door open. "Sorry, sir?"

Nothing. Go get your guns. I'll watch the door.

The three of them slipped into the armory. "Jefferson," said the captain, "you're not combat fit with that arm. Get a real splint from the first-aid kit and then get as much ammunition as you can into that M35 outside. Once you get all of it, start on weapons."

"Copy that, sir."

Freedom grabbed a fresh ammo box for the Bravo and slung a spare on his harness. The Mk 19 grenade launcher caught his eye for a moment but he shook his head. He looked around and also found a trio of drums for Lady Liberty already mounted on a harness.

Across from him Kennedy finished wrapping the Velcro

splint on Jefferson's arm. She reloaded her Bravo with a fresh box and filled a bag with a dozen more. Two boxes of 9mm slid into her thigh pockets.

The captain was heading out when he saw the zip-tied plastic container in the holding cage. He snapped the ties with his fingers, pulled out the twin Glocks and their magazines, and stuffed them into his thigh pockets.

Kennedy watched him stash the pistols. "What are those for, sir?"

He twisted his lip. "If we need a peace offering."

× × ×

Harrison was on point as they moved through one of the underground passages between Krypton's key buildings. It was hot as hell, but he knew it was safer than being upstairs where everything was falling apart. The thought crossed his mind and he felt a twinge of uneasiness. He'd felt it before a few times in his life. It was when he knew he was doing something wrong.

They had Stealth in handcuffs. After seeing her move in Smith's office, he'd used two sets of cuffs. One was latched on her wrists, the other pinched her arms together a few inches above the first set. They'd shackled her legs, too. Polk and Taylor kept her at gunpoint as they marched down the tunnel. The chains rustled and chimed as she shuffled along the hallway.

Harrison turned to Smith. The agent walked between him and Stealth. He didn't seem scared of her at all. "Sir," said Harrison, "may I have a word?"

Smith glanced at his watch. "You do know we're running a tight schedule, don't you, sergeant?"

"Yes, sir. Of course, sir. It's just . . ." Static roared in his head and he had to blink it away. He rubbed his face with his hand and realized his nose was bleeding again. He saw the swath of red on his hand and it helped him focus. "It sounds like there was some truth to what she said, about the Nest units not working. Perhaps we should contact Captain Freedom and make sure . . ."

"Make sure of what?"

"That we're doing . . . that we should be . . ."

Smith watched the blood flow out of the sergeant's nose and tried not to take too much pleasure in it. He twitched when the voice spoke next to his ear.

"He is resisting your attempt to control him," said Stealth.

Polk grabbed her shoulder and yanked her back. Smith could still feel her eyes boring into him. The woman had incredible willpower. He'd asked her to be quiet twice now. He hoped her nose was gushing blood under her mask.

"The sergeant just needs a moment to process his orders," said the agent. He looked at the other soldiers. "We don't need to remember this moment of weakness, do we?"

They nodded with the serene faces of discreet gentlemen. "Of course not, sir," said Polk.

"Excellent. Thank you both." He turned to Harrison. "We're going to follow Colonel Shelly's last orders, remember? We're going to get this prisoner to Groom Lake and establish a base there. It's even more urgent now that this 'Legion' is attacking here."

Stealth spun and brought her arms down over Polk's head. Twin blows to the collarbones stunned him and trapped his neck between the two sets of handcuff chains. She vaulted over him, swung her hips across his shoulders, and dropped to the ground behind the soldier. The cuffs on her wrists pulled tight across his throat. "Release me," she said, "or I will kill him."

Taylor had his Bravo inches from her head, brushing the fabric of her hood. Harrison and Hayes stayed a few feet back with their weapons raised. "Don't be stupid," said Harrison. "You know you can't get out of here."

She tugged on the handcuffs again and laced her fingers over Polk's mouth and nose. "He will asphyxiate in two minutes if you do not place your weapons on the ground and give me the handcuff key."

"Standard procedure for moving prisoners," said Harrison. "The key's never in transit, only at either end of the—"

"The key is in the left front pocket of your pants on a silver ring. Corporal Polk now has one minute forty-six seconds left to live."

"You're supposed to be one of the good guys," said Hayes. "You're not going to kill a soldier in the line of duty."

"One minute thirty-three seconds."

"Oh, for Christ's sake," said Smith, shaking his head. "You're not going to kill him, are you, Stealth?"

The cloaked woman lurched forward an inch, just enough to loosen the chain. Polk took a deep, wheezing breath. "No," she said.

"Would you mind releasing him, then?"

She unlaced her fingers and pulled her arms over his head. In the process she yanked out his earbud, mussed his hair, and knocked off his cap. He took another deep breath. "Fucking bitch," he muttered.

Smith gave her an annoyed look. "Can we make it all the way onto the helicopter without any more outbursts?"

"Of course," she said.

"Thank you."

"Do not expect to bend me to your will," she said. Her voice was loud and clear in the tunnel.

"Lady, you're already bent," he said. "Be thankful I just want to get out of here or you'd be putting on a donkey show for the soldiers."

Taylor chuckled.

"You have demonstrated a small amount of control when I was unprepared. Your limited influence forces you to use more indirect means. If you could assert direct control, you would have done so."

"I've got direct control of half the base already," snapped Smith.

"But not us," said Stealth. "St. George and I are too strong-willed for you to influence directly. I would imagine Captain Freedom is too strong for you as well."

"Freedom will put a gun in his mouth the moment I ask him to," said Smith. His own voice was rising to match hers. "They all would. Don't you get it? This has been my base for almost two years now."

Harrison cocked his head and looked back and forth between the soldiers.

"Is that why you killed Colonel Shelly? Did he become a threat to you?"

"Shelly was my sock puppet up until he died," said Smith. "He had just enough willpower to turn his own brain into mush trying to resist me. He's lucky I let him live as long as I—"

"Sir," barked Harrison. He held up his hand. The soldiers were looking back and forth at each other. The staff sergeant snapped his fingers, then again, then once more. Taylor tapped his collar and Hayes rubbed his own between his fingers.

Polk pulled his duty cap back on his head and coughed. They all looked at him. He blinked. "What?"

"You're keying," said Harrison with a glance at Stealth. "She turned your mic on!"

× × ×

Ummmmm . . . did everyone else just hear all of that?

They'd just made it back to the main gate. Freedom and Kennedy exchanged looks. All the super-soldiers gave each other uneasy glances. St. George looked up at the gleaming wraith.

I never liked that guy.

× × ×

Sorensen sat in the workshop and watched figures stumble by outside. He'd stayed hidden in the back office for an hour, but at some point he'd wandered out without thinking of it. From here, hidden in the shadows of the shop, he could see groups of soldiers running by, or the far more frequent mobs of exes. Several of them wore his nonfunctioning Nest units, but many more did not.

He tapped the fingers of his left hand against his thumb. His right fingers traced lines back and forth on one of the worktables. He was aware he was doing it. It was one of those faint moments of clarity when he realized he looked like a madman. He also realized he needed to trim his beard. Eva hated it when his beard got long.

He heard the cries and the screams, the clicking of teeth, and various shouted calls and orders. Someone would probably come to collect him, soon.

It all seemed distant. The guilty thoughts about the Nest and the ex-soldiers that had weighed on his fragile mind were gone. For the first time in over a year, he felt peaceful.

A trio of exes stumbled in through the wrecked doors. They weren't any of his. These had all been civilians. The woman was dressed in a pant suit, bleached from ages in the sun. The two men were in plaid shirts and jeans. One of them had a thick beard. The other tripped over the edge of the door and fell forward. Its skull hit the ground with a solid crack, but Sorensen could hear its limbs moving on the floor, trying to push it upright. Not enough damage to the cerebellum, but it may have broken its jaw from the muffled sounds its teeth now made.

The dead woman saw him and stumbled forward. Her skin was like leather, and there were a few twigs and tiny leaves in her dark hair. He could see an elaborate cobweb stretched from a ragged ear to her shoulder. Her brittle lips were pulled back in a smile.

"I knew you'd come," he said. "I kept telling them you were out there somewhere. None of them believed me."

He pulled her close. His wife wrapped her arms around him and buried her face in his neck.

Thirty
NOW

"**HOW MUCH LONGER** WE GONNA KEEP THIS UP?" Hundreds of dead faces split into hundreds of grins. "YOU ASK ME, YOU GONNA RUN OUTTA BULLETS LONG BEFORE I RUN OUTTA BODIES."

"First things first," said St. George. "Let's get this gate blocked."

Freedom gave three quick hand signals and the chisel-nosed truck coughed to life. It was a long, eight-wheeled vehicle with a crane mounted on the end of it. They pulled it across the gate and the soldiers fired around and under it as the driver leaped clear.

St. George hooked his fingers under the truck's frame and heaved. The flatbed's side lifted up and he grunted. The damned thing was armored and weighed twice what he'd thought. He got the tires three feet off the ground, then four. He heard a rattling noise as some of the chains on the bed slid off the far side, but he couldn't get it to the tipping point.

His forearm throbbed. He could feel his pulse in the wound and the wet bandage over it. It felt like the fang was tearing into him all over again.

Legion laughed from a hundred throats.

"Unbreakables," shouted Freedom, stepping forward, "give the man some assistance."

The captain's oversized hands slammed into the truck's frame next to St. George's. Pierce, Kennedy, and Garfield added their strength, too. The side of the truck went up another six inches, then six more, and the five of them rolled the ponderous flatbed onto its side across the gate. The soldiers behind them cheered.

"That's not going to hold forever," said St. George.

"Agreed," said Freedom. "The fence line's been compromised in at least three places, and weakened beyond each of them." He pointed at either side of the gate, where the chain-link sagged. "No tension, no strength."

"Sir," said Kennedy, "we haven't been able to reach Captain Creed. If Colonel Shelly is dead . . ." She looked at him with a neutral face.

"Ranking officer?" guessed St. George. "So, what are we going to do?"

Freedom knelt and scratched a rectangle in the sand. "We're here," he said, pointing. He made two quick crosses on the opposite side and gestured to one on the corner. "We've got breaches here and here. That's where your friends are."

"And this one?"

"Most of third company's there. Two more squads on the way."

"How many is that? Fifty, sixty soldiers?"

"More or less," said Kennedy.

"Any of them your people?"

Freedom shook his head. "We've got Twenty-two here. Squad Eleven's still cleaning out the barracks. That leaves Twenty-one escorting Agent Smith." He glanced at the gate.

"First sergeant, now that we're here with St. George let's get Sergeant Pierce and his people to the southeast corner."

"Yes, sir."

"You know this place," said St. George. He nodded at the upended flatbed. "Are we going to be able to block the other holes?"

The captain looked at the map in the dirt. "Maybe," he said after a moment. "It depends on how much Legion has to throw at us."

"Zzzap?"

The gleaming wraith shot into the sky. When he was a few hundred feet above the base he turned in a slow circle, taking in the lay of the land. A moment later he raced back to the ground. *Lots of exes coming,* he said. *I'd guess you're looking at two thousand or more in any given direction.*

"That doesn't make sense," said Kennedy. "Most of them should be coming from the southwest, Yuma. Every other direction is a hundred miles of nothing. Where are they all coming from?"

"They're coming from Yuma," said St. George. "These aren't random wanderers. They've been moved into position. It wouldn't surprise me if he'd been herding them out here for months. He might have half the population of the city here."

There're also a couple good-sized packs inside the fence line. One's coming this way from the north. He looked at Freedom. *I didn't see many of your people, though.*

The officer raised an eyebrow. "What do you mean?"

I mean I don't see anyone. Shouldn't they all be on guard towers or making barricades or something?

"They're probably already in position."

I'd still be able to see them.

"Most of these buildings have a degree of shielding for heat and radiation," said Kennedy. "Once someone's at their post they'd be shielded."

The towers have radiation shielding? scoffed Zzzap. *Still, shouldn't there be a couple stragglers or something? Somebody still moving somewhere?*

"The Army isn't big on stragglers," said Kennedy.

St. George silenced them with a gesture. "What about evacuation, then? You must have a plan. You didn't think some chain-link fences were going to hold forever."

"We can't abandon our post," said Freedom.

"You sure?"

"It's out of the question,"

"Okay, then," St. George said. "Last thing, then. Can all of you hold the gate here while I get to the helipad?"

"Sir," said Freedom, "I think we owe Mr. Smith more than that."

× × ×

Harrison led his squad up the staircase into the records building. Smith was right behind him. Taylor and Hayes dragged the prisoner with Polk at the rear. The sergeant stepped into the dim hallway, checked each direction, and waved them to follow. From the stairwell it was a short jog to the lobby, and the lobby doors were a few hundred yards from the helipad.

Harrison's jacket was stained red just below his chin. There were drops on his collar, too, just below his ears. "Sir," he said, "if we're taking the Black Hawk, what about the rest of the men? Will they meet up with us later?"

Smith sighed. "I'm afraid we're going to have to leave them behind," he said.

"I'm not sure I follow you, sir."

"Getting this prisoner to Groom Lake is our top priority. And don't you remember, Colonel Shelly gave me vital orders that need to be delivered there?"

"Yes, but . . . Sir, there're a thousand soldiers and support staff here. We can't abandon all of them."

"Necessary losses, I'm afraid. You understand, don't you?"

Harrison reached up and wiped away more blood. It flowed from his ears and nose in a set of steady streams. He blinked and his tears were stained pink. "That . . . with all due respect, sir, we can't do that."

"I understand," said the agent with a sympathetic nod. He looked at the cloaked woman. "Moral conflict," he said, shaking his head. "It starts to break down their brains. A vicious circle, really. The degradation of affected areas frees them from my control, which means I need to exert more influence, which leads to more degradation."

The staff sergeant looked up from his bloody hands. "Sir?"

"It's always good to know there are men like you in our armed forces," said Smith. "Men who aren't going to blindly follow orders without at least questioning the morality of them. Could I have your sidearm, sergeant?"

"Of course, sir." Harrison pulled the weapon from its holster, checked the chamber and the safety, and handed it grip-first to the agent. "It's all set to go, sir. You just need to flip the safety."

"That's this one here, right?" He pointed at the tiny lever over the red dot.

"Yes, sir."

Smith flipped the lever with his thumb and fired four shots into Harrison's chest. The sergeant fell back against the wall and dropped his Bravo. His vest had taken most of it, but he still wheezed out some air.

Smith peered down the sights and squeezed the trigger a few more times. One shot went into Harrison's throat. The next one tore open his cheek along his jawline. The last three turned his head into a red and ivory mess.

The soldiers had their weapons up. They'd thrown Stealth to the ground and had Smith in their sights. "Do not move, fucker," roared Taylor.

The young agent blew smoke from the pistol's barrel. "Staff Sergeant Harrison was collaborating with the enemy," he said. "You all knew that, right?"

"Of course, sir," said Polk, lowering his weapon.

"I'm only sorry I didn't shoot the traitorous fuck myself," muttered Taylor.

× × ×

"We're not going to make it until reinforcements get here," the sergeant told Danielle. He had to raise his voice over the chattering teeth. "We're going to have to fall back."

She looked over her shoulder. "Fall back to where?"

The soldier looked at the hordes of undead pouring through the fence. "As far as we can," he said. "Our ammo's not going to last much longer. I think your robot's running out of juice, too. Hopefully we'll meet up with our reinforcements and we can form a new line."

"So, you're talking about a retreat," she said.

"Yeah," he muttered, "basically."

His eyes shifted around for a minute and two or three ex-pressions flicked across his face. Then he swung his rifle up and aimed it past her. She cringed as it went off. Something hit the ground behind her.

A group of ex-soldiers had come up behind them. Almost twenty of them. The sergeant had killed the one reaching for her. He yanked her out of the way and let off a dozen rounds. Three dead men and a woman dropped.

The soldiers shifted into a circle. Four in front, three in back. Danielle could see there weren't enough of them. They were exposed.

She forced one of her Berettas away from her body and tried to remember every offhand comment Stealth had ever made about firing a gun. She squeezed the trigger. An ex-soldier a few yards away jerked up and its shoulder went limp. She fired off two more shots and the zombie dropped.

One of the soldiers facing the fence hollered. An ex had dropped on top of him. He was trying to kick it away and bring his rifle up, but the weapon was tangled in the dead woman's limbs. Danielle shoved the pistol at the ex's skull and blew it apart, but there was already another one clawing at the soldier's feet. She flinched back against the solid safety of the wall.

The sound of teeth was drowning out everything. She barely heard the sergeant yell as his rifle ran dry and he clubbed an ex with it. One soldier wrapped his hands around a zombie's neck and tried to twist its skull off. The circle was overwhelmed.

They were all around her.

She emptied the first pistol, pulled out the second, and looked for a target. There were too many, too close. There were at least a hundred coming through the fence. Still more than a dozen coming from the base. She fired until her fingers ached and the slide locked open. Half the soldiers were down, wrestling with zombies. She was pretty sure two of them were already dead.

One of the exes reached for her with withered fingers. Danielle threw her pistol and it bounced off the snapping jaws. She was exposed. Weak. Flesh. The ex's hand slid up her arm, headed for the exposed flesh of her face.

A metal hand reached down and crushed the dead man's skull. It flung the body back into the mob. "Come on," said Cesar. "We gotta get out of here." He batted away two more exes with a shrug of the battlesuit's shoulders.

Metal fingers closed on her waist and lifted her into the air. She was even more exposed. They set her down on the armor's shoulders and she grabbed the helmet for balance. "Put me down," she shouted. She banged her fist on the metal skull. "We've got to get somewhere safe. We all do."

"Dr. Morris," said the battlesuit, "there's nobody left. It's just us."

She looked down.

The exes had overrun the small defense line. The soldiers were dead. One was still twitching but had a trio of exes gnawing on him. She was pretty sure one had put his rifle in his own mouth and the sound had been lost in all the gunfire.

A pair of exes reached for her feet, but she was high enough up that all they could do was brush her heels. The titan swatted them away. Danielle wrapped her arms tighter around the helmet as the battlesuit stomped down the road.

She looked back at the guard towers flanking the hole in the fence. The soldiers there were still picking off exes with their rifles, but it was pebbles to divert a flood. One of them looked at her and she could see his eyes from fifty yards away.

"We're going to come back," she shouted. "I promise. Just hang on."

He gave her a weak wave that looked like it ended in a thumbs-up. The other one just kept shooting at the dozens of exes stumbling past his tower.

× × ×

Smith had put Polk in front to replace Harrison and left Taylor and Hayes to wrestle with Stealth. They marched through the lobby of the records building and pushed the doors open. Smith took a breath, straightened his tie out of habit, and looked at the scene in front of them.

The Black Hawk rested on the pad about five hundred feet away. Its engines were thrumming, even though the rotors were still. A soldier in a flight helmet pumped fuel into the chopper's tanks and looked over his shoulder.

To one side of the helipad was a mob of ex-soldiers. Sixty, maybe seventy of them. They had the pilot's attention. Smith saw the flash of green on their heads and a few with rifles swinging on straps. Their teeth clacked together, but over the engines it was more a tremble in the air than an actual sound. There were maybe a hundred yards between the first few zombies and the helicopter.

Sergeant Monroe, flanked by Truman and Jefferson, came from the other direction. They were about as far from the helipad as Smith and his group. They were sprinting, even with their oversized rifles.

A shadow flitted across the ground. Smith looked up and saw St. George plunging out of the sky. His boots hit the tarmac twenty feet in front of them. One of them had a ragged heel.

"Well," said Smith, "this should be interesting."

"Stealth," the hero yelled over the helicopter, "you okay?"

"I am uninjured," she said. "I trust you received my message?"

St. George looked Smith in the eye. "Oh, yeah," he said. "Everybody got it."

Smith smiled at him. "You don't think you can beat me, do you?"

The hero stopped in his tracks. Indecision flickered on his face. He glanced at Stealth, then at the soldiers flanking her. His brow knotted up in concentration.

Smith marched his group past the hero. He paused to give St. George a friendly punch in the arm. "I'm sure we'll see each other again," he said. "You've got way too much potential to be running around without guidance."

St. George raised a fist and glared at him.

Monroe and his men were at the Black Hawk, weapons ready. Smith shouted to them while he jabbed a finger toward the exes. "You don't want to let them reach the helicopter, do you? Get in there and protect American property."

A thread of blood trickled out of Monroe's nose, then Truman's. The three super-soldiers fell back and took up position across the helipad. Gunfire drowned out the helicopter. Their Bravos ripped the exes apart one after another. Some of the exes stopped clacking their teeth together and raised their own weapons.

Smith turned to Taylor and Hayes. "Get her on board." He glanced at his prisoner. "You said you wouldn't cause any problems, remember?"

"I do."

"Good." He led them to the Black Hawk. "God, this is almost too easy."

"He will beat you," Stealth said as they marched her forward.

Taylor smacked her in the ribs with his rifle and she stumbled. He yanked her upright. "Not going to happen, you fuck—"

St. George's punch caught him in the back of the head. The hero grabbed Taylor by the jacket, spun, and hurled him back through the doors of the records building. The soldier flew through three of the huge panes of glass and hit the far wall of the lobby.

He turned back to Smith's group and Polk emptied his Bravo at the hero. St. George could hear brass and links from the ammo chain falling like metal raindrops. He tried to brace his foot behind him, slipped, and stumbled back. Polk sprayed another hundred rounds at St. George, then threw the heavy rifle at the hero for good measure.

Smith swung through to the pilot. "Take off."

"Sir, I'm not sure if we have enough fuel," he said. "We're going to have to leapfrog if you want to make it all the way to Groom Lake."

"Are you able to get this damned thing in the air or not?"

"Of course, sir."

"Then do it."

"Yes, sir."

Hayes forced Stealth down onto the bench. It was awkward with her arms twisted behind her, but he pushed her back and strapped the seat belt across her hips. He reached over her for the flight harness. She glared up at him.

✕ ✕ ✕

St. George dragged himself out of his panic and doubt. He could hear the pitch of the engines changing. And below it he could hear shouting.

The exes had expended their meager weapons, but Jefferson had been hit twice in the firefight. He was down, trying to hold up his rifle. The trio of soldiers was pinned down as the exes marched closer. And they were marching in perfect sync.

The Black Hawk lifted off.

He threw himself at the exes. He grabbed one in each hand and used them as flails to knock down a dozen others. Legion glared at him through their eyes and turned to fight.

They grabbed St. George at his wrists and tried to pin his arms. Some wrapped themselves around his legs. None of them wasted time trying to bite. Five bodies had hold of him. By the time he'd crushed three skulls there were ten. He threw off four with a shrug of his shoulders and there were fifteen. They piled on, using sheer numbers to hold him down.

"Gotcha this time, Dragon," whispered one of them.

"Gotcha good," said another.

St. George snorted. "You think you can hold me?"

A musty arm wrapped across his throat. A hand slapped over his eyes. Fingers grabbed at his hair and ears and clothes.

"There's a concrete truck just a little ways from here," said one of the exes. "What if we dumped the whole thing on us? Bury you under all these corpses. What do you think?"

"I think you're still an idiot," said St. George.

He focused between his shoulder blades and shot fifty feet into the air. Over two dozen exes came with him, clutching his body too tight for their own good. Legion had enough time to grunt with surprise and St. George dove back down, flying headfirst for the tarmac. At the last second he shifted direction and hurled himself back into the sky.

The exes rushed past him in a flurry of limbs and bodies. They smashed into the helipad. Some plowed through other undead that hadn't been carried into the air. Skulls shattered, bones snapped, and gore splattered across the blacktop. Close to thirty exes ceased to exist.

St. George hung in the air for a moment over the pile of corpses. A few of them still writhed in the heap. He landed and wrenched their necks the way a regular man would open a twist-off bottle. The last one glowered at him and was taking in a breath to speak when he broke the top of its spine into three pieces.

Monroe and Truman snapped off bursts at the last few exes. "Sir," shouted Monroe. He pointed down the road where another mob staggered toward them.

"Get your man back to the main gate," said St. George. "We don't need to stay here any longer."

"What about Smith? He's still got your partner, right?"

He looked up. The Black Hawk was already a quarter mile away and six or seven hundred feet up, climbing fast even as it tilted away to the north. A body flew out of the side and plunged toward the ground.

× × ×

"Wait a minute," shouted Smith. He'd swung himself into one of the chairs and started to struggle with the harness until something caught his attention. He looked across at Stealth. "I thought you handcuffed her arms in front of her."

Hayes was still leaning over her, adjusting a last strap. He glanced down at his captive and her empty lap.

"We are now on the helicopter," Stealth said in a loud, clear voice.

Her hands slashed through the air, the left arm still trailing both handcuffs. The open palms slammed against his ears and the super-soldier felt a wave of pain and dizziness as his eardrums ruptured. Her legs whipped up and back as she drove her heels into his kneecaps. As he staggered back she grabbed his jacket and pulled herself up to crack her head into the bridge of his nose. The floor tilted and Hayes was pitched out the Black Hawk's open door.

Polk tried to shrug off his harness and stand up. She slammed both heels into his chest. Before he recovered she spun on her hands and circled his head with her feet. The chain of her shackles pulled tight on his throat. She jackknifed her body up and drove four punches into his forehead one after the other. He tried to block them but she was too fast and her calves were in the way. By the fourth one Polk was hanging loose in the harness. She swung back down, untwisted the shackle chain, and flipped back to her feet.

She turned to Smith. The combat knife she'd grabbed from Polk's belt spun in her hand.

Smith yelled something at her. With the engines roaring and the wind coming in through the cabin doors, she couldn't hear what it was.

He realized she couldn't hear him and his eyes went wide.

She saw the pilot glance back at her. He reached for his sidearm.

She threw the knife. It sank into Smith's throat just below his Adam's apple. The blade missed his carotid artery.

It severed one of his vocal cords.

Smith grabbed at his throat and glared at her. She saw

blood bubbling on his lips as he tried to shout commands to the pilot. The deck of the chopper tilted again.

Beneath her featureless mask, Stealth closed her eyes and leaped from the helicopter's open cabin door. The roar of its rotors faded as she dropped away and the Black Hawk continued north.

She grabbed the edges of her cloak, letting it billow out to catch the wind. She was too high up for it to save her, she knew. Almost nine hundred feet. The cloak would slow her descent, and while she would never reach terminal velocity she would still reach a sufficient speed in the next few seconds for the impact to kill her instantly.

Then a strong arm wrapped around her waist and pulled her close. Her descent slowed and stopped, and she wrapped her own arms around his neck.

"I've got you," said St. George.

"There was never any doubt."

Thirty-One
NOW

"YOU ARE BLEEDING," said Stealth.

"I'll be fine," said St. George. "I've had much worse."

They sank down through the air. St. George could go faster on his own, but he was trying to make it a smooth ride. They were heading back into a war, but for a minute or so Stealth was pressed up against him. She was very warm, even in the cool air of higher altitudes.

"How were you able to resist the suggestion Smith gave to you?"

"I thought of *The Twilight Zone*," he told her.

"Again, I do not understand."

"If you watch a lot of *Twilight Zone*s, there're a bunch of them that come down to misconceptions and loopholes," he explained. "People can't do something because they don't understand what's actually going on. I figured Smith's powers might work something like that."

"You sought out a loophole in the suggestion he gave you?"

St. George nodded. "At first I was terrified, because I knew he was right. I couldn't beat him. I was sure of it. I knew if

I tried anything a lot of people would get killed and I still wouldn't stop him."

"Yet you resisted," she said. "You tried to stop him."

"Nope. I told you, I knew I couldn't stop him. It's like he hardwired it into my brain. I know it was some kind of mind control and I still can't make myself believe I could've stopped him."

She hooked one of her legs around his. It took some of the weight off his arm, although it was nothing to him. It also pulled her even tighter against him. "Then how were you able to fight back?"

"That soldier hit you with his rifle. The second he did that, I realized I didn't want to beat the bad guy. I just wanted to save the girl."

"You defeated Smith's powers through a semantic argument."

"I don't know. Did I?"

"So it would appear. It also appears you have heroic fantasies where I am 'the girl.'"

"Well . . ." He tried to figure out what the right response was.

She looked up at him. "Do not worry, George," she said. "At the moment I find your heroic fantasies somewhat endearing."

"Ahhh," he said. "Good."

"I am sure Specialist Hayes appreciates them as well."

St. George glanced down at the soldier hanging from his other hand. "Well," said the hero, "he probably will once he wakes up."

× × ×

So, how'd things go up there?

Stealth slipped free from St. George's arm and dropped the last dozen feet to the ground, her cloak billowing around her. He kept his other arm up so Hayes didn't crack his head on the ground and two other soldiers grabbed the man. "Could've gone better," he said. "Smith got away. I'm sorry."

"Not good," Kennedy said. "If he reaches another base he can start all over again."

Freedom shook his head. "It's not important for now," he said. "Smith's a traitorous piece of crap, but right now our mission's to keep this base safe."

Three lines of soldiers formed a rough triangle. It reached almost a hundred feet on a side, with close to two dozen men on each line in pairs and trios. Jefferson doled ammunition out of a Humvee packed with crates and loose weapons. For the moment, they'd pushed back the exes.

"Where did you say he was headed for?" St. George asked the huge officer. "A lake?"

Freedom gave a single nod. "Groom Lake."

Seriously? Zzzap dropped closer to the ground. *Groom Lake? He's heading for* the *Groom Lake?*

"I am sure the actual base does not live up to the popular urban legends," said Stealth.

"Well," said Freedom, "we can discuss that at another time. For now, we need to figure out how to save Krypton."

The cloaked woman tilted her head. "The base is lost," she said. "The best course now is to prepare an evacuation with as many supplies as possible."

Captain Freedom pulled himself up to his full height. He loomed a good foot over Stealth. Kennedy stood next to him, her arms crossed. "As I told St. George, we are not going to abandon the base," he said. "Even if we wanted to, for a facility this size it's a process of days, not hours. There're too many people for an orderly evacuation in so short a time. It'd cost us too many lives."

"I doubt that." Stealth turned her head to the lines of soldiers. "You claim to have a full brigade here, yet every squad I have seen is four or five soldiers at best."

"Teams are four or five soldiers," said Kennedy. "Squads are eight to ten. If you don't understand the organizational structure it can—"

"I am aware of military command structure," said Stealth, "which is how I know your numbers are incorrect." She looked at the soldiers defending the gate. "Every squad here is undermanned. So are both platoons of super-soldiers."

Freedom shook his head. "You're mistaken, ma'am."

"Counting yourself, captain, I have seen fifteen soldiers on this base wearing the super-forces patch. Shall I name them for you?"

"You haven't seen everyone."

"I believe I have."

There was a burst of gunfire from the fence. A few exes had tried to force their way around the capsized flatbed. They were gunned down.

I kept asking where everyone was, said Zzzap, *and you kept saying they were just out of sight.*

Before Freedom could respond, Cerberus came around the side of a building. It moved with a quick, long stride, and Danielle rode piggyback on its shoulders, her arms around the metal skull. The battlesuit moved past the soldiers and up to St. George.

"Told you I'd keep her safe," said the titan. It set Danielle down on the ground. "You can count on me, man."

"There's a good-sized mob of exes about two or three

minutes behind us," she said. "Legion seems to be focused on them. They're coming after me."

"Lucky you," muttered Kennedy.

"Stow that, first sergeant."

"Sir, yes, sir."

"Man, am I glad to see you," the battlesuit said to Zzzap. "The armor's at, like, eighteen percent power. I'm starving in here, bro."

Yeah, join the club.

"Danielle," said St. George. "You guys were at the northwest corner. How many people did you have with you?"

"Counting the guys in the towers?"

"Include everyone you can," said Stealth.

Danielle skimmed through her memories. "Nine, I think."

The battlesuit nodded. "Nine. Seven on the ground, one in each tower."

"There're always three soldiers in every tower," Freedom said.

St. George looked at the towers flanking the gate. "There's only one up there," he said, "and nobody in that one."

"Specialist MacLeod came down to help secure the gate," said Kennedy. She pointed to the soldier. "That's why it's unmanned."

"If one guy left, shouldn't there still be two people manning it?"

Kennedy looked back at the tower. "He must've been on solitary shift. Sometimes, the way rosters line up, someone gets stuck pulling duty alone."

"Sounds like none of your rosters are lining up, then," Danielle said. She pointed down the fence line at other towers. "One. One. One."

"Smith has been biding his time here," said Stealth. "I

would surmise since the outbreak occurred, his priority has been his own survival and little else. The easiest way for him to maintain control was to let you believe you were performing your expected duties, within the scope that served his purposes."

"Then why recruit people?" asked Kennedy with a gesture. "If you're right, if we were all just drones running the base, why rescue all these people and bring in a bunch of extra mouths to feed? Why put a few hundred civilians through basic? Why . . ."

Her hand drifted down. They all looked at the small squads fighting to defend the gate. Kennedy and Freedom looked over at the empty barracks.

"Oh, God," said Freedom.

Colonel Shelly told me you guys had enough supplies for years, said Zzzap.

"I would surmise," said Stealth, "there were far less recruits and refugees than you remember. It is likely no one was rescued from Yuma. Smith merely convinced you of such to make you more docile." She turned her head to look out over Krypton. "I would not be surprised to discover there are fewer than a hundred soldiers and support staff on this base."

"This isn't a base," said Danielle. "It's a ghost town."

The huge officer looked at the buildings and roads inside the fence. There was no movement. No sound past the chattering of teeth and distant gunfire. "The base fell ages ago," said Freedom, "and we never even knew. They're all dead."

The cloaked woman nodded. "Which is why Smith required the ex-soldiers. If he had a full battalion at his command, why would he waste resources to create such inferior warriors?"

Another burst of gunfire from one of the far lines of the triangle. A mob of exes was coming in from the north. The soldiers were taking slow, steady shots. Almost every one made an ex collapse.

St. George straightened himself up. He was still ten inches shorter than Freedom, but he didn't let it show. "You haven't failed," he said. "If Stealth's right, there're still a lot of people here depending on you."

"I know there're at least two guys back there in towers," said Danielle.

"What are you suggesting?"

"What we've been talking about all along," said St. George. "We merge groups. You come back to Los Angeles with us," said St. George.

Freedom's back got straight. "You're saying we should abandon our post?"

"You do not have a post to abandon," said Stealth. "As you yourself stated, this base has not existed as a functioning entity for over a year."

"Your people are smart and well trained," said St. George. "There's probably stuff we could be doing out there we've never even thought of. You can plan out your next move somewhere safe. Until then, we can help each other out."

Freedom looked past the fences at the dead things throwing themselves against the barriers. "Legion has us surrounded."

"And very outnumbered," said Kennedy.

"His efforts, however, are all built upon the premise that we are fighting to defend the base," said Stealth. "It is possible he also does not realize Krypton's true status. This gives us a tactical advantage."

How's that?

Freedom glanced up. "He thinks we're static. He won't be expecting us to retreat from the base."

Stealth looked up at the captain. "Can your people implement a covert evacuation? We must not let Legion suspect or he will alter his own strategy."

"We've already got a lot of the armory here," said Freedom. "We can gather food, medical supplies, and other expendables under the same premise—centralizing it for the defense."

"Vehicles, too," said Danielle. "Bring them in like you're using them to shore up defenses at the weak points. Then people can pile into them and go on the signal."

Captain Freedom took in a breath and spent half a minute letting it out.

"First sergeant," he said. "We're switching from Red Sand to Dead Moon."

"Yes, sir." Kennedy reached for her microphone but Stealth stopped her.

"You must assume Legion has acquired at least one radio," she said. "The only broadcast communications should further the illusion we are holding positions. The real strategy should be spread by couriers."

"And I want reorganization right now," said Freedom. "Squads of ten, count them off, no assumptions. Everyone goes everywhere together."

St. George glanced up at the pale wraith. "Dead Moon?"

Yeah, said Zzzap, *doesn't sound too inspiring to me, either.*

× × ×

St. George heaved the heavy steel pipe onto his shoulder and kicked another ex away. Dead men and women clawed at him and chipped their teeth on his skin. He shook the pole and the ones walking across the fallen chain-link were knocked off their feet.

Zzzap had done another fly-by and incinerated dozens of zombies as they moved for the gap between the two guard towers. It gave St. George a window. Not a huge one, but hopefully enough. He walked the pole up, foot by foot. The fence rose with it. The chain-link panels sagged, but they went up until the fence was standing again. A few strands of barbed wire rustled loose from the top and hung like creepers. "How's that look?"

Zzzap looked to the towers and both soldiers gave a thumbs-up. *Pretty good*, he shouted back. *I think it'll work for now.*

St. George tried to pack the ground back around the concrete mass at the base of the post. He kicked dirt and sand into the hole and stomped it down. Something tickled his ear and he turned to see another ex reaching for him. He slammed his elbow back and it flew away.

The hero hopped over the sad fence and grabbed two of the exes that had tumbled inside when it went up. Their skulls crashed together with a sound like wood breaking and he reached for two more. Their teeth stopped chattering and they turned to look at him.

"Come on," they said. "You think this'll stop me? I'll have this back down in an hour."

St. George slammed their heads together and the bodies dropped. He grabbed another by the neck and it twisted around to leer at him.

"An hour? Hell, twenty minutes and I'll be munching on your friends."

He pulled back and hurled the dead woman up over the

fence. His wounded arm flared with pain as he did. On the other side exes were pulling at the chain-link, throwing their weight back and forth.

The last ex, a teenage boy wearing a tattered Circle K shirt, glared at him. "Don't you get it? Killing me just made me unbeatable. I'm more powerful than you—"

Yeah, yeah. The air rippled and Zzzap let his fingers sink into the dead boy's skull. The stringy hair and dry skin caught fire. The gray eyes sizzled away. *Struck you down, more powerful than we can possibly imagine, get some original material, you halfwit.* The ex dropped to the ground with smoke pouring out of its skull. The wraith let out a buzzing sigh.

"You okay?"

I'm wiped. I've got to be honest . . . I don't know how much more use I'm going to be to you.

St. George looked over at the tower guards. They'd rushed down to a waiting Humvee. One of them manned the machine gun on the roof. "Can you recharge Cerberus one more time," he asked, "maybe hold it together for a little while longer?"

How long is that?

"If we don't ask you to do anything else but be a presence . . . a day or two?"

Ouch, said the wraith. *You serious?*

"I need you here, Barry. They need to see us. At night they need to see you."

Yeah, yeah, I know, sighed Zzzap. *We're heroes and all that.*

× × ×

Another truck pulled into formation. The back was filled with a heap of coats, boots, blankets, and other dry goods.

The triangle of soldiers by the main gate had been replaced by a ring of almost forty vehicles, all facing the same direction. Humvees, trucks, another Guardian. Soldiers sat in the turrets and used the heavy guns on the exes at the gate.

Stealth and Kennedy agreed regular jeeps wouldn't offer enough protection and skipped over them. It also helped when one of the ex-soldiers stumbled across a parking lot that still had vehicles in it. The cloaked woman looked at the circled vehicles. "How many more?"

"Three. One more truck, two Humvees. But Jefferson hasn't reported in. Neither has King. We may have lost them."

As she spoke another truck rumbled up. It stopped outside the circle and the driver leaped out. His jacket was slashed in a dozen places. He reached back into the cab and dragged Jefferson out. "Medic!"

Two men ran for the wounded soldier. Stealth and Kennedy approached the driver more cautiously.

"Didn't think you'd be joining us, specialist," said Kennedy.

"Yeah, well, you know me, first sergeant," said Taylor. The battered soldier lowered Jefferson into the waiting arms of the medics and then spat out a mouthful of blood. "Always ending up on the wrong fucking team."

× × ×

Freedom had joined Pierce, Twenty-two, and the Real Men at the southern breach. There were only twenty-seven of them left. He wasn't sure how many there had been to start with.

It was a clean break through the fence here. No chance of repairing it. Legion didn't seem to be focusing much here, so at least the exes were providing easy targets. The soldiers had put down so many of them the ground was an uneven morass of bodies. Most of the walking dead stumbled and fell three or four times as they crossed the fence line. The air was filled with the sounds of gunfire and chattering teeth.

Three Humvees had joined them. The soldiers had fallen back around the vehicles. It was going to be tight, but it only had to get them back across the base.

He spun a new drum, his last one, onto Lady Liberty and blew the head off another ex. His radio crackled. "Unbreakable Six, this is Unbreakable Seven," said Kennedy's voice.

"Seven, this is Six."

"Six, this is Seven. Wagons are circled at position one, sir. The Dragon and Sparky are falling back to our position as well."

A new voice broke in on the channel. "You did not just call me 'Sparky,' did you?"

"Seven, this is Six," said the captain. "Roger."

"Seriously. I have a code name."

Freedom pulled out his earbud and looked over his shoulder. He'd done his morning run past this length of fence thousands of times since he joined Project Krypton. He could see the backsides of two barracks. The post exchange was just visible between two of them, on the far side of the street someone had named Deadwood. Far past that, he could see the building with his office and the hospital where Sorensen had made him into the greatest soldier on Earth.

He took a final look at the view and shoved the earbud back in. "We're falling back." He bellowed it for Legion's benefit. "Mount up and back to the main gate."

× × ×

The sun was low in the sky when everyone gathered at the main gate. They had forty-two vehicles. The final headcount was just over a hundred soldiers and support staff. Even all gathered together, it looked like a small amount.

"So," said Kennedy, "how do we get past the truck and out the gate without letting him know what we're doing?"

"We do not go through the gate," said Stealth.

Freedom nodded. "Straight through the fences, just like he did."

"Correct," said the cloaked woman. "There is a point twenty-three yards south of the main gate that is almost free of exes. The Cerberus suit can tear through and we shall follow."

St. George stood on the hood of a Humvee. He'd found Sorensen's mangled body half an hour ago, and his fists were still clenched. Freedom glanced at him. "Do you think this will work?"

The hero glared at the fence. "Despite appearances, Legion isn't what you'd really consider supervillain material. I'd say there's a pretty solid chance. We'd better do this quick, though." He nodded at the gate. "I think he's getting suspicious."

The dead gathered at the gate clacked their teeth less and less. They were moving their heads in sync. Their eyes moved over the circle of trucks and Humvees, then to the heroes gathered with Captain Freedom. A double-handful of heads tilted quizzically at the group.

"Time to move out," said Freedom.

Zzzap flitted over to the battlesuit. It was smashing exes as they made their way around the capsized truck. *Okay, kid,* he said. *No pressure, but it's all up to you.*

The battlesuit nodded. "What do you need me to do?"

Zzzap pointed to the key spot. *Go that way,* he said. *Very fast. If something gets in your way, plow it into the ground.*

"That's it?"

That's it. Once you're through the fence, stomp a few exes and keep an eye out for Danielle. She's in one of the trucks waiting for you.

The suit threw back its shoulders. Barry could've sworn it took a deep breath. "Okay," it said. "Just say when."

When, said the gleaming wraith.

The huge lenses looked at him for a moment and then the suit was running.

"Go," shouted St. George. He leaped into the air next to Zzzap. The two of them darted over the triple fence.

"Seven to all units," Kennedy shouted into her microphone, "move out. Repeat, move out."

The titan kicked up a cloud of dust as it thundered across the packed-down dirt of the base. The first fence exploded outward. It grabbed the second one in its armored fingers and tore the chain-link apart like wet paper. The full weight of the battlesuit hit the third fence and it burst open with the twangs and chimes of breaking wire. The titan fell through and hit the ground.

The convoy rumbled to life. The circle uncoiled like a whip and one long line of Humvees and trucks headed for the opening in the gate.

The exes at the gate saw the trucks move and howled in unison. They ran for the breach in a stiff-legged lockstep.

The Cerberus suit stood up and grabbed one of the tall fence poles. It tore the shaft free and swung it like a bat. The pole swept across a forty-foot arc and devastated the first wave of exes. Then the titan swung it again and knocked down another swath of dead people.

The first vehicles were off the base and roaring into the

desert. One truck peeled off and roared up next to the titan. St. George landed next to it. "Here," shouted Danielle from the back.

The battlesuit hurled the pipe lengthwise at the horde and sent twenty-odd exes crashing to the ground. It took a few steps back to the truck and started to climb in the back. St. George grabbed it by the hips and heaved. The titan crashed into the truck's bed and the vehicle shook. Danielle banged on the cab and the driver floored it.

"NO," roared Legion.

More than half the trucks were through. Some of the exes farthest out from the base tried to intercept the convoy, but they were either run down or gunned down by Freedom and the rest of the Unbreakables. A few closed in from the south but the guns on the Guardians and Humvees kept them at bay.

Zzzap dipped low and burned a path through the last of the gate exes. They scattered and their teeth chattered at him. The pale wraith soared into the twilight sky.

St. George landed on one of the last Humvees next to Stealth. One of her Glocks put a round between the eyes of a dead woman that came running at the vehicle. She spun the other one in her hand and whipped it across the jaw of a dead soldier crawling up the back of the vehicle.

Another ex threw itself against the side of their Humvee. It was a dead man wearing a ragged, bloodstained Army uniform. A large chunk of flesh had been torn from its throat. Its scalp was peeled away down to the jawline on the left side of its face. St. George could just make out the name ADAMS on the front of its jacket.

"You can't get away from me," it growled. The words echoed. All the exes the Humvee roared past were speaking in time with it. "This is my world now, dragon man. I'm ev-erywhere. There's no escape."

St. George grabbed the dead man by the jacket and lifted him up so they were eye to eye. "I guess we'll just have to see about that."

He let the ex drop and it fell beneath the Humvee's wheels. The convoy rolled on, heading west toward California.

Meeting Your Heroes
THEN

"WAKE UP, PEOPLE," Johnson shouted over the headset. "We're twenty minutes outside of Los Angeles. Let's be ready and be focused."

I was sharing the dark crew compartment of a Black Hawk with First Sergeant Kennedy, Platoon Sergeant Johnson, and the men of Unbreakable Twenty-one. The rotors drowned out any sound that didn't come over the comm sets. The helicopter had a hot smell to it. Part of it was the engine, part of it was flying over the desert. Even at night, the desert was hot in the summer.

I wasn't fond of the heat. In my second command position, I'd been in the field for nineteen days when an insurgent fired an antitank round into our Humvee. Somehow I was thrown clear with minor injuries. Three other soldiers survived, two men and a woman. I dragged each of them from the wreck. Each of them had third-degree burns on at least forty percent of their bodies. I remember the smell, which was too much like the scent of fatty ribs grilling in the summer. Someone told me later it was probably Sergeant North. One of her breasts was burned off in the fire.

I needed skin grafts on both hands. The doctors told me

it was a miracle I hadn't suffered nerve damage. There was a minor investigation to make sure I wasn't incompetent or trying for a 4-F. Then I was given another Purple Heart, a Silver Star, and promoted to first lieutenant.

More dead soldiers on my hands. Yet another time I was "one of the only survivors."

The Unbreakables checked weapons and adjusted gear. A few of them had their eyes closed and took slow breaths. "Man," said Truman. "I always wanted to see Hollywood. Never thought it'd be like this."

"Stay sharp, people," I said. "Remember, best estimates say there could be five million ex-humans in the city. We don't know how well these people have secured their borders. We don't even know if they have a solid perimeter. Do not let your guard down. First thing on our task list is protecting Agent Smith. Protecting each other is second. Contact with survivors is third. Clear?"

"Sir, yes, sir," they chorused.

I still wasn't sure why Colonel Shelly had insisted Smith come along, but what's done was done. I didn't like putting a civilian advisor above the safety of my soldiers. He was in the other Black Hawk with Unbreakable Eleven.

"You heard the captain," said Johnson. "You see anything, you hear anything, don't hesitate. Clear?"

They shouted confirmation again.

"No surprises, no screwups," he said. "We're on the ground in sixteen."

Taylor threaded ammo into his Bravo and looked up. "Hey, you know what they got out here? Fucking celebrity exes. Did anyone think about that?" He hooked the box in place and hefted the massive rifle. "We might get to shoot someone famous."

Laughter echoed through the helicopter. Normally I don't condone profanity. First Sergeant Paine hadn't, either. There was a wonderful statement in the first few pages of Vonnegut's *Hocus Pocus*, which I read as a very young man. Simply put, profanity just gives people a reason to ignore you.

It was good to hear them laugh, though. I knew the long months at Krypton had been wearing them down.

Eddie Franklin threw a cleaning rag at Taylor. "You looking for anyone in particular?"

"Fucking Uwe Boll," said the specialist. "If that dumb fuck's a zombie I'm gonna put ten rounds in his head."

Franklin tapped on his knee. "Does a director count as a celebrity?"

"D'you know who he is?"

"I've heard of him, yeah, but—"

"Then he's a celebrity."

"Yeah, but he's not on TV or anything," said Franklin. "If TV doesn't care about you, you're not really a celebrity."

"Did The Rock live in Los Angeles?" asked Jefferson. "That'd be pretty awesome, being the guy who took out the zombie Rock."

"I'd go big, too," said Harrison. "Maybe Tom Cruise or Will Smith."

"Will Smith's too cool to be an ex," said Franklin. "And he was in *I Am Legend*. He knows how to fight zombies."

"Those weren't zombies," said Corporal Polk. His eyes stayed closed. "They were mutant vampires or something."

"Whatever. If he's not still alive, I bet he went down fighting and didn't come back."

Taylor threw the rag back. "What about you, Hayes? Any famous ex-people you want to shoot?"

The specialist mulled it over for a few moments. "David Grant Wright."

"Who the fuck is David Grant Wright?" said Taylor.

"He did all these Jiffy Lube commercials," said the soldier, twisting his lip. "He was their spokesman for a bunch of years. I hate Jiffy Lube. They had this new guy there once and he forgot to refill my radiator. Car overheated and I ended up stuck there for the whole afternoon."

Harrison chuckled. "So you want to kill their spokesman?"

"I like Jiffy Lube," said Truman.

"And he did this crap *Beastmaster* movie I saw when I was a kid. I looked him up once. I'm so gonna shoot that guy if I see him."

They all laughed. So did I.

Hayes threw the rag at the man across from him. "Ryan?"

"Just like *Fight Club*," said Polk. He patted his Bravo. "I want Shatner."

"Oh, yeah," said Jefferson. "Forget The Rock. If he's got Shatner, I'm claiming Leonard Nimoy."

"I'll take The Rock," said Truman.

"How about you, first sergeant?" said Harrison. "There someone famous you'd like to get if they've gone ex?"

Kennedy shook her head. "I wouldn't want some flash-in-the-pan or cult celebrity," she said. "I'd want somebody real. Somebody people are going to remember forever, like Natalie Portman. Or Alex Trebek."

A few of the soldiers whistled and nodded.

They all looked at me.

I shook my head. "I'm not here to play games," I said. I made sure my tone let them know I didn't disapprove of their enthusiasm. "Besides, there's only one person I'm hoping to see." I cracked my knuckles and patted Lady Liberty on my thigh.

A few of the soldiers nodded. "The Dragon," murmured two or three of them.

"You can take him, captain, sir," said Franklin. They hollered and a few of them clapped. They were good people. I wasn't going to lose any of them.

"We'll see," I told them when they stopped cheering. "Dr. Sorensen's done great work, but now we'll see how we stack up against the real deal."

Epilogue

NOW

IT TOOK THEM four days to make their way back to Los Angeles. They lost eight soldiers at a refueling stop just outside Salton City. They found a group of fifteen survivors in Palm Springs.

Now St. George hung in the night sky above the Mount's water tower. One hand rested on the tall spire, anchoring him in place while he looked down at his home. He'd been back for seven hours and already buried with a week's worth of requests, updates, and decisions to make.

He heard boots on the tower's ladder. The conical roof shuddered under heavy footsteps. It wasn't Stealth slipping up behind him.

"Nice view," said Freedom.

"That it is," agreed St. George. He glanced back at the huge officer. "I never get tired of it."

"How is Mr. Burke doing?"

"He's okay now. He went into shock as soon as he changed back. Dr. Connolly got him on a glucose drip or something like that. She says he'll probably be eating and requesting DVDs tomorrow."

"And that's good, right?"

"Well . . . it's normal. Let's leave it at that."

The huge officer coughed once, then cleared his throat. "I wanted to apologize, sir," he said. "For everything that happened back at Yuma."

"Don't worry about it."

"I could shift the blame and say I was following orders, but I think on some level I knew a lot of it didn't make sense. I knew it was wrong. I take full responsibility for my actions."

"Don't worry about it," repeated St. George. "Smith was screwing with your head. It wasn't your fault."

"I'm still sorry for what happened, sir, and for how I treated you. You and your woman."

"Oh, jeeeez." St. George shook his head and glanced over at the Roddenberry building. "Don't let her hear you say that or she'll beat you senseless."

Freedom smiled. "I'd like to see her try."

"Yeah, don't say that either. Seriously, it's like tempting fate."

"Not wearing your coat, sir?"

St. George glanced down at his patchwork flight jacket. "I've got to be honest. Digital camouflage isn't really my style. Plus, it's hot as hell."

"You get used to it."

"Maybe when winter rolls around." He let his feet settle down onto the roof of the water tower. "So, captain, what are you going to do now?"

Freedom looked out at Los Angeles. "I'm not sure, sir, to be honest. First Sergeant Kennedy and I discussed it several times on the trip out here. The men want me to stay in a command position, but I think an active military presence doesn't fit with what you've established here at the Mount."

St. George shook his head. "Not really, no."

"A few of them have even said we should strike out on our own. Try to make it back to Yuma or maybe Fort Bliss. See if there's anyone left there."

"Could you make it?"

"Probably."

"Do you really think you'll find anyone?"

He shrugged. "I don't know."

"Doesn't sound like the best tactical decision."

"Maybe not, sir. But it's the one that fits best with who I am."

St. George smiled. "What if I could give you another option?"

"Like what?"

The hero bent down and picked up the bundle resting against the spire. He grabbed it by the corners and shook it out. Freedom raised an eyebrow.

"Is this a joke, sir?"

"Not at all," said St. George. "The position's been empty for nine months now. A couple people have tried to fill it unofficially, but I think you might be just the man for the job."

Freedom stepped forward, his boots clanging on the tower. "You're serious?"

"Very. I talked it over with Danielle on the trip, and she agrees this is the way to go. And that you're ass-kicking enough to deserve this. So does Stealth. We got someone to let it out for you."

The larger man took it and shrugged it up over his body. "It's tight in the arms. And across the chest."

"Do you own anything that's not tight across the chest?"

"Not at the moment."

"He can probably add in some more material or something. What do you think?"

"It is appealing, sir, but I can't abandon my commission. Or my men."

"I'm not asking you to," said St. George. "I'm just hoping you can do this for now. Help us protect these people and keep this place safe and peaceful. It gives your men a purpose. It gives you a purpose."

Freedom stretched his arms. It was tight, but he could still move. "You know, I've got to be honest, sir. I've wanted one of these coats ever since I saw *Hellboy*."

"You can lose the sir. It's just St. George. Or George, even."

"I'll hang on to sir for now, sir."

Voices echoed up to them from the base of the tower. Two men were shouting at each other. St. George recognized one of them as Roger Mikkelson. He was waving his arms at one of Christian Nguyen's regular lackeys.

"Duty calls," said St. George with a smile.

The large officer smirked and bowed his head to the hero. Then he leaped off the water tower and plunged down to street level.

Captain Freedom hit the pavement and it cracked under his heels. The two men leaped back, their argument forgotten. He straightened up and brushed back the lapels of the leather duster to let the light hit the seven-pointed silver badge.

"Let's take it easy there, gentlemen," he said. "Now, what seems to be the problem?"

Acknowledgments

One of the worst sensations in the world is writing your first book. Don't let anyone tell you anything different. In many ways it's glorious and thrilling, but there's always that nagging fear, the one gnawing away at the writer each night. Am I wasting my time? Will anyone ever read it? Will they like it?

As such, the second-worst feeling is when that first book *wasn't* a waste of time, was read, and was liked. Because now you have to write another one and figure out some way to make that lightning strike twice. Worse yet, as Hollywood has shown us again and again, there's no such thing as one sequel. If the first one works, you have to aim for a trilogy. At least.

Of course, I couldn't've handled all this alone. So some deeply felt thanks must be given to . . .

The folks at Permuted Press, who originally published *Ex-Patriots*. Jacob Kier let me work on *The Eerie Adventures of the Lycanthrope Robinson Crusoe* before diving into this book. Jessica, the original editor, caught far too many things that slipped past me, in spelling, grammar, and structure. Also a belated thanks to Matthew, who did a fantastic job as the first editor of *Ex-Heroes*. A discussion we had about sonic booms and the nature of Zzzap's energy form became the talk between Barry and Sorensen.

Mary, soon to be Dr. Mao, pointed me in all the right directions to begin my superhuman research project. Another big thanks to my college roommate, who now goes by Dr. John Tansey, director of the Interdisciplinary Program in Biochemistry and Molecular Biology of Otterbein University. John helped fine-tune the project and made Dr. Sorensen's work sound far more plausible than I ever could. Any vagueness, errors, or open fabrications are there to serve the needs of fiction and came from me, not either of them.

The U.S. Army plays a huge part in this story as well, and I know just enough about that life and career to know that I know very little about that life and career. Definitely not enough to do it the justice it so rarely gets in zombie stories. My friend Jeff talked to me at length about his decision to join the military, as did my dad, Dennis (who spent Vietnam aboard the *Will Rogers*). Staff Sergeant Lincoln Crisler—a fine author himself—helped with military call signs and communications. My stepsister, Carolyn (Master Sergeant Dade, Ret., to the rest of you), spent ages teaching me about command structure, ranks, and life in the military. My best friend, Marcus, who has forgotten more about every branch of the military than I will ever learn, answered questions about weapons, vehicles, tactics, and more at all hours of the day and night. Again, any mistakes or exaggerations in these pages are entirely my own and not theirs.

I am indebted to Jen, Larry, and John (Surfin Dead over at zombiezonenews.com), who all read early drafts of this book, offered many comments and critiques, and let me know where I'd gone horribly wrong and where I'd gone somewhat right.

David Fugate at LaunchBooks Literary Agency was excited enough by the second book that he contacted me and brought the series to Crown Publishing, where Julian Pavia and the team there somehow pushed it through the most insane publishing schedule ever imagined.

And a very special thanks, as always, to my lovely lady, Colleen, who listens patiently, criticizes fairly, prods gently (or not so gently), and has far more faith in me and my ability than I do at times.

—P.C.

Los Angeles, January 9, 2013

Read on for a taste of Peter Clines's

EX-COMMUNICATION

Prologue
NOW

"**THIS IS THE** northwest corner," shouted a man on the radio. A gunshot blasted over the open channel. "Twenty . . . something. We're under attack! Two, maybe three hundred of them. We need help!" The call was punctuated by another shot.

Captain John Carter Freedom of the 456th Unbreakables, considered temporarily on leave from his post at Project Krypton, heard the two sharp pops echo between the buildings. He was a few blocks from that corner of the Big Wall. The sound of gunfire in a quiet city. There was nothing else quite like it.

They were rifles, but unfamiliar to his ears. Civilian weapons. That lined up with the voice's confusion at radio protocol. Freedom was pretty sure it had been the wall guard who went by the name Makana.

He looked down at the kids in front of him. Two boys and a girl, barely into their teens. All three of them sat on the curb with their hands zip-tied together behind their backs. They'd been trying to steal a car for a quick joyride when he found them. They'd been cowed by his appearance and surrendered without a fuss.

Most people were cowed by Freedom's appearance. He was

a bald giant of a man, almost seven feet tall and over three hundred pounds of solid muscle. A leather duster hung open across his broad chest, and a silver sheriff's star sat on one lapel. Underneath the duster he wore a tan T-shirt and pants checkered with digital camouflage. Strapped to his thigh was a holster the size of a loaf of bread. He rarely had to draw the pistol it held.

A third and fourth shot rang in the air. The kids went back and forth from Freedom's face to the direction of the sound. One of the boys had gone wide-eyed with terror. They knew what the shots meant. They were aware of how vulnerable they were, tied up on the ground.

"You'll be fine," Freedom told them. "There's a deputy on the way to take charge of you."

Three more gunshots. And between the rounds he could hear a growing noise. The click-click-click that made life near the Big Wall so rough for some. The sound of teeth.

The girl opened her mouth to say something, but it vanished under the snap of his leather duster as he spun and bolted for the northeast corner. The captain had been quick for his size before joining the Army's super-soldier project. Now he could run a three-minute mile without breaking a sweat, do five of them before he even started to feel winded.

The gunfire was near-constant by the time he reached the northeast corner. It made Los Angeles sound like Iraq. He could see the half dozen guards on top of the wall. Four of them were shooting down into the area beyond the barrier. The other two were pushing back the figures climbing onto the upper deck.

Freedom never broke stride. His legs flexed and hurled him twenty feet into the air. His duster flapped around him, and he steeled himself for combat.

The top of the Big Wall was a continuous platform made from old pallets and plywood. A double line of rope served as a railing. It was a temporary fix until a more permanent bastion could be built. Freedom hit the wood surface just south of the large square that was the northwest corner and took in the situation as he straightened up.

This corner of the Big Wall sat at the intersection of Sunset and Vine in downtown Hollywood, right at the center of the road. A Borders bookstore and a vandalized Chase bank stood just outside the barrier.

Almost a thousand exes stood outside the wall, too. Thirty months since the world ended and people still called them exes rather than zombies. "Ex-humans" was just easier to deal with somehow. Even the military had used the term.

Back when there had been a functioning military, the captain reminded himself.

The former citizens of Los Angeles crowded the intersection beyond the wall, filling the air with the endless sound of chattering teeth. Even when there was nothing in their mouths, their jaws gnashed open and closed like machines. Some of those mouths were lined with gray teeth. Others held a mess of jagged stumps which splintered even more as they banged together. Most of them were coated with blood and gore. Their flesh was the color of old chalk, spotted with dark bruises where blood had pooled inside the skin. Their eyes were mostly dusty and dull, but more than a few of them had empty sockets gaping in their faces. Many of the exes had deep cuts or punctures which would never heal but also didn't stop them. Some were missing fingers, hands, or whole limbs.

Something was different about the horde, though, and Freedom couldn't put his finger on what.

The wall guards fired into the crowd with their motley collection of weapons. Rifles scavenged from personal collections or motion picture armories. A dreadlocked man he recognized as Makana was trying to keep them organized, but there was an air of desperation around the guards. One of them swung his rifle like a baseball bat and clubbed a thin figure off the platform. The guard turned and swung again. It was wild, but it caught his next target in the side of the head and tipped it back off the wall.

The guard was scared. They were *all* scared. Freedom wasn't sure what had them spooked. He drew his massive sidearm, a modified AA-12 shotgun which had been cut down to a pistol for his huge hands. The armorer had nicknamed it Lady Liberty. His gaze went down to the horde again.

Some of the exes were moving quicker than the others. They ran at the Big Wall and lunged up. They grabbed handholds and kicked with their feet, pulling themselves up the barrier. A handful of exes turned their attention to Freedom as he landed. Behind their dead eyes, Legion glared out at the giant officer.

On their own, the undead were almost manageable. Over the years, the people of Los Angeles had developed methods and procedures for dealing with them. The mindless exes were still a threat, but it was a contained threat. One they had lots of practice with.

Legion had changed everything. The exes were pawns for him to control. He could slip from zombie to zombie, using them as his puppets. They could be his eyes and ears. Or his hands and teeth. He made them smart. He made them unpredictable.

Freedom pulled back his boot and kicked a climbing ex

just as its head rose above the top of the wall. The dead man flew back into the crowd. It took Freedom's military mind a moment to register what he'd seen in that instant, and then he realized what had caused the panic.

Most of the exes storming the Big Wall were wearing helmets.

Several of them wore motorcycle helmets with Lexan visors. A few looked like SWAT or National Guard issue. Freedom saw a few football helmets and hardhats. Even a few gleaming bicycle helmets, useless as they were. Killing exes had always been a numbers game. Legion had shifted the numbers more in his favor and shaken the guards in the process. Their practiced methods and procedures were crumbling. They were hesitating and second-guessing shots.

Freedom had to restore morale and get their fire focused before things fell apart. The Big Wall was on the edge of being overwhelmed. The attack was spread across a section almost forty feet long and, from the look of it, another twenty or thirty around the corner. Legion had at least four hundred exes under his control. Half a dozen civilians to defend seventy feet of ground against a few hundred opponents.

Not great odds.

A dead man with a red construction helmet climbed onto the platform. Its fingernails clawed at the wooden platform. Freedom stomped on one of the hands and took the ex's head off with another kick.

Makana and another noticed him and he saw their shoulders relax. The sheriff's star and his Army uniform still had that effect on people.

"Take your time," ordered Freedom. His voice bellowed out of his barrel chest, louder than the sound of teeth and rifle reports. He stabbed a thick finger at the horde. "Make them count." To accent his words, Lady Liberty roared and threw two more dead things back from the wall. The round couldn't penetrate, but at close range a 12 gauge packed enough raw force to shatter a skull even through a bullet-proof helmet.

The panicked shooting slowed. A dead man with a biker helmet staggered back and fell. One in National Guard headgear stumbled from a shot, then threw itself back at the wall. A figure in a football helmet dropped with a bullet in its eye.

More of the exes fell, but more of them reached the wall. A dead woman made it to the platform, but a guard smashed her off with a baseball bat. Another withered hand slapped onto the platform. Captain Freedom grabbed it by the wrist and pushed it away. The ex, a dead man in an Oxford shirt, fell back into the horde and was crushed under dozens of feet. Captain Freedom turned and cracked Lady Liberty's muzzle across the jaw of a teenage boy with a batting helmet and a bloody porn star T-shirt. The dead thing staggered back from the blow and vanished over the edge.

Captain Freedom shouted a few quick orders and got the guards spaced out to cover more area. "All units," he called over the radio, "this is Six. We have a major incursion at the northwest corner of the Big Wall. Request immediate assistance."

At least two people replied, but their words were drowned out by another burst from Lady Liberty. One of the rounds shattered a bicycle helmet and pulped the skull beneath it. The ex dropped and vanished into the tide of dead things below. Two of the others he hit struggled back to their feet.

The guard closest to him, a rail-thin woman with gray-streaked hair, paused to reload her rifle. It was an old M1, and Freedom was impressed how fast she loaded the clip without pinching her thumb. She brought it back up just in time to shoot a chalk-skinned man in the face. The round took a chunk out of the Lexan visor of the ex's helmet and knocked it back off the Big Wall.

A dead body threw itself up onto the platform a few feet away and struggled to its feet. Freedom took four quick steps and clotheslined it with a sweep of his massive arm. The ex pinwheeled back off the wall.

Another guard near the far end stopped to reload, but an ex crawled over the edge of the platform just as he pulled the magazine. He slammed the rifle stock into the zombie's face, right below the brim of its yellow hardhat, then smashed it again when the dead woman grabbed at his knee. The ex trembled and fell limp across the plywood.

The guard with the baseball bat, a wiry man with Asian features, swung a line drive that knocked one of Legion's puppets into the air. There was too much force behind the swing, though, and the man stumbled forward on the follow-through. His body bent over the ropes and the lines flexed. He dropped the bat, flailed for the lines, and added to his own momentum. An ex grabbed one of the waving hands and threw itself off the wall, dragging the man with it.

Freedom leaped to help the man, soaring two dozen feet along the top of the wall, but it was too late. The exes closest to the wall passed the guard back over their heads, carrying him away from safety. He had time to look back at his friends before the dead things dropped him on the ground and fell him. Then he started screaming.

The captain clenched his jaw. He fired three bursts into the swarm of exes before his pistol ran dry. Half of the exes dropped and the guard stopped screaming. Freedom half-hoped he'd put the man out of his misery.

He kicked away another ex, loaded a new drum onto Lady Liberty, and sized up the situation. The line was too thin. It was down to himself and five guards. It wasn't even five minutes into the assault, but he knew which way it was going to go if something didn't change.

Movement caught the corner of his eye as his pistol spat out three-round bursts at the undead. Back at his position another ex had made it onto the platform, a gaunt figure with a bare chest and a black SWAT helmet. It crawled across the platform and rolled over the far edge.

Legion was inside.

Freedom tensed for a moment as the dead thing crawled to its feet. One ex compromising the security of the wall could mean the end of everything. It was too far away for a sure kill, and he couldn't risk leaving the wall.

Then he realized what the ex had landed next to. Huge armored fingers wrapped around the zombie's helmet and lifted it into the air. Legion batted at the steel digits and swore in Spanish. Its voice was a dry rasp that barely carried over the sounds of gunfire and teeth.

The blue and silver titan stood just shy of nine feet tall and six feet wide. Flags decorated its shoulders, and each of its metal arms ended in a three-fingered fist a little bigger than a football. The battlesuit swung an arm and hurled the undead creature back over the wall. It sailed through the air and hit the pavement outside.

"Situation?" barked Danielle Morris from inside the armor. She had the suit in public address mode and her voice echoed across the corner.

Freedom fired three more bursts into the horde. The Cerberus Battlesuit wouldn't've been his first choice for backup. It was powerful, but it no longer had ranged weapons. It was also too big and heavy for the platform on top of the Big Wall.

"You're the second line," he told her. "If anything gets past us, it's yours."

Legion took that moment to send another ex scampering over the wall. Cerberus took two steps, scooped up the dead teenager, and threw it over the barrier. "Got it," she said.

The huge officer turned and found himself face to face with a dead woman in a football helmet. The ex lunged at him, but its gnashing jaws were blocked by the face mask. Freedom gut-punched the creature and it flew back down into the chattering horde. He moved down the wall back to his starting position, blasting exes wherever he could. They'd put down close to a hundred since he arrived on the scene, and the dead were still coming.

Two more guards, a man and a woman, ran down the Big Wall from the east. They added their fire and helped hold everything beyond the corner of the barrier. It meant somewhere else had thinner defenses now. Freedom hoped they'd hold.

He heard Cerberus move behind him, the muffled clomp of metal toes and the hiss of servos, and another ex came sailing back over the wall. He hadn't even seen that one get past them. Not a good sign.

The thin woman with the gray streaks reloaded her M1 again. She shot him a nervous look he'd seen in other firefights. It was the last of her ammunition. He fired two bursts to cover her and Lady Liberty's slide clanged empty again.

The guard heard it and looked up. As she did, an ex wrapped its pale fingers around her ankle and yanked. She screamed and slid toward the edge as the dead man pulled itself up onto the platform. It was wearing a gold CHP helmet.

She kicked it once in the head with her free leg. It snarled at her.

Freedom took two steps and slammed his boot into the ex's chin. The head whipped back and its neck snapped with a sharp crack. It tumbled off the platform and knocked another one off the wall on its way down.

The woman scampered back and grabbed her rifle. Freedom grabbed another drum from his belt. He had one more after this.

He turned his attention to the horde and something fluttered in the corner of his eye. His weapon came up. And then he realized they might have a chance.

A woman stood a yard to his left. She was dressed head to toe in skintight black leather, crisscrossed with charcoal straps and belts. Holsters rode low on her thighs, like the ones on a special forces soldier or an old-time gunslinger. A wide hood hid her face in shadows, and her cloak settled around her like a parachute.

"Took you long enough," snarled Cerberus from somewhere behind him.

Stealth's pistols were already out. For a moment Freedom thought the Glock 18Cs were on full automatic. Then he saw her aim twitch and realized she was firing single shots, each one finding a new target.

Over a dozen of Legion's puppets dropped, their strings cut. Stealth took a step forward and her cloak swirled in the night breezes. The pistols never stopped. Every round found the open space in a helmet.

Within thirty seconds she'd dropped as many exes. Maybe more. She spun on her heel and kicked another as its head cleared the platform. The hardhat it wore cracked under her boot.

The pistols spun in her hands, came in close to her waist, and her fingers whirled. The Glocks came back up with fresh magazines and continued to fire. Freedom knew decorated marksmen and snipers who would've been in awe of the woman's accuracy.

He fired off another burst from his own weapon and saw an ex in a military helmet drop, its face an unrecognizable mess. A zombie slipped over the wall closer to the corner and flew back out a moment later. A second form followed it. The ex hit the ground hard. The second figure hovered in the air on the far side of the intersection.

St. George, the hero once known as the Mighty Dragon, was a solid six feet tall, and the muscles of his wiry body were visible even under his stitch-covered jacket. His golden brown hair gleamed in the spotlights from the Big Wall. It brushed his shoulders and matched the leather of the jacket.

Freedom felt his own shoulders relax a bit.

× × ×

St. George settled in the air above the crowd of exes. Even with a quick sweep across the horde, he could pick out unique features on each of them. They'd been people once, after all. Before they'd died.

A gore-faced girl with a bright green tank top and charred-black hands. A Hasidic man whose beard was caked with blood. A dark-skinned woman with a quartet of bloody bullet holes in her chest. A little boy missing his lower jaw. A knife-thin man in a leather trench coat. About half of them wore some kind of protective helmet. One large, bald ex glared at him through a hockey mask before it gave him the finger with both hands.

He took in a deep breath, felt the tickle of mixing chemicals in the back of his throat, and sent a wave of fire washing down over the swarm. It lit up the intersection with golden light. He swung his head and washed the flames across the back line of the horde.

Half of the exes stared at the flying hero even as their hair and clothes caught fire, their teeth still clicking away. The others, the ones wearing helmets and hardhats, flinched. They moved in perfect synchronization, all turning their heads away to the right as they raised their left arm to shield their face. A handful of them glared up at him.

St. George drifted down into the crowd, grabbed a few exes by their necks, and hurled them back away from the wall. He moved through the horde like a man weeding a garden, plucking one dead weed after another. Over a dozen of them crashed against the buildings and pavement before all of them shifted their attention to him. The horde took in a rasping breath and spoke with one voice.

"Next time, *pinche*," they growled.

Their expressions sagged and their teeth started clicking again. A shift rippled through the crowd of exes as Legion's guidance vanished. The ones closest to St. George stumbled toward him on unsteady legs.

He drifted into the air, away from the grasping hands, and back to the platform. A few more gunshots rang out, but he could see the horde was settling down. There were still a few dozen exes pawing at the wall, but without Legion controlling them it was a mindless action that would never get their feet off the ground. Climbing was too complicated for them.

"I think he's gone," St. George called out. Wisps of smoke drifted out of his mouth and nose, like an idling engine. His boots thudded against the platform across from Stealth. "Everyone okay here?"

Makana shook his head. "We lost Daniel."

Another guard raised a trembling hand. There was blood on his fingers. "I . . . I think I got bit," he said.

The thin woman eyed the man and raised her rifle a few inches. "You think?"

"It was all so fast," he said, his eyes locked on the rifle's muzzle. "I mighta just cut myself on something. That's probably all it is."

"Get over to the hospital," said St. George. "Get checked out. Cerberus, can you go with him?"

The battlesuit tipped its head and focused on the man. He walked down a wooden staircase and headed down the street. Cerberus followed a few steps behind him.

"Thanks for the assist, boss," Makana said to St. George, and then added a nod to Freedom that made his dreadlocks swing. "Bosses. Didn't think he'd have so many bodies ready to move that fast."

Captain Freedom gazed down at the exes. "Helmets," he said. "This is new."

Stealth looked at the guards, then turned her head to Freedom. "How much ammunition was expended in this assault?"

"Most of it," said Makana. He glanced at the other guards. They added shrugs and nods. "I've only got one mag left after this."

"I'm almost out," said the thin woman.

"I think I've got a couple rounds," said another man, "and two clips after that."

Twin streamers of smoke curled up and out of St. George's nostrils. "I guess we got here just in time."

"Let's get a resupply out here," said St. George, "and some relief guards. Captain, can you stay with them until everything gets here?"

"Of course, sir," said the giant officer.

"And somebody find out if Daniel has . . . had a family."

"I think he had a boyfriend," said Makana.

St. George nodded. "Let's get word to him then."

"It is unlikely Legion will make another attempt tonight," said Stealth. She holstered her weapons and focused on the crowd of exes below. "His demonstrated impatience and the mix of headgear imply that this was the majority of his scavenged armor, possibly all of it."

St. George raised a skeptical brow. "Are you sure?"

"He has never returned in less than five hours once he has been driven back. It is more likely he may strike at another part of the wall, but I would say the odds are against that as well."

"So, is this what things are going to be like now?" asked the thin woman. "Because this sucked."

Stealth's expression was hidden beneath the blank fabric of her mask. Her body language was another story. St. George had known her long enough to see the subtle signs.

"Okay," he said, "if you've got this in hand, Captain, we'll leave you guys to it and get back to our patrol."

Freedom gave them a quick salute. St. George held out his hand and Stealth grabbed his wrist without a word. He focused on a spot between his shoulder blades and rose into the air. He lifted the woman and they shot into the sky, her cloak billowing behind them.

St. George sailed up to the top of the half-finished building at this corner of the Big Wall. If the world hadn't ended it would've been an office building or apartments by now.

Instead, it was a framework of rusted girders and sheetrock. It gave them a good view of the north and west sides of the wall.

Stealth lowered herself onto one of the beams. She held onto his hand even though her balance was perfect. She had a firm grip. St. George hung in the air near her, his fingers threaded between hers. "You've been expecting something like this, haven't you?"

"I have," she said. "It was only a matter of time before Legion realized he could use the resources of the city to outfit the exes. This will complicate matters for a time. Our ammunition stores are strained as it is."

"But you've already planned for it?"

"I have."

"So what's bothering you?"

"Before the assault, Captain Freedom detained three teenagers attempting to steal a car."

"So?"

"Petty crime has risen almost ten percent in the past few months since the Big Wall was completed. It is a distraction we do not need now that Legion has discovered these new assets."

"Yeah, but it's a good sign, in a way," said St. George. "If we're getting big enough to start having a crime problem, it means we've got a pretty sizeable population. Things are getting better overall."

All around the Big Wall, and as far as they could see, figures shuffled and stumbled in the streets. The sound of their teeth popped and cracked in the night like a hundred distant bonfires. Even at night, St. George could see thousands of them, and he knew there were thousands more out there in the darkness. Stealth said there were just over five million exes in Los Angeles. In three years he hadn't seen anything to make him think otherwise.

At the best, every one of them was a mindless machine with no purpose past killing and feeding. A pack of ten could strip a person to bones in less than half an hour. At the worst, the undead were harboring Legion.

Stealth shook her head inside her hood. "As always," she said, "you are an optimist."

"Well, what is it they say?" St. George shrugged. "'Better the devil you know . . .'"